"HAS THE* ENTERPRISE *BEEN RECALLED?"

"Emphatically not," Pike said. "Our mission is to continue, duration unchanged."

"Then I resubmit my request for an expedition to Pergamum 85752-B."

"Susquatane."

"As the preface to my report details, that name was recommended to the Federation Astronomical Committee by members of the 2244 survey voyage. But it has yet to receive formal approval." Spock looked keenly at the captain and added, "Nor has my expedition."

Pike inhaled deeply. "Well, we're retracing our steps. We should be able to see it again." There were another half-dozen candidate planets for study—but frankly, Pike didn't give much of a damn which one they went to. He stood. "Spock, I should let you know I didn't agree with our return to the nebula. With the war on—well, I can think of better things to do than to spend months in the middle of nowhere studying the effects of exotic radiation on space daffodils."

"We are unlikely to find any members of the Earth genus *Narcissus*, Captain. But the range of biomes does look promising for other discoveries, as—"

"As mentioned in your report," Pike said, walking toward the door in hopes of cutting the disquisition short.

Realizing that Spock hadn't moved, he stopped and looked back. They'd shared many experiences, including the Talos IV incident—yet there was little getting close to a Vulcan, and even less of a chance with Spock. "Is there something else?"

Spock spoke. "Captain, the Klingons pursue violence. We would pursue knowledge. For now, they are more likely to convince the Federation to join them in their violence. By our remaining here—and continuing with our plans—we assure them that we will never abandon our path."

Don't miss these other
exciting books in the world of

STAR TREK®
DISCOVERY

DESPERATE HOURS
David Mack

DRASTIC MEASURES
Dayton Ward

FEAR ITSELF
James Swallow

THE WAY TO THE STARS
Una McCormack

STAR TREK®

DISCOVERY

THE ENTERPRISE WAR

JOHN JACKSON MILLER

Based on *Star Trek*®
created by Gene Roddenberry
and
Star Trek: Discovery
created by Bryan Fuller & Alex Kurtzman

G

GALLERY BOOKS

New York London Toronto Sydney New Delhi

G

Gallery Books
An Imprint of Simon & Schuster, Inc.
1230 Avenue of the Americas
New York, NY 10020

This book is a work of fiction. Any references to historical events, real people, or real places are used fictitiously. Other names, characters, places, and events are products of the author's imagination, and any resemblance to actual events or places or persons, living or dead, is entirely coincidental.

This book is published by Gallery Books, an imprint of Simon & Schuster, Inc., under exclusive license from CBS Studios Inc.

First Gallery Books trade paperback edition July 2019

GALLERY BOOKS and colophon are trademarks of Simon & Schuster, Inc.

For information about special discounts for bulk purchases, please contact Simon & Schuster Special Sales at 1-866-506-1949 or business@simonandschuster.com.

The Simon & Schuster Speakers Bureau can bring authors to your live event. For more information or to book an event, contact the Simon & Schuster Speakers Bureau at 1-866-248-3049 or visit our website at www.simonspeakers.com.

Manufactured in the United States of America

10 9 8 7 6 5 4 3 2 1

Library of Congress Cataloging-in-Publication Data is available.

ISBN 978-1-9821-1331-5
ISBN 978-1-9821-1332-2 (ebook)

To Michael Stackpole,
with thanks for years of guidance and support

The world itself to some men is a prison, our narrow seas as so many ditches; and when they have compassed the globe of the Earth, they would fain go see what is done in the Moon. . . . What is a ship but a prison?

—Robert Burton
The Anatomy of Melancholy

HISTORIAN'S NOTE

The main events in this story begin in October 2256, five months after the Battle of the Binary Stars—and two years after the *Enterprise*'s first mission to Talos IV.

Prologue

2236

I'm dead. They buried me.

Christopher Pike awoke to those thoughts—and to pain. He felt as if the world had fallen in on him and, indeed, a portion of it had. Alone in the dark, on his belly with blood streaming from his chin and a mountain crushing his back, he found every breath a chore. No asthmatic episode from his childhood compared with the agony he felt now.

But he felt it, and that told him something.

I'm not dead. I just can't move.

The seventeen-year-old blinked dust from his eyes and fought to focus. There was nothing to see. He remembered in disjointed flashes. He'd started running when the rumbling began. In truth, "running" had meant skittering like a prairie dog, ducking tunnel ceilings barely a meter high in places. "Rumbling," too, barely described what had felt like being sealed inside a snare drum. Then he had tripped and fallen flat, losing his flashlight.

How long ago had that been?

He called out. Nothing. Pike wilted. He could barely hear his own voice, the way the mountain was still groaning.

He turned his attention to uncovering his left arm, numb and partially pinned under debris. Doing something cleared his head. He recalled the hot California morning, and how he'd given up an afternoon on horseback to break a few laws and visit a local shrine to perseverance.

The tunnel was the work of a lone twentieth-century miner, William "Burro" Schmidt, whose nickname came from the animals that carried his gold ore across the El Paso Mountains to Pike's hometown of Mojave. Seeking a shortcut, Burro had burrowed, using hand tools and explosives to hew a narrow passage into a ridge. Long after a road through Last Chance Canyon eliminated the need for his tunnel, the miner had kept at it, finally punching through nearly a kilometer of granite after more than three decades. The man some called the "human mole" never transported a load of ore through it—but he had succeeded.

Such a combination of determination and defiance was irresistible to Pike and his friends—particularly one Evan Hondo. A Starfleet dropout, the twenty-year-old Hondo served as ringleader for area kids with time on their hands. Having entered the tunnel before, he'd proposed the adventure not as a dare, but an expedition—a framing sure to interest Pike. So as not to be tracked during their trespass, they'd left their communication devices at home.

Pike soon understood why the entry had been barricaded. In an earlier time, the United States had festooned the Mojave Desert with military bases: tempting targets during the Third World War. The Hermosa Quake of 2047 had also weakened many underground features. And while modern spelunkers had cleared paths with phasers, they'd also added side tunnels of questionable stability—as Pike had painfully discovered. He'd never been claustrophobic; now, he could only think that evolution had failed him by not instilling in him a preternatural dread of confined spaces.

Buried but not dead, he thought again as he flexed his freed left arm to restore blood flow. It felt like caressing a porcupine. Palms down, he tried to push himself up. Pain erupted again as something moved in his chest. The weight on his midsection shifted, but not enough to free him. He'd have to pull himself out.

He clawed at the surface in front of him. Something metallic was in the rubble. It was a rail, a remnant of the line Schmidt had laid for his ore cart. Pike dug with his fingernails until he could curl his hands around it—and then heaved.

You've done a million chin-ups, Chris. Pull!

Pike screamed in agony as he dragged his body forward and into the main tunnel. Farther behind, more of the passage gave way, proof he had acted just in time. He crawled to the opposite wall of the tunnel and rolled over, bracing himself against the surface in an attempt to sit up. More blinding pain, as something inside him shifted again. Finally upright, he sat petrified in the dark, clutching at his chest. *A broken rib for sure, maybe two.* His legs seemed fine, although leaning over to examine them nearly caused him to black out.

He needed medical help—but he couldn't think about that now.

"*Hondo! Freena! Dosh!*"

Still nothing. Freena and her boyfriend, Hondo, inseparable, had gone ahead on their own. Sick of listening to the teenage know-it-all Dosh, Pike had sent the chatty Tellarite off to join them. Wincing as he stood, Pike hoped to hear Dosh's nasal voice again. He used the craggy wall for support as he worked his way farther into the darkness, meter by miserable meter.

He passed one phaser-cut corridor after another, hearing only his own voice when he called out. Down the fourth passage, he heard weeping. Pike moved down it, teeth clenched against the pain. There was a pile of debris ahead—and beyond it, a light. Pike pitched against the pile of rubble and methodically cleared a person-wide opening.

Through it, he saw Dosh sitting against the wall, arms

clutching his knees, tearful and disoriented as he stared at a lantern on the floor in front of him. "Dosh, are you all right?"

"N-no. I mean, yes."

He didn't *look* all right. Pike could see Dosh had tried to dig himself out, only to give up. "It's okay, pal. Just hold on." Steeling himself, Pike shimmied through the aperture. More agony. He crawled down the rock pile to Dosh's side. "Where's Evan and Freena?"

Dosh gestured weakly. "Ahead. They left me."

Pike looked up the phaser-cut tunnel. "We've got to find them."

Dosh didn't respond. The kid was shaken, shattered. He wasn't going anywhere, not alone. "Wait here," Pike finally said.

"D-don't take my light."

"I won't."

That made it harder. The mountain rattled some more as he fumbled forward in the dark. But he heard something: coughing. It had to be Freena. A few dozen meters later, around a turn, he saw light again. Pike hurried toward it. His eyes adjusting, Pike called out to her. She was on the ground at the end of the chamber, facing the wall and looking down.

"Chris!" She tried to stand, but faltered. He caught her. Caked in dust, she looked rough. "Hondo's there!" she said, pointing at the dead end.

The passage stopped at a sheer wall, slick to the touch. Pike stared, confused, before Freena pointed again. "Look down!"

At the foot of the wall was half a meter of blackness. Pike peered into the nothingness. "It's the rest of the tunnel!" He got on his hands and knees and peered down inside. "*Hondo?*"

"Chrissy!" a voice called out from below. Only one person called him by that hated nickname. "Buddy! That you?"

"Yeah." Pike brought Freena's lantern to the opening.

Several meters below, he beheld Hondo's smiling face. "It's like the mountain just shifted down—and took half the tunnel with it."

"I guess I got a little happy with the phaser," Hondo said.

Phaser? Pike looked to Freena.

She shook her head. "Hondo wanted to cut a new passage."

"Took Burro thirty-plus years," Hondo said. "Hey, everybody tries it."

"Well, now you're in a hole," Pike said.

Another rumble. Freena clutched Pike's shoulder to steady him. "Every time there's shaking," she said, "the tunnel shifts down some more."

Blanching against the pain, Pike dropped to his stomach and stuck his arm over the ledge. "Hondo, can you reach me?"

"Can't. It's too high. And I think my leg's broken."

And no medical kit at all on this trip, to go along with no communicators. Pike had harbored serious reservations from the start. How different might it have been if he were in charge?

He couldn't think about that. He had to act. "Hondo, I have to get Freena and Dosh out. But I'll bring help. Okay?"

"You just want to be the hero," Hondo said.

That was the furthest thing from Pike's mind, but he wasn't going to argue. "Maybe that's it." He stood.

Shaking, Freena objected. "I'm not leaving him."

"Go with Chrissy," Hondo called out from below. "It's all right."

Pike touched her wrist. "I swear, we'll come back."

She looked down for a long moment, before nodding. "Okay."

"Hey, if you find a phaser," Hondo yelled, "I want it back."

Pike's path back up the tunnel was much slower with the hobbling Freena in tow. All the while, he calculated. Mojave had an emergency services shuttle, one with an onboard transporter. He'd find a way to call them from outside, and then head back in, providing information on where Hondo was. Would that be enough for them to get a lock? Could transporters do that? He didn't know. But he had to find out.

Finding Dosh unmoved from his location, Pike and Freena worked to clear a larger opening to the main tunnel. All that time—and during the trio's long rush back toward the entrance—the creaking ridge reminded them to hurry. Every little tremor nearly sent Freena back for Hondo, but Pike kept the group moving onward.

Finally, he saw the light—blinding and brilliant. Muscles tensed up since the start of the ordeal began to relax. It would work out. He was getting the others out of the mountain. He'd get Hondo out too.

And then he'd have a serious reassessment of his friendship with him.

—

It had *not* worked out.

With Dosh and Freena collapsed outside the entrance, Pike staggered to the old miner's dwelling, where Hondo had hidden his vehicle. He activated the emergency communicator on board. A hovercraft arrived minutes later, followed by another, and another; more authorities than he ever expected to see, so swiftly. Pike was elated—

—at first. He learned they were in the vicinity because of the Garlock Fault, which ran across the northern edge of the Mojave Desert. It wasn't an especially active system; Pike had never felt a quake while living in the area. But it was prone to sympathetic seismic events, responding to stimuli as small as ill-advised disintegrations.

And before the authorities could get a transporter fix on

Hondo, it had responded again. Sensor readings suggested his death was instantaneous.

For an hour, Pike sat outside the miner's shelter, feeling numb—and not from what the medic had treated him with. He'd consoled his tearful friends as best he could—until they realized he needed consoling too.

"They just told me they're calling off the search." Pike shook his head. "I wasn't fast enough."

"Don't say that," Dosh said. "You were helping us."

"Then I should have tried something else. I should have shimmied down to help him out."

"Then you'd be gone too," Freena said. "We all would be." Her blue eyes were all cried out. "Chris, I love him and I didn't stay."

Yeah, but I promised. Pike looked back at the tunnel opening. *He was counting on me. I just wasn't smart enough.*

With the adults gathering, he knew the trouble was only beginning. There would be explanations. Angry parents and guardians. Sanctions from the authorities who managed the land.

Pike had already decided he would take it all on himself.

It was going to be bad—real bad. The sort of thing that might well put an end to his hopes for the future. *Piloting shuttles. Running his own ranch. Starfleet?* It would be foolish to dream of anything now. His destiny was buried under a mountain of granite.

Buried, but not dead.

He would keep on digging.

DETONATION

October 2256

INCOMING TRANSMISSION

TO: CAPTAIN C. PIKE • *U.S.S. ENTERPRISE* • NCC-1701

FROM: VICE ADMIRAL K. CORNWELL, STARFLEET COMMAND

ALERT. HOSTILITIES OPENED WITH KLINGON EMPIRE. STATE OF WAR EXISTS.

LOSSES INCLUDE *CLARKE*, *EDISON*, *EUROPA*, *SHENZHOU*, *SHRAN*, *T'PLANA-HATH*, *YEAGER*.

REGRET TO INFORM YOU CAPTAIN GEORGIOU MIA/PRESUMED KIA.

ENTERPRISE TO REMAIN IN PERGAMUM NEBULA, MISSION UNALTERED.
DO NOT RETURN.

ENCRYPT ALL FUTURE COMMUNICATIONS PER REGULATION 46A.

END TRANSMISSION

1

U.S.S. Enterprise
Pergamum Nebula

"*Ram us through!*"

Captain Christopher Pike called out a second warning to the *Starship Enterprise* bridge crew, but even he couldn't hear it. The black cloud that had loomed on the main viewer for the last few minutes devoured the screen—and the vessel shook wildly. The ship's gentle sonorous hum gave way to the din of quaking bulkheads.

"Kappa band entered!" shouted Lieutenant Jamila Amin. One of several recent additions to the crew, the navigator was barely audible despite sitting meters away from the captain's chair. "External boundary breach in twenty seconds!"

I don't care for the word "breach" in the current circumstance, Pike thought to respond—but against the roar he worried someone would think he was trying to say something more important. He looked up and around. Pike had grown accustomed to nearly everything the universe had to throw at a starship, but flying through dense material was his least favorite by far.

Enterprise was up to it, of course; space wasn't fully a vacuum, and a starship needed to be able to traverse areas of plasma unscathed. But a starship still responded to the outside environs, buffeting as material impacted its shields. Accelerating quickly through a thick medium somehow managed to transfer enough stress through the shields and hull to make the bulkheads complain.

Some Starfleeters had likened the eerie sound to the creaking of a wooden ship of old. To Pike, it was like being back inside a mountain that didn't want him there.

Slowly, the shaking and racket subsided, and the viewscreen image shifted from oily black to just oily. "Kappa nebular band cleared," Lieutenant Raden said from the helm. "But we may want to go back and pick up the rest of the hull!"

"Relax, Raden," Amin said. "Your beauty's intact."

"I'll believe that when I can inspect it myself," the Ktarian replied. "Not before!"

Pike's forward station was completely new, with Yoshi Ohara and the veteran José Tyler off to well-deserved commands of their own. While Amin had settled in, Raden still treated *Enterprise* like his parents' hovercraft—one he was terrified to leave a scratch on. That had given the otherwise fully competent helmsman a jittery demeanor to match his animated golden eyes.

"Lambda band detected," called out the wavy-haired young man from the science station. "Measuring particulate velocity, direction, and composition."

"Thank you, Mister Connolly," Pike said. "Sad news for you, Mister Raden. This wall of guck has as many layers as the Greeks had letters."

Two fewer, actually, but Spock wasn't there to correct him. That was just as well: the Vulcan was where he needed to be. Pike had ordered *Enterprise*'s premature return the second after he'd read the message from Starfleet about the declaration of war. At the time, Spock had been forward in the stardrive section, working on a new program for the navigational deflector. Pike expected he was still there, shoveling facts into the system to adjust for every new region they encountered.

"Lambda region readings confirmed. Conveying to engineering and nav," Connolly said. "Carbon monoxide and nitrogen, dust particles in suspension. Less ammonia in this one. Outer boundary is majority formaldehyde."

"That's fine. I'm feeling ready to be embalmed." Pike grinned at the lieutenant. He never liked to show concern before the young ones—especially in a place as hellish as the Pergamum Nebula.

The adjective was apt. The colossal astronomical body known on deck just as the Pergamum was named for the city that held Satan's throne in the Book of Revelation. It lived up to the title. Superheated reds and oranges alternated with deep blacks of absorption formations, giving it such a levels-of-hell feel that even Starfleet's staid astronomical naming body felt the need to get poetic. While distant from the core of Federation space, it stood near the intersection of routes popular with civilian prospectors—and a number of vessels had never returned from the region. Pike's orders had been to find out why, while conducting a comprehensive survey designed to take an entire year.

Pike had only needed a few days inside the Pergamum to know that the hazard wasn't its proximity to the nearby Ionite Nebula, rife with Lurian pirates. The Pergamum was simply too harsh a place for ships that weren't built for it. *Enterprise* was up to the challenge. Pike had been able to scout a handful of target worlds for closer study before the war news came.

It was just a brief repeating text message sent in the open on an extremely low-frequency subspace channel, the only one where signals could even occasionally penetrate the clouds. From the time code, Pike could tell Starfleet had first started broadcasting it earlier—*months* earlier, mere days after he had entered the nebula. That made it easier for him to decide that the part about staying in the Pergamum might no longer be operative.

Maybe it was a fig leaf, but he didn't care. *Shenzhou* was gone. *If the best of us are falling already,* he'd told Number One in the turbolift, *we're needed.*

And he wouldn't spare the horses. An orderly departure would have meant taking days to go around the Acheron Formation—the river-to-hell–named gauntlet of space chemistry bounding the Sol-facing end of the Pergamum. The Federation might not have days to spare.

"Lambda in ten seconds," Raden said. He looked back. "Still time to change course, Captain, and find a cleaner lane."

"Always appreciate hearing the options, Mister Raden," Pike said. "Brace yourselves."

Another cloud, another shipquake, worse than before. Ahead, Pike watched his tireless first officer, Commander Una, keeping an eye on the vessel's condition from the bridge control station. "Shields holding," Number One called out. "Hull integrity nominal."

"Burro" Schmidt would laugh, Pike thought. *My "shortcut" might take longer than his did.* But his crew wouldn't let that happen. Between the bridge officers, main engineering, and Spock, *Enterprise* was constantly reshaping her shields to find the best angle of attack—even as the cloud formation threw surprises at them.

"This is a bad patch," Raden said, wiping sweat from his large forehead lobes.

He wasn't alone in his concern this time. Una glanced back at the captain. It was as close to *"Are you sure you want to keep doing this?"* as his closest advisor was likely to get before the crew.

"Steady as she goes."

Five minutes later, an interstitial void allowed a brief respite—and time to explain briefly to the bridge crew the reason for their sudden return. It mattered that they felt the same urgency he did. A couple had friends and classmates impacted by the Klingon attacks, and everyone knew *Shenzhou* from their shared Sirsa III adventure the year before. Scientist Connolly, he thought, was about ready to transfer to security then and there.

Pike hadn't made an announcement shipwide, though, and he wasn't going to now. Michael Burnham was aboard *Shenzhou*. He knew Spock had a familial connection to her; it wasn't the sort of news to learn over the public address system.

"New region approaching," Amin said.

Raden looked at her. "I thought we were just up to Mu."

"No, I meant *new* as *new*. Not the letter, as in—"

"Never mind," Pike said. With another opaque wave growing in the viewscreen, levity had found its limit.

"Dense but narrow." Connolly studied his readings. "Shouldn't be so bad on the other side."

Pike blanched at the sight. "Are you willing to swear there's another side to it?"

"Spock is reshaping shields for maximum efficiency," Number One reported.

Well, I wanted to do this, Pike thought. "Here we go again."

Enterprise pierced the blackness. There were some light shakes, but the starship found a corridor with easier going. Pike breathed a sigh of relief on behalf of everyone. "Well, that one wasn't so—"

A shock wave struck the ship, pitching *Enterprise* forward, stern over bow, and throwing several crewmembers from their seats. Artificial gravity and inertial dampers could accommodate for a lot of jolts, but not that one. Alarms screamed on the bridge as the tumbling continued.

Pike, thrown forward, had wound up between Raden and Amin, knocking both of them from their chairs. The helmsman hung onto the console and worked control after control, trying to restore the ship to an even pitch. Several moments later, *Enterprise* was stable again.

"Full stop." Pike looked around. "Everybody okay?"

Connolly stood up from where he had been thrown backward against the command well railing. "Lucky this fence was here."

His helmsman and navigator reclaiming their seats, Pike climbed back into his chair. "What the hell was that?"

Number One had been working the problem already. "There was a concussive force in our wake."

Raden frowned. "What would do that?"

Connolly studied his readouts. He spoke tentatively. "The shape of the blast—" he began, before pausing.

Pike faced him. "Come on, what do you think?"

"Maybe I'm still dizzy. If I didn't know better, I'd say it looked like . . . a photon torpedo blast, detonated somewhere in the soup behind us." He looked at Pike. "But I know better."

A torpedo? All eyes darted to Commander Nhan at tactical, their new head of security. Until now, the long-haired Barzan woman had little to do at her station but to hang on. "Most of our sensors were directed forward," Nhan said, "just like our shields." Nobody argued the wisdom in that. "But I didn't see anything aft. We haven't seen anyone for weeks. Just probes."

"And half of them ours," Pike said. Old and spent, from previous surveys. "How could a torpedo hit us that hard?"

"It's the medium," Connolly said. "All that debris hit us like a tsunami. And we couldn't have gotten a visual if we'd wanted one. Not in that morass."

"Check the logs anyway," Pike ordered. "We must have gotten a reading from something."

Nhan set to it.

"Damage reports coming in," Una said. "Whatever it was, we weren't shielded aft."

Pike frowned. He had someplace to be. He looked to the

engineering station, and the Tellarite lieutenant who served as departmental second officer. "Jallow, will we still have warp drive when we exit?"

Jallow worked his interface furiously. "I don't know, sir. I'm checking for reports now."

Una's eyes narrowed as she turned to face Pike. "Should we stop, Captain?"

Always trying to save me from myself. "No," he said, standing. "You have the conn. Resume course as soon as impulse power and engines allow." He made for the turbolift. "I just remembered we have a superstar belowdecks."

She looked quizzical. "Captain?"

"Our new chief engineer. Maybe he can rub his two Cochrane Medals of Excellence together and get us home before the war ends."

2

Warship *Deathstrike*
Pergamum Nebula

"Vauss, you are a true imbecile. There is no prevarication about you; you are every bit as stupid as you appear." Gripping his lieutenant by the throat, Baladon crushed him against the bulkhead. "Were it not for the lie Mother tells of our kinship, you would find yourself floating with the jetsam outside."

Vauss struggled against his massive older brother's hold. He attempted to speak, without success. Hulking and yellowish gray, Lurians had faces that normally looked like shriveled pieces of fruit. His had turned nearly fluorescent.

"What's that?" the gravel-voiced Baladon asked, baring his teeth. "You wish to admit your first mistake, surviving childhood?"

Back at a control station, Baladon's navigator—also a brother—mumbled without much interest. "He's choking. Or something."

"Hmph."

Baladon had attempted to strangle his siblings many times before; he usually knew when Vauss was about to expire. It wasn't easy to kill a Lurian. Their bodies were stuffed with redundant organs, as if evolution had predicted just how stupid some of Baladon's relatives would later be. Someone who might drink used reactor coolant on a dare could use a spare stomach or two.

Baladon brought his head centimeters from his brother's face and glared into his bulging yellow eyes. "We had *one* photon torpedo, Vauss. And you wasted it."

"*Nrfflmph*," Vauss replied.

Baladon decided to take that as an apology and released his hold. Vauss fell to the deck, gasping.

"The detonation was too soon. You cost us *Enterprise*."

"Not . . . me," Vauss muttered between wheezes. He pointed. "Blame Jeld! Ship . . . too far."

The navigator, younger brother to the two of them, snapped back, "Clouds too thick."

"Ship too far. I said get close!"

"We'd be in their galley!"

Galley. The word, and its suggestion of food, calmed them all. Baladon knew this was normal for Lurians, and indeed offered their society what stability it had. It was also the longest word many of his relatives knew.

Baladon turned from his brother and stalked about *Deathstrike*'s dilapidated bridge. "There is no need to argue," he said, adopting his most leaderly tone as he plopped down in his command chair. "You are all *equally* incompetent. You function together as parts of a machine that does absolutely nothing. When the end comes, I will be able to say with pride: each crewmember aboard brought me to it."

Several on the bridge erupted in self-congratulatory cheers. Baladon closed his eyes and groaned.

It was not true, as a spacers' joke went, that in the land of the Lurians, the one who knew how to operate an automatic door was king. Many leaders Baladon had known would've failed that test. It was why he had left. Born into a family of privateers, he had the requisite brutality—but also a gift for words. That set him apart from most Lurians, who kept their thoughts to themselves—when they had them. His smart-sounding talk attracting attention, Baladon had promised great wealth to warrior families that would join him in his piratic exploits outside the Ionite Nebula. The nearby Pergamum, as stolen Starfleet charts called it, was larger and mostly unknown, easy to sell as a vast realm of plunder and profit.

He'd misjudged on two counts. The recruits that he'd hoped would be sharper than his relatives turned out to be equally useless, barely able to operate a starship at all. And they wasted his precious black-market ammunition on the few targets they'd found. Those pickings were meager, indeed, because conditions in the Pergamum were far harsher than in their home nebula. They hadn't seen as much as a workpod in weeks—

—until *Enterprise* appeared. The frozen image of the starship still remained on the screen on the starboard wall, taunting them for their failure. *Deathstrike*'s surveillance drones had spotted her days before; building stealth probes for use in nebulae was one thing Lurians *were* good at. Baladon had stalked the Starfleet vessel, using the clouds to cover his approach. And then, just as *Enterprise* lingered near a colossal planet known in records as Susquatane, the starship turned and rocketed for the nebular boundary.

"No one saw us," Jeld said. "We had a clear shot."

"Don't start," replied Vauss, rubbing his neck. "And it was just one torpedo." That was the other long word Vauss knew. He gestured to the *Enterprise* image. "What could it do to *that*?"

"The same thing we always do," Baladon growled. "Strike the unshielded aft—then send over the boarding pods. They couldn't have more than a couple hundred people over there. We have that many belowdecks, eager to kill on command."

"They want food," Jeld said. "So do I."

Baladon didn't want to hear it—but he was hearing *something*. Yellow eyes shifted. "What is that sound?"

"Rogall is beeping," Vauss said, pointing to the comm station—or, more precisely, the corpse slumped over it and bleeding out. The comm operator had announced during the earlier pursuit that he was going to hail *Enterprise* to ask the Starfleet ship to slow down. He'd gotten his hand to the send control when Baladon relieved him of his duties. The leader's knife still protruded from the unfortunate Lurian's back.

"What is it?"

"Message," Vauss said after shoving the corpse to one side. He read aloud from what sounded like an intercept: "*Alert. Hos . . . til . . .*"

"Hostilities," Baladon said.

"*. . . opened with Klingon Empire . . .*"

After the interminable wait while Vauss finished reading the entire message, Baladon punched his hand with his fist. "That explains it! Why they were in haste to leave the nebula—and why they were willing to take the worst route possible."

Jeld frowned. "Then they won't come back."

"They aren't out yet—which means we still have a chance." Baladon regarded the image on the wall and rubbed his hairless chin. "A Starfleet ship fancier than any we've ever seen. I ask you, Vauss—what might that be worth to the Klingons?"

"Klingons like fancy ships?"

"No, my good dolt. If we've never seen anything like this *Enterprise* before, it's a lock that they haven't. If we bring that ship to them—or even just a shuttle, a sickbay couch, a serving spoon—it might be worth more to them than it would be to us!"

"How much?"

"Fortune will tell." Baladon cracked his knuckles. "Follow the *Enterprise,* brothers. This time, we're going to get it right."

And if not, he thought, *I'm soon to be an only child!*

3

U.S.S. Enterprise
Pergamum Nebula

"*Captain!*" Avedis Galadjian nearly vaulted the computer console he was working at when he noticed Pike's arrival in main engineering. "Welcome!"

"Lieutenant Commander."

"*Doctor* is fine." The human in red seized the captain's hand and shook it vigorously. "I so rarely see you here. It's an exciting day, and we're delighted to have you."

"Thank you, Doctor—but we still don't do handshakes."

"How foolish of me." Bald with a finely coiffed gray goatee and beard, the sixtyish Galadjian released Pike's hand. "That is a pity, but needs of the service."

"Right." At least he wasn't saluting anymore, Pike thought. "We're nearly through the Acheron Formation. What's your status?"

"Excellent! It has gone very well."

I'd have won the pool on that answer, Pike thought. Galadjian's first name meant "good news" in his native language, and that had quickly become his nickname. The captain surveyed the junior engineers bustling about at their assignments. "I don't suppose you noticed the shaking down here?" As if on cue, *Enterprise*, moving again, shuddered around them. "Like *that*?"

"Of course I felt it. Very exciting."

"Was the excitement in any way concerning?"

Galadjian walked toward one of the engineering displays before turning, apparently having had a flash of insight. "You see, Captain Pike," he said, gesturing with his hands, "the calculations for the creation of a magnetodynamic envelope in which a vessel, *V*, travels through a medium, *M*, without harm to occupant *O* are a simple mathematical matter. What is unusual in this case is that I am inside the problem myself."

"You're *O*."

"*Doctor O.* But yes. My presence makes me more than a mere observer in this system. And that is a hazard. If I were to allow my feelings as a sentient being to enter into my thinking, it might influence my calculations and introduce error."

"Or give us a less bumpy ride."

"Ah, but the tolerance levels of our occupants have already been taken into account, and our journey has been entirely within prescribed parameters."

That's a relief, Pike thought. "How about that big bump earlier?"

"Big bump?" Galadjian looked at him attentively. "Perhaps some clarification."

"When the ship went pinwheeling. You must have noticed that."

Galadjian nodded. "Again, very exciting. There are no moments like this back home at the institute."

"Lieutenant Connolly seems to think it might have been caused by a photon torpedo."

"A photon—" Galadjian repeated. His head tilted forty-five degrees. Dark eyes stared into space for a moment, as if the new information needed to be submitted through internal channels only the engineer could see. "That is a remarkable possibility," he said after a few moments. "We will turn to our good and trusty friend, the sensor logs."

"Commander Nhan has already started collating data."

"Magnificent! I will see if I have anything to add." As Galadjian headed to a far terminal, several engineers stepped from their stations to join him.

Pike braced himself against a bulkhead and waited—and looked again at the busy officers about. He saw nothing unusual: if *Enterprise*'s rough transit was posing a crisis, there was little trace of it. This was an experienced team—

—save one. Even the ensigns had been in Starfleet longer than Galadjian.

The problem with *Enterprise* being a showcase for Starfleet was that the coveted chief engineer's post had become something of a revolving door. People came and went, often taking personnel with them; sometimes they even came back. Kursley, Marvick, Grace, Burnstein—even Transporter Chief Pitcairn briefly had filled the top slot for a mission. Caitlin Barry had been the most recent chief engineer to depart, taking several assistants on a leave of absence before the Pergamum mission to advise Starfleet's shipyards about the *Constitution* class. Now, with a war on, Pike had no idea whether they'd return. He hoped they would. One of the junior officers Barry had taken, Scott, had seemed pretty bright.

Galadjian was as accomplished in warp physics as Richard Daystrom was in computing—and if anything, he was more famous, because he welcomed interactions with laypeople and the media. Where other theoreticians tended to be distant and obscure, Galadjian thought his complex models were never complete unless he got the average person excited about them.

Galadjian's mastery in the physics of shields and their interactions with nebulae had made him Starfleet's choice for the Pergamum mission. Many of his ideas had gone into the most recent refit, reshaping and optimizing *Enterprise* for nebular travel. While Pike could understand why Galadjian had been awarded a commission—if not the lofty brevet rank—the captain still had no idea why the man had wanted to go to space.

But his credentials impressed Spock and Number One, and he had seemed to settle in well. Among his engineering colleagues, Galadjian's exuberance kicked into overdrive. Lately, every trip Pike had taken to main engineering had felt like wandering into the after-party of a Cochrane Medal awards ceremony, with Galadjian quipping about the latest discoveries as if they were the juiciest bits of gossip around.

After about a month of that, Pike had decided to let Number One handle making the rounds.

The latest confab broke up. "Captain, I have my analysis," Galadjian said, stepping away from the terminal as his juniors returned to their stations. He picked up a cup and saucer from the deck where they had fallen during the tumult and held them up before Pike. "Let us consider this saucer as *Enterprise* and this cup as a high-speed projectile—"

"I have a grounding in physics, Doctor. Starfleet likes that in its captains."

"Yes, of course!" In their short time together, Pike had found he could be a little acerbic with Galadjian because the man either didn't register sarcasm or didn't resent it. The chief engineer set down the dishes and led Pike to the terminal.

Galadjian pointed to the display. "Based on the distribution of damage to the aft section and the nacelles and the surge of particular particles, I project to ninety-five percent certainty that we were exposed to the reaction of antideuterium with magnetic borotenite, four-point-eight kilometers behind our position."

"Just ninety-five percent certain, huh?" Pike stared at the findings. "That sounds like a torpedo—and not one of ours."

Galadjian grinned. "If such reactions happen naturally, we have come to the right place—because there is definitely a paper to be written here."

"After people are finished shooting at us. Damage assessments, Doctor. Can we safely go to warp once we're outside the nebula?"

"I believe so, but would like to have Spock's opinion, when he is done with his work on the deflector dish."

He's not a member of your section, Doctor. "It can't wait. There's an emergency—as you might have surmised." He gestured to the nearby cup, which was starting to rattle. "I need your best judgment now."

"Ah," Galadjian said. He pursed his lips. "Yes. Yes, all systems should function normally. I guarantee it." He clasped his hands behind him and straightened at dutiful attention—a pose that broke when the ship shook violently, once again knocking the nearby saucer and cup to the deck. *Enterprise* had entered another area of dense material. He looked at Pike. "I'm afraid I've lost track of which zone we're in. Was that Upsilon or Phi?"

"I leave the alphabets to Spock." Pike headed toward the exit. "Oh," he called back, "as long as you're working together, tell him I want to see him when he's available. I have some news for him."

"Aye, Captain!"

Inside the turbolift, Pike clapped his hand on the control lever and made his way to the bridge. The doors opened to a welcome sight: stars on the main viewer.

"Captain on the bridge," Una announced, rising from the command chair. "Sir, that was the final layer of the formation. We are in the clear."

"I'd almost forgotten what 'clear' looked like," Pike said, relieved to be out of the giant chemistry set. He wandered toward the screen, admiring the open expanse.

Amin nudged Raden. "We just shaved a month off the transit."

"Yes," the helmsman whispered. "And a few centimeters off the hull."

Pike's jaw set. They'd done it; now it was time to report for duty—whatever duty—Starfleet required.

He turned to the bridge crew. "My mother used to say, 'It's better to ask forgiveness than permission.' I told you all that the message I received from Starfleet was broadcast a long time ago; what I did *not* say—except to Number One—is that we were also ordered to remain in the nebula."

He paused, waiting for a reaction. Seeing his crew strangely relaxed, he plowed ahead. "Obviously, I have disregarded that order, judging that enough time has passed since it was sent that circumstances are likely to have changed. I accept full responsibility; none will fall on you. That said, I don't want any of you thinking this is an okay practice when it comes to orders from *me*—or any future captains you may serve under." *Perhaps sooner than I'd like.* "Is that understood?"

He got nods and statements of assent from the bridge crew. "Fine. All hands, prepare for warp. Lay in a course for—"

A chime sounded at communications. Lieutenant Vicente Nicola touched his earpiece. "Captain, we're being hailed."

Pike's brow furrowed. "Is it whoever shot at us?"

"No, Captain. It's Starfleet Command. They want to speak with you—immediately." The dark-haired man hesitated. "It's Admiral Terral, sir."

Terral? Pike had clashed with him before over matters of policy, without ever once winning an argument. A joke around Starfleet had called him "the only Vulcan who could read minds remotely." But the timing of this call was on a whole other level. "Vic, how would he even know we were here to—"

He stopped in midsentence and looked at Una. The woman's expression was mild and serene, as it often was; as a human who grew up in the Illyrian colonies, she had adapted much of that placid species' emotional self-control. Pike interpreted the current look to be the Illyrian version of trying to appear innocent.

"Never mind," he said, heading back to the turbolift. "Keep the conn, Number One. I'll take the call in my quarters." He looked over his shoulder. "Unless somebody else wants to come along and enjoy the fun."

There were no takers.

4

Warship *Deathstrike*
Pergamum Nebula

Baladon did not say that he had a realistic hope—that in exchange for *Enterprise*, the Klingons would give him one of the Federation worlds they had conquered. There, he'd set up his own Lurian society, free from the ruling Gheljiar and their dynasty of dunces. Humans favored luxurious planets for their homes; why they set off to study the reeking armpits of the galaxy was beyond him. Baladon would be happy to set up court and allow the privateers to come to *him* for jobs.

That is, if Klingons made deals.

"Are we still following *Enterprise*'s course?" he asked.

"Yes," Jeld replied. "But they go fast."

Baladon nodded. He had little worry about losing his prey. Tracking a vessel through a nebula was one of the few Lurian flight-deck talents, honed by operations in the Ionite. The nebula would slow *Enterprise* down again eventually.

At the tactical station, Vauss tentatively raised a finger. "Something's out there."

"Aha!" Baladon clapped his hands and sprang from his chair. "Sooner than I expected. They've been forced to stop. Perhaps we did damage after all." He stepped to the bloody comm station and activated the shipwide address system. "This is Baladon, my legion. Even fools can find redemption, it seems, when history takes a hand."

Jeld quietly grumbled, "They have no idea what you mean."

"Consider that last attempt merely a drill," Baladon continued. "Reassemble at the assault pods, weapons at the ready. On boarding *Enterprise*, you will deal with any Starfleet personnel with extreme malice." He laughed. "They aren't conquerors by reputation, so it should be—"

At once, a deafening boom. *Deathstrike* rocked, knocking Baladon from his feet and several of his officers away from their stations. Alarms screeched.

"They shot at us!" Vauss yelled over the din.

"Nonsense," Baladon said, using a console for support as he got to his knees. "Remember where we are! *Enterprise* is far ahead. You have driven us into a wave of dense material, or possibly a—"

Another clamor, another impact put him flat on his back. Baladon rolled over on the deck, seething with fury. This time, before he could say anything, a third blast struck.

Deathstrike shuddered, the sound of its impulse engine dying.

"*Now* we've stopped," Jeld called out. "Still think they're far ahead?"

Baladon gritted his teeth and looked at the forward viewport. Dark gases—maybe a moving silhouette? He stood. "Charge weapons. Find them!"

Vauss, huddled behind his control station, rose and tried to get his bearings. "Can't see them."

Baladon bolted toward the tactical station. He would sort this out himself. As he reached it, a clang reverberated through the overhead.

What in—?

One clank after another, and a little jolt to *Deathstrike* each time. Baladon was still piecing together what was happening when Vauss grabbed his arm. "Brother, look!"

Outside the forward viewport, a stubby cylinder hurtled

toward *Deathstrike*'s bow, propelled by attitude-control jets on its rounded surface. It looked for a moment as if the object would strike the viewport, but it instead slammed, flat-end first, into the hull a few meters to the right. It was the loudest clang they'd yet heard.

Baladon instantly realized what would come next. "They're cutting us open!" Several points on the bulkhead inside the impact location glowed as laser torches began cutting through. *Deathstrike*'s assault pods operated in a similar manner, but with a difference: there were Lurians piloting the small vehicles. These things didn't seem to be carrying anyone—and that made them weapons. "They're going to decompress the bridge!"

Chaos ruled, as Lurians rushed willy-nilly to find environment suits that nobody had thought to stock the room with. Time ran out quickly. The three-meter-diameter circle of metal that had been part of the bulkhead began to give way. Jeld shouted a warning—and everyone reached for whatever handhold they could find.

The panel fell in and slammed to the deck. Through the smoke from the cut, Baladon saw not the open space of the nebula, but another door, a few meters beyond. A moment later, that view vanished as a second, nearer door, flush to the outer hull of the ship, slammed shut.

They're installing their own airlocks? That suggested to Baladon that the boarders might intend to keep *Deathstrike*'s occupants alive—which would track with Starfleet's soft-hearted practices. But who knew they even had such capabilities?

Bipedal figures were now coming into view outside, carried along on jets of their own. Baladon cursed. His crew had been searching for spacesuits when they should have been looking for weapons.

"Repel boarders!" the pirate yelled for the first time in his life. Elsewhere on *Deathstrike*, something was already happening. Extremely high-pitched screeches intermingled with lower-pitched sounds of certain violence. Baladon, who always carried a sidearm for disciplinary purposes, raised his disruptor and trained it on the new doorway—

—not anticipating the powerful sonic wave that erupted from a device on the impromptu airlock doors facing them. The shriek knocked Baladon and others off their feet, even as the airlock doors cycled open again.

What passed that new threshold was unlike anything Baladon had ever seen—not in battle, nor in any records of warfare. A titan two and a half meters tall entered, completely protected in armor made from some kind of reddish composite. The outfit was anything but sleek, with multiple protrusions, including a large jetpack, equipment cases of various sizes, and gear asymmetrically stowed. Some parts of it looked newer than others; much of the plating was pocked and dented, as if by combat. The armor bristled with offensive systems: built-in energy weapons, what looked like grenades, and even some kind of white staff—which the faceless figure drew and thrust against the deck. An electric shock went through the floor, causing bridge crewmembers—but not the invader—to jump.

Baladon and a couple of others recovered and tried to fire on the attacker, but their shots glanced off something, not even making contact with the armor.

Energy shielding too? Baladon frowned. He had no time to strategize, as several more warriors poured through the doorways aft of the bridge. Unlike the first intruder, their gear seemed less battle damaged—but they bore just as many weapons.

The ensuing melee was as brief as it was surprising to Baladon, who knew fighting to be the one thing, besides eating, that every member of his crew had some talent at. He had all he could handle himself. As more intruders cycled through the new bridge airlock, the mighty Lurian flailed wildly at the warrior who had entered first. Baladon's knuckles slammed against the armor, a painful act evoking no reaction. Nor did the next blow, or the next one, bloodying his hands but doing nothing else. Then in a movement faster than the Lurian could see, the intruder's hand lanced forward, seizing Baladon's beefy neck in a powerful grip. The warrior's arm rose, lifting the hefty Baladon centimeters off the deck.

The fight was over—for everyone. More armored characters streamed onto the bridge. As Baladon struggled helplessly, some carried off his companions; his crewmates seemed dazed, not dead. Other new arrivals produced power tools, which they deployed to begin removing control stations from the deck. This included the console of *Deathstrike*'s late communications officer, whose body was unceremoniously shoved onto the floor.

"I am Kormagan," the invader said in perfect Lurian, easily audible through the warrior's faceplate without mechanical amplification. The figure returned Baladon to the deck and released him. "Speak if you understand me."

Baladon coughed—and nodded. "You're from *Enterprise*."

"What's an *Enterprise*?"

Baladon slouched, only able to watch as the boarders did to his ship what he had done to so many others in his career.

Too late, he realized he had just discovered who the *real* pirates of the Pergamum were.

5

U.S.S. Enterprise
Outside the Pergamum Nebula

"You are not where you're supposed to be, Captain. If you were, I would not be able to talk to you at all." On the computer on Pike's desk, Admiral Terral's steely gaze cut across light-years. *"Calling this moment a surprise would be an understatement."*

Leaning back in his chair, Pike had already decided there wasn't any point in denying anything—so he started by being pleasant. "It's good to see you, Admiral. You're the first person I've seen in months that's not a member of my crew."

"That is another surprise," the bald-headed Vulcan said. *"I expected to see you as a hologram."*

"More trouble with the system." That was another understatement. The holographic recorders and projectors had never really worked; *Enterprise* had rejected them like a transplanted organ. With no one to transmit to while in the nebula, there had been little impetus to get the systems going.

"I suppose you are going to tell me that trouble also explains why you disobeyed my order. Your mission isn't even half over."

Pike shifted in his chair. "Your message was sent months ago, Admiral. I thought it was prudent to come out and get an update."

"The fact that we continued to transmit that message should have told you the order was still operative."

"It could also have meant that nobody was left to turn it off."

Pike blanched a little. It was a dark place to go for a defense—and Terral's tone grew icier. *"I highly doubt you emerged simply to check the news, Captain. You were about to warp home."*

He smiled awkwardly. "How could you tell?"

"Your first officer, in her *prudence, logged into the astrometric subspace database as soon as you left the nebula, to check what interstellar routes were occupied by Klingons."*

So that's it, Pike thought. Una would have needed to consult the database in preparation for carrying out his order to return—and she also had to know the action would alert Starfleet of their location, perhaps in time to stop him before he did something he would regret. *She's as sly as ever.* "Well, I guess I'm found out."

"She did you a favor. She knows your mission there isn't supposed to be over for months."

"Admiral, we are at war—" He paused and tilted his head. "We *are* still at war, right?"

"Very much so."

"Sorry to hear that. But we can help. I have a pretty amazing ship, and a lot of great people. The problem is we're about as far from the action as we can be."

"We have ships farther out than yours."

"Every light-year we go deeper into the Pergamum is like a hundred somewhere else, Admiral. We just found that out the hard way. Little to no contact with the outside universe, and you've got to fight to leave it."

"And you left it to fight. It is irrelevant. Your presence is not required."

"Admiral Cornwell sent me a list of starships that were destroyed. Am I right in saying that we've lost more since?"

"We are fully capable of handling the threat."

Pike studied the dark-skinned Vulcan's face. He might have been able to read Katrina Cornwell, but it was impossible to tell how much confidence Terral had in what he was saying. On the chance that conditions had worsened, Pike thought it might be better to dial down his appeal and take a different tack.

"I apologize, Admiral. It was my decision; it's on me." He clasped his hands together. "Look, I got to know Philippa Georgiou at the Academy. I can't remember what brought her back there, but I've never met a more consummate professional. That business back at Sirsa III last year where she and I were put at cross-purposes—that could have worked out badly. But it didn't, because of her and her people."

"And also, I understand, because of yours."

"Thanks. I don't have to tell you what the 'captain's club' means to those who are in it. When you tell me we've lost so many, so fast—"

Terral shook his head. *"I admire your loyalty, Captain. But we are adequately defended—and we have other plans for* Enterprise. *The mission you already have."*

"A mission assigned before war broke out." Pike didn't know how hard to push. "Navigating the Pergamum's like swimming in glue. Whatever we're learning here—well, I'll be honest, it can wait."

"That is not our judgment." Terral paused. *"Are you certain that is the only reason you wanted to return, Captain?"*

Pike was caught off guard. "Yeah. I should think it's enough."

Terral didn't seem so sure. He looked down, referring to something off-screen. *"I do not see anything about personal connections at home that would command your attention. Or,"* he said, raising an eyebrow, *"does it relate to two years ago?"*

Pike blinked. Terral meant Talos IV, and the incidents surrounding his visit there in 2254. The admiral would have been one of the few people brought into that mass of secrets. "No, that's all fine," he replied. "I'm not having any problems."

"Then it comes back to something your science officer would

agree with, Captain. Logic. Intended function. Production for use. Enterprise *is a science ship."*

"You know, people keep saying that. It's strange, because it feels an awful lot like a warship." They'd found an old sore spot, long a point of contention between him and Starfleet. "Just about every time I've come back to port since my missions started, we've been refitted with weapons that have only grown more lethal. And those were for peacetime."

Terral scowled. *"This again."*

"It's the truth, Admiral. Two years ago, we were outfitted with lasers; now it's phasers. There are single armaments on this ship with more firepower than was expended in the last war. *H.M.S. Beagle* carried four six-pound guns and two nine-pounders. I have more destructive power attached to my belt. I have the most overpowered 'science ship' ever conceived." He chuckled. "Now, maybe my history's wrong, but I don't think Jacques Cousteau ever needed to flatten a city."

"It is a dangerous galaxy. How often has Starfleet discovered that?"

"A few times. I just worry that we're starting to get so obsessed with that fact that we're losing perspective. We're going to wake up one day and find out we all joined a military outfit after all."

Terral gave him a chilly Vulcan stare. *"Moments ago you wanted to come back to fight. You are a pacifist now?"*

"I didn't know I had to choose. I even worry that, eventually, just carrying around all these weapons is going to make *us* the target."

"Then you have little to fear. If somebody comes for Enterprise, *you'll be able to fire back."*

Curt words, the latest in what had been a volley between them over Starfleet's direction going back years. But they also jogged Pike's memory. "There's something else you should know, Admiral. We think somebody shot at us."

That got Terral's attention. *"I thought you said nobody was there. When did this happen?"*

"It was today, on our way out. Galadjian thinks it was a photon torpedo."

"If he says so, it was."

"Agreed." Pike didn't mention the five-percent chance that it wasn't. "We didn't see who fired it."

Terral's eyes narrowed. *"There have never been any reports of Klingon activity near the Pergamum. It is not in their quadrant."*

"I grant it's not much of a tourist destination. But they're not your usual tourists."

"Very well," Terral said. *"Then you have just given yourself another reason to stay. If you find Klingons, certainly, emerge long enough to get us a message. Starfleet Command will issue further orders then. Otherwise, we will see you when your mission is complete."*

Pike slouched a little in his chair. Another trademarked Terral logical trap—and he'd walked right into it. "Aye, Admiral."

"The nebula sounds like a strong defensive position," he said. *"If you want to contribute to the war, finding planets there that can be safely inhabited would be a job of high importance."*

Pike swallowed. *So things* aren't *going as well as you say,* he thought. "We'll do our best."

"Excellent. I am sending a report on the Battle of the Binary Stars."

"It has a name already?"

"Enough memorials and that will occur." Terral spoke clearly. "*It is for your information, and should not affect your intentions. Is that understood?"*

"It is."

"Trust us to win the war, Captain, and we will trust you to find something interesting we can all study when it's over. Starfleet out."

6

Warship *Deathstrike*
Pergamum Nebula

One thing was true of just about every sentient species, Kormagan thought. As a creature's rank and privileges rose, so did the complaining when all that was taken away.

Ever since her warriors captured his ship, the fat grayish thing with the shriveled face—now manacled to a bridge support—had never stopped yammering. She had inferred from his clothing that he had superior rank, and that had been proven correct. But even a short time with him was enough to make her regret ever loading the Lurian language into her armor's audio systems.

"You are making a colossal mistake," he declared. "All of you! Do you have any idea who I am?"

"Baladon," she replied. *Unless it changed since the last time you told me.*

"I am ambassador extraordinary for the ruler of Luria, visiting this nebula on a fact-finding tour. On behalf of my government, I demand compensation for damages to this vessel!"

"You said that." The Lurian's vocabulary was as big as he was—and while the temperature on the bridge was lower than Kormagan's species liked, her armor's sensors told her that it was slightly higher surrounding him. *Probably from all the words.*

"And you will return my crew!"

"They're already in Processing."

Baladon's eyes widened. "You intend to *eat* them?"

"Not that kind of processing." Kormagan looked up from the console she was studying. "Your ship's labeled *Deathstruck*. Maybe there's a problem with our translation. In our language, it sounds as if *this* is the ship struck by death."

"It was meant to be *Deathstrike*. My cousin has trouble with verbs."

"Because when we started trailing you, we were concerned it was a plague ship. The way the name was hand painted."

"The only plague is on me."

That's a relief, Kormagan thought. Bacteriological and viral hazards came with the territory on this kind of mission, and they could ruin the worth of a good prize in a hurry.

"Wait," Baladon said as she moved to another terminal. "*You* were stalking *us*?"

"You weren't hard to find. Skulking just inside the nebula—not something an outsider does unless they're hiding from someone. You sure you're a diplomat?"

Baladon's eyes narrowed. "I refuse to answer."

"So you know how to remain silent."

"You're the one who kept me here. If I am so disturbing, you are perfectly welcome to leave!"

This is a waste of time. Kormagan caught the attention of one of her companions and pointed to one of the remaining consoles. The armored figure set to work examining it.

Kormagan stood to her full armored height, towering over Baladon. "I know your language because we've encountered your people before—and we know what *they* were up to. I also saw your spacepods back there. This is a pirate vessel."

"A scurrilous accusation, I deny!"

"Your crew didn't."

Baladon sputtered for several moments before going silent. He rested his head against the column he was secured to. "Ruin. They have brought me to ruin."

"That's where you're wrong."

"How?" the Lurian asked. "When you started taking equipment, I thought you were privateers—but your questions prove otherwise. You are authorities of some government!"

"We have our own ships—we don't need yours. Though if there's a good idea in here," she said, referring to the console being carted out, "we'll use it. No, what we want is *you*."

"Me!"

"And any more of those torpedoes we saw you fire."

Baladon snorted. "What we had, you saw. If we had more, I would've sent one to you to inspect close-up." He bared his teeth. "But you would not have had long to study it."

Kormagan disregarded the attitude. "Maybe there *is* one more thing. *That*." She gestured to the screen on the starboard bulkhead, where the image of a colossal starship had been present since her arrival. The smooth curves fascinated her. It looked nothing like Baladon's ship—nor any vessel her own people had. "What is it?"

"Why should I tell you?"

She put an armor-encased finger under Baladon's stubby nose. "If you've found something that'll help us, you're going to want to share it. If not now, in a couple of weeks, when I put your speckled ass on the front lines."

"On the what? What are you talking about?"

There was no point in answering. Kormagan's recently arrived companion was already having some success in operating the Lurian's computer systems. Captions appeared next to the ship on the wall. "*U.S.S. Enterprise*," she read. "Did you chase it into the nebula, Baladon, or were you following it *out*?" She couldn't tell from the data on the display. "A warship, for sure."

Baladon stared at her. "I thought you said you weren't pirates."

"I didn't say what we were. Enough." Kormagan toggled

her armor's onboard communicator. "Redsub, give me two to get the *Deathstrike* captain out of here."

"Affirm."

Baladon groaned and stared at the deck. At last, he addressed Kormagan. "If I tell you what I know about *Enterprise*, will you let me go?"

"No."

"What if I lead you to it?"

"No."

Baladon frowned. "If I help you capture it!"

"You're going to do that anyway." A pair of Kormagan's comrades entered the bridge. She pointed at Baladon. "Put him with his friends—and scrub them down the second they reach Processing. Jayko hates people smelling up his deck."

"Wait!" Baladon said, launching a stream of protestations that continued for his entire journey out of the room.

Kormagan looked to her other companion, still standing over a console. "You have the data on *Enterprise*?"

"That's affirm, Wavemaster." She heard his voice clearly through his faceplate, a battlesuit feature that helped reserve comm channels for true distance communications. "The info is duplicated in the datacore we already brought out. This console just operates the screen."

"Then leave it here. Anything else worth a look?"

"*Deathstruck* isn't very interesting."

"No, the name is—" Kormagan started to say. "Never mind. Dismissed."

Alone, she studied the *Enterprise* image. Her armored hand touched the screen, and she traced its long, sloping lines. Inside her headgear, her eyes narrowed. Warp nacelles. Weapons banks. Some kind of emitter. And was that a shuttlebay in back?

Whatever you are, Kormagan thought, *you're worth more to me than these people.*

7

U.S.S. Enterprise
Outside the Pergamum Nebula

Pike had done as instructed. He had not gone to the bridge to issue his order to return to the nebula, but rather had sent the command over the comm system. He hadn't had the heart to order it in person. It was easy to imagine the reactions across *Enterprise*. They'd just gone through hell to leave the Pergamum the fast way—and now they had to turn back and re-enter the slow way.

If there's a Starfleet citation for going in circles, we're a shoo-in.

Pike had used the time instead to absorb the report Terral had sent him about the battle. It devastated him. After their heated conversation—he hoped it wasn't an argument—the admiral had undermined his cause in sending the file, because it certainly didn't make following the order any easier. He wondered whether Terral would have sent it at all, had Pike's mention of the torpedo not made it imperative that he know the Klingons' latest—and horrific—tactics.

But there was one other element in the report that *was* relevant—immediately, he saw, as his door slid open to admit a visitor.

"Spock. All wrapped up behind the deflector dish?" Pike asked.

"Yes, Captain." The crew had gotten bright new uniforms

during the last refit; the young Vulcan's was stained with lubricant. "You will forgive my appearance, but our transit necessitated frequent equipment repairs, and I was told you wanted to see me directly."

Pike's brow furrowed, but not solely because Galadjian hadn't mentioned any repairs. "Lieutenant, I have some news for you. You may want to take a seat."

"I am not tired. Or is there excess detail in what you have to say?"

"It's the weight, not the volume." Pike figured he had better get to it. "The Klingon Empire has gone to war with the Federation."

"I learned from Yeoman Colt on my way here. I inferred it was behind our sudden departure." Spock's head tilted. "How large is the engagement?"

"The Federation's entire Beta Quadrant frontier with the Empire, as well as raids at other locations. You'll get a full accounting. In short, they surprised us."

Spock thought for a moment. "The Klingons must be responding to some stimulus."

"It's out of proportion to anything we did, so far as I know."

"That is further evidence to suggest there are factors involved we do not understand. Something must explain the difference in scale between provocation and response."

"I wouldn't rule out pure meanness." Spock always tried to find answers even when logic did not apply; it was a trait Pike admired in him. The captain took a breath. "There's more. A number of starships were destroyed in the engagement." He paused. "*Shenzhou* is one of them. Captain Georgiou and many of her crew were killed."

Spock took in the news. "A regrettable waste. The captain was a most qualified commander."

A succinct way to put it, Pike thought, but one he agreed

with. He expected Spock might have more to say about the next news. "Michael Burnham is alive. I was assured of that."

Spock said nothing.

"There's more, but she's okay. I thought you'd want to know." Pike squinted. "I've known since the mission on Sirsa III that there's a connection between the two of you."

"We are Starfleet officers."

"Yeah, well—" Pike started, before stopping. He decided to spare the details of Burnham's imprisonment. *Maybe they weren't that close.*

"Has the *Enterprise* been recalled?"

"Emphatically not," Pike said. "Our mission is to continue, duration unchanged."

"Then I resubmit my request for an expedition to Pergamum 85752-B."

"Susquatane."

"As the preface to my report details, that name was recommended to the Federation Astronomical Committee by members of the 2244 survey voyage. But it has yet to receive formal approval." Spock looked keenly at the captain and added, "Nor has my expedition."

Pike inhaled deeply. "Well, we're retracing our steps. We should be able to see it again." There were another half-dozen candidate planets for study—but frankly, Pike didn't give much of a damn which one they went to. He stood. "Spock, I should let you know I didn't agree with our return to the nebula. With the war on—well, I can think of better things to do than to spend months in the middle of nowhere studying the effects of exotic radiation on space daffodils."

"We are unlikely to find any members of the Earth genus *Narcissus*, Captain. But the range of biomes does look promising for other discoveries, as—"

"As mentioned in your report," Pike said, walking toward the door in hopes of cutting the disquisition short.

Realizing that Spock hadn't moved, he stopped and looked back. They'd shared many experiences, including the Talos IV incident—yet there was little getting close to a Vulcan, and even less of a chance with Spock. "Is there something else?"

Spock spoke. "Captain, the Klingons pursue violence. We would pursue knowledge. For now, they are more likely to convince the Federation to join them in their violence. By our remaining here—and continuing with our plans—we assure them that we will never abandon our path."

"Yeah, that case has been made." Pike led him into the hall. "It's a nice sentiment. We should send you to the peace talks."

Spock raised an eyebrow. "That would be a waste of material." He turned and departed.

I can never tell if he's making a joke or not, Pike thought. Maybe someone else would figure Spock out someday.

He called for the turbolift—only to see Una inside when it arrived. He gave her a playful glare. "It turns out I'm still the captain."

"That was my hope."

"More months in the chemical stew," he said as he stepped inside. "That was some dirty trick you pulled. You tipped off Terral that I was coming home."

"It would have been . . . *irresponsible* not to check for Klingon incursions on our possible route."

"That's what makes it a dirty trick. You did it in a way that I can't get mad at you." Pike kept his stern gaze on her—until he broke into a grin. "Well done, Number One. Where to?"

"I was coming to see you. Amin has the conn. We are approaching our nebular entry point from five months ago."

"And around and around she goes." Pike grabbed the control handle. "Let's explore this god-awful thing."

From his seat on the bridge, Pike had found the sight was

no better the second time: an endless quagmire—only now, without the mystery of what they'd find on their journey inside. Most of the crew weren't looking at the main viewscreen at all—and none were looking at him. Certainly they'd been stressed by the day's efforts, only to suffer a literal reversal. Pike figured Galadjian was still belowdecks, planning his next symposium and wondering what the hell kind of outfit he'd signed up with.

Pike's eyes fixed on the advancing cloud formations—and he tried his best not to look away too. Terral had been right: there *was* something else, something that he'd managed to keep out of his psych reports.

He had survived his teenage spelunking expedition; his hopes for the future had survived too. Evan Hondo's death had been attributed to his own negligence with a phaser, and Freena and Dosh had testified to Pike's attempts to save all of them. In so doing, *they* had saved *him*. There had been near-term consequences, as he'd expected, particularly from his parents—but in the longer view, having the incident on his record had helped, rather than hurt, his case for entry into Starfleet Academy. It wasn't something he wanted to profit from, of course—but the admissions officers were impressed by someone who would risk life and limb to not leave anyone behind.

What they didn't know was that he'd left a chunk of his nerve back there. For a long time, Pike hadn't known that claustrophobia had followed him out of the tunnel. Desert horseback riding had been an excellent balm, and while starships were enclosed, they opened a window onto the biggest sky in creation. But his aversion to confinement had recently crept back, reactivated by his captivity underground on Talos IV, two years earlier.

That experience had produced such a tangle of confused emotions for Pike that he'd barely noticed that element of it—until the *Enterprise*'s arrival in the Pergamum. And now he was going back in—twenty years to the day after his escape from the tunnel. Angry pillars of oppressive darkness loomed ahead, ready to crush them all.

He looked down. His right hand hovered over his left wrist, as if poised to clear invisible rocks.

He quickly brought it back to the armrest and used it to toggle the shipwide comm. “Attention, all hands. We’re going in.”

8

U.S.S. Enterprise
Pergamum Nebula

Spock meditated.

Despite his assurance to Captain Pike, the efforts of the day had taxed him. Galadjian's calculations had been instrumental in effecting their quick exit from the nebula, but the theoretician—rightfully renowned, in Spock's judgment—had little discernible experience in putting his findings quickly into action. Spock had served as the conduit, understanding that his skills were, on that occasion, superior. It was what officers did on an efficiently functioning starship.

Spock had taken a small meal and recorded a personal log in his quarters, after which he had read the report on what had happened to *Shenzhou*. It had been troubling. Ostensibly, Michael Burnham had acted to protect her starship and others from an anticipated—and, it turned out, correctly predicted—Klingon attack. But assaulting a superior officer in that cause was beyond the pale. Spock could not visualize any situation that would lead him to commandeer *Enterprise*.

But while the episode was shocking, the fact that Burnham had committed the acts did not come as a complete surprise. Their connection had been fraught and complicated. The brief joint mission at Sirsa III had been productive, but their interaction had not changed the basic facts of their relationship. It already felt like many years since he had spoken to her, and he expected she felt the same way. Spock was gratified that she had survived *Shenzhou*'s destruction, but her fate did not move him.

His mother, he expected, would differ. *That*, he cared about.

His eyes fixed on the light from the candle he had lit in *Shenzhou*'s memory. The glow lingered when he closed his eyes and bowed his head. He knew the effect: a physiological afterimage created by retinal photoreceptor cells continuing to send impulses to his brain. A negative afterimage followed. It was reproducible but not pathological, as it might be if he suffered from an ailment that caused palinopsia.

There was no magic to it. Just as there was none to the stars, to *Enterprise*—or even to the place where their sojourn would now resume. Despite the insistence of its discoverers to imbue the Pergamum Nebula with some mythological significance, there was nothing paranormal about its arrangements of atoms, its varieties of rays. Science had brought them safely in and out once before. It would do so again.

He extinguished the candle and went to sleep.

INFILTRATION

January 2257

INCOMING TRANSMISSION (ENCRYPTED)

TO: CAPTAIN C. PIKE • *U.S.S. ENTERPRISE* • NCC-1701

FROM: REAR ADMIRAL TERRAL, STARFLEET COMMAND

HOSTILITIES WITH KLINGON EMPIRE CONTINUE. MULTIPLE ENGAGEMENTS.

AMBASSADOR SAREK PEACE BID UNSUCCESSFUL.

REGRET TO INFORM YOU VICE ADMIRAL CORNWELL MIA/PRESUMED KIA.

ENTERPRISE MISSION UNCHANGED. DO NOT RETURN.

END TRANSMISSION

9

U.S.S. Enterprise
Orbiting Susquatane

Someday, Pike thought, *they need to build a starship that's got its own nature park. A few months stuck aboard the ship, and everybody wants to go for a hike.*

Pike had returned from his lunch to find a line of off-duty personnel outside the officers' lounge. He'd commandeered the facility as his temporary expedition staging area because its ports overlooked Susquatane, an enormous orb painted with strokes of green, blue, gold, and white. And all of Pike's visitors wanted the same thing: the chance to beam down to it.

There was no surprise in that. Spock had been correct, as usual. Of all the planets *Enterprise* had surveyed in the Outer Pergamum, as the outermost layers were called, only Susquatane, sitting in one of the rare zones free from dangerous radiation, had looked viable for extended surface exploration. Its varied terrains and climatic regions tantalized a crew that had been cooped up for months. *Enterprise*'s puny botanical garden had no chance of competing.

Dutifully, he had seen all but one of his visitors, delighting some, disappointing others. This final appeal, he could tell, was going to be another heartbreaker. He looked up from the written request to the young lieutenant who'd delivered it. Seeing that the poor kid was on tenterhooks, Pike decided to end his misery quickly. "I can't put you on the ground, Connolly. Your expertise is gravimetrics. You can get your data from orbit."

"Captain—"

"If you saw some of my Academy scores in science, you'd lose all respect for me. But your particular brand doesn't get you onto a lot of landing parties."

Connolly boldly launched into what Pike figured was a rehearsed spiel about how much time his on-site microgravimetric analyses could save Spock's teams on Susquatane. "I can locate hideouts for subsurface life-forms we could never detect from orbit. Underground liquid reserves too. I can even find all the great places for spelunking."

Not a selling point. Pike clasped his hands together and leaned across the table. "Why don't we skip past the sales pitch to where you tell me you've got cabin fever, like everyone else on the ship?"

Caught, Connolly smirked a little. "Just trying to say I'd be down there to work. I'm not looking for shore leave, sir."

"And I'm not issuing it. Not on an unknown planet."

"We've been out eight months. I'd just like to see a sky from underneath."

"This planet is Spock's project. He's indispensable to it. That puts his relief in science on the bridge and that means you."

"Ensign Dietrich could—" Connolly began, before he caught Pike's expression. "Aye, Captain."

"If it makes you feel any better, I'll make sure they don't have too much fun down there."

Connolly lingered. "While I'm here, I was wondering if you'd gotten any news. You know, from back home."

He studied the young man. So many had friends and family behind the lines. Pike read him the latest missive from Starfleet. Short, as usual, given the restraints on their ability to receive—and devastating. When he was finished, Connolly looked abashed. "Believe me," Pike said, "you're not the only one who doesn't want to be where he is."

"I don't know what to say, Captain. Sorry to hear about the admiral."

"So was I." Pike could sense the young man's unease. "Was there something else?"

"No. I mean, well—now I feel bad about what I was really trying to ask about." Connolly shifted from one foot to the other as he fumbled for words. "It was about baseball."

"About *what*?"

"It's a game."

"I know what it is. I've seen it."

"There's a revival league back in Florida where I'm from. They post results to the Federation news feed. I know we got a databurst while we were outside the nebula—"

"Classified. About the war."

"—but our fall classic would have been done by then. I was just wondering who won." He smiled awkwardly. "And if there's final standings, I'll take those too." Another pause. "You know, because we went in the nebula just a few weeks after opening day."

Pike stared. "Go back to work, Lieutenant."

Sheepish, Connolly straightened and turned. He opened the door to find Doctor Boyce waiting outside. The two passed one another, with the doctor's eyes following Connolly on the way out.

Boyce looked back to Pike. "Problem?"

In their mutual language, it was more of a prompt than a question. "Just somebody else who wants to jump ship. He was the seventh one today."

"That got past Una, you mean." Boyce smiled as he took a seat. "Suddenly everyone wants to join the science team."

"We've got twenty people going already."

"Twenty-six. That's Una's latest count. She's just gotten Nhan's security recommendation."

"That's right—I asked her to increase it." Pike nodded and gestured to the door. "Better not tell the last guy who was here. He'd put on a red shirt if it meant he could beam down."

"Evan Connolly? He's always raring to go."

"I think he wants to start a baseball league down there."

"He'd get takers."

Pike stood and walked about the room. "There was another kid I knew—also named Evan. From Australia, living in California while his parents served in Starfleet. He was pretty gung ho too." Staring out the port at the planet's night side, he decided to forgo the story. "Things happened."

"Would anything happen on Susquatane?"

Pike shrugged. "How should I know? How do we *ever* know? Could be carnivorous rock creatures this time, or hypnotic bees. Or maybe it's the summer home of whoever lobbed that torpedo at us weeks ago."

"And have you heard any more about that?"

"No. I'm no longer even sure it was what we thought."

Boyce studied him before speaking. "Permission to make a comment the captain may find patronizing."

"Patronize away."

"If you keep trying to protect every person that steps on the transporter pad, Chris, nobody's ever going to leave the ship."

"I gather that."

Boyce shook his head. "I'm definitely in the wrong line. They need to send counselors instead of physicians. You haven't talked like this since after Rigel VII."

Pike droned, "I'm past that."

"I thought you were too. You didn't have a problem going into action at, what was that place, Sirsa III? And weren't you just wanting to run off and join the war a couple of months ago?"

Pike looked back at him in frustration. He walked around to the desk and called up the data on his computer. He swiveled it to face the doctor. "Check this out."

Boyce studied the dots on the screen. "Looks like a bad skin condition."

"It's the Beta Quadrant."

"The quadrant has a rash."

"Klingon space. Starfleet Intelligence can only count the stars—no idea how many ships or warriors there are." Pike sat down and waved his hands. "Now here I am. I know what I've got. One ship and two hundred and three people who can surely do some good. Only we're being kept on the shelf for some reason. Terral's reason, perhaps—maybe even Katrina Cornwell's. But she went MIA a while back, and I can't even get a message out to ask what happened, much less why Starfleet sidelined us."

"I doubt she made the decision alone."

"Maybe it's me. Or maybe it's because they think *Enterprise* is too precious to lose, that they'll need us. In which case—"

"—they'll need *every one* of us." Boyce's eyes lit with amusement as he considered. "This is classic. You want to get involved—but you can't, so the only way you can do anything is to sit on all your eggs and make sure nothing happens to them. Starfleet has just put Chris Pike's mania in the captain's chair." He chuckled. "And me without my emergency cocktails."

Pike stared at the wall for a moment, before looking back at Boyce. "Twenty-six people?"

"Latest count I heard. I'm sure Spock will tell you soon."

That's a lot of eggs.

Boyce leaned toward him. "Spock also told me there wasn't any danger on the planet."

"So far as we know from orbit. Nhan is still looking."

"You've found angry natives? Hungry animals? Plants with teeth?"

Pike shook his head.

Boyce patted the desk and rose. "Well, then. Have Adventure Pike tell Protective Pike to take it easy for a change. Maybe go down there yourself. Contemplate a creek."

"I'll still have a hundred seventy-seven people up here."

"Counting yourself." The doctor chuckled. "I'll see myself out."

Pike stared. "Wait. Why were you here?"

"I was going to report some minor allergic reactions to a new solvent being used in the hangar deck, but I don't think you can take the worry." As Boyce approached the door, it opened. "Oh, hello again, Mister Spock."

"Doctor." Spock entered holding a manifest. "Captain, I have an update about the personnel necessary for the Susquatane survey. I will require two additional teams for the southern biomes—and someone with gravimetric expertise to assist in my studies of the polar ice shelf."

"Excuse me," Boyce said. "The captain needs me to bring back my medical bag, fully stocked."

Spock heard Boyce's comment, and turned to study Pike. "Are you unwell, Captain?"

Pike looked daggers at Boyce.

10

U.S.S. Enterprise
Orbiting Susquatane

At Starfleet Academy, Pike had seen archival video of mission control operators during some of the earliest robotic missions to planetary bodies. No lives at stake, but there were white-knuckle moments nonetheless. Projects developed across decades and mounted at incredible expense all came down to one single moment: landing.

Workers who had labored in anonymity for years would wear their matching mission polo shirts for what would either be a birth or a funeral while the whole world watched. There would be long stretches of worried silence, punctuated by indecipherable status reports announced in hushed tones—and then applause as each intermediary milestone was reached. Finally, if all went well, held breaths suddenly released as cheers. Later missions with human crews were the same, times ten.

Meanwhile, Pike had agreed to the Susquatane expedition more or less because there was nothing better to do, and while the journey had taken time because of the need to go around the Acheron Formation, the landing phase hadn't sped his pulse in the least.

"Standing by to beam first party down," said Lieutenant Pitcairn over the comm.

Pike stood by the entry of the bridge turbolift, coffee mug in hand. "Go."

Nicola spoke, scant seconds later. "Incoming transmission."

"On."

"Landing party on the surface," Spock reported. *"Conditions as expected. Initial survey underway."*

"I guess that's that," Pike said. He turned back into the turbolift in search of a refill.

—

This feels like I'm leaving for a ski trip, Pike thought as he walked into the transporter room a week later. It felt bizarre to be the only one in the hallway wearing thick boots and thermal cold-weather gear; at least it wasn't a parka. He wasn't planning on staying on Susquatane that long.

He hadn't intended to go, but after days during which he had done little more than keep tabs on his half-dozen landing parties from above, Una and Colt had conspired to convince him to spend some time on the ground. "Energize," he said—

—and took his next breath on an alien world. He coughed, his lungs protesting against the sudden presence of chillier air. But the discomfort was over soon enough—and what filled him next was wonder. The brief winter day at the polar exploration site had just ended, unleashing a sky awash in color. Birthing stars peeked through narrow gaps on the inner side of a black nebular wall while, much closer, sheets of aurora draped underneath. Between the stars and snow, Pike crunched about in a vibrant twilight.

"Captain," Spock acknowledged, approaching from the north with his tricorder in hand. He was dressed in his white thermal uniform, apparently feeling no discomfort in this region much colder than his homeworld. He had also mastered the knack of walking in the snow without making a lot of noise. "Camp Five is ready for your review."

"This isn't an inspection, Spock. I just wanted to check the place out."

Spock seemed to understand the distinction. "I have visited all our expedition sites on planet. Susquatane is ideal."

"There's usually a 'but' somewhere." Pike didn't believe in Edens naturally occurring in hellish places. But if there was something wrong with Susquatane, he hadn't heard of it. This location was cool and sterile, but others were warm and teeming with life.

"Perhaps I should say that finding a Class-M planet here was improbable." Spock gestured to the sky. "But not impossible."

The Pergamum Nebula was an active body, with many regions of matter and energy in motion. Most had emissions hostile to living beings. But the Susquatane system sat in a bubble safely apart from the greatest dangers. "We're in the eye of the hurricane," Pike said, looking up.

"There are parts of the comparison which are not apt, Captain. Susquatane is not affixed to this location, such that it would be overtopped by the storm as time elapsed. Rather, it is traveling in space *with* the protected pocket. To know the permanence of the situation, it is imperative to study the atmosphere and geology of the world and the condition of its life-forms, both now and in the past."

"Spock, you sold me months ago. We're here." Pike looked about. "You think your surveys will soak up the remaining weeks of the mission?"

"Without difficulty." Spock eyed him. "You are willing to remain?"

Pike was surprised by the question. "Yeah, of course. We were ordered to stay in the nebula."

"I ask because travel is the function of starship captains—and for many, their preferred state."

"Not this one." Pike gestured with his gloved hands. "For

centuries on my world, captains have had to learn to live with time in port. This place seems reasonably safe—and as interesting as you say. I could kick around here for a while."

"Excellent."

"But it'd be nice to have a horse," Pike said with a smirk. "I don't suppose you've found any?"

"There are land-traversing cephalopods in the temperate zone which are sized similarly with ungulates on Earth," Spock said.

"Then I need a saddle."

"They would interpret any attempt to approach them as a challenge."

"I've broken a bronco or two."

"The challenge would not take physical form. The cephalopod would sing to you, and expect you to harmonize. If you fail to satisfy, it would immobilize you with a harmless ink spray while its companions educated you."

"Maybe I can do without that."

Pike heard the others approach before he saw them. It was the sound of the R3, one of the small surface vehicles *Enterprise* kept in its stores for expedition sites. Generically known as a snow scouter, it resembled a three-person version of one of the open-air Earth snowmobiles of old. With sleds at its base and antigrav-assisted repulsors for occasional use, the device cut a clean path across the slope, barely disturbing it. Pike's footsteps were leaving more of an imprint.

The driver disembarked first. Ghalka, a silver-haired Andorian biologist, looked as if she felt right at home. "Welcome, Captain," the chipper ensign said. "We've established a post above a subglacial lake. Would you care to see it?"

"Maybe later." Pike smiled at the second occupant. "Wheedled your way down, did you, Connolly?"

Connolly stepped off the snow scouter and smiled. "I said I'd be useful."

You and a lot of other people, Pike thought. A fair chunk of his staff was on the ground. This team's safety was coordinated by the third rider. Nhan was still seated in the vehicle, cinching her uniform and examining her phaser. The replacement for longtime Security Chief Mohandas had insisted on taking some of the shifts personally, perhaps not bargaining for the weather. "Ready for the next safari," the Barzan said, moisture crystallizing in the air in the space before her breathing device. "They should put a roof on this thing."

Spock conferred briefly with his colleagues and then approached the vehicle. "Commander, I must go back to the lake. There is an instrumentation problem."

Nhan shivered. "Glad I didn't bother to get off."

"You must. There are only three seats and I will need both my colleagues with me."

"That's not the arrangement, Mister Spock. The camps are under shipboard surveillance, but nobody leaves without a security officer."

"I can vouch for their safety."

Nhan stood and looked to Pike. "Captain?"

Pike's eyes widened. *Wow, a command decision*. "This is the deadest place on the planet, right?"

"Until you get a kilometer down," Connolly said.

Pike nodded. "It's been a week with no incident. And we don't want to beam when it's short distances." Even in this relatively safe spot of the Pergamum, *Enterprise*'s crew had decided not to overuse the transporter until they knew more about interactions with the particle environment. "Your call, Nhan."

She looked at the scientists. "Who doesn't have a sidearm?"

Ghalka looked puzzled. "I don't, but—"

"You do now." Nhan stepped off the snow scouter and placed her phaser in the ensign's hand. "I want that back."

Ghalka stared at it. "It's your only one?"

"It's not even the only one on me," the security chief said. Her devotion to her personal weaponry was well known. "Report back to *Enterprise* every fifteen minutes."

Well done, Pike thought as the snow scouter powered up again. Nhan was new, but his crew was in good hands.

Boots crunching snow, she began to walk around the camp with him. "I was going to see you after my shift down here," she said, "to report on the torpedo detonation."

"This is as good a place as any."

"It's as *cold* a place as any. I'm freezing my ass off—Captain."

"Sorry." He'd always known her to speak her mind. "We can always go back up before we talk."

"Are you kidding? After all those months I thought the walls were closing in."

Pike well understood. "The torpedo. What are our theories again?"

Nhan began numbering with her fingers. "One: that Good News—I mean, Galadjian—is wrong about it being a torpedo."

"The five percent possibility. A natural phenomenon."

"Two: that it was a mine that somebody left." Nhan waved randomly to the sky. "A mine in defense of what, I have no idea."

"I hate mines," Pike said. Every spacefarer did, with a passion.

"Three—and I used to like this—that the weapon had gone off track from some previous war, seeking a target until it had found the Pergamum—and *Enterprise*."

"You don't like that one anymore?"

Nhan pointed to the horizon, and the receding snow vehicle. "Spock did the math for me on how infinitesimal such an accidental meeting would be. I believe him."

"I can believe he said 'infinitesimal.'" Pike began to wish

he'd brought the parka after all. "What about hostile actors firing with intent?"

"That's always been the zero option—as Spock would say, the null hypothesis—to be disproven." Nhan shrugged. "But we've found absolutely no supporting evidence for it in eight months here. There's more life under our feet than in those clouds."

"At least in the parts that we've seen." Pike kicked at the snow. "Conclusion?"

"I'll keep looking. Hell, we're not going anywhere for a while." She gritted her teeth. "How long *are* we here?"

"The rest of the tour. The full four months."

"Ouch." Nhan shivered again and looked around. "I think I'll let my staffers handle the detail at this site. Enough of them want down here, they can have it."

Pike clenched his teeth and nodded. "Yeah, the night air's starting to get a little brisk. Let's both go up. I think Spock can take care of himself until your relief arrives."

"No argument here."

Pike flipped open his communicator. He was already thinking about a change of clothes—and a trip to one of the warmer zones. *Whichever one doesn't have the singing cephalopod.*

11

Combat Module Carrier 539-Aloga
Approaching Susquatane

The Lurians were right, Kormagan thought. *There it is.*

The wavemaster couldn't believe her luck. Dozens of duty cycles had elapsed since *CMC539-A*—more simply known around the unit as *Carrier Aloga*—had captured Baladon and his crewmates. In that time, her people had come to think of *Enterprise* as unreal. An imaginary ship, inserted into the database on *Deathstrike* for no good reason other than to prank anyone who came along to steal their vessel. Kormagan couldn't buy that. She'd spent enough time with the Lurians to conclude that none of them had the requisite imagination.

But Baladon, the only one with any intellect, had been considerably more pliable in the weeks since his capture—and had provided her with the location where he'd first spotted *Enterprise.* His ship's records called the world Susquatane. Kormagan's people were aware of the planet, naturally. They knew every drifting pebble, every flamed-out cinder of a star, in the nebula. Susquatane was too far from the places they cared about to be of interest, though, and so they'd never even named the place. That wasn't unusual. Their nebula didn't have a name, either. It was nothing to get sentimental about.

Kormagan had thought Baladon's intended quarry was worth playing a hunch, and between missions had launched probes into the debris clouds surrounding the Susquatane system. Sure enough, the robotic scouts later reported that *Enterprise* had returned to the planet, prompting her to retreat hastily from another engagement. Soon, her five carriers had joined the probes in the clouds, straining for a look at the mystery vessel.

For what seemed like the hundredth time that day, she cast her eyes upon it—or rather, on the latest imagery, projected in front of her by the graphical interface in the armored cupola that served to protect her leathery head. The pictures had come from her stealth probes, still at work; they'd gotten in a lot closer in recent days. *Enterprise* hadn't visibly responded to them, suggesting that its sensors weren't something her people hadn't encountered before.

The rest of the ship, though, was something else. Since her flotilla's arrival in the cloud, she had studied *Enterprise* whenever she had the chance. During meals, exercise—

—and briefings.

"Wavemaster! Are you listening?" asked someone unseen.

"Affirm." With regret, Kormagan toggled the *Enterprise* image to disappear, revealing her aide-de-camp. His name appeared in soft green lettering superimposed over his armored form, which was in all other ways identical to hers. "Sorry, Oppy. Where were we?"

"I know where you were," Opmaster Sperrin replied with a laugh. "We haven't gotten to *Enterprise* yet."

"Then go faster." Kormagan looked down at the armorer toiling at her feet. "You, too, Jayko."

The chief armorer stopped tinkering with her shin plating long enough to swear. Then it was back to work. Other wavemasters took their briefings in more formal surroundings, but Kormagan never had time for that—certainly not when there was impending action. So she stood in Jayko's bustling workshop, getting a replacement knee joint fitted as Sperrin droned on about the details of the day.

"You should let us supply you with a whole new outfit," Jayko grumbled.

"Never," Kormagan replied. "This armor's kept me alive—"

"—for sixty trillion years!" he retorted. Nobody in the wave quite knew what the real number was. "I'm tired of patching you up." Jayko looked up at her. "And this would be easier if you removed the assembly."

Kormagan stared down. "Am I on duty?"

"I guess."

"Are *you* on duty?"

"What does it look like?"

"I can't tell. You're working so slowly, my movement detector timed out."

"I'm not surprised," Jayko grumbled under his breath. "It was probably built by my grandfather."

Kormagan crossed her arms. Her preference to remain suited up most of the time wasn't unusual in the service; there were plenty of members of species aboard *Carrier Aloga* who needed the environmental protections for reasons beyond the radiation areas the vessel often had to traverse. But Kormagan's insistence that all those in her wave remain armored while on duty was unusual.

Outsiders called it eccentric; she called it sensible. It underscored that they were all one unit, regardless of species. But there was a more important reason. The nebula was the most dangerous place in creation. You never knew when you might have to go into action.

"I almost forgot," Sperrin said. "The packet drone came in from Five-Four-Four just before we reentered the cloud."

The Forty-Fours. What a joke. Kormagan looked at her aide. "What's old Hemmick want now?"

"He took your deal. The forty Lurians we sent in exchange for some of those new combiner gate valves they came up with for disruptor cannons."

"How many valves did he send?"

"Ten."

"He paid too much." Baladon had sworn about his forces' incompetence during his first meeting with Kormagan; as it turned out, he was being too generous by half. Kormagan relaxed. "I think that was the last of the bad ones. Hemmick must be desperate for reinforcements. Maybe he can do something with them."

"K'davu save us from the Lurians!" Jayko looked up, disgust doubtlessly hiding behind the opaque ports of his headgear. "They keep fouling up their circulation units. Every time they pass gas, the warning systems think there's an armor breach during a chemical attack."

"Were we talking to you?" Kormagan asked.

The armorer answered by taking a laser torch to her kneecap covering, still gnarled since her last engagement had turned part of it to scrap.

"Skip to it, Oppy. What's on the ground?"

"Readings from the probes' passes are in," Sperrin said. "*Enterprise* has occupiers on Susquatane."

"How many?"

"Approximately thirty. Six camps, all on the same side of the planet. It's mostly land there. Observe."

Kormagan watched as inside her headgear a map of Susquatane appeared, along with glowing markers where non-native life signs had been detected. "Looks like it's mostly humans."

"We've seen them before," Sperrin said. "I've never met one."

"I have. They're more useful than Lurians." But toggling to see the surveillance shots, Kormagan noticed something was missing. "How did they get down there? In those shuttles we thought *Enterprise* had?"

"Unknown. We don't see any down there now."

Kormagan switched to the close-up images. "They just plop their forces down there with no way back. What kind of invasion force is that?"

"Maybe it isn't one," Sperrin said. "They could be prospecting."

"With a ship that size? Negative." A plan forming, Kormagan dismissed the imagery from her sight. "This'll be easier than I thought. A basic snatch-grab."

Her aide was startled. "You're bypassing *Enterprise*?"

"For now. We don't know its capabilities. So we harry, take her measure—keep her from launching those shuttles." It could work, she thought. And thirty people below was a good number. A classic ground operation, like her very first mission decades before.

She turned, her sudden movement nearly taking the still-laboring armorer with her. "Wait," Jayko cried, chisel in hand. "I'm not done."

"I'll fix it myself." Kormagan looked at Sperrin. "I want all the carrier chiefs on the low-band in ten. Get the probe runners in on it. And find Baladon. If there's anything he hasn't revealed about this 'Starfleet,' I want to know it."

"Affirm."

"We're doing this today. *Enterprise* is about to meet the Boundless."

12

Susquatane
Polar Expedition Site

". . . really, sir, it's all math. And geometry and physics—and gravity, of course." Connolly smiled at Spock. "That's part of what drew me into this line of work—imagining how the game would have transpired on other planets. Space travel completely transforms everything we know about sabermetrics."

"Lieutenant, I am gratified that your interest in an ancient human sport brought you to science," Spock said as he knelt over the data collector. "But I repeat that I have been sufficiently informed about baseball."

"Sorry," Connolly said, his breath shimmering in the night. "Here's the pliers."

Spock took them. He could not regret including his relief in the expedition, for the most interesting information about life on Susquatane was bound to come from deep under the ice shelf, in places Connolly could locate. Whether fossilized or somehow alive, any beings there would explain much about how stable the planet's ecology had been over time. Susquatane was a fair-weather island in a perpetual storm; future settlers would want to know how long that weather might last.

Still, Spock had calculated that by working with Connolly's team instead of the other ones on Susquatane, he would be able to get the lieutenant back onto *Enterprise* as soon as possible. That would spare the ship any more time without a senior science officer on the bridge—and would have the added benefit of removing Connolly and his speculations about "what must be happening in the winter meetings back home," whatever they were.

Ghalka brought another tool kit from the stowage on the snow scouter. "How's our baby doing?"

"The geocorder, which you persist in likening to a living being, is still not calibrated to within acceptable limits," Spock said. "The magnesite deposits below interfere with its sensors."

"Magnesite's not bad for deflecting radiation," Ghalka said. "In this nebula, it could be good to have some around."

"The fact remains it is inconveniently placed for this instrument." Spock's communicator beeped. He drew it from his belt. "Spock."

"Enterprise *to landing party,"* Nicola said. *"The captain informs you that he and Commander Nhan have returned to the ship. Her relief, Ensign Gupta, has been transported to your camp."*

"Understood. We will return there shortly. Polar expedition out."

Connolly leaned against their vehicle. "Kind of glad there's only three seats in the scouter. I'm starting to like this idea of no red-shirt babysitters."

"They are here for our protection," Spock said.

"Protection from *what*?"

"Repeating myself would not be productive." The Vulcan pointed behind him, to where several spars were deeply embedded in the distant snow. "Move each of the probes five hundred meters north. I will attempt new readings then."

"We can walk that," Connolly said.

"I'll bring the power tools." Ghalka slung a case over her shoulder. As she and Connolly began walking away into the night, she whispered, "Is he *always* this serious?"

Connolly smirked. "Your first tour, right?"

Spock heard them both as he donned his parka, but it was not worth a remark. Not when part of the reason he had sent them away was to exit the conversation. He wanted to focus on the work and another theory he had developed. A few quick taps on the geocorder brought up the seismometer screen. It was just possible that some of the errors he was seeing came from plate activity.

He stopped when he saw the readings. A quake had rocked the dayside of the planet scant minutes earlier. The instrument couldn't say much about where the temblor had struck, just that it was far away—and not deep at all. Spock was beginning to consider the possibilities when another tremor was detected, also on the dayside but well apart. Its intensity was identical; it did not appear to be an aftershock.

Something is happening. Spock reached for his communicator.

U.S.S. Enterprise
Orbiting Susquatane

"We're on it," Pike replied to the hail. Spock and Connolly's stand-in, Salvadora Dietrich, was checking the sensors. "What do you see, Ensign?"

"Same as Mister Spock," the young woman said. "Two impacts, right at the surface. We'll need to approach to see more."

"Hail the expeditions." *Enterprise* sat in a geosynchronous orbit above the planetside expeditions; the starship had occasionally left briefly to study a moon, but never strayed far. Nicola signaled when Pike was on with all of them. "Landing parties, this is the captain. We're going to leave station to check something out," he said. "*Enterprise* out."

"Sun's set on most of the camps," Nhan said. "We're leaving them in the dark."

"We won't be long," Pike repeated. "Engage."

Enterprise's impulse engines hummed to life, their gentle push enough to send the ship cruising toward daylight. Dietrich began receiving more data almost instantly.

"There's the vibrations," she said. "Two quakes, fifteen hundred kilometers apart."

Pike peered at the main viewer. Their dayside destination was under heavy cloud cover. "I don't remember the map. What's the surface like at those coordinates?"

"Open steppe and jungle plateau," Una replied.

Pike's eyes narrowed. Something was off with the clouds in those two spots. Oily smears on white, just starting to spread with the trade winds. "Are there . . . volcanoes in those locations?"

"Not that we'd recorded." Una increased the main viewer magnification of the dayside. "How would *two*—?"

A bright flash appeared on screen, blazing brilliantly for a moment before *Enterprise*'s main viewer filter kicked in. "Another quake!" Dietrich announced.

"Fifteen hundred kilometers from *both* the other impacts," Una said. She looked back to Pike. "A perfect triangle."

Dietrich kept reading her scope. "Intense heat . . . *radiation*?"

As the third cloud formation grew an inky and angry black, Nhan shouted what they all had just realized. "They're nuclear blasts!"

Troop Module Aloga-One
Approaching Susquatane

It was an old diversionary tactic, one Kormagan had learned back in the first wave she'd served with. The nukes her engineers had armed her stealth probes with weren't likely to do much to *Enterprise*, which surely would have detected the threats before they got close. Baladon had told her that unlike *Deathstrike*, *Enterprise* was likely to have functioning shields.

But nothing would stop the weapons when directed at the ground—particularly when the starship was on the other side of the planet. It had only remained to see whether *Enterprise* would take the bait.

It had. The vessel from "Starfleet"—that was the odd word Baladon used—had abandoned Susquatane's nightside. Kormagan had given the command then for her troop modules to emerge from the nebula. Twenty-four assault transports, just like hers, screamed toward the planet and its camps, unbeknownst to *Enterprise*'s crew.

Of course, the starship would try to return as soon as those occupants heard there was a threat. They would be stopped. Not by Kormagan, but by the capital ships of her flotilla: the combat module carriers. With their troop modules detached, the streamlined vessels that remained were nimble battleships, awaiting their cue in the nebula over the dayside. Kormagan looked at the synchronized timer on her helmet interface.

All right, carriers, you're on.

And so was she. *"Atmospheric entry in twenty seconds,"* her navigator called out over her comm system.

She looked to her troops, lined up before their drop doors and ready to be deployed. "You know the objective," she called out. "Every target you kill is like wasting one of your own people. They *are* your own people. So take care of our cargo." She raised an armored fist. "For K'davu!"

"For K'davu!" the warriors shouted.

Kormagan gave her gear a last check and stepped into her own drop bay. The wavemaster *always* went with the strike teams; any other practice would be foolish. She shuddered to imagine any military so fearful that it would protect its superior officers like precious plants. No, she had to show her forces the way—and besides, she loved it.

She had ever since the first time she had put on armor and joined her fellow warriors. Different species, all given equal abilities and united for one great cause. Her kind had evolved to live in the desert, seldom entering the cold. Since donning armor, she'd fought in every clime imaginable—and she was about to set foot on an icecap.

"Starfleet," Kormagan thought as air buffeted the ship. The word sounded so arrogant. *They certainly think a lot of themselves.* She would soon make up her own mind.

13

U.S.S. Enterprise
Over Susquatane's Dayside

"*Red alert. Shields up!*"

As the siren blared and red lights flickered on the bridge, Pike leaned forward in his chair. "Information, people. Did those blasts originate on the ground, or did somebody bomb them from above?"

"Cannot determine, Captain." Dietrich worked her console's interface. "Checking the recording of the moment before the third detonation."

Number One looked to Pike. "We haven't seen sentient life, Captain. It can't be a local disturbance."

"I'm not waiting around to find out. Lieutenant Amin, plot us the fastest course to evac all six camps. Raden, punch it as soon as she's ready."

"Aye, sir."

Behind Pike, the turbolift doors opened. Galadjian emerged and looked at the flashing lights, baffled. "So we *are* at red alert. Is there an error?"

"Glad you could join us, Doctor," Pike said. He'd forgotten it was time for his chief engineer's shift on the bridge. "We have a situation. We're going to need to do a lot of transporting."

Galadjian's eyes fixed on the main viewscreen—and nodded. "Oh, yes, the full withdrawal. As in the drill."

"That's the ticket. Number One, fill him in." Galadjian gamely took his station.

Pike's eyes narrowed. One blast might not have been noticed; indeed, it hadn't been. Only Spock had noted the second. But the third, in defining a triangle near the equator, had made it glaringly obvious that whatever was happening there was a deliberate and unnatural act.

Too obvious—certain to draw *Enterprise*'s attention. What was special about that spot?

At once, he knew. He stood and walked behind the navigator. "Jamila, those blast coordinates. Invert them and overlay atop your new course."

"Invert them?"

"Latitude and longitude."

Amin caught Pike's drift—and in a moment, Pike saw what he was afraid of. The triangle of blasts was centered on a point exactly on the other side of Susquatane from the geographic center of all *Enterprise*'s camps.

"We've been fished in!" Pike turned back toward his chair. "Raden, get us moving. Don't wait for—"

Enterprise shook. Pike pitched sideways, nearly losing his footing. "Was that—?"

"Nuclear blast!" Nhan yelled. "Not antimatter. Same as on the planet."

"Torpedo? Mine?" Pike asked as he found his seat.

"New contact," Una called out. "One vessel, one-five-seven mark one." Before she could say anything else, another blast rocked the bridge, this one producing a flash visible on the viewscreen. "Correction, two vessels. Second contact, one-two-two mark four. Both closing fast."

"Shift power to shields and keep making for the nightside. Nhan, prepare to return fire."

Number One checked her readings. "Captain, they entered the Susquatane nebular pocket from the innermost cloud band."

"Third vessel," Nhan said. "No, *five*!"

Pike asked what everyone was thinking. "*Are they Klingons?*"

Susquatane
Polar Expedition Site

"—on our way," Pike said over cascading waves of static. *"Return to your camp and await—"*

Spock adjusted the comm unit on the snow scouter to no avail. Just like his handheld communicator, it was receiving nothing but interference. This was no atmospheric phenomenon, connected to the cloud formations. They were being jammed.

Spock looked to the north. Connolly and Ghalka were half a kilometer away, repositioning one of the sensor spikes. Out of earshot, certainly. He climbed fully into the driver's seat of the scouter and activated the engine.

It was then that he saw it—bright lights blazing down across the night sky, touching off a sonic boom that arrived quickly. They were vessels, several times longer than shuttles, with engines both aft and beneath. One soared over Connolly and Ghalka's location, to hover a few dozen meters beyond. A series of flaps sprang open down the long side, disgorging airborne passengers.

Not passengers, Spock saw as he neared: jetpack-wearing warriors, clad completely in armor. Their propulsion units fired, carrying them the final few meters to the surface. Billowing snow raised a cloud as they touched down, but Spock did not need to see them to guess their intention.

He tried his transmitter again. "*Enterprise*, we are under attack!" But he could hear nothing as the low whine of the racing scouter was lost in the thunder of another transport heading his way. No, not one, but two—descending perilously close to the ground on either side of him and preventing him from going any way but forward. Spock dared not look back, but he surmised there was a fourth one trailing behind.

Spock remembered a term Pike had used: he was being corralled.

Ahead, he saw Ghalka and Connolly running in his direction, pursued by troopers who had landed. In between them and the snow scouter was one of several exposed patches of ice. Spock saw his opportunity. He raced for the frozen surface and activated the emergency brakes the instant he reached it, turning the control yoke hard to port as he did so. The snow scouter spun wildly, causing the transports hemming him in to bank farther away in response. Arriving at the far side fully a meter off the ground, Spock reactivated the engines and regained control just in time for the vehicle to slam into the snow between his fellow officers and the advancing troops. Spock spun the scouter backward, its runners digging in and throwing sheets of ice crystals in the direction of the newcomers.

The scouter vaulted forward, grinding to a stop beside Connolly and Ghalka. Their weapons were out, their faces flushed. "Klingons!" Connolly shouted.

Spock had no basis upon which to agree or disagree. He had never known Klingons to wear armor of this kind, but it was hardly the time to wonder about attire. The make of the transports was also new to him. The two that had closed off his escape did so again, settling in front and releasing troops of their own. Spock saw a fourth transport even farther to the south, closing on the camp. *After Ensign Gupta*, he thought.

"Board quickly," he barely needed to say, as Ghalka and Connolly were in the process of doing so. But a sonic shriek threw them right back off. Spock, his ears ringing, hung on—and then went sideways as more intense sound waves struck the vehicle, flipping it.

On his shoulder and half buried in the snow, Spock looked at the advancing intruders marching deliberately toward him. Except for one whose armor appeared battered and worn, they all looked alike. He found his phaser, set to stun, and fired—only to see the blast dissipate off some invisible personnel barrier protecting the armored figures. His second shot was joined by a third of higher intensity from the other side of the overturned snow scouter; it had clearly come from Ghalka or Connolly and a phaser that had been set to kill. It likewise had no effect.

The arrivals from behind joined a perimeter, surrounded the Starfleet officers and advanced. "Wrap them up," he heard someone say in words he could understand. Spock got to his feet—

—and fell backward as a transparent substance struck him hard, enveloping him. Webbing, clearly designed to incapacitate personnel—and which tightened around Spock as he struggled to free himself. Beyond the snow scouter, he heard a loud chuff of air, followed by another—probably, he surmised, the same sort of weapon being used on his comrades.

Struggling for breath inside the cocoon, Spock beheld one of his attackers, looming over him. He could not see through the bulky armored figure's opaque headgear, but he had already calculated that they were not Klingons for one simple reason.

They had not killed him.

Spock knew that could change.

14

U.S.S. Enterprise
Over Susquatane's Dayside

This is a bullfight, Pike thought. *And we're the bull.*

He'd only seen archival video of the ancient activity, long considered barbaric—but was aware of the tactics involved. A matador attempted to control the movements of an enraged bovine, assisted by lancers on foot and horseback. An escalating series of pokes and prods reduced the great animal, concluding with the *tercio de muerte*—the "part of death."

The vessels assaulting *Enterprise* had neither hailed nor responded, but it was clear to Pike that they were working in tandem with one another, effectively controlling the direction and movements of his starship. First through their torpedoes—the source, he now knew, of the initial strikes against his shields—and later through disruptor fire as they closed in on *Enterprise*. Every time Pike tried to make for the nightside, some new attacker intervened.

"Shields at ninety-one percent," Una announced. "And holding."

"Kid stuff," Pike said. *Nuclear blasts?* Where were the antimatter weapons? Did they even have them?

He found out. A shining spark sailed through the space before them, almost like a phosphorescent shell in an ancient war—until it exploded, hammering *Enterprise*'s forward shields and deflecting the starship's progress.

"Evasive maneuvers," he called out. "Oh-nine-oh mark one!"

"Antimatter reaction," Nhan said. "*That's* the real stuff."

Damn it. Pike pounded his armrest with his fist. "They're just toying with us. Nhan, are you having any luck?"

"I'm firing away, Captain. They've got shields too—and we can't focus on one for more than a few seconds the way they're buzzing around."

One of the nearer attack vessels came more clearly into view. A long prism, close to *Enterprise*'s length stem to stern; it didn't appear Klingon. The thing looked vaguely like a bomb-shaped frozen confection Pike had enjoyed on Mojave afternoons as a kid—and the bomb connection was apt. Perfectly pentagonal in lateral cross section, its five edges were festooned with weapons arrays running the length of the vehicle. Fixed disruptor cannons, ball turrets, and what appeared to be torpedo launch tubes. Between the rows of death, the faces of the vessel were barren, except for what appeared to be multiple docking clamps and airlocks.

"Are they battleships or carriers?" he asked aloud—only to have his words muted by another antimatter detonation off *Enterprise*'s bow.

"Directing power to shields," Galadjian said. The researcher was shaken, but holding up. "These have not been direct hits."

"Maybe that's the idea," Pike said. They'd known from the beginning of the mission that pirates might be in the nebula; had they accidentally found, at Susquatane, their hideaway? It was possible there might not be a *tercio de muerte*—but that wasn't something he was going to take a chance on.

"Recording analysis complete," Dietrich said from the

science station. "The nukes we thought were volcanoes were delivered by probe-sized vessels. We saw the last one go in."

"That's about six crises ago," Raden snapped.

"Stow that, mister." Pike still thought the blasts occurred to attract attention—and not to target *Enterprise* or its people directly—but a weapon was a weapon. He looked back to Dietrich. "Feed the visual to Nhan. Get a tactical analysis. If we've got two kinds of hostiles running around out there, I want to know."

More antimatter near misses and disruptor direct hits pounded the shields. "Say again, Lieutenant, I cannot hear," Nicola shouted. His earpiece pressed to his ear, the communications officer looked fraught to Pike. "That was the tropical-site team, Captain. I was only getting a word here and there—now I can't get them at all."

"You can't get them, I can't get *to* them." He had barely finished the sentence when it dawned on Pike: that might be the whole point. "Enough of this. Do we have any of the landing parties in line of sight?" Pike looked over to the port side, and Galadjian's station. "Doctor, what's the status on our people?"

"I am online with the transporter rooms," the chief engineer replied. He looked flustered, overwhelmed by input. "I—I don't believe they can get a fix."

"I don't want beliefs. I need certainty."

Galadjian pressed a control and spoke. "Lieutenant Pitcairn, you have the coordinates. Can you get a fix on anyone?"

"Not through a planet, Doctor."

Pike thought Pitcairn hit the last word a little hard, but he understood the frustration belowdecks. He felt it too. "Raden, try to put us in range of the closest camp."

"That'd be Spock," Raden said, feeling *Enterprise* quake from another barrage. "I'd be happy to, if these characters would let us!"

Susquatane
Polar Expedition Site

The communication from Kormagan's transport was piped directly into her headgear. *"Carriers report engagement,"* one of her warriors declared. *"Target* Enterprise *has put up shields and is returning fire."*

"Did they launch shuttles before they raised shields?"

"No, and they can't do it now. The carriers have made sure of that."

That was the plan: bottle up *Enterprise*, preventing it from recovering its people. The fact that she could hear the call from her junior at all meant something else. While several of her combat modules aloft had been jamming the Starfleet camps on the nightside, *Enterprise* hadn't done anything to retard her forces' ability to communicate with her ships on the dayside. The nebula blocked most subspace messages of longer distance; at least so far, her ability to communicate in the operational theater was unhindered.

The clingtrap cocoons had been successful in immobilizing the three Starfleet people; in hundreds of exfiltration operations, she had never known a bipedal life-form to escape one yet. Her specialist went from one captive to another, running quick scans on the captives. He read the results. "Subtype human, first encountered by Wave Five-One-Nine. Subtype Vulcan, Wave Four-Eight-Oh. Andorian, Wave Five-Three-Nine." He laughed. "One of yours, Chief!"

"All exfils are alike to me," Kormagan said. "Do they need to breathe?"

"I think so."

"Stick 'em and punch 'em."

Dutifully, the specialist and two of his comrades knelt over the prisoners, injecting sedatives through the clingtrap envelopes. Immediately afterward, they cut larger holes in the bags for breathing tubes. "These three won't need special equipment on the ship."

Kormagan wasn't surprised, given that the three were clad only in their all-white thermal uniforms. Baladon had suggested Starfleet was some kind of multispecies militia, ranging in parts of the universe where existence was easier.

"Four troop modules is a lot to extract three people," the specialist said.

"'No second chances means nothing left to chance,'" Kormagan said, repeating something her mentor used to say. "Enough delay. Back to the troop module."

Six of her warriors went into action as bearers, carting the captives through the snow. Any one of them would have been able to handle the weight alone, of course; the servomechanisms inside their armor multiplied the strength of wearers manyfold. But the cargo was too precious to damage—at least for now.

The exfils safely loaded, Kormagan took a call from another troop module. It was Sperrin, who had been coordinating the mission from aloft. *"All opmasters have reported back. Quarry obtained. Repeat, quarry obtained."*

"Good. Tell everybody to raise ship and await my command." Kormagan had no expectation of taking *Enterprise*—not this time—so a little trail covering was in order. She toggled a control to talk to someone else. "*Aloga-Five*, did you plant the cleaner at the camp?"

From the troop module parked farther south, a deep voice responded, *"That's affirm, Wavemaster."* It was Baladon. *"Looks like I finally got my shot at* Enterprise.*"*

The elation in his voice amused Kormagan. Perhaps there *were* second chances—at least for Lurians. "Lift off."

15

U.S.S. Enterprise
Over Susquatane's Dayside

"I've had enough of this game," Pike said. "Time for a new move."

The engagement had started less than ten minutes earlier—and yet *Enterprise* had actually lost ground, thanks to the efforts of its attackers. The fact that those attacks were more harassment than attempts at destruction had made him reluctant to unload on the stalkers with his most powerful weapons; as unlikely as it seemed, there might still be a conversation to be had with such people.

That left a theory he'd been developing since seeing the docking ports on all five horizontal faces of the warships. "I don't think those things are designed to land. Concur, Number One?"

"Aye, Captain."

"We're going down. Raden, take us into the stratosphere. We're going to the nightside that way."

Raden's eyes bulged. "But those mushroom clouds we saw down there—"

"Came from something else. And it can't be any rockier than flying through the Acheron Formation."

Raden adjusted course and took *Enterprise* downward. As the first licks of atmosphere became bites, the starship juddered. *Enterprise* wasn't designed to land, either, apart from its saucer section—and that was only after separation from the stardrive section in the gravest of emergencies. But that capability meant that she could handle the descent.

The starship's pursuers did not follow—but neither did they depart, and they began firing their weapons into *Enterprise*'s path. Pike's abrupt move seemed to have thwarted their targeting, however, and now, rather than barring his way, the blasts were in his wake.

"Approaching the terminator into night," Amin said.

"Take us up." Pike tensed. The act had bought them moments, yes, and thousands of kilometers. But he couldn't risk any more ordnance being directed downward. He hoped he had done enough. Outside, the nebula-bounded sky reappeared above, with a growing patch of bowl-shaped darkness below.

"Bogeys adjusting and gaining on us," Nhan said.

That'll have to be enough, Pike thought. "Shields down. Doctor, do you have a fix on Spock's party?"

"It's difficult," Galadjian said, nearly hypnotized by his displays. "We are looking for their communicators to get a fix on them. But . . . I do not trust the readings. There is jamming."

Una looked to Pike, her demeanor unable to hide that she, too, was growing alarmed. "You don't need to send them a message," she said. "At this distance, the sensors should be able to spot the transporter lock confirmation circuits in their communicators. The antenna grid would work even if it's powered off."

"I . . . know that." A blast struck somewhere behind the now-vulnerable *Enterprise*, giving the bridge a big jolt. Galadjian wiped sweat from his brow. "But there is such distortion, still. I do not trust what I see."

Another blast. "I'm running with shields down, Doctor," Pike said.

Galadjian began scrolling through screens again. "Perhaps if I do the math again. Something is the matter. The readings—"

"*Doctor!*"

"—the readings are unclear. I would like more time to—"

Pike hit an armrest control. "Transporter room one! Beam aboard the team at—"

Dietrich shouted, "Ground detonation, nuclear, two thousand kilometers ahead!"

Pike's eyes locked on the flash on the horizon. *No!* He clapped his hands on the armrest control. "Pitcairn, the polar camp!"

He couldn't hear the response, as overlapping shouts came from Nhan and Dietrich. "Another detonation, fifty-five south latitude, thirty east—"

"Detonation, Camp Four!"

"Detonation, equatorial—"

"Camp Two!"

Pike grew hoarse. "Pitcairn!" No response but the alert klaxon, still going. He looked at Galadjian. "Did you get anyone out?"

"I have no word from the transporter rooms."

"The status is on the interface in front of you." When Galadjian froze, Pike leapt up. "Dammit, man, I have people down there!" He caught a chilling glimpse of Una, her face white, as he rushed over. Galadjian withdrew from the terminal. "This isn't even the right menu," Pike said, astonished.

"Our attackers are withdrawing," Nhan said. The captain barely heard her.

"Pitcairn to bridge," came a voice from the console.

Pike didn't bother to identify himself. "Did you get anyone?"

"Negative, Captain. Our targeting sequence reset when the X-ray pulse hit."

He slumped over the console. "And now?"

"I'm sorry, Captain."

Pike's face fell. He lingered for several moments before closing the channel and turning his back to his crew.

"I . . . I am sorry," Galadjian said, quivering. "We haven't transported many people this trip—and I was rarely at station then. I was trying to make sense of the data. I thought I knew where to look . . ." He sat back at his station—and saw the interface Pike had pulled up. "Oh."

Pike gawked at his superstar for a moment—and shook his head. "The attackers fired them?"

"No, Captain," Dietrich said. "They were ground based—or could have been dropped by probes, like the first ones we saw."

"There's no one in the area above the nightside," Nhan said. She looked impatient. "I'm tracking our attackers. They're making for the nebular cloud, different headings."

"Get after these guys," Pike said, before checking himself. "No, wait. Launch probes of our own. Have them lock on the bogeys and tail them. We've got to check on our camps."

"Yes, Captain."

In silence, he walked to the bridge support station, pausing at one point to touch the back of a chair for support. Arriving beside Una, he spoke quietly to her, even as he kept his eyes averted. "How many?"

Una looked at the duty roster. "One member had cycled up on a shift change. Another had obtained a sample and returned."

"*How. Many.*"

"Thirty."

"That's . . ."

"Yes." Una looked down.

Pike wandered back to his chair in a daze. He fell into it, as if struck by an unseen blow.

They're all gone.

Across the bridge, Avedis Galadjian stood, straightened his tunic, and walked to the turbolift. He had not been dismissed. At the door, he listened for an objection—but none was heard.

Troop Module Aloga-One
Departing Susquatane

The nebular clouds billowed thick, but *Aloga-One* had no trouble finding its parent vessel. *Carrier Aloga* and its four companion capital ships—battleships, when they were not functioning as carriers—had been designed to navigate such places.

They had also been built for two other purposes. For the war, of course; that everlasting conflict required starships that were versatile, able to be reshaped to meet the particular threats posed by the Great Enemy. And they had been designed for one other purpose: the type of mission Kormagan had just flawlessly executed.

Recruiting.

There was nothing like a good, clean takedown when executed by a crack organization. But she already knew the armored warriors on her team were the best, for a simple reason: they were still alive. That made this part of her job especially important. The war required an endless supply of soldiers. For every battle she fought—and survived—her wave needed replenishment to go on. Her people represented too many different species; multiplication the natural way would never be enough to keep up with casualties.

Fate had sent her people to war, but it had also provided. Lurians, Batakas, humans, Gorodese—those were but a fraction of the peoples that had blundered into the cosmic trap. It was a wonder that the nebula, as hostile as it was to life, continued to attract so many curious travelers. Some "exfils" claimed to have entered the nebula to prospect, to colonize, to hide. She had a different word for entering the nebula: "volunteering."

And when they brought their own technology, like *Enterprise*? That was just a bonus. Time spent thinking up new things could be better spent fighting.

Yes, Kormagan had quotas to meet before taking to battle, but she had always taken pride in that part of the work. The Enemy punched holes in whatever warriors they found. Someday soon, the forces Kormagan had just plucked from Susquatane would be all that stood between her and that fate. A bad warrior might die. A bad recruiter was already dead.

Through her armor, she felt the deck quake. *"Docking completed,"* chirped the automated message in her headgear. *Aloga-One* was once again part of *Carrier Aloga*, her home for decades and one of the mobile centers of civilization for a people who lived for one thing: to reclaim that which had been taken from her people so long ago.

The people of *Enterprise* belonged to Starfleet no more. Like her, they were something better, something vital, something necessary.

For as long as they lasted.

16

U.S.S. Enterprise
Orbiting Susquatane

For those aboard a starship, the turn of the new year was a strange thing. Alongside stardates, the calendar year had continued to be used as a marker for many things having nothing to do with the length of the planet Earth's revolutions around its sun. Academic periods. Tours of duty. The occasional birthday. But divorced from seasons, there was little to differentiate one time of year aboard a starship from another.

Wherever he had lived, Pike had nonetheless seen New Year's Day as a psychological marker worth celebrating. The official date passing during his science team's deployment, he had postponed the ship's party until everyone's return. The party had never happened. Instead, he belatedly rang in 2257 with funeral bells. It was one of several services he had officiated, ceremonies delayed while his crew attended to more urgent matters.

Making certain, first of all, that the thirty indeed had fallen. Of that, there had been little doubt. Susquatane was a vast planet, already healing itself—but the blast sites at the former camps would stand as memorials for years to come.

The second matter, answering how the camps had been targeted in the first place, took longer to resolve. Most of the science team had been annihilated, leaving Ensign Dietrich the senior officer of a near-empty department. Pike had appointed

Number One to step in and try to reconstitute the unit with whatever skilled hands she could find. Together, they had pored over gigaquads of sensor data, not just from *Enterprise*'s sojourn at Susquatane, but also its earlier survey visit, and everything before and after. Someone had known they were at the planet, and had seen the camps.

It had taken a week before a shadow was spotted on a few milliseconds of imagery—material recorded not by *Enterprise*, but by the explorers at the equatorial region. An early attempt to telescopically record the habits of a nocturnal avian on a far ridge had picked up the overflight of a probe identical to the one Dietrich had seen before the third bomb fell on the dayside. Pike suspected that was both how the attackers knew what to strike, and where.

Just not why—and he still had no idea who they were. It was glaringly obvious that the five attacking starships were not alone in their actions; nonetheless, for operational purposes *Enterprise*'s crew had named the assailant group the Susquatane Five, "Essfive" for short. Finding Essfive was the third mission before them, and he could not imagine it would end well. *Enterprise*'s probes had been able to transmit clearly only until the attackers they were following reached the nebular clouds surrounding Susquatane. *Enterprise* then received partial signals for a day, and nothing thereafter. In the Pergamum, there was no way of knowing whether the probes had lost their targets, been destroyed, or were simply wandering around aimlessly.

That had left Nhan with the barest of clues regarding where to start looking—quite a contrast to the wealth of data *Enterprise* had recorded about the bogeys. The shields and hulls of the Essfive starships were quite strong, hardly unexpected for vessels that navigated the nebula; as a result, sensors had not been able to peer through to take life-signs readings. But enough physical features on the vessels had been examined that Nhan was almost ready to say that the hostiles were not Klingons. The technological differences observed in the ships were just too great.

What she could not say, of course, was whether Essfive was in alliance with or in the employ of the Empire. That would be another matter.

Whatever the answer was, Pike knew the Federation would definitely need to know about the attack—and the attackers. That made his course clear.

They would leave Susquatane today, following Vector One into the soup for as far as that long-cold trail would last. Then, in the very likely case that they found nothing, they would exit the nebula, informing Starfleet.

And Pike would inform them of something else: his resignation.

He could see no other path for himself—not when so many had been lost. Rigel VII had devastated him. It was barely a scratch. Three had died there. This was thirty. He had been fooling himself to think that he had the talent for the job—and he certainly didn't have the stomach for failing at it. He wouldn't tell anyone. Not Boyce, not Una. No one would change his mind, this time.

But right now, he still had his duty.

"We are assembled here today to pay respects to an officer who served with distinction. I first met Lieutenant Spock of Vulcan . . ."

—

The walls in Galadjian's quarters were a shrine to science. On the wall hung diplomas and commendations from the Zefram Cochrane Institute for Advanced Theoretical Physics, the Alpha Centauri Academy of Science and Technology, and a variety of other places of the highest learning. One was entirely written in Vulcan. The professor had further accentuated the sitting room with a bookcase filled with the works of the great engineering masters. And in place of family pictures, Pike saw images of Galadjian shaking hands with three different former presidents of the Federation.

He's living in his résumé.

Galadjian emerged from his bedroom wearing the dark gray civilian suit Pike had seen him in when he first reported for duty. "Thank you for waiting, Captain. I wanted to change after the funeral."

"I appreciate your attending. I know you have been on personal leave."

That was what they were calling it.

"I could hardly have done otherwise," Galadjian said. "Spock's was a fine mind. It is a tremendous loss." He gestured to the chairs by the bookcase. "Please sit."

Pike did so. He knew attending the funeral could not have been easy for Galadjian—and what he had to say next wasn't going to be any easier. "Doctor, we have to talk. The Susquatane incident—"

"I take full responsibility for it, Captain. And I assure you I am doing everything in my power to make things right."

How, exactly? Pike wondered. Galadjian had been holed up here since the disaster. "Since the action, I've heard from a number of staffers. Your division—some others. That moment on the bridge—that wasn't the first time, was it?"

"Of course, I have not been in action before. That is a unique experience—"

"I don't mean that. I mean the not-knowing-how-things-work."

"I do know how things work." Galadjian gestured to the books. "Captain, the principles on which your shields operate were based on papers I wrote twenty years ago."

"I applaud that, Doctor." Pike frowned. He was going

to have to get at this another way. "Place your right hand in the air."

"Excuse me?"

"Indulge me." Pike lifted his right hand into midair, palm out. "Like you were activating the shields at station."

Galadjian smiled. "Ah. Like this?"

"That's right. Now increase the intensity of the deflector beam." He spoke abruptly. "Quick, where's your hand?"

Galadjian, tentative, drew his hand back. "I cannot see the console, sir."

"You have to commit it to memory. The greenest ensigns on my bridge can see the interface in their sleep. Nhan could probably do it with her feet."

"Oh." Galadjian nodded, understanding.

"There will be times when there will be no power. No gravity. No lights. Failing life-support. And your crewmembers' lives will depend on your knowledge not just of how things work, but of how to make them work."

"We knew this would be the case. It is my first starship, after all."

"I hear things as captain. You're right—I haven't gotten down to main engineering enough. I've failed you in that. But engineers have come to other officers, who have come to me. They all respect your accomplishments—" Pike stopped, not wanting to continue.

"Please be frank, Captain."

Pike winced. "They don't call you Good News. They call you Doctor Oh."

"Ah, because of my 'Doctor *O*' example." Galadjian managed a weak grin. "Yes, I have used that before with others."

"It is the example—but they don't mean *O* the variable. They mean 'Oh' as in . . ." He stopped.

Galadjian blanched. "*Oh.* As in 'Oh, the old professor doesn't know what the hell he is doing.'"

Pike spoke quickly. "Doctor—*Avedis*—I want to apologize on their behalf and say that this is not normal for Starfleet. Our officers are expected to be people of the highest moral standards, who are trained to treat everyone with respect. Especially superiors. This isn't the ancient military—we don't do pejoratives."

"But your organization's normal function is also to promote from within, based on merit awarded while on active duty. I have bypassed that."

Pike couldn't deny that. "I didn't object to Starfleet because so much of the current refit came from your work—and none of us expected there would be anything we couldn't handle. I figured things would improve. But we're more than halfway through the mission." He clasped his hands together in advance of the most difficult part. "I took the impression from evaluations that your staff has been covering for you, as much as collaborating with you."

Galadjian looked lost. "I thought we were working as a team."

"But you have to come out of the ivory tower and use an actual spanner a time or two. Or, at least, they think you do."

"Is this what would make me effective? To crawl around in a Joshua's tube?"

"Jefferies." Seeing Galadjian's face fall further, Pike leaned forward. "Look, the service isn't always fair about these things—and the paths forward aren't always linear. I started as a test pilot years ago. That's as solitary as it gets. I didn't want others dependent on me for their survival—not directly. Not until later, when they flew vessels I'd found to be safe. I wasn't planning on being responsible for *two* other people, much less *two hundred*—and I'm still not sure I'm ready for it."

Galadjian took a deep breath, as if taking it all in. He straightened. "I am a rational man, Captain; my life is equations. I am no Vulcan or Illyrian, but I admire their discipline, and try to emulate it. When I am shown a problem, I can work it out." He locked eyes with Pike. "What must I do?"

Pike stood. "Keep my ship running long enough to help me find whoever did this—and then get us out of this hellpit. By yourself or with help, I don't care which. When we're out of the nebula, I'll breathe again."

Galadjian watched him, before nodding with somber recognition. "And also at that point, I will no longer be your problem."

"Kind of."

"Very well. It will be done."

Pike thanked the doctor. He had told the truth: Galadjian *wouldn't* be his problem. None of it would—one way or another.

He saw himself out.

17

Mobile Processing Center 539
Pergamum Nebula

Spock awoke fighting.

He did not awake *to* fighting, though it would not have surprised him if he had, given that the last thing he remembered before he was drugged was struggling against the armored attackers on Susquatane.

No, he found that *he* was the one in armor now, and that he was punching another warrior. Hard.

"Keep at it," shouted a gruff voice into his ear. *"We know you have a circulatory system. Get it working!"*

For a long moment, Spock thought he was having a dream, or some kind of aftereffect from the sedative. But the material encasing his body was real, as was the motion of his arms and the impact—much muted—when his blows struck the other party. He could also feel tiny prods touching his skin near his joints, generating tingling electrical impulses. Those, Spock surmised, were combining with the mechanical armature inside his armor to produce his movements.

Movements that were involuntary on his part—but certainly according to someone's will.

Spock's protected fists slammed against his opponent's headgear. It was no helmet, he saw, but more of an angular dome: it resembled half a dodecahedron, with a flat side on top and the forward, left, and right faces appearing as blackened window panes. Spock had the same three ports to look through—and now he noticed data projected on the inside of the panels. *A visual interface.* Text appeared superimposed over his fellow pugilist's massive form: "*539A-2/Green-3*" moved as his opponent moved. The characters were recognizable to Spock, if their meaning was not.

Since the combat seemed to pose him no danger, Spock took the chance to look out his left and right ports. Two other titans—*Green-4* and *-5*, his interface read—clashed with one another. Both were two and a half meters tall. Spock realized part of his disorientation came from the fact that he, too, was made taller by bulky boots and what he now perceived to be a sizable amount of gear mounted on his back.

"Your center of gravity's going to be off for the first couple of days," the voice said. *"The gyros in the unit will accommodate—until you start adjusting. You cretins might as well start now."*

Spock looked around for the speaker, whose voice seemed an odd mix of erudition and meanness. All he could see were black walls, with glowing red lights beaming down, defining a round room a dozen meters in diameter. Too small for an arena, he thought. Inferring that he was sparring rather than fighting, he guessed the room might be a gym.

It was time to say something. Not knowing the appropriate protocol between marionette and puppeteers, Spock simply said, "Greetings."

"Ah, another sleeping fool has decided to join us," responded the voice.

"I am Lieutenant Spock, of the United Federation of Planets *Starship Enterprise.*"

"You're Green-Two until I say otherwise."

Spock threw another punch. "I wish to stop this activity."

"I'm muting you now."

Spock's further entreaties went unanswered. Nor was he able to communicate with the individual he was trading punches with. The pointless pummeling went on for another three minutes before the motions of his opponent subtly began to change, becoming less robotic, more uncoordinated.

"Looks like our last one's finally awake," the voice said. *"At ease. Stow headgear, all units."*

All four combatants stopped punching. The compartment around Spock's head snapped open at the seams, with the left, right, and forward panes withdrawing into his armor like an automatic door into a wall. Above him, the solid top casing folded and retracted into the bulk on his back.

As his eyes adjusted to the low light—it was *much* harder to see without the faceplate in front of him—Spock found that his legs were immobilized. He could move his arms, however. The armored limbs were overly large relative to his body, but with the servos assisting, he was able to move them with surprising ease.

In the suit of armor across from him, Spock made out the narrow, frightened face of his opponent.

"I'm so sorry," the gray-haired male said. Spock could not place his species. "I don't know why I was striking you." He looked down at the armor encasing him, clearly disoriented. "Who are you?"

"Spock."

"I am Malce. What *is* this?"

"It would seem we are prisoners." To the side, Spock saw the other two pugilists had been revealed as Connolly and Ghalka. Each of their suits had a single small, green light glowing near the left shoulder assembly; Spock hadn't noticed that when his headgear was in place. He looked back to his opponent.

"Mister Spock, where are we?" Connolly asked, tense.

"Unclear, Lieutenant." The air outside the armor wasn't as fresh as what he was breathing when his suit's cupola was closed. He felt a light tremor, followed by a wash of light as the walls of the room descended into the floor, revealing a much larger space. What had been their gym, he saw, was one of five round structures encircling a wide pentagonal dais. It was too tall to see if anyone might be atop the platform, but he could make out a railing.

In the better light, Spock realized he knew Malce's species. "You are Antaran. But there are no Antarans on *Enterprise*."

"My colony ship was cutting across a nebula. We were attacked."

Then we were not alone, Spock thought.

Malce winced. "I feel like I've been out for days."

"That is possible." If their captors were in the habit of drugging their victims, he could see recovery rates differing. How long had any of them been in this predicament?

Another rumble, and the massive dais started to retract into the floor. It stopped with a meter's height to spare, revealing several armored figures inside the railing, bustling around a circle of consoles. Some of the individuals' gear was bulkier than others'. A warrior with black shoulder plates stepped to the railing to address Spock and his companions.

"So this is Green Squad," he said in the same voice they'd heard earlier. The words were audible through the faceplate of the speaker's armor—and Spock realized he was hearing a translation coming from his own. "I've seen better-looking warriors in graves."

"What is this?" Connolly asked. "Why are we here?"

Spock had his own question—inspired by the Federation's recent state of war. "Why can't we see your face?"

"I do the talking!" The black-shouldered warrior gestured—

—and Connolly turned and gave Spock a teeth-jarring slap with the back of his reinforced hand. Immobilized in the armor, the senior officer had little chance of avoiding it.

Connolly looked at Spock, horrified. "Lieutenant! I didn't—"

"Do not explain," Spock said, doing his best to ignore

the pain. "We do not control our actions here." He turned his head to focus again on the speaker on the dais. "Who does control them? Are you Klingons?"

Black Shoulders simply laughed. "Klingons!"

"What's a Klingon?" asked a voice from the middle of the crowd on the dais.

When the speaker stepped forward, Spock recognized the older, pocked armor worn by one of his attackers on the ice. "You were the one that abducted us. Who commanded you to do so?"

"History did. And in this fleet, I'm the one who commands." The battlesuit's cupola retracted, revealing a ruddy brown face that could have been seen on a Vulcan lizard. Golden eyes, little more than slits between the scales, looked down upon the foursome. "My name is Kormagan," she said, pointed tongue slipping out. "I am of the Boundless. And now so are all of you!"

18

Mobile Processing Center 539
Pergamum Nebula

Kormagan walked among the statue-frozen assemblage. What she was about to do, she had already done three times that day with other groups—and thousands of times before over her long career. Other wavemasters left orientation chores to their underlings—but then those other fleet leaders slept occasionally too.

Not Kormagan. She wanted to see what she had to work with. They could take it easy. She had a war to win.

"You are of the Boundless, Wave Five-Three-Nine," she said. "I don't know the names of all of your species. That is unimportant. I barely remember the name of my own. Your battlesuits will adjust to your individual anatomies, making you all the same. You, we—are all one."

"What are you talking about?" Malce cried. "Where is my family? Where are my people?"

"Some are still getting suited up." Kormagan gestured to the four other rounded walled areas. "Some are acclimating, like you were."

At that, the dark-haired one with the ears looked keenly at her. "Did you take more of our people from Susquatane?"

Kormagan responded matter-of-factly. "I took them all. The ones on the ground, anyway."

"Careless of you to leave them about," the black-shouldered warrior hissed.

She flashed a stern look over her shoulder before returning her attention to the Starfleet officer. "You were driving the snow vehicle." She nodded. "You have spirit."

"I am Spock."

"To you, maybe. To me, you're Green-Two of the *Aloga-Five* platoon. That may change as you perform and as events warrant—but one thing won't. You're a Thirty-Niner. It's all the identity you should ever want." She gestured to the others. "Even after the rest of your unit is gone, you will remain Thirty-Niners in your hearts—or whatever organs are most vital to you."

"You are a military organization," Spock said. "We are not warriors. We are scientists, who come in—"

"Save it." Starfleet members of the first two groups she had spoken with had tried to plead the same thing. *Nonsense.* Spock and his companions down on the ice had been armed, even fired at her—hardly the demeanor of peaceful people. And *Enterprise* had entered the nebula armed to the teeth. Clearly they had either expected to meet trouble—or to make some.

Besides, the Boundless needed scientists too. If that was indeed what they were, that would come out in time. *If they lasted.*

Spock stared at her, undeterred. "You also said 'recruited.' We were kidnapped."

"Kidnapped, drafted—I've responded to that question since before you were born," Kormagan said, beginning to walk again. "Nothing you would have ever done in your lives is as important as what you are going to do for us."

"And what is that?"

"Eager." Kormagan smiled. "I like that." She continued to pass among them. "You are Thirty-Niners, but there are other waves, known by other numbers: Forty-Sevens, Fifty-Ones, Fifty-Fours. They are Boundless, like you—and yet they are not like you, because they are garbage. *You* are the pinnacle of existence, the ones who will take back what was lost. They dress up in armor and pretend they're soldiers. You live to kill. When they fall back, you charge ahead."

The white-skinned recruit squirmed in her battlesuit. "This thing is miserable. Let me out!"

"Silence!" the black-epauletted warrior still on the dais snarled.

"Ensign Ghalka, do not provoke them," Spock warned.

Kormagan saw Spock look with caution to the railing. "Has my subaltern been slapping you around?"

"By proxy."

"Unsurprising. He's new on the job—he's got the zeal. But don't worry. He may be in charge of the rest of your life, but only after I'm done talking." She approached the one Spock had called Ghalka. "That battlesuit is your home, Green-Five, from this day forward—powerful and self-sustaining. You will breathe, if you need to. You'll receive nourishment and fluids, if you need them."

Circling Ghalka's battlesuit, Kormagan proudly pointed out features. "The biopacks mounted to your sides and in the cavity of your chest protector constantly recycle the solids, liquids, and gases you expel—transforming them into the compounds you need to survive. The radiations of the nebula are nothing against you. As long as your onboard generator functions, you will live." She walked back to the center of the group. "We have inducted members of more than a dozen different species into our ranks, and never yet has an individual died because of armor rejection."

Behind her, the new subaltern piped up again. "Quite a few have died from *my* rejection, after they have failed me. Do not be one of—"

"That's enough, *Baladon*!" Kormagan looked back. "I just said they weren't yours yet." At her mention of the name, the subaltern's canopy recessed into his armor, revealing the Lurian's rubbery face. Kormagan glared at him. "Why did I promote you?"

"Because of my results on Corva Mundu, Wavemaster." He smiled toothily. "And because you traded my superior to Wave Five-Five-Three for an isolinear chip rack."

"That probably made sense at the time." Kormagan faced the recruits. "Baladon is Green-One, your subaltern. Not a mere squad leader: a teacher, a liaison with command."

Spock studied Baladon. "I am aware of your people. The Lurians—of the Ionite Nebula."

"That was before," Baladon said. "I never would have believed it, but it only took weeks for me to realize the Boundless are everything my own people were not. You will discover the same thing." Baladon faced the captives and scowled. "Unless you fail me and I kill you."

"Save it for the Enemy," Kormagan said. She liked a little exuberance, but she liked his example more. "Baladon was a pirate captain, running some of the least competent people ever to make it into space. But even some of *them* have prospered with us. Because here, you only need to be able to count to five."

Baladon shouted, "*Five soldiers to a squad! Five squads to a transport module! Five modules to a carrier! Five carriers to a wave!*"

"Your first drill," Kormagan said.

"Six hundred twenty-five to a wave," Spock observed.

"Joy," Baladon growled. "I have a Federation scientist to command."

"Three," the blond-haired male said.

The Lurian gawked—before his head sank a little into his armor. "Three scientists," he said mournfully. "Another promising career destroyed at the start."

Spock looked to Kormagan. "If we are Wave Five-Three-Nine," Spock said, "that would seem to suggest a much larger force." His eyes narrowed. "But you refer to other units by two digits."

"It's because there are no survivors of the first five hundred waves."

Spock's head tilted. "They exceeded their life spans?"

"I'll say." Baladon guffawed. "Once you hit the battlefield, you'll find out why."

"*Battlefield?*" Malce moaned. "What are you talking about? I'm a financial examiner!"

Puzzled, Kormagan looked back to Baladon. "What does that mean?"

"Money."

"*That.*" Kormagan chuckled. "The Boundless manufacture only four things. Battlesuits, starships, and munitions are three. If you survive and become too old to fight, due to your species' infirmity, you will wind up building them. And you *will* survive, because we are very good at manufacturing the fourth thing: troopers. You now are raw materials, nothing more—until you prove to us you are something else."

Kormagan had given variations of this speech innumerable times. Some beings responded well. Others, with fear—like Malce—or discomfiture, like the Andorian, Ghalka. Seeing her had jogged Kormagan's memory of capturing Andorians years earlier, on another operation. Ghalka looked to Spock. "Lieutenant, what are we going to do?"

"One thing is you're going to stop using that word," Kormagan said. "Know this: all your obligations to previous hierarchies are broken. You will not defer to others, or refer to them by their old titles. You are of the Five-Three-Nine—that is status enough for any being. Master and slave, captain and warrior, president and peon are equal in the ranks of the Boundless."

"Just don't get the idea that includes you and me," Baladon said, grinding his armored fist into his hand.

"I need my medication," Malce said. "I can't stay in this thing!"

"What you four were wearing when you were recruited is in compartment seven in your backpack gear," Kormagan said. "We fit armor to people—we don't have time to be their tailors. Any personal effects or devices you had are in there too. Except weapons, of course—and communicators. Neither would do you any good." She faced Malce. "If you have a medical need our sensors haven't picked up, talk to Jayko. Our armorer can add it to the compounds your unit is synthesizing for you."

Across the way, another silo descended into the deck, revealing four other battlesuited figures, all immobile. Spock recognized another science officer, Godwin, as well as two more Antarans. Kormagan looked back at them. "Looks like I have another speech to give. If there are no more questions—"

"Many," Spock said.

"Two."

His eyes narrowed. "It was the Boundless who fired a torpedo at *Enterprise* four months ago."

Baladon laughed. "No, that was *me*."

"You fired it *for* the Boundless."

"No—during my old career. We captured ships for profit. The Boundless do it because they are born to do so and are exceedingly good at it. If they had fired, it would have struck you."

"What's your other question?" Kormagan asked.

"I get two," Spock said. "There was not an interrogative in that sequence. I advanced an incorrect theory."

"You got information."

"From Baladon, not you."

Baladon chortled. "You've caught yourselves a Vulcan," Baladon said, rubbing the back of his head. "This will be an experience."

"What," Spock asked, "is the enemy you spoke of?"

Kormagan lowered her voice. "The Rengru." She shook her head. "You're just going to have to see."

"And why should we fight in *your* war?"

"Because it's everyone's war. It's the right thing to do. And as for you specifically," she said, stepping over to Spock, "you'll fight because your battlesuits will make you."

"As they did earlier, you mean." Spock shook his head. "Illogical. We would be little more than robots."

"If you were, it'd be a lot easier. Sadly, our AI technology isn't advanced enough yet. Maximum unit efficiency requires a sentient operator. But if you're reluctant, we can still make it charge the line." She stared coolly at Spock. "We never run out of battlesuits—or recruits."

She turned from him. "Oh, yes: some of you may be considering escape. We monitor your suits all the time. All deserters are assumed to be tainted by the Rengru, and incinerated as spies." She stopped to pat Malce's armor. "I'll leave you to figure out how."

Malce quivered, his eyes wide.

Spock spoke up as she started to walk away. "Perhaps there is an exchange I could make on behalf of my people—"

"They're my people, Green-Two. We're done here. Baladon's your liaison now."

Baladon called after her. "If you want better technology, ask them about *Enterprise*, and its secrets!"

"We'll tell you nothing!" the wavy-haired human shouted.

"Lieutenant Connolly is correct," Spock said.

"I told you, enough with the titles," Kormagan called over her shoulder. "And in due time, you'll give me everything I want to know about *Enterprise*. And after that, you'll help me take it. *Willingly*."

19

U.S.S. Enterprise
Pergamum Nebula

Una found Pike where she expected to. The "observation deck" was really more of a wide hallway, with ports overlooking the hangar deck on one side and space on the other; with no operations involving shuttlecraft and not much to see while traversing cloud formations, the place had seen little traffic. Earlier in the mission, *Enterprise*'s first officer had used it herself, finding it a good place for reflection.

She had skipped her sessions ever since the ship departed Susquatane. The hunt for the attackers deserved her every spare moment. But it was a trail already cold when they set out. Day after day of fruitless searching had worn on everyone. The captain most of all.

"Congratulations, Number One." Leaning against the port looking onto the hangar deck, Pike didn't turn to face her. "You found me."

She entered the room slowly. "I thought you would want to know—our engineers have completed the download from the Alpha probe."

Pike looked at her. "You didn't call me in?"

"You didn't leave instructions to do so."

He tilted his head. "That's because I didn't think we'd learn anything."

"You were correct."

"Right now, I hate being right." He returned his gaze to the shuttle deck.

Number One approached him. "The probe only had a lock on the attacker for a few minutes. It's been running blindly since."

"No readings on the bogey?"

"It was flying through that muddle," she said, gesturing to the sauce outside. "We got a better look at Essfive's starships when they were shooting at us."

"I guess we couldn't have expected more." He shook his head. "We should have left earlier. I mean, right away. Chased them down ourselves."

Her brow furrowed. "You made the right decision, Chris. We had to see if anyone had survived. We couldn't—"

"Bull." Pike tapped on the port he was facing. "I could have left shuttlecraft here to check on the camps while we gave chase. Colt even volunteered."

"And you could have lost her, and everyone with her, to a return by the attackers. We could only follow one ship." Una turned around, leaning her back against the port so she could see Pike's face. "Whatever we would've accomplished wouldn't have been worth it."

He gestured. "It would have been intel for Starfleet. Justice for the families. Retribution."

"And whom would *that* have been for?"

"Revenge isn't just for Klingons." He pushed himself away from the port. "Hell, they still could have *been* Klingons, for all we know." He took a deep breath. "Una, I just want to know *why*."

She had no answer.

For several minutes, they remained silent. Pike meandered to the opposite wall, gazing out the port to the nebular gases outside.

She simply watched him—until he noticed her reflection in the pane. "You can stop looking at me at any time."

"Is that an order?"

"Those Illyrians may have taught you a lot, but they can't read minds."

"You're thinking of resigning your commission."

"What?" Pike looked back. He shook his head vigorously. "Wow. No."

She pursed her lips. "Hmm."

He frowned. "What's that supposed to mean?"

"It means that we have a long while before we reach the nebular boundary, which means we could have the same conversation for many days to come."

"And you'd like to skip ahead to the point where I give you a different answer."

"It *would* save time."

"Time I could spend doing something more useful, like writing my memoirs." Pike looked back out the port. "It wouldn't be much of a read." He exhaled. "How did you know?"

"Because I know how you felt after Rigel VII, when we lost people there. I was afraid you were going to resign right there. Then the Talos business happened."

"A burn over a cut," Pike said. "The cut doesn't stop hurting."

And neither does the burn. She suspected he had *never* stopped thinking about Talos IV and the mysterious woman he had met there, Vina. But the first officer had decided long before that the best way for their working relationship to go forward would be to allow Pike to bring her up.

Una stepped to the port—not beside him, but farther up the way, and looked out at the roiling blackness. "You're committed to this?"

"Yes. I mean, no." Pike balled his fists. "I mean—here I was, thinking we'd been exiled, kept away from the one place where we might do some good: the war. Instead, we lost more than I imagined possible. So you tell me, Number One. Where am I supposed to be?"

She looked down. "I'm not in the destiny business. I evaluate orders. I thought your orders at Susquatane were correct—and I think your orders since then have been correct. We have followed the trail to its end. It remains to leave, to contact Starfleet as quickly as possible."

He said nothing.

"In fact," she said, "I think we should go back through the Acheron Formation."

That got his attention. "I wasn't expecting that."

"It makes sense." She touched her cheek softly—in Illyrian culture, a microgesture of contemplation. "That's where we were attacked with a torpedo—meaning it's possible we might see our attackers there. We know it will save weeks on the return, weeks that could be important for Starfleet. And we did it before."

"Yeah, but with Spock." Pike left his vigil and approached her. "Galadjian farmed out the deflector attunements to him last time."

"But we have a record of what they were—and if you don't need me on the bridge, I can go down and take Spock's place. Or oversee engineering while Galadjian makes the adjustments on the fly."

"Maybe we should stick with little steps there." Pike shrugged. "Well, there's certainly no reason to be on the bridge. You've seen all the sights before." He let out an exasperated chuckle. "Hell, I'd hide in a windowless room, if I could."

"Hiding doesn't work. You've taught a lot of cadets that."

He exhaled. "Okay, I don't know if I'm going to quit. But I am going to face the music—and that might be the same as quitting. I guess I don't need to decide anything but the destination."

"And then the destination will decide." She nodded. "Starbase One—via the Acheron."

He turned toward the door. As she walked at his side, he smiled gently. "We really are going in circles, aren't we?"

She didn't have a clever response—but then she was already busy calculating. She only had a limited time to think of a way to keep him from quitting, and she'd just moved her deadline up. *A lot.*

20

Troop Module Aloga-Five
Pergamum Nebula

"Bottom of the third. Jericho walks. Leary grounds to Connolly, force-out at second, six-four. Santis HBP, Leary to second. Tamerlin grounds to Connolly, double play, six-four-three—"

Spock looked up from his meditations. Across from him stood Connolly, uncovered blond head bowed turtle-like in his battlesuit. The man was mumbling. Spock spoke loudly to be heard over the troop module's thrusters. "I do not understand you." His instinct, to add "Lieutenant," had been slapped out of both of them by Baladon's sadistic attempts at puppetry. "I thought I heard you say your own name."

Connolly looked up from his near trance, seeming to notice the rumbling of the transport for the first time. "It's nothing," he said. "Sorry—it probably didn't make a lot of sense."

"It did not."

"I'm going over the last ball game I played back home," Connolly said, looking about in the darkness at the cramped surroundings of Green Squad's drop bay. "It was our league final."

"You remember a sporting event with such clarity?"

"We keep written records—a *lot* of them. I know it's kind of arcane."

"The same is done in chess."

"Yeah. It helps me relax."

"Then it is only important that *you* understand it," Spock said. In truth, there had been many times in his life in which he had done the same thing. Reciting to himself the precepts of logic had helped him to organize his thoughts when they were the most chaotic.

Across from them, Ghalka was mouthing something too: *aloga, vesht, dezik, krall, urdoh.* The Boundless alphabet, or rather the part of it they had been told they needed to care about. Five call signs were all that had been drilled into their heads. They had been taught those, and how to move and fire their weapons—but little else.

It was baffling. "I didn't think we'd be out here so fast," Connolly said, looking about in agitation. "I thought I'd seen this story before—that they'd keep us in training longer, kind of like Starfleet."

"The Boundless have no time to spare for that," Baladon said, stopping for a sip of nutrient from his onboard feeder tube. "It's all recruiting and dying with these people."

"But at least they could show us what we're up against!"

"That would be a mistake." Baladon pointed downward to the drop chute doors. "You think you're worried *now*? If you knew what you were heading toward, you'd be soiling yourself faster than your composting systems could handle!"

Spock looked to Malce. He was in the corner, staring into nothing. The Antaran hadn't spoken in days, earning him Baladon's wrath. The best news had been that despite Baladon's threats, the Boundless did not believe in physically harming their recruits. Battlesuit operators were a precious resource, worth risk—significant risk, in the case of the *Enterprise* abductions. Baladon might batter them mentally and have them smash at one another's armor, but that was the limit.

It did not make it any more pleasant.

Spock moved his hands to his temples. The reflex was far

from helpful to his concentration, given the size of his covered fingers. They had not seen Kormagan again after that day on the training floor; Spock understood from Baladon that her domain extended to all five carriers, as well as the processing vessel and multiple support ships. He had spotted other members of *Enterprise*'s crew, dispersed among the other squads aboard the processing ship. He had counted seventeen, himself included—but had no idea whether he had encountered everyone. They seemed healthy, if just as bewildered as Spock's companions were.

The problem was, he had not seen most of them in some time. After a few days in training, Spock and his group had been marched—there was not a more accurate way to describe a process in which one's legs walked against one's will—aboard *Combat Module Carrier 539-Aloga*, reputed to be Kormagan's flagship. Their squad had been assigned to *Aloga-Five*, the modular troop transport they were in now. Nowhere in between had Spock seen any of the other *Enterprise* captives, save Connolly and Ghalka. Baladon, who was always willing to answer when he thought his words could cause unhappiness, had suggested they could be on Kormagan's other ships or possibly traded to some other wave.

If the latter, Spock wondered, *how would we ever find them?*

Navigational thrusters sent a horrid creak through the ship. Another black-shouldered warrior entered—this one with an identifier light shining ruby-red. The unmasked being's hairy orange face marked him as belonging to one of the more common species within the Boundless—and his armor markings made him the red squad subaltern. He greeted Baladon. "How's command treating you, Greensub?"

"We'll see after today, Redsub." Baladon cast a leering eye toward his teammates. "My curse in life is to bear the failings of others."

"You'll live."

"I'm surprised that *you're* alive. I thought you did a recon this morning."

"We did. I lost one on the way out. One of your kind."

"I know who you mean," Baladon said. "That was Garnam. A consummate oaf. It always surprised me he lived past birth."

"Yeah, no great loss."

"So the Rengru know we are coming."

"They always know we're coming." The subaltern looked to Baladon's troops. "Listen, I've got a slot to fill."

"You want one of these?" Baladon laughed. "Rookies, all. They haven't seen a thing."

"A body's better than nothing. What'll you take?"

Baladon's eyes focused on one of the weapons affixed to Redsub's armor. "I like that assault cannon."

"The Ripper? For one of *them*? You're crazy."

"And you're a trooper short—and we're about to go in."

The subaltern listened to the straining of the transport and growled. "All right. But I get to pick."

"Not a chance, my friend—not when the store is about to close." Baladon looked over to his squad. "You there. Andorian!"

Ghalka looked up, broken from her fretful haze. "What's happening?"

Spock fixed his eyes on Baladon. "What do you intend?"

"It's a deal," Baladon said. He spoke into the mic before him. "Transfer personnel, Aloga-Five-Green-Five, to same, Red."

"Accept transfer," the other subaltern said, and the light on Ghalka's shoulder assembly went from green to red. Redsub passed the weapon to Baladon. "Have fun."

Ghalka couldn't see the light directly given its position on her armor, but she could see its glow—especially when she brought her hand up before her to block it. Her eyes widened as she saw the changed color. "Spock, what's going on?"

Spock's eyebrows lowered. "Baladon has traded you. *For a gun*."

"For *what*?" Connolly erupted. "What, no draft pick to be named later?"

"Stow that nonsense," Baladon said, admiring the weapon. "Or I'll throw you in for free."

"Sorry, pal," the Red Squad subaltern said. "We're full up. But maybe soon." He pointed to Ghalka. "Come on, Red-Five."

Ghalka jerked upward from where she was leaning and lurched into motion. "No!"

Connolly and Spock reached for her, but Baladon barred the way. "Stay put. Either the surveillance tech on the deck above can stop you, or I will."

The two Starfleet officers could only watch as Ghalka followed her new leader out, objecting all the way. "We will see you again," Spock said, unsure of how he might make good on the promise. He felt as if he had to say something.

A klaxon sounded—and at the same moment, the transport banked. "That's us," Baladon said to his squad, now down to three. "This is Shivane, a Rengru forward depot. Destroy everything that moves. That's it." Baladon made purposefully for his drop alcove.

"That's *it*?" Connolly gawked as Baladon stepped onto the sealed trapdoor. "We don't even know what kind of environment we're going into."

"We're in a higher radiation zone, so keep your headgear deployed. Beyond that, these units can handle anything."

"Except whatever hit that guy that Ghalka's replacing!"

Spock spoke firmly. "Baladon, I will not attack someone who is not my enemy."

"Then I'll have *two* openings to fill," Baladon said, disgusted. "The Rengru do not care about your morals, Vulcan. Now button up and get into position before I have to walk you there myself!" Baladon's angry face disappeared behind his reactivated headgear.

Spock watched Malce walk, hypnotized, into the Green-3

drop chute alcove. Connolly looked at Spock, rattled. "Tell me you've thought of something. A way out of this—anything."

"I have not. Perhaps we will find a way below." With that, Spock stepped onto the plating assigned to him.

Hearing the rumbling grow thunderous outside, Connolly reluctantly went to his own spot. "Are we going to be okay?"

Spock did not respond. "Insufficient information" felt unsatisfactory, even to him.

21

Rengru Depot
Shivane

Evan Connolly's Starfleet career, an ex-lover had once said, resembled the sport that so fascinated him: years of training followed by a lot of standing around, waiting for something to happen. The words had been spoken in unkindness—and were, he thought, unfair to baseball. But only to the game: about his work, it rang true. A specialist in planetary gravimetrics didn't have a lot to do until they actually got someplace—and as nearly happened at Susquatane, he didn't always get to leave the ship even then. He longed to hit the dirt at every opportunity.

Twenty seconds on Shivane gave him a sudden determination to never leave the confines of a starship again. There had been no ports on the troop module for passengers to see where they were; Connolly now understood that to be a right and sensible decision. The sky alone was an abomination: a cacophony of nebular gases, nauseating in color. It served as backdrop to more than a dozen combat modules landing or leaving—and a variety of other Boundless fliers of a kind he hadn't seen before.

Shivane itself, meanwhile, was a filthy sponge. What passed for "ground" was a fetid mat of slick moss that gushed oils with the least provocation. Connolly and his teammates had descended to the surface using their battlesuits' jetpacks, but even controlled landings couldn't keep them from sinking knee-deep. Further—and far more alarming—was that the ground responded to their jet exhaust by catching fire. It posed no threat to his armor, and so for a long moment, Connolly simply stood, wondering what the proper response was to standing in fire.

Out of earshot, Baladon called over his comm linkage to the team: *"Quit daydreaming. Form up!"*

Throwing up seemed more appropriate to Connolly—and he could hear that was exactly what Malce was doing. The Antaran had been the first to spot their destination, the Rengru depot, close to the horizon. Multiple dark structures huddled in a half-kilometer-wide circular area, covered by a dome of magnetic shielding that appeared in red on his headgear's visual interface. At regular intervals outside its circumference were five raised openings into the ground, dark maws that led into tunnels beneath the protective shield. Surrounding the portals were gun emplacements, firing disruptor bolts at the Boundless ships.

Connolly looked up to see several hits being scored, blasts deflected by the troop transports' shields. The oddball Boundless vehicles were in play now; gunship and bomber modules, according to the text that appeared on his interface when he looked at them. The vehicles dropped ordnance near the Rengru cannons in an attempt to cover the landings.

"Lieutenant!" Spock called out, pointing to a descending transport whose markings both of them had seen before on Susquatane. As then, Boundless troops debarked from meters in the air—also setting the spongy moss on fire as they landed. One, however, acted differently. Kormagan, distinctive in her older armor, triggered her jetpack again until she hovered just above the flames. Then she unleashed flames of her own—a cauterizing chemical spray from a weapon attached to her armor. Within seconds, she had burned a dry crater within the morass.

"Follow the lead!" Baladon pointed to one of the weapons protruding from his backpack gear. "Deploy Agent Urdoh-Forty, triple strength!"

Connolly saw the same instructions appear in text on his interface. He reached over his shoulder with his right hand—and felt the proper weapon leap into his hand. *Some caddy,* he thought, pulling the hose-connected sprayer forward and pointing it. *Easy enough!*

But while Connolly had been taught to use his jetpack on the processing vessel, he hadn't been much in the mood to learn anything else, including how to hover. Thus, his attempt to replicate Kormagan's maneuver sent him spinning in the air, spraying chemical fire wildly before pitching back into the guck. The flaming reagent, disliking close contact with its target, caused the tool to explode in Connolly's hands. A loud clang announced ejection of the remainder of the chemical canister from his gear. Dazed, Connolly found himself on armored hands and knees in a burnt-out pit of his own making.

Baladon looked down into the hole at him. "Are you sure we're not related?"

"I didn't know how to—"

"Never mind! Get out of there!"

Determined not to try the jetpack again, Connolly clambered up the charred and smoking bramble walls. Doing so with more than a hundred kilos of extra mass was no easy chore even with mechanical assistance, but after repeated tries, he was back on the surface. Spock had burnt a proper shoulder-deep foxhole, he saw; Connolly made for it and entered.

Before he could say anything, Kormagan transmitted. *"All squads from* Dezik *and* Krall, *infiltrate opening and destroy depot shield.* Aloga *and* Vesht *squads, provide fire support and prepare to reinforce!"*

Warriors from Kormagan's other carriers charged—and

Connolly could see in his interface that they had glowing personal deflector shields of their own, protecting them as they moved forward. *I have to figure out how to turn that feature on*, he thought. Something was also happening above: the Boundless gunships were firing frenetically, trying to protect the warriors on the move.

That was when Connolly saw the black opening to the depot grow cloudy, and then white with movement.

"The Rengru," Spock said.

"I don't see—"

"Your armor has telescopic capabilities. Focus your eyes and use vocal commands to enhance."

Connolly did—and wished he hadn't. The faraway "cloud" was a stampede. Countless creatures, alabaster white, exploded from the tunnel onto the grounds before the depot. They bounded, twisted, and ran, seeming to take new shapes as they went, the wretched soil no impediment to them at all.

They were mesmerizing. "It's somewhere between a trilobite and a crustacean," he said. "If they grew three meters long."

"The Japanese spider crab does," Spock said. "But your comparison is apt. The Rengru do almost appear arthropoidal." Spock seemed steps ahead in his observations of the creatures, still distant. "Exoskeletons with multiple body segments and paired jointed appendages. Shielded carapace, also jointed, running the length of the body and topped with a crown. Robust motor abilities, almost protean in movement."

You forgot "scary as hell," Connolly thought. Some internal musculature within the Rengru's long limbs allowed each one to move independently and be used for support. As he increased magnification, he realized the many limbs were themselves multijointed and prehensile, miniature versions of the Rengru body plan. And they, too, had smaller limbs at their tips. "Fractals in action," he mumbled.

"Indeed. Observe, north of the gateway." There, Connolly saw something he hadn't noticed before: the anti–air battery on that side had several Rengru perched on it, manipulating it. "Here as elsewhere," Spock said, "fine motor skills are nearly a prerequisite for a spacefaring society."

They didn't look like they had any society at all to Connolly. Mesmerized by the sight, without thinking, he drew his disruptor rifle from his gear.

"They are highly intelligent," Spock said. "I see them reacting as a group. They must be transmitting information to one another."

Connolly wasn't interested. "Spock, I think we'd better—"

"Rengru!"

"Spock?" Snapped from his trance, Connolly looked up to see that Spock had jetted out of the depression and onto the surface. "Spock, get down!"

The Vulcan stood with his weapon stowed, his hands out. Connolly heard him over his comm system. *"Rengru, if you can hear this broadcast: I am Lieutenant Spock, of the United Federation of Planets. I wish to communicate!"*

22

Rengru Depot
Shivane

"I was delivered here by your enemy," Spock broadcast, *"but I am not your enemy. I do not wish combat."*

An answer came in the form of a nearby explosion. "They *do* wish combat!" Connolly called out. Rengru guns opened up on newcomers to the scene: Boundless land vehicles being disgorged from one of the specialized transport modules. Across the blasted fens, Kormagan issued a command to them to move out—just in time for the Rengru cannon to find its mark. Shrapnel rained down, causing Spock to dive back for cover.

"Shivane sucks," Connolly said, covering his head despite the fact that it was already armored.

If Spock had a rejoinder, it was lost in the screams coming over the comm. The squads from *Dezik* and *Krall* had used their disruptors to clear some of the swarm blocking their approach to the tunnel opening, but several individual Rengru had gotten through. One had leapt upon a Boundless warrior whose shields had evidently failed him, using its limbs to wrap around the unfortunate fighter. The warrior writhed, trying to get free—

"Breach! Breach! Dezik-One-Blue-Two!" warned an automated voice—and a black "X" blinked, superimposed, over the struggling pair.

"This is Dezik-One Bluesub," called out a frantic warrior. *"Purge protocol engaged!"*

At once, the nearby Boundless fighters turned, robotically, and unloaded their weapons on the Rengru and its victim. After a couple of seconds, something in the warrior's armor reacted, producing a colossal explosion that immolated both the wearer and the Rengru. The Boundless warriors then appeared to regain control of their bodies and continued fighting.

"We've got self-destructs!" Connolly said. "We're walking bombs!"

Spock didn't sound so certain. "There must be some fear of pathogens, enough that they systemically overrode the protections against friendly fire."

"Spock, they killed their own! They were made to kill their own!"

"I did not say I approved, Lieutenant."

"You two, step up!" To the left, Spock and Connolly saw Baladon emerge from his makeshift bunker. "We go next!"

Connolly's eyes bugged. "Go where?"

There was no answer, because Baladon had already clambered into another depression—and a second later, Connolly saw another Boundless warrior scramble out. As the armored figure broke into a run, Baladon emerged from the hole and yelled, *"You're running the wrong way, you imbecile!"*

Spock and Connolly looked at one another. *Malce!*

The Antaran had buried himself in a pit at the start of the action, and was now running as fast as his mechanical legs could take him toward the drop zone. It seemed like the right idea to Connolly—but not Baladon, who broadcast an alert to the Boundless's watchers in the air. *"Specter, specter. Aloga-Five-Green-Three—turn him around!"*

At once, Malce's jetpack ignited, lifting him into midair. Rotating there, he hit the ground and ran back toward the fray, no longer in control of his extremities. *"Help me!"*

"Point your damn weapon!" Baladon yelled. When Connolly and Spock climbed out of their crater and began to move to head off Malce, Baladon pointed at them. "Do you want to be next?"

"Baladon, look out!" Spock yelled.

The distraction had proved destructive for Baladon. Two Rengru, having broken loose from the scrum outside the gateway, charged the Lurian, one striking low with its hardened carapace, the other high. Surprised, Baladon lost his footing in the moss and staggered. *"Get off!"*

Spock, who had not drawn his weapon in the entire engagement, did so now. He fired a disruptor blast that flashed off Baladon's armor, temporarily knocking the attacking Rengru off. Then he bolted toward the group. Connolly was unwilling to join in the rescue, but a nearby blast got him moving.

"We must prevent a breach," Spock yelled, arriving at the fray, "or we will be forced to kill him!"

Connolly wondered why Spock would want to save Baladon after what he'd just done to Malce—but the subaltern's howls of horror moved him to action as well.

"No disruptors this close!" Spock called, drawing a different weapon from his arsenal. A powerful sonic blast emanated from it, knocking the two Rengru off Baladon's prone form. Connolly found his own device and used it in unison with Spock's, the shrieking waves forcing the squirming Rengru back.

We can't keep this up for long, Connolly wanted to say, knowing he wouldn't be heard. But then two powerful disruptor blasts rendered the warning unnecessary.

Malce stepped up to the motionless Rengru, rifle in hand. "I . . . didn't do that on purpose," he said.

Spock moved back to Baladon, who had not moved since the attack. "He is in cardiac distress."

"I would be too," Connolly said.

"Armor . . . helping," Baladon said. They'd been told that the battlesuits could play medic when needed. "Just need . . . moment . . ."

There was no moment. *"Fall back!"* Kormagan commanded from afar. *"Troop module evac to the rally points, now, now, now!"* Connolly looked back to the depot to see that the assault wave had been completely repulsed. Boundless warriors, whose jetpacks were of limited help on planets with significant gravity, were using them for all they were worth, trying to retreat across ground teeming with Rengru.

Connolly saw a blinking arrow appear on his visual interface, pointing to the left. He turned to see a flashing marker superimposed over a hill—clearly his pick-up point. A timer and distance meter had numbers in motion, depicting how far away *Troop Module Aloga-Five* was from the site. Malce, in control of his legs or not, was already on the way there. But Spock was trying to help Baladon up.

"Spock, let's just get out of here!"

"We cannot escape on this planet, Lieutenant. Our prison is the only sanctuary."

"But he would've sent Malce to his death. He was about to send us!"

"He is a prisoner, just as we are. Captain Pike would not leave anyone. Neither will I."

Spock was right, of course. Connolly helped Spock get Baladon on his feet.

Aloga-Five appeared above, heading for the rally point. They had only gotten a few dozen meters toward it when a disruptor bolt from one of the depot's cannons struck it amidships, sending it crashing down. Connolly and Spock shoved Baladon into a blast crater and dove in after him.

Shivane shook around them—and soon the rain of debris began. The flashing marker—indeed, all the telemetry Connolly had been receiving from aloft—disappeared.

Connolly plopped down, his armored butt on the ground. "What do we do now?"

"New . . . rally point," Baladon said between coughs.

"How do you know?" Spock asked.

"Subalterns get . . . a different data stream."

Sure enough, new telemetry loaded—and Connolly saw they'd been reassigned to *Aloga-Three*, currently making its way to a clearing nearby. Outside the pit, he saw Kormagan leading a firing line screening the approach; one by one, Boundless warriors escaping the failed assault made their way safely through it.

They moved with Baladon to the evac area. There, already, was Ghalka, with the Red Squad subaltern; astoundingly, so was Malce, who had just missed being killed earlier by the crashing transport. As *Aloga-Three* came into beautiful sight, Connolly heard Kormagan—but not over the transceiver.

"The Starfleet crew," she said, stowing her weapon as she approached. If she was wearied at all, there was no way to tell. "Looks like you made it. Not bad for your first day."

"Not bad?" Connolly blurted. "It was a massacre!"

"That just means it's time for more recruits." Anything else she said was lost in the din of the transport's engines.

23

U.S.S. Enterprise
Pergamum Nebula

It had haunted him all day. A simple phrase, part of a conversation Pike had overheard that morning in the galley at breakfast.

"Calling off the search."

They were among the worst words in the language to Pike, almost always the end of hope. He couldn't remember ever hearing the phrase in association with a happy ending. When Hondo had died, the emergency crews had known just where in the mountain to look thanks to Pike's information—and yet it still took them time to scan the ridge and definitively locate his corpse. He had heard the phrase then.

Pike had resolved never to say the words in association with the Susquatane attackers. Yes, *Enterprise* was making its way toward the Acheron Formation and its exit from the Pergamum, effectively ending his search; and yes, he still felt he would be forced to resign. But if Starfleet wanted him to reenter the Pergamum and continue searching for the murderers of most of his science team, he was willing to become a permanent resident. He would search until Hell froze over.

He didn't think he would be allowed to do that—and, clearly, neither did his crew. No one had protested to him directly; they were too professional, all fully certain that Pike shared in their mourning. They also understood that such a major incident had to be reported. If the attackers were in any way affiliated with the Klingons—if they *were* Klingons—they posed a significant danger to the Federation. That could not be done from within the nebula; the *Enterprise* simply *had* to leave.

And yet—as at breakfast—he saw only sullen faces, averted when he looked. And the words, in hushed tones.

". . . never find them . . ."

". . . got away with it . . ."

". . . didn't do anything . . ."

". . . gave up."

Pike heard them all again in his mind as he awaited the turbolift. He stared at the deck, fist and teeth clenched. *Somebody,* he thought, *give me a reason to stay.*

The turbolift doors opened. Mia Colt smiled at him. "Captain!"

"Yeoman." He stepped inside. "You're happy."

"Something interesting down in science."

"Is that so?" He had seconded his assistant to the science team, to help cover some of the jobs done by the departed. The move had the side benefit of giving Pike more time to stew alone without someone always asking after him. Colt had changed a lot from the green yeoman he used to know, but her devotion to him hadn't altered in the slightest.

"It's better to show you. I'm headed to the cargo bay."

Cargo bay? Pike followed.

Far aft in the stardrive section, Pike and Colt descended the stairwell into the cargo transporter complex. There, they found Ensign Dietrich and Nils Pitcairn huddled over the control consoles. "You're right. It's out there," the transporter chief said. "Just on the edge of what we can pick up."

Pike approached. "What's out there?"

Dietrich showed him a small dot on the interface. "You remember, Captain, the probe we spotted just before the third nuclear blast? Colt and I have been scanning every formation we pass through." She brought up magnification. "That reads as a probe—and it's not one of ours."

"Has it responded to our scan?"

"No. But it's about to pass out of range."

I can fix that. "Pike to bridge."

Number One responded. *"Bridge."*

"Full stop."

"Full stop, Captain. Are there further orders?"

"Stand by." Pike looked at the others before the console. "You want to approach?"

"No, sir," Pitcairn said. "That did it. I think I've got it now."

"Scan for hazardous content. I don't want to bring aboard a mine."

Pitcairn nodded. That was part of the usual protocol anyway.

A high whine followed—after which a large, gangly device materialized on the cargo transporter pad. Heavily scored by impacts during its nebular transits, it didn't look much like anything that attacked them at Susquatane.

Colt walked around it. "It's Lurian."

Pike's eyes widened. "*Lurian*? How do you know?"

She waved him around. The opposite side of the probe bore the words:

PROPERTY OF THE KINGDOM OF LURIA

PLEASE RETURN

"That's helpful," Pike said. "Looks like the words 'Kingdom of Luria' are crossed out."

"With a knife."

"A dull one."

Dietrich approached with a tricorder. "No explosive aboard. Just an exhausted dilithium crystal. I'd say our foundling ran out of steam."

"When?"

"I ought to be able to tell from the decay rate," she said, adjusting her device.

Before she could follow up, Nicola called from the bridge, which was still on standby. *"Captain, we're receiving a transmission."*

Pike looked up. They hadn't gotten a message from Starfleet in a long time—and he sure wasn't expecting to pick one up deep in a cloud. "Where's it coming from?"

"From there, sir. Whatever you brought aboard is broadcasting. It's a very weak signal—I don't know that we'd even notice it if we weren't carrying it."

Pike looked to where Pitcairn was stationed. "Nicola, pipe whatever it is to the terminal down here."

"Aye, Captain."

Pike and Colt stepped over and saw a sequence of images appear on-screen. Most depicted nothing at all—but several near the end looked very familiar.

Colt pointed. "That's us!"

"It sure is." Pike shook his head as he framed through the shots. The earlier ones were hazy, *Enterprise* a dark blur amid nebular gases. Later images were much sharper. "How did it get that close without us seeing it?" Pike asked.

"We'll want engineering to look at it," Dietrich said, kneeling beside the probe. "But it seems to be conditioned both to function out here—and to do so stealthily."

Like a Lurian pirate would want, Pike thought.

The final image was the clearest, and most surprising. It showed *Enterprise* orbiting Susquatane. "Is that from when our people were attacked?"

"Look at the icecap," Colt said, still enlivened by her discovery. "That's from our first visit there. The encounter would have been back last year, just before we found out about the Klingon war and turned for home."

"That matches what I have over here," Dietrich said. "The probe tried to follow—and seems to have died not long after sending its images."

"Sending—to the Lurians. So *they* killed our people?" Pike wasn't sure he believed his own words.

"What are Lurians?" Pitcairn asked.

"Small-time Alpha Quadrant operators. Out of the Ionite Nebula—not too far from here. They're barely on Starfleet's sensors. Maybe they're very nice people, but they seem to generate a lot of petty crooks," Pike explained.

"Could they have gone in with the Klingons?"

"They'd have to be pretty stupid to do that." Pike shook his head. "I don't even know if there have been any formal contacts with the Federation."

Pike looked again at the image of *Enterprise*—and then stared for long moments at the probe.

"Are we staying, sir?" Colt asked, hopeful.

Pike frowned. "I need something more. Keep at it."

24

Combat Module Carrier 539-Aloga
Pergamum Nebula

Not long after Shivane had acquainted Spock and Connolly with Boundless combat, the two experienced what was apparently a post-battle ritual aboard *Carrier Aloga*: being berated by Jayko, the chief armorer.

"This might be the dumbest class of recruits I've ever seen," Jayko said as Spock watched him circle Connolly's armor. The explosion of Connolly's chemical agent canister had charred his dorsal gear. "The Boundless I was born into had a policy," the armorer said. "We only inducted *intelligent* life."

Spock ignored the insult and focused on the tidbit Jayko had just revealed. "You were not pressed into service, as we were?"

"What did I just say?"

"Would you be of the same species as Kormagan, then?"

Jayko's headgear split open and recessed into his battlesuit, revealing a yellow face with vaguely avian features. "Do I *look* like her kind?"

"No."

"If I did, I'd want to stay buttoned up all the time too." Jayko snorted and began tinkering with Connolly's gear. Other staffers were doing the same, in one of the larger rooms Spock had seen aboard the carrier. It appeared to be part workshop, part sickbay—though it soon became apparent that for many, their battlesuits were already doing the medical work.

That included, across the room, Baladon. He bellowed something Spock could not make out. Jayko responded with a stream of epithets that crossed cultural boundaries and left Connolly's side to deal with the Lurian.

Spock stepped close to Connolly, whose headgear was likewise not deployed. The Vulcan spoke quietly. "I saw the list of casualties from Shivane at the armorer's station while he was working. It only mentions species typologies, not names—but I infer from it that none of *Enterprise*'s crew were among the fallen."

Connolly let out a huge breath. "I was terrified. That planet was hideous."

Spock looked around the room at the warriors whose battlesuits were being tended to. "There is apparently more than one core race to the Boundless. Like Jayko, not everyone we have seen has been abducted. I also believe some of Kormagan's speech about the Boundless during our induction was aspirational, and not representative of true practice."

"How do you mean?"

"Racial and status barriers still matter to them."

As if cued by Spock's statement, across the room, Jayko loudly proclaimed that Baladon and his people were a foul pestilence sent to ruin his laboratory.

"I see what you mean." Connolly snickered. "I've been trying to get more data about the battlesuit's systems, but it doesn't have much. So much of everything around here is need to know."

Needlessly, Spock thought.

"But the stuff I have figured out is amazing. If we could take one of these suits back to the Federation, it'd go a long way to evening up the score with the Klingons."

"That is not a priority, Lieutenant. We must establish the

status of the other members of our landing parties. Concurrently, we must locate *Enterprise*. When those two things are accomplished, our mission is clear."

"Which is?"

"Escape."

Connolly stared at him—and then winced, as he heard someone approach.

"The two of you, whispering there—I see you!" From behind, they saw Baladon's lumbering approach. His face, uncovered, looked a little paler than they had seen it before—but he still had the energy to intimidate. "You two did a terrible thing. Don't think I've forgotten it!"

"What," Connolly said, "saving your life?"

"Forget that!" Baladon spat—a mistake, as his spittle struck the open collar of his battlesuit and stayed there. "I'm talking about my assault cannon. I lost it when the Rengies attacked—and you didn't pick it up. I didn't even get to use it!"

Spock did not always know when others were being serious—and to him, it seemed that Connolly could not tell either. But then Baladon broke into a smile. "But at least you got there before they punched a hole in me."

"Malce did that."

"I'm sure he regrets it." Baladon pointed a thumb at Jayko too. "That one certainly does."

Seeing the gesture, Jayko stormed back. "Would you like me to tell your squad what great injury felled their oh-so-great subaltern?"

Baladon shrugged. "I couldn't stop you."

"*He had a heart attack!*"

"That is what I thought from the readings," Spock said. "But I was curious how it was possible. The battlesuits' health management subsystems are designed to regulate our bodies, in combat and out."

"That only works if you ever regulated your body on your

own," Jayko said. "The Lurians' consumption habits have thrown all the modeling off. The feeder systems think they need more calories than a whole squad—"

"Don't forget the drinking," Baladon said.

"—and they consume so much alcohol that the battlesuits have started to assume that they need it for survival. He's been walking around half-inebriated!"

Baladon patted his armored chest. "I only wish I had a suit like this when I ran my old crew. I guarantee I would never have settled for *half*-inebriation!"

Disgusted, Jayko tromped off.

Spock looked to Baladon. "You are recovering?"

"I will be back on the line the very next fight." The Lurian smiled broadly; Spock began to feel that the Shivane episode had created a bond. "On the subject," Baladon said, smiling, "did you enjoy your introduction to the Rengru?"

Connolly rolled his eyes. "It left something to be desired."

Spock wanted answers. "What is the Boundless's complaint against them?"

The question caught Baladon off guard. "I have no idea."

"Do the Boundless desire the Rengru's planets?"

"Just as places to fortify. They're not like your Federation, always colonizing. They just fight."

"But for what reason?"

"Since when is a reason necessary?" Baladon shook his head. "All I've heard is that maybe the Rengru did something to someone named K'davu."

Spock's and Connolly's eyes met. The word sounded vaguely Klingon. "Who is K'davu?" Spock asked.

"I don't know. Only the old-timers in the units ever say the word, usually to rally us. I never wondered much about it. A fight is a fight. I go where they say."

"You do not mind being subservient after commanding your own ship?"

"It wasn't much of a ship to command," Baladon said. "I had hoped to start something new somewhere—perhaps my own settlement. But that requires finding a place to conquer and someone to conquer them with. In my case, the Lurian element was lacking."

Spock listened. While brusque, Baladon increasingly struck him as a highly intelligent member of an often-brutal society, trying his best to succeed; that experience had evidently served him well in the Boundless so far. "Perhaps," Spock said, "you could have tried it without conquest. I know of a planet the Vulcans abandoned that might be suitable for your people. There is an existing infrastructure on Garadius IV which may be of use to you in—"

"*These* are my people," Baladon said loudly, eyes shifting left and right to see if anyone else in the armory/infirmary was listening. Then he said more quietly, "What's the idea, Spock? Helping me off the battlefield isn't enough—you think you can get on my good side with a bribe?"

"My intentions in both cases were altruistic."

Baladon regarded him with suspicion for a moment. "Maybe they were. I've heard about Vulcans. But it doesn't matter. There's no sense plying me, Spock. You're no longer under my command."

"What?" Connolly blurted, stunned. "What did you do, trade him for another gun?"

Spock's brow furrowed. "I understood that the *Aloga-Five* squads were being merged with the others, but—"

"They are," Baladon said. "This is about splitting the two of you up. The opmaster aboard *Aloga-Five* died along with the cabin crew when she went down, but her telemetry all streamed back to the carrier—including all the armor feeds. They saw your little stunt."

"I had a stunt?"

"What do you call standing up and waving to the Rengru like you're inviting them to dinner?"

Connolly's head sank a little into his armor. "Yeah, he did that."

"Might as well make it official," Baladon said. He toggled his mic and spoke a stream of call signs—and the light on Connolly's armor went from green to blue. "We're on *Aloga-Four*, now, Blue-Two."

Connolly shook his head. "From *Five* to *Four*. I guess we're moving up."

Spock's light had turned yellow. "You're Gold-Five on *Aloga-One*," Baladon said. "You're to report there now."

"That is the vessel Kormagan deploys with," Spock observed.

"Bright one. Yes, she wants to keep an eye on you." Baladon snorted. "I can't imagine why." He nudged Connolly. "Come on, let's try to find what garbage chute Malce has tried to crawl into."

Connolly looked back wanly at Spock, who needed no telepathic powers to read his thoughts. Every option he had considered for escape was likely to require cooperation. Now each of them would be acting alone—

—and worse news yet arrived over their comm systems.

"All commandos, report to your troop carriers," Kormagan said. *"We're going back to Shivane. And this time, we're going to win!"*

25

Warship *Deathstrike*
Pergamum Nebula

In the days following the discovery of the Lurian probe, Pike had slow-walked the return approach to the Acheron Formation to give Dietrich and Colt time to continue scanning. It had been a worthwhile decision, for they had discovered another probe, one identical to the Essfive bomb-delivering drone Dietrich had seen over Susquatane. That was the one upside to the Pergamum: the nebula made it difficult to find things, all right, but it was so hostile that it also had a way of trapping failing vessels like flies in amber.

The Essfive probe was too large to beam aboard, and scans had shown that it carried an explosive device: an end-of-mission self-destruct mechanism. White-knuckle moments had followed as an *Enterprise* EVA team discovered the truth: radiation had caused the probe to fail, and its detonator along with it. Removing the explosive, they had beamed the probe's central command module to the cargo bay.

An up-close look made it doubly obvious to Pike that it had not been built by the same hands as the Lurian probe. However, the two drones proved to have engaged in similar activities. The Lurian device had stalked *Enterprise*. The Essfive probe had imaged a completely different ship, evidently, a Lurian one. Better, its data core still had a record of where, generally, it could be found. The "Pergamum paparazzi," as

Number One had called them, had been the bloodhounds leading them to their quarry: a derelict starship, half the size of *Enterprise*, adrift in one of the denser structures of the Acheron Formation.

Pike was more excited during the approach than he'd been in a year. Closing in on the vessel, however, the questions all started anew. Beginning with one voiced by him on the *Enterprise* bridge:

"*What the hell kind of name is* Deathstruck*?*"

The ship itself was old, except for half a dozen fresher-looking airlocks on the hull, all of which were placed strangely and at odd angles. It had all the appearances of a plague ship, and the word haphazardly painted on its hull sounded more like a warning than a name. With no life signs reported, he'd expected to find disease—or a massacre.

An hour having passed with no toxins discovered, Pike felt free to transport over and join the investigative team. After two minutes aboard, however, he still wasn't sure what his team *had* found—except for an awful stench. Some of it came from garbage; clearly, a whole lot of people had been living on top of one another in the vessel.

And none of them were still aboard the ship.

He saw his security chief make her way around a corner, phaser drawn. "It's only me," Pike said.

"I don't know why I even have this out," Nhan said, reattaching her weapon to her belt. "Nothing here any larger than the flies—or whatever they are."

"I've noticed." Pike flicked one of the bugs away. "What do we have here?"

"Parent vessel of the Lurian probe, for sure—we've found more like it aboard. The ship appears to be called *Deathstrike.*"

"What, was that a typo outside?"

"No idea. It's a classic privateer model, matching the sort operating out of the Ionite Nebula."

"I wondered if they would make their way over here." The Federation had long been aware of the problem of Lurian piracy—some of it state sponsored—but had treated it as a minor nuisance. The Orions were much better at it, and a lot nearer to the member planets. He followed her down a hallway. "No transporter rooms?"

"Too old a ship."

"How did they conduct . . . *business*?"

"You saw the rows of doors down the starboard hall?"

"The lifepod stations?"

"You and I would use them that way. The Lurians have weaponized them, adding magnetic clamps, laser torches, and everything one would need to crack open another starship once its shields were down. If it had shields at all. I suspect this bunch sticks to the smaller fish—unless something falls into their laps."

"Like a Federation starship rushing hell for leather to escape the nebula? With its aft shields down?"

"I can show you something on that score. This way." Nhan led him briskly toward the bridge. "Unless you have a breathing filter like mine hidden somewhere, you may want to cover your mouth."

Pike had already started to do that on his own. By the time he reached the wide area, the stink was making his eyes water. He soon saw the source: the blackened corpse of a Lurian, on the floor amid several burnt-through stumps where pedestals for consoles had been. "This guy was stabbed and bled out," Nhan said.

One of her officers, wisely masked, was working the forensics. The woman shifted the body to reveal the murder weapon, still in place. "Whoever it was left the knife."

"Meaning they didn't need knives," Pike said, "or left it here as an example."

"And there's another clue," Nhan said, gesturing to starboard.

Pike looked over—and his eyes bulged. Still on screen—the only thing active, besides life-support—was the image of *Enterprise*, sent by one of the probes now sitting in his cargo hold.

"I guess that closes the loop." Pike shook his head in sadness. "Sorry Spock didn't get to share in the detective work."

"Yeah."

Nhan hadn't been aboard long enough to know Spock well, but Pike knew they had been collegial. "Is this the ship that fired the mystery torpedo last year?" he asked.

"I don't know how we'd begin to confirm that, with the weapons control systems all pulled. Maybe our superstar engineer knows some trick I can't imagine."

I wouldn't be so sure about that. Pike dismissed the thought and walked over to the impromptu airlock, seated to the right of the forward port. The circular opening was off-center, entering the vessel a meter or more above the deck plane—and a large piece of *Deathstrike*'s burnt-through hull was sitting on the deck. "This was punched in from outside!"

"Yep," Nhan said. "Somebody wanted in, and didn't bother to knock. There's six of these holes, leading to all decks of the ship."

Pike looked around at the debris and weapon score marks. "Definitely a fight here. How many more bodies besides our pungent friend?"

"None."

"*None?*"

Pike was still trying to choose which question to ask as a follow-up when he heard a chipper voice from down another corridor. Galadjian, back in uniform, entered smiling. "Doctor."

"Good morning, Captain." The older man looked up and around. "I have to say this is something, being on a real pirate ship. Do they all smell like—" Then he saw the corpse—and took three steps back. "Oh, dear. I didn't know."

Pike tried to get his attention. "What have you found in engineering, Doctor?" He paused. "*Is* there an engineering section?"

"Oh, yes." Galadjian recomposed himself. "Not to reclaim my nickname, but I have good news. First off, this ship is definitely the source of the photon torpedo we suspected was fired at us last year."

Pike looked at Nhan, who stared at Galadjian, skeptical. "Everything up here is gutted," she said. "How can you tell that?"

"I would love to say it was by a snap analysis, based on my mastery of systems employed universally in spacecraft."

Pike's eyes narrowed. "But instead?"

"Someone on the weapons deck handwrote a note on the wall outside the loading chamber listing the date and target," Galadjian said, consulting his notes. "Oh, yes, and the words, 'Need more torpedoes.'"

Nhan blinked. "Wow. I have *got* to meet these guys."

Pike rolled his eyes. "I don't suppose the Lurians wrote down what happened to everyone aboard while they were at it?"

"My regrets, Captain, but no. The chalk was abandoned on the floor." He stepped gingerly around the bridge, trying to reach Pike and Nhan without getting too near the corpse. "But there are better sources for that information." He looked to the *Enterprise* image on the starboard display. "That image is coming from there, correct?" He pointed to one of the few consoles still standing.

Nhan nodded. "I think so."

Galadjian approached the terminal. "This equates with what the team has seen below. Consoles and data cores torn cleanly out, by people who wanted to preserve anything on them. They seem to have been interested mostly in offensive systems, as well as anything having to do with warp drive and propulsion."

"Why didn't they take the ship with them?" Pike asked. "Who were they?"

"I want you to see for yourself—" Galadjian said, trying to work the controls. Pike and Nhan waited and watched—

—and waited some more, as frustration began to replace the chief engineer's confidence. "Unfamiliar systems. I am sorry."

"Do you need a hand, Doctor?" Jallow called out from the passageway Galadjian had entered from.

"Ah, very good. If you would, please."

So close, Pike thought.

Galadjian's second-in-command stepped to the terminal—and moments later, the image of *Enterprise* disappeared. "The only surveillance imagers in the whole ship are in main engineering," Jallow said. "I guess whoever was in command didn't trust the crew."

Galadjian, a bit abashed from his momentary failure, seemed to bristle a little from that. Pike hurried past the moment. "Jallow, is this from the boarding?"

"Yes, Captain." Where the visual of *Enterprise* had been, a silent tableau depicted the searing installation of a new airlock, followed by the entry of armored figures, even taller and bulkier than the panicked Lurian engineers trying to stop them.

The quartet watched the drama, spellbound. Combat, yes—ineffectual on the Lurians' side. But on the attackers' side, something else.

"Do you notice something about the invaders?" Nhan pointed at the screen. "They're holding back. Doing their best not to kill anyone."

"Definitely isn't the Klingon way," Pike said. He gestured to the corpse. "But what about our guy over there?"

"These attackers are high-tech," Nhan said. "They don't look like the stabby kind."

"Speed it up," Pike ordered. Jallow complied—and he saw the invaders forcing Lurians through the airlocks they'd made. "*Prisoners.*" He looked to Nhan. "Theories?"

She was obviously still working on them. "Serious operators.

Surgical strike. Took everyone. Probably not rivals or ransom—could be slavers. Could be political."

"But why swipe all this stuff? And leave the surveillance imagery?"

"They seemed not to care about being seen. Certainly they didn't mind leaving any of the rest of the evidence."

Pike stared at the moving images—and reached for his communicator. But before he flipped it open, he received a hail. "*Enterprise to Captain Pike.*"

"Yes, Number One?"

"We've analyzed the airlocks. They match the features on the warships at Susquatane."

"How close?"

"Identical. Essfive boarded this ship."

Excited, Pike looked to the others. "If Essfive went to such effort to keep the Lurians alive, then maybe our people—"

"Yes," Nhan said, reading his thoughts. "And they might be in the same place."

Galadjian nodded. "A testable hypothesis, is it not?"

Pike brought the communicator before his face—and smiled for the first time in weeks. "*Enterprise*, cancel plans to leave the nebula. *I think our people are alive!*"

26

Troop Module Aloga-One
Approaching the Darvus Straits

Spock meditated.

Or he tried, at least. His father had told him that a Vulcan could meditate anywhere. Near mummified in his battlesuit, Spock had trouble believing that. The ingenious suits' internal mechanisms worked in many ways to comfort their occupants and keep muscles from cramping during inactivity. But the Boundless armorers had only designed a few postures for resting positions: all seated, never reclining—or kneeling.

Spock had no personal quarters, either. His battlesuit was his billet, never removed while on alert. And they were always on alert these days. In the weeks since his transfer, he had participated in three more battles, including two assaults on Shivane.

The first return had been even more catastrophic than Spock's initial visit, with the landing repulsed almost immediately and a troop transport from another carrier destroyed. The next assault had been different, with Kormagan acting in concert with another Boundless wave. Numbers had made a difference, allowing her forces to infiltrate the Rengru outpost and disable the shields. Spock and his fellow troops had been quickly extracted in advance of a rain of photon torpedoes from the sky: no meager nuclear weapons here. Spock doubted anyone would ever know either party had visited Shivane.

The third action had taken place in space, with Spock and his squad utilizing their jetpacks on EVA to seize a Rengru spacedock. After Kormagan's carriers cleared the space fighters—there was no better term for the small, disruptor-armed shells with engines that the Rengru zipped around in—the station's occupants had been "cleansed" via acid grenades delivered by Boundless infiltrators. Dilithium crystals and other resources had been harvested before torpedoes destroyed the station.

On none of the occasions had Spock been forced to kill a Rengru, as his fellow warriors had often done. He worried that it was only a matter of time before he would be made to follow suit. The creatures weren't giving him much choice. The Rengru fought opposing ships and hovercraft with whatever weapons they had, but when encountering personnel, their tactics changed. As Spock had first seen on Shivane, the Rengru sought to envelop Boundless warriors, piercing their headgear with a peculiar appendage that functioned like the biological equivalent of a powered auger.

They were certainly intelligent, architects of a society that had somehow reached the stars. But all else about them remained a mystery. They had never responded to any of his attempts to communicate.

The experiences had been troubling for one taught to value peace. He had participated in battles while aboard *Enterprise*; the starship was heavily armed, perhaps too much so for its own good. But Starfleet's mission was to avert conflict, not seek it. The Boundless seemed to exist entirely to fight—and their veterans thought nothing of it, considering their reasons perfectly logical. *Had he not seen what the Rengru did to those they fought?*

And while Spock had only participated in offensives while under Kormagan, he had been assured that the Rengru attacked the Boundless just as often. The troop module he was in was on its way to protect Boundless positions in the nebular region known as the Darvus Straits. The point of view of the Boundless might not be correct, but it did rest on some evidence.

For one who lived a life devoted to peace, Spock was more than familiar with conflict. The logic extremists, whose bombing of the Vulcan Learning Center nearly killed Michael Burnham, continued to use violence. How different were they from the Boundless, who did not feel remorse about the steps they took? Wasn't "feeling" the thing he had been told to avoid for so long?

No, he thought—trying to focus again on the candle-flame image he had asked his headgear's interface to project before his eyes. Living beings could create a fire to burn for a purpose, some reasons worthwhile, others not. So, too, did they create conflict. It was still moral to question, to challenge, the use of force. And if he could not refuse to serve the Boundless, he could still try to moderate their violence, even as he considered means of escape.

Outside, he heard the troop module braking. They had arrived at the Straits—and the next engagement. He dispelled the candle image and headed for his deployment station. It was time to fight. Again.

SEPARATION

April 2257

INCOMING TRANSMISSION (ENCRYPTED)

TO: CAPTAIN C. PIKE • *U.S.S. ENTERPRISE* • NCC-1701

FROM: VICE ADMIRAL K. CORNWELL, STARFLEET COMMAND

REALIZED I HAD NOT MESSAGED PERSONALLY SINCE MY RETURN FROM CAPTIVITY. IT HAS BEEN BUSY. GLAD ADMIRAL TERRAL HAS KEPT YOU APPRISED.

STATE OF WAR CONTINUES. KLINGON ATROCITIES AT KELFOUR VI AND ELSEWHERE.

U.S.S. DISCOVERY STILL MISSING. NO CHANGE IN *ENTERPRISE* MISSION. DO NOT RETURN.

END TRANSMISSION

27

Combat Module Carrier 539-Aloga
Pergamum Nebula

After each operation, Spock had returned to *Carrier Aloga* for what had become his best source of information about the organization and its practices: the combination armory and infirmary operated by Jayko. This time, to his surprise, he found Ensign Ghalka there, studying telemetry from the battlesuit worn by a now fully-bearded Connolly. It was the first time he had seen the other two since his transfer, weeks earlier.

"I am pleased to see you in this role," Spock said to Ghalka. "You are a technician now?"

"They figured out I was telling the truth about being a scientist and not a security officer," Ghalka said. "They need biologists to help the battlesuits acclimate better to our species."

"I knew I studied the wrong things in the Academy," Connolly said. "Could you tell them *we're* scientists too?"

"Sorry," Ghalka said, gesturing to Connolly's readings on her monitoring device. "They think you're in great physical shape. Even in the battlesuits, athleticism counts."

"Damn cross-training."

"And Spock's Vulcan physiology gives him endurance that supplements his battlesuit." Ghalka shrank a little, embarrassed. "Sorry. But it was a great day when Redsub said I belonged 'in the rear with the gear.'"

Spock's brow furrowed. "That is a peculiar expression," he said. "Your subaltern said it?"

She nodded.

"I've heard it before," Connolly said. "Earth, way back. Tooey Monahan was the last first-round draft pick ever to be Rookie of the Year—until they drafted him for the Third World War. They put him in the rear too."

"I do not understand," Spock said.

Neither did Ghalka. "He was drafted—then he was drafted?"

"That is not what I was referring to," Spock said, forestalling another digression into Connolly's hobbies. "Why would a phrase known on Earth be employed in this nebula?"

"Oh," Ghalka said, understanding. "Their first medical file on a human is well over a century old. Clearly somebody wandered in. They've been at this a very long time."

Ghalka had learned more. There were many species serving in the Boundless, but there were five founding member races—Kormagan and Jayko belonged to two. Child-rearing took place on the support ships that followed the waves around. The founder species were highly committed to the fight against the Rengru, Ghalka said, but they also understood that their numbers and weapons were insufficient to the task—hence the military units doing double-duty as pirates and press gangs.

"There's a good reason we have such an easy time communicating with the others here," she said. "Apparently the outer spacefaring cultures have been influencing them for decades, whether we knew it or not. They're mimics about more than just technology."

"You have learned much." Spock looked about at the bustling center. "Is it wise to speak so openly?"

"They don't seem to care about what people say," Ghalka said. "The Boundless encourage conversations between old troops and new to facilitate integration—and don't mind them between fellow abductees, as long as they don't lead to actions against their authority. Some of these warriors were born into it—I assume their parents actually had to meet."

"That's how it usually works," Connolly said.

Ghalka looked about at the various technicians and their subjects. "You have to understand how much they all really do believe in this fight. Even the abductees eventually come around."

Connolly stifled a laugh. "Seeing the Rengru will do that to you! It only took Baladon two months to buy in."

"We have been here longer than two months," Spock said, "and encountered the same things."

"I know. Still," Connolly said, "I was afraid this part would be a lot worse." He gestured to the overhead, indicating the whole ship. "More brutal, with everyone acting like Baladon was at the start. But they seem to save the violence for the Rengru."

"We are Starfleet officers," Spock said firmly. He studied Connolly. "Where does your commitment lie, Lieutenant?"

Connolly seemed gobsmacked. "That's a crazy question, sir." He shook his head. "I mean, the Boundless do seem to be under threat—they have a need. It might even be legitimate. But this isn't the way to fulfill it."

Spock looked to Ghalka. "Ensign?"

"Screw the Rengru," she blurted. "I want to go home."

"Very well. Continue to learn what you can."

Across the infirmary, he saw Kormagan enter. Spock had seen earlier that her armor had been scored by acid, from a dousing that had come when she had led the assault on the Rengru station. Jayko spotted her and called out. "Welcome, Wavemaster. Pray tell did you spare any of that acid bomb for the Rengru?"

"Shut up," she said. "Just make sure everything's working."

As Jayko left his patient to attend to her, Spock spoke

quietly to Ghalka. "Your observations about openness noted, Ensign, perhaps it is better that I step away."

He had gotten only a few steps away when the Andorian whispered loudly to him. "*Spock!*"

He turned amid the noisy room and saw Ghalka looking—not even pointing—directly at the wavemaster and the armorer. Spock casually followed her glance and saw that Jayko was tending to a rounded module behind Kormagan's right shoulder. Like the rest of her armor, it bore scars.

"I hate to tell you this," Jayko said to her, "but you're going to need a new governor."

Spock blinked. He had never heard of governors in the Boundless before. Then Kormagan responded: "Fix the one I have."

"I don't even know why you have the thing," Jayko said. "You're not going to run away. How long have you been in charge?"

"We're all the same here," Kormagan said. Seeing Spock listening, she repeated it more loudly. "We're all on the same team."

Spock watched her—and nodded gently in assent before heading into the hallway. Once there, he reached around and touched the nodule behind his shoulder. Everyone in the Boundless might indeed be equal—but they were all governed. And now he knew what and where the mechanism was.

28

U.S.S. Enterprise
Pergamum Nebula

"We may not be able to find these guys," Amin said. "But we sure can tell where they've been."

"Convenient for us," Pike said. "Not for their targets."

More Essfive victims had been discovered two hours earlier, prompting the staff meeting. Their detection was the result of cooperation by a crew newly enlivened with hope.

During *Enterprise*'s stay alongside the Lurian derelict, Galadjian's engineers, assisted by Una and Dietrich, had focused on one of the earlier clues: the Essfive probe that had led the kidnappers to *Deathstrike*. No one understood how it had contacted its creators. Subspace communications only worked locally in the nebula before dissipating in an ocean of interference. So how, his officers had asked, had it executed its mission?

On partially reviving the Essfive probe, Pike's team had discovered a clever program driving its actions. After sensing a potential target vessel, the drone traveled through the clouds to a checkpoint where it looked for other probes in local subspace range to communicate with. If it found none, it would head to a second checkpoint—and then a third, and a fourth. The "couriers," as Una called them, allowed the attackers to use a relatively small number of probes to communicate across a vast amount of nebular space. What they sacrificed in timely communication, they made up in extended range.

So after *Enterprise*'s team had wrung every last bit of valuable information from *Deathstrike*, the Federation starship had methodically visited each of the Essfive probe's checkpoints. At the third, Dietrich detected faint subspace emissions on the expected frequency; those led *Enterprise* to yet another probe. That one, tagged *Courier 2* for convenience, *did* successfully self-destruct on *Enterprise*'s approach—but a split second too late. Pitcairn and his aide, Sam Yamata, had already transported the probe's data core safely to the Starfleet vessel before the blast.

"Give me a schematic of an unshielded ship," Pitcairn had said, "and I'll beam the donuts right out of the mess hall."

The data was sweeter than any confection. It had not led to the attackers but, instead, another derelict. Pike walked to his chair in the conference room and sat down as Nhan and Colt, his landing party, entered. "Looks like the victims list is getting longer all the time," he said. "What did we have over there?"

"The ship is called *New Tomorrow*," Nhan said, taking her seat. "An Antaran colony ship. Their onboard surveillance coverage was more widespread than on *Deathstrike*—still no sound, sadly. But we saw the same people attacking, same result. The two ships could be twins."

"Except *New Tomorrow* was easier on the nostrils," Colt added. "It looks from the time codes like Essfive struck it just hours after they hit *Deathstrike*. So they weren't done hitting people—and we're headed in the right direction."

"Antarans," Pike said. "Enemies of the Denobulans, right?"

Una nodded.

"Could our kidnappers be Denobulan? They were pretty warlike a few centuries ago."

"Not lately," Una replied. "And I can't see them going after a Starfleet crew. We've also checked the armor we saw against every known civilization in the database. No obvious connections."

"So we're still playing catch-up." Pike stifled a sigh. "Okay, here we go again. *Courier 2* must have told somebody on its mail route that *New Tomorrow* was here. We follow its earlier checkpoints, we might find the next link in the chain—or our people."

Una looked toward him with small trepidation. "I'm not sure that's going to be possible."

"What now?"

"Captain, we've been in this mess for the better part of a year and we've only begun to figure out what's where," Amin said. "There are more layers to this nebula than—"

"Than an onion. I get it."

"So we only know what we're able to see from here," the navigator said. "Our survey shows this particular mail route goes into rougher territory than we've seen. I don't think we can make our way through it."

Pike blinked. "We handled the Acheron Formation."

"Radiation sources are more exotic here, Captain. The plasma's thick enough to serve with a spoon. And there's another difference," Amin added, touching her ear with her fingers. "We weren't trying to use our sensors for anything on that trip. This time, you're looking for something."

"So we'd be going slower—which is more exposure." Pike shook his head. "That adds risk for all of us."

Colt looked to Amin. "Couldn't we just wait to scan until we're at the checkpoints? That's what worked before."

"You could, but the medium we're traversing gets hairy in places. I can't give you anything close to a straight line unless you can find a way to punch through material thicker than any *Constitution*-class starship has ever encountered." She sat back. "I'm sorry, but I can't change the weather."

This sounds like an engineering problem, Pike thought. Thing was, he already had an engineering problem. Galadjian had been uncharacteristically quiet ever since his little console-operating slip aboard *Deathstrike* had negated his previous triumphant mood.

There wasn't anything to be done about that. "We're starting to run up against our end-of-mission time—and with the war, I think we at least owe Starfleet a check-in." Pike felt the air go out of the room. "Believe me, I don't want to start to leave *again*, especially when we've just made some headway. But unless we find more, someone's going to have to make a—"

Galadjian snapped from his trance and slapped the table. "*Eureka!*"

"I was going to say, someone's going to have to make a sudden discovery that solves everything." Pike really wasn't, but he looked to Galadjian nonetheless. "Something you want to share with the group, Doctor?"

Galadjian's eyes focused on a point far away—and he spoke. "As you know, normal penetration through plasma and other gaseous material requires the projection of magnetic shields, which are shaped to envelop the vessel while providing the most efficient angle of attack. Plasmadynamics is different in key ways from aero- or hydrodynamics, but the practice is similar: to place our vessel within the blade of the knife as it cuts."

They all knew that. "And your plan?"

"Consider a different analogy, but also relating to sharp things. In my native Armenia, there was an ancient blade called the *tsakat*. It was used to cut vegetation."

"Like the machete," Amin said. "The thing they cleared paths through bush with."

"Yes, though ours had a longer handle—our vegetation was not so tall. Now consider this: we do not place ourselves inside the blade, but rather as the worker holding the tool. Rather than generating shields to envelop *Enterprise*, we direct our systems to shape a high-intensity three-dimensional force envelope along the length of the deflector beam. Simultaneously, we continually rotate and refresh the shaped field—both opening our path and sweeping it clean."

"It sounds like an old weed whacker," Nicola said.

"Yes, but spinning many times faster."

"One ancient agricultural analogy at a time," Pike said. He blinked. "You say we'll be able to navigate gases far denser than we have before. More than in the Acheron Formation?"

Galadjian nodded. "I calculate up to twice as dense."

"Because that was taking a boat into a pond full of molasses."

"I don't know what that is," Galadjian said. "But I can say that the procedure will ease our passage."

Dietrich looked shaken. "I've never heard of shields being used like that."

"I understand, my young friend. I helped to invent the specific kind that are aboard this ship—my first model was called the 'meteorite beam.' And while that name may not have caught on, I am still considering ways in which the systems can be used." Galadjian sat back and crossed his palms, a grin on his face.

"But if I understand correctly, it sounds like the ship itself wouldn't be shielded."

"You have it," Galadjian replied. "We would rely on our hull to withstand any impacts the shield did not protect us from—and also against the radiation. In this case, yes, we would want to traverse quickly."

Nhan gawked. "Did I hear this right? We're expected to give up our shields?"

"That's correct, Commander." His smile faded a little at being questioned. "We would not want anyone to shoot at us."

"The people we are after *have* shot at us, Doctor. This could be a problem. How fast can you revert to normal operation?"

"Quickly. But we would have to come to a full stop."

Pike saw the looks around the rest of the table. He worried, as he assumed they did, that their onetime superstar was pushing too hard, seeking some kind of redemption through the thing he knew best. "I'd like the room, please. Doctor, you stay. And you, too, Number One."

Galadjian looked uncomfortable as the others dutifully filed out.

Pike spoke in even tones. "Doctor, we had discussed earlier that some of the operational matters aboard the ship might be beyond you—"

"I have been working on that, Captain."

"I know, I know. But my concern is whether your plan might be beyond the limits of your staff to execute. It's pretty cutting edge."

"An apt term," Galadjian said, "considering we are constructing a beam that will—" Noting Pike's wooden expression, he stopped. "Captain," he said, more slowly, "the entire reason I am here is to push your staff beyond. If this is successful, the things we learn here will make all future *Enterprise*s able to traverse many varieties of space."

"Forgive me if I'm more concerned about the current *Enterprise*."

"It can be done, Captain."

Pike frowned. He'd lost thirty people; he didn't want to risk anyone else on a science experiment. He looked to Una. "Does this make sense?"

Cautiously, she nodded. "Yes, I see where he is going. He'd need people behind the deflector dish in the stardrive section again, as Spock was last year in the Acheron transit."

"We are without Spock."

"I could do it, Captain," Una said. "I understand the principles involved."

Pike looked to Galadjian. "If she's working the dish, can you run this thing from the bridge?"

"Yes, Captain. I can understand why you might want to—"

"Can you be *ready* to run it?"

Galadjian appeared to catch Pike's meaning. "Yes. I will have mastery of all the interfaces."

"Then get started. Dismissed."

Galadjian stood and quickly departed, not noting that Pike had motioned for Una to hang back.

"Are you sure about this?" Pike asked her.

"It's advanced," she said. "But it's in his wheelhouse."

"Yes, but you'll be working in it. I'd rather have you on the bridge. I may want your guidance."

"I won't be far. You can call down whenever you want."

29

Combat Module Carrier 539-Aloga
Pergamum Nebula

"I am here, Wavemaster."

"Enter, Gold-Five."

Spock had spent the previous hour mentally preparing for departure on another mission. He had not lost count of them yet, but their frequency had been enough to introduce a fatigued indifference to the specifics. He had been ready to board *Aloga-One* for the drop when the summons from Kormagan arrived.

He had never before been allowed anywhere near *Carrier Aloga*'s command bell, much less in the room he now entered. The room was a perfect sphere, clearly the center of the forward section of the ship. But the place was pitch black.

"Step over, Spock." Kormagan stood atop a pedestal at the room's center. Spock complied. When he reached the platform at its base, she—or someone else—took control of his armor systems, activating his jetpack and lifting him to her level. *"Button up."*

Spock deployed his headgear—and saw before him what Kormagan was looking at. In place of the walls he saw swaths of color, punctuated here and there by points of light—and populated everywhere by blinking icons. *Enterprise* had been hoping to finish mapping the Pergamum. The Boundless, he saw, had already done it.

In the nearest foreground to his right, he saw the indicator for *Carrier Aloga*'s five transport modules, all heading to the nearby globe of Ghaffah. "You are not going on the mission?" he asked.

"It's just a reconnaissance operation." Kormagan stepped in front of him—and he found that he could see her in front of the stars. "I'll come to the point. I want to know everything there is to know about *Enterprise*."

Spock had expected such a talk—only much earlier. "You saw her in action when you apprehended us. That must be enough."

"We were too busy trying to keep from being annihilated," Kormagan said. "Those photon torpedoes of yours are more powerful than anything we've been able to construct."

"May that serve to prevent you from harassing *Enterprise* again—presuming you find it." Spock studied her for a moment. "Unless you *have* found it," he added, looking around the room.

"They didn't stay at that planet—the one the Lurians called Susquatane—long," Kormagan replied. "By the time one of the other waves went back to check, it was gone. We thought *Enterprise* had left the nebula entirely."

It made sense to Spock that Pike would give the order to depart. If he hadn't, that order must surely come soon, as the vessel's one-year mission was nearing its end.

"Last week, things changed." Kormagan paced around the circumference of the platform. "Some of our early-warning-system satellites in the middle-density regions noticed something passing through, pounding with shield projection in a way that none of our ships—or the Rengru—would ever do."

Spock's eyes narrowed. "You are certain of this?"

"I think *Enterprise* has stumbled across the path of one of our other waves. They have no idea the force that captured you is one of many. I think they're headed toward Little Hope."

"Excuse me?"

"A rift between cloud complexes. It's named for a battle that—well, you can guess how it went." Kormagan waved her hand—and a region came into view before Spock. It appeared to be a void populated by stellar remnants. "Nothing there of value, just the wreckage of colliding solar systems," she said. "A few failed stars and dead planets."

Spock studied the place. "Significant dense formations surround it."

"It sets up perfectly for an ambush. I know because the Rengru did it to me, when I was part of the Five-One-One. That's how the place got its name—and how I wound up in another wave."

Spock had nearly taken a step back at the word "ambush"—but did nothing. Kormagan had definitely noticed. "You control your emotions well."

"Yes."

"They tell me your kind tries to do that. It's one reason I've kept you out on the line."

"As opposed to what?"

"You know there are safer places to be." She faced him. "What you may not know is this: right now, all your people are still alive. All thirty."

That startled him. He hadn't known the exact number—or the fact. "They are unharmed?"

She shrugged. "They're armored, they should be. It wasn't easy to find out. Some of them are with different waves now."

"Traded like chattel," Spock said, his voice chilly.

"I can get them back."

Spock froze. *What is she getting at?*

"Not right away," Kormagan said, pacing again. "It would take time. But at a minimum, I can negotiate with my opposite numbers to get them taken off the most dangerous details.

Most of them are already in support roles, like your friend in Jayko's workshop."

"What is it you want?"

"You will lead an assault on *Enterprise*."

"I will not."

"This won't be like Susquatane. We weren't trying to take her then—just you. This time, I'm bringing in a couple of other waves that want a piece of the spoils. And your former comrades are going to have a hard time fleeing from Little Hope." Kormagan gestured. An image of *Enterprise* appeared in the location, followed by more than a dozen Boundless carriers and their constituent transport modules, surrounding it.

The plot had not surprised Spock at all. "Return me to the deck, Kormagan. I will not betray my people."

"You betray them by *not* helping."

Spock couldn't see how.

"You don't realize what I'm offering," Kormagan said, stopping. "No peoples in the Boundless are afforded special status. But I am willing to see that the thirty we have now—and however many I capture from *Enterprise*—wind up in manufacturing divisions. No fighting."

"I see. And if I refuse, you will act in a sadistic and punitive manner toward them."

"Have I acted that way to you?"

"Would you call abduction the act of friends?"

"You don't know what you're facing," Kormagan said, turning her armored back to him. "And I mean *you*—because if we don't stop the Rengru, they will next become a problem for your Starfleet or the Klingons or whoever lives outside. We're the *heroes*."

"You are acting in your own self-interest, in the name of someone—or perhaps some *thing*—called K'davu."

Kormagan didn't seem surprised he had heard the word. "That too."

"What does it mean? What is your conflict about?"

Kormagan spun. "It wouldn't help you to know. You'd simply try to communicate with the Rengru again—yes, I know you've never stopped trying. And they will pierce your armor and knife the back of your skull, and you will die having been of no use to us."

Spock was unmoved. "To my captain, we thirty are already dead. I will not trade the freedom of *Enterprise*'s occupants to improve our lot—or to lessen the putative fate of the entire company." He crossed his arms. "You may speak until these stars burn out."

Kormagan stared at him. "Are all Vulcans so unreasonable?"

"Reason is our greatest treasure."

"Reason this: I don't want to kill your people. But they entered my war of their own volition, with weapons and technology never before seen in this nebula. I have to have what they have. Or I have to keep it from the Rengru."

"If you fear the latter, we will leave."

"It's too late!" Kormagan shoved at Spock, nearly knocking him off the platform. She pointed at the star field. "Your people sealed their fate by not leaving when they had the chance. Now they're out there, banging about—it's a miracle the Rengru haven't found them yet. If *they* claim *Enterprise*, we will never get our chance to—"

She paused. Spock watched her take a step back. In a more composed voice, she said, "If you will not help, you lose any say in what happens."

Spock considered her words. *Enterprise*, he now knew, was the key. He began to pace. "I have a counteroffer, Kormagan. Am I correct in assuming the starship is more important to you than the personnel?"

"I always need personnel."

"But there are many things you can learn from *Enterprise*—and which its personnel will never teach you, under any form of duress. I certainly will not. Surely adding to the efficiency of your future troops is better than a marginal number of new recruits who were never bred for war?"

Kormagan regarded him cautiously. "Logical."

"Yes," Spock said, "it is." He stopped and turned toward her. "So if I help you take the ship in such a manner that results in no casualties—"

"I can't guarantee that. Your people may act against us. And I don't control the other waves."

He began again: "If I help you take the ship so the Rengru do not have it, the cost would be the thirty—plus the people of *Enterprise. All* of them—provided with a vessel or vessels capable of making it home. With the promise that they may traverse your space unmolested."

"You don't ask for much!"

"You ask for more than you know." Spock went silent.

Kormagan studied him for several long moments before looking back at the image of *Enterprise*, surrounded. Then she studied the blinking icons across the sky—all, Spock suspected, representing Rengru forces. They seemed particularly clustered around one cloud-laden region which had a small white light at its center. Kormagan looked at it the longest before speaking again. "I have a counteroffer to your counteroffer."

"I will not haggle over my crewmates' lives."

"This is a little thing."

"Proceed."

"You can have every crewmember—but one."

Spock shook his head. "My captain is not for sale."

"I don't mean your captain. I need one of you to remain, to help me make sense of the technology aboard *Enterprise*."

"I already said no one would help you."

"Except, perhaps, the one making the bargain."

"You want *me* to stay."

"It makes sense. You know our needs—and you know

your technology. If you help me seize their ship, I don't know how welcome you'd be with them anyway." Kormagan opened her gloved palm. "I would give you a place of importance in the wave."

"I would take no reward for separating my crew from its ship. Not even if it saved them."

"But you would save them."

Spock looked at *Enterprise*'s image—and then looked down. "I will give the matter thought."

She gestured—and Spock's jetpack ignited. He lifted from the platform and drifted down to the deck and its entryway. "I can't give you much time," she called down. "We're going to cross paths with your starship one way or another. Once that happens, either you're in or you're out. In which case, all your people are in."

Spock nodded. "You were wrong about something, Kormagan."

"What?"

"You said the Boundless had no use for economics. But you are more accomplished at trade than you know."

30

U.S.S. Enterprise
Departing Shivane

Nearly a year into his mission to the Pergamum, and a number of things no longer seemed funny to Pike. One of them: Amin's joke about being able to tell where the Essfive attackers had been. Not after *Enterprise* visited Shivane, a planet named in the records of *Courier 4*, the most recent probe his team had captured. A significant portion of the world's surface had been purged by antimatter blasts.

"Essfive sure didn't spare the gigatons," Nhan said, studying her recordings of the blast zone from her bridge station. "We can't find an atom of what was there before."

"It was a colony," Raden said. "These characters steal people. That's all."

Pike couldn't imagine it had been anything but a settlement either. "But why," he asked, "does Essfive cover its tracks on planets but not spaceships?"

"Possibly two different kinds of raiders," Nhan said. "Maybe even two unrelated groups?"

Let's hope not, Pike thought. He was all theorized out—and the *tsakat* protocol, as Galadjian's nebula-navigating procedure had come to be known, was rattling enough to make the transits between clues as off-putting as the stops.

Nhan spoke again. "Huh."

"Something else, Lieutenant?"

"Sensors thought they saw something in the rear-view tactical display—just for an instant." She shook her head. "It's gone now."

"Should we investigate?"

"No, not for this," Nhan responded. "This nebula is a floating trash heap."

"If you're sure," Pike said. "What's next?"

"Back onto *Courier 4*'s mail route," Amin said. It had led them to Shivane. "Three stops yet where we might find more probes waiting."

"Or something else," Pike said. *Like our people—or maybe another Shivane.* Touring ghost towns and ships of the Pergamum had turned all their lives ghoulish.

"Course is laid in," Amin said, looking at the massive swirl of gas on the viewscreen. "I feel like we're about to fly into yesterday's tapioca."

That, Pike laughed at. He touched his armrest control. "About to be *tsakat* time again, Number One."

From the stardrive section, Una responded, *"It's a little crowded down here, but we're ready to go."*

"I just realized I am the only engineer currently in the saucer section," Galadjian mused aloud from his station. Pike knew there had been a time when the engineers would have preferred that state of affairs—but hopefully success ahead would get his chief engineer past all that.

"We're here to keep you company," Pike said. "Engage *tsakat*. Mister Raden, hit the trail."

Combat Module Carrier 539-Aloga
Approaching Little Hope

"Thank you for what you are doing, daughter. The Rengru are destroying our lives. Your duty honors all of us."

Seated again—as she often was these days—in the carrier's spherical strategic-planning chamber, Kormagan thought back to the message she had first seen as a child. It had not been written by her mother, but rather was an exchange between two of her ancient forbears. The message of gratitude had inspired Kormagan as she was growing up in a Boundless mobile educational facility—and later, she had made sure to hand it down to her own daughters and granddaughters.

They were long since dead. The Rengru knew no mercy. Not on her ancestors—nor her children.

Still, Kormagan wondered. *Who were you, Greatmother Eudah? How did you meet your end? And what would you say if you knew what we still do for you?*

"Troops are prepared, Wavemaster."

Kormagan opened her eyes. When she looked down and to the left, Opmaster Sperrin appeared superimposed over the nebular imagery. "Thanks, Oppy," she said, snapped back to the job at hand. "You're blocking my view of Wave Five-Four-Four."

Sperrin chuckled. "I'm doing you a favor. Couldn't we get anyone better for the right flank?"

"Not a lot of choice—not with eleven waves tied up at Varadah." She didn't add "at the moment," because her updates were limited to what their network of messenger probes had delivered—but it was a safe bet. The Varadah Gap was a massive engagement that was into its seventh year. "Besides," she added, "Hemmick said I owed him for the Lurian trade."

"They're better his problem than ours," Sperrin said. "So you're going to stay here for the operation? Not like I mind getting back into action."

"Three waves, fifteen carriers. Somebody's got to play commodore—and it was my idea, after all."

"The master of the Fifty-Twos is all mouth," Sperrin said. "If this doesn't work, Quadeo will ensure the other waves never let us lead anything again."

"Like they have any better ideas. This war has gone on for centuries—*Enterprise* is the first chance we've had to break it wide open. I'm not letting it go." Kormagan repositioned her map point of view and opened the channel for Sperrin to see what she was seeing. "Just about figured out all the positions. What do you think of the plan?"

Sperrin looked up. "I think it's overkill."

"It's fine. Is the trap baited?"

"Affirm. We've launched several probes to places where *Enterprise* ought to be able to find them, all directing them straight to Little Hope."

The moderate clearing in the nebula was right before Kormagan's eyes. "You took that name out of the probes' navigational databases, I assume."

"We changed the entry, as ordered."

"Good. Spock cooperated on that too. Did you get him what he needs to break into *Enterprise*?"

"Requisitioned. You're sure you trust him?"

Inside Kormagan's headgear, reptilian eyes narrowed. "I don't trust anyone," she said. "But I didn't see any way he could have been fooling us. From what I hear from Baladon, I don't think Vulcans lie."

"Great! He can become Hemmick's new opmaster for the Damn Fool Brigade. And speaking of dumb ideas," Sperrin asked, "are you really going to set Spock's people free after we capture them?"

"If he does as instructed—yes. *Enterprise*'s tech is such a force multiplier we won't need as many warriors."

"K'davu by the equinox," Sperrin said. "*That* would be a capper to your career."

"To everyone's." Kormagan breathed easily, her whole being full of the certainty that this was the best hope for her people. "Get our ships into position. I'm expecting guests at any time."

As Sperrin faded from view, Kormagan looked at the icons indicating assembling forces and thought again of the message from the woman she had never met. Greatmother Eudah's daughter—and so many more—had fallen. It had convinced her: inspirational words were not enough to give future generations of Boundless. She would give them *Enterprise*—or she would reduce it to atoms.

31

Troop Module Aloga-One
Near Little Hope

"Now listen up, people! This isn't your standard exfiltration."

It wasn't a standard mission, either, Spock knew. *Carrier Aloga*'s Opmaster Sperrin had taken Kormagan's place aboard *Aloga-One* as ranking officer, meaning he was addressing Gold Squad in person. His words were being broadcast not just to the other squads aboard the ship, but also to those aboard the other four troop carriers.

"We're not going to be able to fire our docking ports into *Enterprise*'s hull," Sperrin continued. "We've got an operative here who says it won't work. The hull's too damn thick. So it'll be laser torches to the hatches if his entry codes don't work."

Spock said nothing. He had asked Kormagan to keep his name out of it. It had been a long time since he had seen Connolly or any of the other *Enterprise* officers; if the wavemaster had told the truth about all the abductees being alive, Spock thought it was likely that they had all been moved into support roles. But he wished his involvement to remain secret, just in case. If any of his fellow officers listening heard his name, they might cause a disturbance, demanding to see him and interfering with the operation.

The significant shame involved in hijacking *Enterprise* did not enter into it.

Sperrin continued his briefing. "Little Hope is a Class-Twelve gaseous zone—forming star systems slammed into one another and failed, leaving a lot of junk. Gas, debris, brown dwarfs. Our bet is that *Enterprise* will make for the fragment clusters and use them for cover. We'll let them."

The opmaster looked to Spock. When he did not react, Sperrin continued. "There are hatches on the outside of *Enterprise*'s hull. Once her shields are punctured, you will jet to the hull and lock on magnetically. We've loaded you with enough jetpack fuel to launch you to the next galaxy."

"So don't get shot at," interjected the Gold Squad subaltern, a harsh veteran of many campaigns. The other members of Spock's squad laughed.

"Always there with the good advice, Goldsub." Sperrin continued undeterred. "There's debris all over Little Hope. If for some reason you get cut loose and can't communicate, try to get to something with a surface. Your armor can keep you fed, watered, and breathing for three or four months, but you'll last a little longer if you're someplace where it's got resources to draw upon. I'm not saying we'll come back and look for you right away, but you won't be an immediate casualty."

Sperrin announced that *Enterprise* was expected any time—and that several troop modules would be deploying in advance of its arrival. "This is a big one," the opmaster announced. "Do it right—for K'davu!"

Having signed off, Sperrin looked to Spock. "Did I forget anything?"

"You did not tell them where the hatches were."

"We found those in the imagery from the earlier encounter. They matched up with what you told us."

"I know my starship." Spock had known already that the Boundless had images of *Enterprise*; there was no point in lying about the hatches. It suited him to appear cooperative.

"You know how to activate your own torch?"

"Affirm," Spock said, using the Boundless's term.

Sperrin stared at him. "All right, then," he finally said. "I'm here to keep an eye on you, but you sound committed."

"He's a good soldier," Goldsub piped in. "Smart. Doesn't shoot at much, but he's gotten us out of some jams. If we find some more Vulcans, send them my way."

In fact, Spock had yet to commit fully to his next steps. He lacked information. He knew he would apprise Pike and *Enterprise* of the situation, as quickly as possible, once he encountered them. But what happened next would depend on the starship's chances against the Boundless.

If *Enterprise* looked a match for Kormagan's forces, it might be able to demand release of the other twenty-nine officers, once Spock made contact and explained where they likely were. That was the best case. The intermediate case was of more concern: *Enterprise* might be forced to flee. In that event, Spock would have condemned his fellow abductees to whatever punishment Kormagan sought to deliver. Still, that saved one hundred seventy-three lives at the cost of just thirty—thirty whose fates might already have been sealed on Susquatane.

If crushing Boundless superiority forced him to actually follow through on Kormagan's plan, he would see that the *Enterprise* crew and the other captives safely departed the nebula. And then, instead of assisting in the theft of the ship's secrets, he would scuttle it, with himself aboard. That would at least partially satisfy Kormagan, by keeping *Enterprise* from the Rengru—and it would free the maximum number of people.

That left only the worst case—that Kormagan was lying, and had no intention of freeing his crewmates once captured. He had not sensed any prevarication in her, yet it seemed wrong to ascribe a code of honor to a people who kidnapped others and forced them to fight their wars. For that reason, he had used his collaboration with her, days earlier, to plant a small seedling, one with the potential to avert the encounter entirely. It was the longest of longshots—

A klaxon sounded, dashing that last hope once and for all. "Stations!" Sperrin called out. Spock knew why. One of the probes placed as bait was approaching Little Hope, with the indication that *Enterprise* was following. He touched the laser torch in his gear and steeled himself. He would have to go through with this, one way or another.

U.S.S. Enterprise
Pergamum Nebula

On the day *Enterprise*'s original one-year mission to the Pergamum was to have ended, Pike had finally caught the break he'd been waiting for.

Courier 5, found days earlier, had not even tried to self-destruct, making the harvesting of its data core easier. It had pointed the way to a sixth probe, whose trail they had already picked up. And *Courier 6* seemed to be going somewhere in a hurry. It was not a behavior they had seen in the other probes; Nhan inferred that it was likely about to report in to Essfive. So *Enterprise* was cutting through the plasmic seas again, *tsakat* protocol in operation and all hands on high alert.

"What do we make of this region it's headed for?" Pike asked from his command chair. "Ensign?"

Colt answered from the supplementary navigation station on the starboard side of the bridge. "It's a nebular rift. It appears from the probe's records that it once had been a cluster of evaporating gaseous globules," Colt said. "EGGs, as they say."

Just a little late for Easter, Pike thought. *I wonder if that's the basket my lost eggs are in.*

The formations swept up dust and hatched protostars—when they weren't crowded and colliding into one another.

That appeared to have happened here, Colt said. "The result is kind of a muddle. A patch with less radiation, but more widely distributed debris."

"Do the probe records have a name for the rift?"

"Sovital," Colt said, placing the stresses as in the word *nominal.* "Actually, it sounds a lot better pronounced this way: *So vital.*"

"The place you describe sounds neither nominal nor vital."

"Odd coincidence," Nicola said from the comm station. "The spelling's likely solid, but I haven't loaded all the audio from the primer into our systems yet."

That had been another break: *Courier 5* had been found to have a language primer aboard, attached to one of the messages it was carrying. It connected its creators' language to Lurian and Antaran, among others—and Starfleet Standard English, which Pike assumed the attackers had found in the Lurians' databases. It made sense that pirates would want to understand languages as an aid to future boarding operations.

It had also given *Enterprise*'s enemies a proper name. If the primer could be trusted, Essfive called itself the Boundless. Pike found that a little amusing. For all their destructive power, the name sounded like posturing by common thugs.

"*So-Vital* sounds like a good pronunciation to me," Amin said, adjusting her records on the region. "Like it's a pleasant place—or an important one."

"Yeah, a nice contrast from Pergamum and Acheron," Raden said. "I'm just glad we haven't found any place called Hellmouth."

"Okay, okay." Pike put up his hands. "Any other information?"

"Dates," Colt said. "One is when the probe last visited. It's recent, as you'd assume from the mail route. The other date appears to be older. Possibly a date of discovery, or of the last time the Boundless visited the place."

Pike nodded. They had figured out the attackers' time system by studying a revived probe's processing unit in action. "What's the older date for Sovital?"

"It's in 2236."

Pike froze. It was a year he would never forget—the time of the tunnel collapse that had taken the life of Evan Hondo. And it was also something else. In another of the eerie coincidences—how many had there been?—that he had discovered in the aftermath of his most jarring mission, Pike had learned that 2236 was the year of another disaster.

It was when *S.S. Columbia* had crashed on Talos IV.

The ship that had carried Vina.

The exact date of the crash had never been discovered; only the time of the disappearance, eighteen years before Pike's visit to the planet. But the specific number seemed designed to get his attention, and it put him on edge. "Colt, the name of the region. How'd their English transliteration spell it?"

Surprised at the request, Colt complied. "S-O-V-I-T-A-L."

His hands fell to his sides as he felt his heart begin to race.

Colt looked concerned. "Captain?"

He mouthed his response three times to himself, before repeating the letters to her, anagrammed: "T-A-L-O-S-I-V."

Raden blinked. "*Talos IV?*"

"We're nowhere near Talos," Amin said. "And this is a nebular rift, not a planet."

"A region tagged with the year of *Columbia*'s crash," Pike said.

"Huh," Colt said. Of the others on the bridge, she alone had been aboard during the Talos IV incident. "That's spooky."

"It's more than spooky," Pike said, standing up. He crossed to her station and looked at the map display. There, he found the name of the place they were headed for located on *Courier 5*'s onboard map—and with his finger, traced the letters in his chosen order.

Colt fixed her eyes on him. She'd known what he had gone through on the planet—and since. "Captain, you heard Nicola. Their translations might be wrong about what the letters represent."

"Why do we have them at all?" Pike looked abruptly to his right, to the science station. "Dietrich, didn't you say *Courier 5* didn't even try to self-destruct?"

"Correct. And the files were unencrypted. That was new."

"This probe didn't try to self-destruct because the Boundless wanted us to find it, see their maps, and follow it to Sovital. Maybe they even wanted us to read the word, because the surface meaning is inviting in our language. Maybe not." He looked not at Dietrich, but at her chair. "But if you wanted to send a message about a place that only the crew of *U.S.S. Enterprise* would understand, what would the name Talos IV tell you?"

"*Keep away*," several people said in unison.

"That place was named by Spock." Pike hurried to his chair. "Doctor, disengage the *tsakat*. Full stop, shields up. Red alert!"

32

U.S.S. Enterprise
Pergamum Nebula

"Captain," Colt said cautiously, "with the *tsakat* protocol disengaged, I could go down and relieve Number One behind the deflector dish. She could take my place up here. If you needed her."

"A sound idea," Raden said. "Er—if you approve, Captain."

They think the old man has cracked, Pike thought as he looked around. *But I'm not an old man—and I'm not losing one more person to another ambush.* "Request partially denied," he said. "We are going to be using the protocol—but I will be sending you down there, Ensign. I need a hand that knows the ropes, and who knows what I'm planning here."

"Sir?"

"We're going to put the warp drive through its paces," Pike said. He stood and faced the mass of clouds on the main viewscreen. "I don't care how you pronounce the place. It's a trap—a box canyon. We're supposed to follow *Courier 6* into there. I'll bet the Boundless have those battleships hiding in the clouds on every side but the one we're going into."

Nhan's brow furrowed as she looked at him. "Sensors aren't reading anything."

"I just said they wouldn't be where we are. Where's *Courier 6*?"

Nhan consulted her readings—and her eyes went wide. "It's slowed down. Happened when we stopped."

"It thinks we lost track of it," Pike said. He pointed to the main viewer. "It's a damn Judas goat, leading us to the slaughter."

"Which is why you mentioned the warp drive," Amin said. "Should I plot a course away from here?"

"No. We're going in."

His response stunned the bridge crew. Nhan produced words first. "We're *what*?"

Pike stalked around the command well. "We've been chasing these people for months." He looked to Galadjian. "Doctor, the *tsakat* protocol works best at low speeds, so we've been sticking to warp two and below. Will it still protect us if we go faster?"

"Its efficiency will be much reduced. I would not advise it for very long." Galadjian's mouth was dry. "Captain, I am not sure that I understand—"

"Our friends out there beat us once by limiting our mobility. We won't be making that mistake again." Pike faced his security chief. "Nhan, you've been working on what would happen if we encountered Essfive—I mean, the Boundless—again. What's your tactic?"

"A right to the jaw. With one hand tied behind our back," she said, "in case our people are aboard any of the ships."

"Can you disable them without making a kill?"

"If I can get past their shields? Oh, yeah. They're fast, but all that armament is hiding some nice big, flabby impulse engines. Just get me behind them."

Pike spun back to Amin. "You've got *Courier 5*'s internal maps on the region, correct?"

"Sovital? Yes."

"Forget that name. We're calling it Hellmouth now—make the change." Amin did so as Pike continued. "Can we go to warp just this side of the region, heading for the clouds on the other side—winding up, say, no more than twenty kilometers deep?"

Raden considered it. "We'd want the *tsakat* operating, considering the medium—"

"Can you do it?"

"Aye, sir."

"Great," Pike said. "Can you do it a few dozen times?"

Raden's mouth hung open. Across the bridge, Nhan smiled broadly. "Damn!"

The two at the helm station looked baffled until Pike laid out the rest of his plan. "I think it'll work," Raden said. "But there's no regs on something like this."

"Perhaps we are writing one now," Galadjian said, staring at his console.

"Okay," Pike said. "Colt, go fill Commander Una in. Dietrich, I need instant scans of the clouds each time we come out of warp—for Nhan's targeting, and for future jumps. And scan the hell out of anyone we encounter. We couldn't detect specific life signs before, but we weren't really trying. It'd also be nice to make sure they're our hostiles from Susquatane. Got all that?"

"Yes, Captain." It was a lot for an ensign elevated to the bridge, but she seemed game.

The communications officer spoke up. "What do you need from me, Captain?"

"I want to record a hail for as soon as we see anyone. Keep it repeating—in our language and theirs."

"What message?"

Pike grinned.

Combat Module Carrier 539-Aloga
Little Hope Boundary Region

Kormagan had managed several fleet actions in her long career, but never one so important—and rarely had she done anything significant without Sperrin at her side. But she had known Dreston, the captain of her lead carrier, for the better part of a century, and they spoke the same language when it came to managing the movements of dozens of vessels at once. He knew what things Kormagan would and wouldn't be able to see in the strategic chamber; he wouldn't tell her anything she didn't need to know.

"The probe reads Enterprise *as approaching the cloud boundary,"* Dreston said, his voice transmitting to her from the bridge. *"At its current speed, it will enter the stellar graveyard in two minutes."*

"Excellent. Where's the probe?"

"Plotting it for you now. It has fully entered Little Hope, and is heading for the brown dwarf star indicated before you."

Good enough, Kormagan thought. It really didn't matter where the probe went, or how long *Enterprise* followed it. Wherever the Starfleet vessel went within the ruined region, it would find skies filled with Boundless troop modules. The carriers, fifteen in all, would enter the fray, preventing *Enterprise* from leaving Little Hope—and eventually battering down her shields. Then whatever troop modules were closest would take the prize.

Her bet was on *Aloga-One* to execute the first boarding, and not just because it was her usual troop module to command. Sperrin knew what he was doing, and had Spock along. Hopefully, the latter's presence would make *Enterprise* surrender quickly. Her wave would follow her orders to limit the loss of lives, but she wasn't as sure of her allies. They'd do harm not from intent, but out of inexperience or ineptitude.

"We have the first reading from the carrier nearest Enterprise*'s point of entry.* Five-Five-Two-Krall *reports—"*

The captain stopped speaking. "What is it, Dreston?"

"They report that Enterprise*'s shields are down."*

"See if we can get secondary confirmation without being

detected," she said. *Shields down while stalking?* She couldn't imagine that the Starfleet captain was that foolish. Spock had seemed to hold him in some regard. She had allowed the Vulcan to contribute ideas during the preparations for the assault, including finding something innocuous to name the region in the records of the probes *Enterprise* was expected to intercept. Were Starfleeters so trusting that a mild word on a map could move them?

That seemed unlikely. Maybe there was something wrong with the starship's shields after being battered for a year in the nebula. If so, it would make her comrades' mission much easier.

"Something's happening," Dreston said. *"Hail from Wave Five-Four-Four."*

"Put it through." She looked to the tactical map ahead of her—and the name of the wavemaster of the Forty-Fours appeared in her helmet interface. "What is it, Hemmick?"

"Something just materialized behind us and blew my thruster mounts all to hell!"

What? She looked at the display ahead of her. The lead carrier in Hemmick's wave blinked red, but it was not alone at its position. "You've got *Urdoh* off your bow. Order them to target the—"

"Target what?" Hemmick cried. *"It's already gone!"*

Her fellow wavemaster had only started to swear when Dreston broke in with another hail. He patched it through.

"This is Five-Five-Two-Dezik*!"* said a female voice. *"We've been hit—multiple high-energy bursts, aft!"* Kormagan had to turn ninety degrees to the right to see the ship's icon blinking. It was just off the far end of Little Hope.

"Shields up, all carriers!" she commanded. "You hear me, Dreston?"

"Wavemaster, in this soup, that could give our locations away."

"I think that's not a concern right—"

"Another hail," called Dreston, the ice in his voice cracking a little. Kormagan saw another of Hemmick's carriers start to blink—and then felt a barrage shake her own vessel.

"Dreston, how bad is it?" she shouted. The strategic interface wasn't updating fast enough; *Enterprise* hadn't even been plotted on the map yet.

"Our shields went up just in time. Can't speak for the others yet." Kormagan saw that more carriers in her strategic display were reporting strikes than not—and several of the early victims looked as if they would be unable to advance. Dreston spoke again. *"Hail coming in!"*

"I can see what's happening," Kormagan snarled. "I don't need to hear—"

Dreston piped it in anyway. The voice was human, like Connolly's—but older, more confident:

"Attention, Boundless. This is Captain Christopher Pike. I have you surrounded. Surrender!"

33

U.S.S. Enterprise
Little Hope Boundary Region

"Jump fourteen," Pike called out. "One-thirty mark two."

"One-thirty mark two, aye," Raden repeated.

"Confirm *tsakat* orientation."

Galadjian responded. "Shields are shaped and ready."

"Warp two point five. Engage."

Enterprise lurched, another short hop in a series. While the Hellmouth was a relatively small local region by Pergamum standards, the feature's outer boundaries covered a significant area. The starship's first jumps across to the clouds on the other side had been blind, but each crisscrossing trip afterward had revealed more information about where the Boundless ships were.

Moments later, *Enterprise* was across the stellar graveyard, amid the clouds on the other side. Before Pike could make sense of any features on the main viewer, Amin shouted, "Boundless hostile detected, two-seven-five mark one."

"That's our one from jump five," Pike said. "Bring us around, Mister Raden."

Pike sat back. So far, they'd seen ten starships, twice the force at Susquatane. He'd considered the vessels there to be battleships, but now he knew them to be carriers. Several of the heavily armed vessels had large modules attached lengthwise to their flat sides; excursion vehicles of some kind, likely able to carry forty or fifty. A couple of the carriers had five of the things attached, covering all the free sides, making him wonder if the other ships' modules existed. Might they be elsewhere? He hadn't seen any floating loose.

"Phaser range," Nhan said. "Targeted."

"Fire."

She did. "Their shields are raised, Captain. That's two in a row. They've wised up."

"So they can talk to each other, even if they're not answering us," Pike said. "Switch to photon torpedoes for the next ones—let's bust those shields."

Amin looked back. "I have jump fifteen calculated, sir."

Pike looked to Galadjian. "Doctor?"

The gray-bearded man gave a thumbs-up. He seemed to be having the time of his life.

Pike smiled. "Jump fifteen . . ."

Combat Module Carrier 539-Aloga

"What's going on here, Kormagan? What have you led us into?"

Kormagan fought the impulse to mute the transmission from the leader of the Fifty-Twos. Decades her junior, Quadeo ran one of the newer waves; she had an answer for everything, which seemed to be the way with the current generation. Kormagan had seen a dozen others like Quadeo rise through the ranks just to die horribly, smothered by their own hubris. Kormagan wouldn't have minded so much if the commanders were the only ones who died on those occasions.

"Answer me," Quadeo said. *"You said we were just after one starship!"*

"We are," Kormagan replied, her eyes scanning the data from the map displays ahead of her. She was not entirely sure her answer was the truth. Pike's "surrender" message had

all pitching forward against their consoles. There was no falling out of chairs or stations as aboard a larger bridge; there simply wasn't room here, a small blessing. Una looked at her colleagues. *Did we do something wrong?*

Galadjian called down. *"We emerged into the aftereffect of an antimatter detonation."*

"Damage report?" Una asked. It was information she could find from where she was, but the shield work kept her monitors occupied.

"The tsakat *took the impact. A glancing blow. The captain is turning us about now."*

Mann frowned at Una. "It didn't feel like a glancing blow."

"Is a diagnostic necessary?" Galadjian asked.

Una called up. "Doctor, I think definitely that we—"

Pike broke in. *"We're under attack, Number One—with no shields. We're going back to home base."* Back across the Hellmouth, that was the location *Enterprise* had started from. No Boundless ships had been present—at least, not then. *"We'll run the diagnostic then."*

"Aye, Captain." Feeling the starship quaking from nearby detonations, Una agreed with the plan. She read the data for the new heading, piped from Galadjian above. "Jump seventeen. Modulation change, one point two, deflector beam protocol *Tsakat*-Five."

"*Tsakat*-Five, aye."

Enterprise went to warp again—and left it just as quickly, with a bang that threw the room's occupants into the air. The narrow space was no help this time, its fixed furnishings giving painful landings to the officers present.

Seeing the state of her comrades, Una fumbled for her communicator. "Doctor Boyce to auxiliary control!"

His acknowledgment was drowned out by another call from the bridge over the comm panel. *"What's going on?"* Pike asked. *"We just dropped out of warp in the middle of the Hellmouth!"*

Una worked her way back to the console. The data on the monitors didn't make any sense. Her breath caught in her chest as she realized she knew what this particular brand of nonsense meant. "Captain, we have a failure in the field attraction sensors."

Silence.

There was a reason for it. Housed outside in the three bulges surrounding the deflector dish, the sensors provided practically every fact the shields needed in order to operate.

The next words they heard were from Galadjian. *"The* tsakat *appears to have distributed the shockwave from the torpedo earlier as feedback into the ship."*

"I agree. We have overvoltage failures in a dozen subsystems back here."

"Can the system be reset?"

Una and Mann exchanged stunned glances. *Of course it couldn't.*

"No," she answered. "No field attraction sensors means no shields. I can't tell you what else may be down. Stand by."

She was starting to look when she noticed Colt behind her. The young woman had recovered from where she had fallen backward; now, she was struggling to exit. "I want to check on main engineering," she said, "but I can't get the damn door open!"

She knelt, activating the manual override. The door cranked open, admitting wafts of smoke high in the air. "Oh, that's not good."

"Where's the fire?" Mann asked.

That wasn't the only question Una had. "Why haven't we heard an *alarm*?"

34

Combat Module Carrier 539-Aloga
Little Hope

"We got 'em!" Dreston called out. *"Target's position is on your display."*

Kormagan saw it. *Enterprise* had dropped out of warp and stalled, drifting, amid the mingled debris of a pair of failed stars. One was a brown dwarf; the other, a massive gas giant where fusion had fizzled out. And all around, dust and rubble. Just like the rest of Little Hope, the system was a wreck.

The wavemaster had a hunch that *Enterprise* might be one too. This was no calculated move, no planned place of cover to which the starship had retreated. She didn't know what magic Captain Pike had been using to swiftly traverse Little Hope, heedless of the nebular material in his path, but he didn't seem to be able to use it now. The trick was one more discovery she would pry from the ship. Perhaps Spock could explain it.

"The torpedo was ours," Quadeo transmitted. *"My carrier fired it!"*

Kormagan was glad anyone had hit anything, though she knew this success would only make her rival more unbearable. It didn't seem like a good time to remind Quadeo whom it was that had given everyone the orders to fire in the first place. There was more important business.

"All operational carriers, close in," Kormagan said into her armor's mic. "Assume positions to block avenues of escape. Disable shields if they come back online—otherwise, harassing fire to cover troop module approach and prevent the launching of shuttles. Troop modules, zero in on *Enterprise* and commence operations."

Pike had fought with cunning, but his gambit had failed. It was just a matter of time.

U.S.S. Enterprise

"Captain, main engineering is on fire."

It was not a thing captains—or anyone else aboard a starship—liked to hear. "What happened, Number One?"

"That feedback appears to have damaged the warp control systems. Some equipment exploded when we tried to jump."

Pike heard shouts in the background. "The warp core. Is it intact?"

"Still trying to get close enough to evaluate. The fire retardant systems are offline." More sounds of chaos. *"Stand by."*

Pike hurried to the bridge support console. "Report."

"Many systems appear to have gone into diagnostic safe mode," Dietrich said.

"Even the safety systems?" Pike couldn't make sense of the data he was seeing. *Enterprise* seemed to be speaking another language. "What do we have that's up?"

"I've got tactical sensors," Nhan said. "We've got inbounds. Looks like those modules that were attached to those carriers. Ten—maybe twenty of them."

"What weapons do we have?"

"Phasers. Which would be helpful, if the plasma regulators were online." The phasers were another new addition to *Enterprise* since Talos IV; some bugs were still being worked out. Without the regulators, Nhan had no way of controlling the intensity of the bursts they fired. She hammered at her interface in frustration. "Give me something that works!"

"I've got thrusters," Raden called out.

Pike looked back. "Impulse?"

"Honestly, I'm afraid of it. I don't like these readings. I don't want another blowup."

He trusted his helmsman. Impulse movement was out, at least until he got an update from below—and warp certainly was off the table. "What kind of feedback would cause all this?" Pike asked. "I wouldn't think ODN cabling could even transmit something like that."

Hunched over his station, Galadjian stared at his screen. "Given the electromagnetic properties of the shielding systems and the energies generated by—" He stopped in midsentence and rubbed his temples. "I don't know."

Pike looked back at his chief engineer for a moment—until an intraship hail turned his thoughts to a doctor of a different kind. *"Boyce to bridge!"*

"Pike here. Where are you, Doctor?"

"I'm . . . in main engineering," Boyce said between wheezes. *"There are injuries from the sudden stop . . . and from damaged consoles."*

"Phil, are you all right? Is it the fire?"

"Nearly . . . under control."

"But the way you—"

"*Bulkheads didn't drop . . . smoke retardation systems inoperative. Turbolifts out—tough getting to people."*

"Keep me posted." Pike looked at the turbolift doors. "I guess we're *really* not going anywhere." He stepped back to the center of the room and turned to face the viewscreen. That was still working, at least—although he quickly saw that the Hellmouth didn't look any more hospitable up close. They had dumped out of warp in a gravity well. A gas giant loomed; in the sickly light of a nearby brown dwarf, the sphere appeared as a colorless blot. All around, moonlets and asteroids tumbled aimlessly in the dust.

No—there were shapes with direction out there too. Heading Pike's way. He looked back to his engineer. "*No* shields?"

"Or transporters." Galadjian shrugged, palms open. "I have a dead board here. Useless."

"*You're—*" Nhan started, before closing her mouth. She shot a furious look at him and turned away. Wounded, Galadjian faced his station and looked down.

"Don't do this," Pike said with a pointed glance at Nhan. "Not now." He couldn't have the staff melting down, not under these conditions. "We pushed the limits. We shouldn't be astonished that we found them. Sometimes even the best horse bucks."

He gave a look back at the viewscreen—and turned, striding purposefully toward an equipment cabinet. "We're going to use the thrusters to keep moving—make this difficult for them. We've got to buy Una time to get things sorted out."

Looking back at him, Raden nodded. "Aye, sir. Anything else?"

"Yes. Stand by to repel boarders."

Troop Module Aloga-One

"Now!" Goldsub shouted. One by one, the doors over the heads of the troopers in the depressurized chamber blew open. The panels they were standing on shot upward, catapulting Spock and his squadmates into space.

Spock hurtled wildly for several moments before the jets affixed to the mass on his back fired, stabilizing his orientation.

"Just look at the target. Once it's in your reticule, toggle your booster," Goldsub called out over Spock's comm system. *"You'll home in automatically."*

All Spock saw was the gas giant and debris—and dozens of other warriors, soaring on back-mounted rockets of their own. But then something else entered his view. The deployment area of the Boundless troop modules had no ports to look from, in part to keep soldiers calm about what they were heading toward. *Enterprise* had existed for him only as a memory and a goal—but now it rose into his field of view.

It didn't look normal. Several of its brilliant lights had been extinguished. Was it Pike's plan to hide in the nebula? If so, it had not worked.

"What are you waiting for, Gold-Five? Set your course!"

Spock focused on a section directly astern from the bridge dome. There was an airlock there. He oriented toward it and triggered his jets. A surge went through his armor to his body as he shot forward, leaving his companions behind. Moments later, they were alongside.

"That's it!" his subaltern said. *"Lead the way, Gold-Five."*

"We're with you too," announced another voice. It was Opmaster Sperrin, still aboard the troop module, which was now following the warriors through space. *"We'll cover your approach."* Spock knew there was another reason Sperrin was monitoring: to keep an eye on him.

In fact, it was becoming hard to know where to look, especially as *Enterprise* opened up on the troop modules, battering their shielding with phaser fire. It was not particularly effective, Spock saw; each shot seemed to vary with intensity. Some Boundless modules fired back, attempting to target the weapon emplacements—with the floating warriors soaring in the territory between.

And now the carriers approached, strafing the space nearby in an attempt to make *Enterprise*'s attempts to evade costly. The unshielded starship's response had been far more limited than Spock had expected; it was using its thrusters only to escape the tightening net.

Something must be very wrong.

He couldn't think about that now—not with the dorsal hull of the saucer section filling his view. *Enterprise* dipped abruptly, heading away from him; he could see other Boundless warriors overcorrecting, sailing right on past. As the ship lurched again, others slammed off the hull, hurtling back into space.

Spock adjusted his jets to bring himself into contact with the hull—and then magnetized the palms of his gloves. He cut his engines the second his fingers made contact with the smooth surface. Then it was a matter of hanging on until he affixed his boots to the ship's skin as well.

He looked back to see several other warriors on the hull. Some nearby, others farther away at the other objective points. Goldsub, standing, saw Spock and gestured to the bridge dome.

Trying to keep his balance, Spock looked at it. There was no channel he could access on which he could open communications with anyone aboard *Enterprise*: to it, he resembled just another boarder. *"Call the shot,"* Goldsub said.

"Their standard procedure will be to block all manual airlock overrides," Spock said. "The mechanism cannot be defeated. It must be removed."

"Affirm." Goldsub nodded and patted his utility casing. That was where the laser torches Spock had requested resided. He turned to wave his arriving squadmates in.

Spock began the plodding magnetic walk up the sloping hull toward the bulge of the bridge assembly. The destination had been inevitable since Spock learned of Kormagan's plan. She had figured that by having him with the troops assailing the bridge, he might forestall a costly fight. He had theorized there was no rescuing his comrades unless *Enterprise* learned the full story of where they were, and how they were being held. They just had very different ideas about what he would do when he got there.

It was time to act. Seeing Goldsub's back turned, Spock began to reach for his own laser torch.

"All squads, stand by!"

Spock stopped in midmotion. The call had come not from his squad leader or Sperrin—but from Kormagan.

"Over there!" Goldsub cried out. *"It's the Rengru!"*

Spock turned—looking to the sky above his squad to see what they were pointing at. Hundreds of Rengru fighters swarmed through space, a torrent of raindrop-shaped propulsion shells. Something was protruding from them; his telescopic sights showed them to be the Rengru's limbs, evidently invulnerable to the hostile environment of space. The fighters served as a vanguard for larger pyramidal ships of a kind Spock had never seen before—all headed his way.

He and Kormagan had envisioned quite different fates for *Enterprise.* Spock realized now that the Rengru had ideas of their own.

35

Combat Module Carrier 539-Aloga
Little Hope

Not here! Not now!

Kormagan had thought most of the nearby Rengru forces were bottled up in the endless engagement at Varadah. Somehow, they had discovered that *Enterprise* existed—and that the Boundless wanted it.

"Enterprise *chasing us must have tipped them off,*" Dreston said. *"Their sensors aren't perfect, but even they can see an arsenal like that blundering about."*

She cursed herself for a fool. Shivane had been one of the planets along the trail *Enterprise* had followed; surely the Rengru would have sent a scout to check on the outpost Kormagan had destroyed. Odds were that was where the Rengru had stumbled across *Enterprise*—and noticed the ship. They would have naturally assumed the Boundless's interest in it.

Interest, of course, that had to be thwarted. Everything in the nebula was a zero-sum game between the Boundless and the Rengru.

"Looks like we have between three and four hundred Stingers, leading eight Hiveships," Dreston said. *"That's a lot."*

It surely was. More than enough to take on three Boundless waves—and she could see that several of her carriers were still out of action from *Enterprise*'s surprise attack.

"Orders, Wavemaster?"

Kormagan had to think. This was a new phase. It wasn't the first time the Rengru had tried to interfere with one of their boarding attempts; the intelligent creatures knew very well how the Boundless improved their numbers and technology. They'd destroyed many a find before it could be exploited.

The new element was that *Enterprise* was a victim capable of fighting back. It was still actively doing so, even though many of its phaser shots had been underpowered and ineffective. How could she fight to take the Starfleet vessel and keep it from the Rengru at the same time?

Hemmick called in, sounding shaken. *"Should we withdraw our boarders?"*

"Negative. This could be our only shot. We've got to protect *Enterprise* from them. Give our people time to board!"

U.S.S. Enterprise

"What the hell are those?" Standing in the pried-open doorway to the turbolift, Pike stared at the main viewscreen, stunned.

"More inbounds, Captain," Nhan said. *Enterprise*'s malfunctioning systems had reduced the security chief to the role of observer. "Lots more."

Pike's eyes goggled at the swarm of newcomers. Unwilling to have Nhan leave her station, he'd popped down the ladder of the turbolift shaft for just a minute to retrieve some heavy weaponry from a security locker. In the Hellmouth, apparently, it was impossible to step away for a second without everything changing.

"We've got small fry and large out there," Pike said. "Hail them. No—a distress call."

Nicola sent it. "No response."

"Look there!" Amin said, pointing. On screen, three of the big pyramidal newcomers simultaneously fired orange disruptor blasts into one of the Boundless troop modules. The white flash of overloaded shields was replaced an instant later with a spectacular explosion.

"Whoa!" Nhan blurted. "I guess they're friends!"

"This is bizarre," Amin said. "Does this nebula have antibodies or something?"

"It's a big galaxy," Pike said. "Who knows?"

"I think I saw these guys in the probe's dictionary," Nicola said, checking his database. He nodded when he found the image. "They're called the Rengru."

"Go, Rengru!" Nhan said.

As the arrivals assaulted the Boundless ships, Pike walked the bridge distributing weapons. "We've got our own problems. Which boarding team is closest?"

Nhan found the right feed. "Docking port two, stardrive section."

"On-screen."

Pike saw Boundless warriors clustering on the hull near the deflector dish that had caused so much trouble. The view was coming from surveillance sensors on the underside of the saucer section. They clearly still worked, but a lot of the subsystems that could have helped him defeat the intruders were unavailable. "Pike to engineering."

Colt answered this time. On hearing that boarders were at an airlock, she responded with what Pike almost thought was a laugh. *"They're going to get a face full of smoke. It's spreading through the Jefferies tubes—and the systems aren't cycling it out."*

"Can you post more security?" He saw one of the boarders ignite a laser torch. "They could be in at any time."

"If they know how to fix a warp drive, we'll give them oxygen masks and a place to sit." More noise in the background. *"I'll try. Colt out."*

Pike looked around, frustrated. "We've got to do something from up here. Raden, intensify evasive action."

"I don't think we'll knock them loose," Raden said, shaking his head. "But aye."

Enterprise changed directions abruptly again, but it barely budged the break-in artists. Pike was nearly out of options. "I suppose we should quickly go over our self-destruct protocols, in case they—"

Before he could finish, a white blur raced across the screen. One of the tiny Rengru ships swooped in, ripping the Boundless warrior at the airlock cleanly off the side of the hull. Another did the same—and another, until the entire boarding party was gone.

Astounded, Pike pointed to the receding Rengru attackers. "Close-up on that!"

The nearer view brought into focus two figures of similar size—the Boundless warrior and the Rengru fighter—wrestling as they rocketed through the dust. The Rengru seemed as much living being as vehicle, clutching at the armored soldier with powerful limbs that extended outside its shell.

That's something you don't see every day, Pike thought. But before he could make a remark, both figures vanished in a blinding blaze of disruptor fire.

"That came from one of the big Boundless warships," Nhan said. "They killed their own guy!"

Pike didn't like any of it. And he liked it even less when the viewscreen switched back to a view of the saucer section. The Rengru fighters were in running disruptor battles with several Boundless boarding parties on the surface of his ship.

All was madness. It was time to chance the impulse drive. "Raden, I think we need to—"

A sudden blast quaked *Enterprise*, throwing Pike against a console. His heart nearly stopped. "Was that the warp core?"

"No," Nhan shouted as another explosion hit. "The big Rengru ships are shooting at us!"

The Boundless capital ships had treated *Enterprise* with

kid gloves, unwilling to risk their prize. The Rengru, whoever and whatever they were, didn't seem to care. He saw the little fighters lighting on the skin of the *Enterprise*, pincers clawing at the hull. "Okay, they are definitely not friends!"

"Maybe they're firing at the boarders?" Galadjian asked, nearly overwhelmed.

"No, they don't like anybody." Some of the little Rengru were firing their disruptors point-blank at *Enterprise*. Their guns were no larger than rifles, but they were firing them nonstop—and without apparent care. Pike's worries had gone from precision lasers against the airlocks to brute force against everything.

Nothing had prepared him for the moment. And nothing could have prepared him for the next.

"This is Una." She, who never sounded stressed, did not hide her alarm. *"We have a possible warp core breach. That last impact was bad."*

"Can you control it?"

"I can try. But you have maybe a minute to get the saucer section separated and clear!"

It was the capper. Pike had never seriously considered splitting up the ship before; he barely remembered the procedure. But Number One would never exaggerate the danger. "Forget staying down there. Get everyone back up here!"

Galadjian was on his feet. "I must go down! I will take care of—"

"It's too late for that," Una said, having overheard. *"Turbolifts are down—and the smoke's still thick in the Jefferies tubes. Not even sure the escape pods will deploy. Captain, I need to get back to work if I want a chance!"*

Pike closed the channel. There was no other way. He returned to his seat and looked around the bridge. "Emergency saucer separation."

36

Outside U.S.S. Enterprise
Little Hope

Connolly had gone through so many emotions in the last hour he could barely process them. Commanded to board *Enterprise* as part of Baladon's squad, he'd been filled with anger and expectation. Outrage at being ordered to take his own ship; happiness at the thought of seeing it again. Before he could object, *Enterprise* had struck at the Boundless ships. He'd wanted to cheer then, and had not objected to the mission in the expectation that it was safer to be standing outside *Enterprise* than to spend another day inside a Boundless battlesuit.

Seeing the wretched defense *Enterprise* was mounting had given him pause, however—and finally, he had been standing on the lip of the saucer section when the Rengru had attacked.

There hadn't been time to breathe since.

"This is insane! We've got to get out of here!"

With a newly traded-for disruptor cannon in his gloved hands, Baladon laughed. *"They don't frighten me,"* he said over his battlesuit comm, unleashing hell on every Rengru that flew past. *"I could barely get within torpedo range of this ship before. Now, I'm standing on the hull. I am not going anywhere!"*

It wasn't as if there was anywhere *to* go—not with *Enterprise* lurching to and fro and fire coming in from the Rengru warships. The blasts seemed to be targeting the stardrive section; that was the only reason Blue Squad hadn't been vaporized. As it was, only Baladon, Connolly, and one other trooper remained—

—and that number immediately went down by one as Blue-5 was ripped from the surface by a Rengru fighter. *"Help!"*

"*Becko!*" Connolly called out. He hadn't known his newest teammate long at all—but reflexively he prepared to deactivate his magnetic boots and ignite his jetpack.

Before he could, however, Baladon adjusted his weapon and fired at the struggling pair in the sky, annihilating both the soldier and his abductor.

Connolly shoved at Baladon. "You killed Becko! What did you do that for?"

"That's what we're supposed to do!" Baladon shouted, turning to fire in a different direction. *"Like we always do!"*

"We didn't hear a breach warning. He still had a chance!"

"Rengies don't breach armor in a vacuum. They wait until they get you home."

At the word *home*, Connolly boiled over. "I'm done!"

"They're hearing your chatter," Baladon said. *"Stick to the program. Get down there and sabotage the impulse engine."*

"No!" Connolly pointed at the airlock behind the bridge. Several Boundless had arrived there earlier—and were waging a defensive war against the swooping Rengru. "Baladon, forget this! Come with me. *Enterprise*—she'll save us, take you wherever you want to go. Home, or—"

"The Boundless *are taking me where I wanted to go! My home was nothing. I led an army of fools. Now I'm part of something!"*

"Forget it." Connolly released the charge he'd been ordered to set, allowing it to float away. He started a mad dash across the rear of the saucer section, heading for the bridge airlock.

"Little ingrate. They're watching you! Get back here before—"

Connolly didn't hear the rest of Baladon's sentence, because the audio in his armor cut out, along with everything else on his interface. Blind in the dark, he felt his magnetic boots disengage from *Enterprise*'s hull—and his jetpack activate.

"No, no, no!" He wanted to flail in anger as he rocketed away. Away, surely, to the troop module that had launched him, where he would be disciplined for his attempt at desertion. But his battlesuit would not let him move. His part of the battle was over.

Combat Module Carrier 539-Aloga

"We've got runners," Dreston said. *"We're bringing them back."*

Kormagan didn't care a whit about deserters, not now. She was trying to save her wave—three waves—from destruction. She had never before known the Rengru to hit so hard over a spoil of war.

"We're going to recall everyone and get out of here," Quadeo transmitted. *"I've just lost a carrier!"*

Kormagan knew. *552-Urdoh* had been caught in crossfire between the Hiveships. Three hundred hands would have been lost, minus whatever warriors were out in the modules or in space. "Don't go yet," she implored, "or this will all have been for nothing."

"It already is for nothing! Don't you see it?"

The wavemaster was momentarily confused, thinking Quadeo was speaking generally. But Dreston piped in to explain.

"Something's happened to Enterprise,*"* he shouted. *"It's split in two!"*

The image appeared before her. The saucer front of *Enterprise* had separated from the rear section, even as both portions were still under attack by Rengru. Several of her troops were still aboard the dish.

"Should we order our people back?" Dreston asked.

She hesitated. It really did look like the end of her prize.

The starship had come apart at the seams—but there still was a chance that somebody could get aboard for a minute and find something of use. She'd come too far to walk away with nothing.

And with the damage done to three waves, that might be all that remained of her career tomorrow.

"Hemmick, Quadeo—back your carriers out to the cloud line and recall your modules. The Thirty-Niners are going to see this through!"

Outside *U.S.S. Enterprise*

The chaos surrounding Spock had not abated since the Rengru arrived. What he needed to do involved concentration, a feat nearly impossible given the running battles on the surface of the ship and between ships. Seconds after watching a Boundless member astern from his position rocket away, he had felt one jolt after another shaking the starship under his boots. Powerful explosive bolts fired, propelling *Enterprise*'s saucer away from the stardrive section.

Things are worse than I surmised, Spock thought. He could wait no longer for the perfect chance. He had to act.

The only shadow he still had to contend with, the Gold Squad subaltern, was engaged in a firefight while covering him at the airlock. That was satisfactory. Spock disliked taking advantage of someone defending him, but he had no choice. Facing the airlock, he activated his laser torch—

—and turned it on himself. Or, rather, the governor module jutting from his back. He had studied it since learning of it in Jayko's lab; it was supposedly impervious to sabotage, by the battlesuit wearer or a companion. Except in one case: a precision burn by a laser torch, an item not usually in the Boundless warriors' complement of tools.

It was a dangerous act: like doing laser surgery on himself.

The burn had to be in precisely the right place and of the right intensity and duration. He could cut himself, breach the huge reservoir of jetpack fuel he was carrying, or touch off one of his munitions with the tiniest miscalculation. In a bit of irony, his battlesuit's AI helped him keep his hand steady.

An alarm sounded briefly in Spock's ears, but nothing in his interfaces changed. He wondered if he'd done something wrong.

"Hey!" Goldsub spun around. *"What are you doing there?"*

"Apologizing," Spock said. He fired his disruptor at the hull near his squad leader's one planted boot. Only partially affixed to *Enterprise*, it gave way—allowing Spock to fire again. The impact on Goldsub's personal energy shielding propelled him away from the saucer.

As Goldsub swore, Spock stepped forward, thinking he might need to fire again. But the saucer section was in motion now, heading forward and away from the engineering hull. That made sense; if such a measure were necessary, the crew would be using the saucer to escape a catastrophic blast.

He stowed his weapon, reset his comm channel to one previously prohibited by the governor, and spoke quickly. "Captain Pike, this is Lieutenant Spock. I am on the hull of *Enterprise*, requesting transport!"

There was no response. He could well imagine no one listening at such a juncture; the transporters might be inoperative as well. He turned back to the airlock—and saw a warrior standing before the closed accessway.

"Well, if it isn't Spock." Baladon's name appeared in Spock's interface. *"Don't tell me you're homesick too."*

"What do you mean?"

"Connolly just tried to run. Being at the doorstep seems to have an effect on you people." He gestured to Spock's governor unit, still sparking. *"Obviously Connolly didn't have your smarts. It's a neat trick. I can't override your battlesuit."*

Spock regarded Baladon. The warrior seemed heedless of the fighting and destruction around him. "What do you intend?"

Baladon pointed to the stardrive section, still being battered by Rengru. "*Enterprise* is no prize now—for the Boundless, or for me. But I'm sure they'd like a word with you after all this. I'll settle for bringing you to them instead!"

37

U.S.S. Enterprise
Saucer Section
Little Hope

"I have the tally," Nicola announced. Since nobody outside *Enterprise* had seemed interested in talking, the comm officer had switched to the more urgent task of contacting other decks on the saucer section. It was another place where the ship's computer wasn't being its usually helpful self. "We have ninety-nine aboard."

"Which means we have seventy-four aboard the stardrive section," Pike said. Since Susquatane, it had become the unbearable arithmetic of his life. "Status?"

"Still not moving," Nhan said. "Some of the Boundless ships are leaving—and a lot of Rengru are following. Maybe they all think we're worth less, broken in two."

Or maybe they're afraid the engineering hull will explode, Pike thought. He dismissed the idea as quickly as he could. He already knew there was nothing to be done for Una and the others. "Look for escape pods."

Nhan called out. "Captain, we still have boarders on the hull, both sides."

"Both the Rengru and the Boundless, or both sides of the saucer?"

"Sorry. *Both* both. The Rengru are just tearing into the hull. Some of the Boundless are at the airlocks."

"Show me." With security already stationed inside some of the airlocks, he had delayed checking the feeds from the hull to deal with more pressing matters.

The main viewscreen lit up with the display from the airlock just behind and beneath the bridge. Pike had expected to see armored warriors there, laying siege to his ship. Instead, he was surprised to see the two Boundless warriors outside were battering not the airlock, but one another.

"They're fighting!" Amin said. "What the hell?"

Nhan squinted at the scene. "Is everyone doing that?"

"I don't care," Pike said. "They're not in yet. Raden, the thrusters are still nominal?"

"Aye."

"Angle the dorsal exhaust ports perpendicular to the center, as far as the gimbals will allow. Ventrals the opposite direction."

Raden smiled with recognition. "I think I get you."

"They want to ride along so bad? Take them for a spin!"

—

"Baladon, this is unnecessary," Spock said.

"Really? I am quite enjoying it!"

With hell breaking loose in the space all around, the two armored warriors, made titans by their battlesuits, pounded at one another as they rode the hurtling saucer. With their feet magnetically planted on the hull, there was little either could do to dislodge the other.

Unfortunately for Spock, that fact—plus the bulk of his gear—made it difficult to bring his *Suus Mahna* training into play. Every step off the surface was a danger, a chance for one of the combatants to knock the other off the starship.

Now there was a new element: the saucer section had started to spin.

As the rotation accelerated, Spock saw Rengru and Boundless warriors alike losing hold and tumbling off the saucer into space. Baladon saw it, too, and laughed. *"Wonderful! Hilarious!"*

"Some of those are your own people," Spock said.

"You fret about everything, Vulcan. I'm having the time of my life!" Baladon brought both fists down on Spock's headgear again and again, jolts that his battlesuit barely cushioned. *"You need to smile more!"*

Spock hunkered down beneath the rain of blows. He could not defeat a brawler without footwork—and as *Enterprise* spun ever faster, centripetal force came into play. All the boarders closer to the edge of the saucer were already gone, flung into the dust; only he and Baladon, near the center, remained.

Soon Baladon was all he could see—as the surrounding war and debris vanished into a whirl. Baladon flailed against him, broad blows beginning to miss more than connect—but each strike from the more massive warrior nearly sent Spock to the hull.

The hull! As Baladon wound up for another haymaker, Spock realized what he had to do.

Spock ducked the blow, as he had before—only this time, he did not rise back up to a fighting posture. Instead, he went down to a crouch and slapped his hands on the hull. "*Magnetize!*"

Baladon laughed—and grabbed Spock in a wrestling hold. *"It's time to go, Vulcan,"* he said, and his jetpack activated. It was all physics—Spock's four points of adherence fighting against Baladon's upward thrust, even as both struggled against the force generated by the saucer's now-frenzied rotation. Alarms went off in Spock's interface. Too much stress on his armor, stress on his body.

Baladon spoke again. *"Hey! Don't—"*

An orange flash filled the visual receptors of Spock's battlesuit. Baladon released him. Spock lost hold of the hull and tumbled outward and forward, barely catching on with his hands. He looked up to see Baladon hurtling end over end into the morass, his jetpack blazing away.

His feet no longer affixed, Spock tried to mash every molecule of his gloves to the hull. Under the ripping force of the saucer's rotation, his torso and legs floated from the surface, pulling against his grip on the ship.

A phaser blast struck nearby, causing his right hand to reflexively move—an act translated by his battlesuit as an order to let loose. Clinging and dizzy, he looked up—and saw in the open airlock what had happened to Baladon. A spacesuited Christopher Pike stood braced inside the aperture, pointing a phaser at the people he thought were trying to board his ship.

"*Captain, it is Spock!*" he called out.

Whatever channel he was on, it wasn't the right one. He did finally think of a way to send a signal—but a second after he did, his left hand came loose too.

Enterprise vanished—along with everything else.

—

"I think I'm going to be sick," Nhan said as Pike clambered back up the ladder and out of the turbolift shaft.

"Mark the inertial dampers as 'also barely working,'" Amin said.

"I figure that got rid of the boarders," Pike said, removing his helmet and staggering toward his chair. "Please tell me that's everybody."

"We were down to two," Nhan said. "I saw you shoot the one."

"The other fell off," Pike said, collapsing in his chair. His helmet tumbled to the floor and rolled, curving away. "But it was strange. Before he let go, I could have sworn he made a Vulcan salute."

The mystery moment had little time to sink in, for before Pike could order a stop to the spinning, a final colossal blast ended the conversation altogether.

38

Little Hope

Spock meditated.

Or he thought that was what he was doing. He was back in his quarters on *Enterprise*, his focus on a candle. A candle for a lost ship. *Enterprise* was a lost ship. His impulse to reason naturally tried to connect the two—but logic said he could not be on a vessel and mourning it at the same time.

Still, the candle burned.

He thought to close his eyes, to see if the light would disappear or linger. He realized then that they were already closed. He still saw the light. It was red. A kind of red that only existed in the deepest recesses of his memory, where he had forcibly hidden it away.

He had been a child on Vulcan when it had appeared to him. Crimson, glowing rays emanating—no, extending—from a figure that was there, and yet not there. It had hovered over his bed, instilling in him wonder—and also bone-chilling fear. There was no logic to the thing's presence then—nor in his mind now.

I will not have this dream again. I will not!

Spock opened his eyes to darkness—and breathed the cool reprocessed air of his battlesuit. It had indeed been a dream, he thought, caused by exhaustion or injury. Or a hallucination caused by a flaw in his oxygen mixture—or perhaps nitrogen narcosis from the pressures exerted on his body. He had been spinning, hadn't he?

It was then that he realized where he was: in space. The darkness, he now realized, wasn't complete. A brown dwarf sun sat dully off to his right, a fuzzy blob hardly visible through the dust of the region. Much nearer, to his left, was a gas giant; his body had joined its family of satellites.

Spock had been aboard *Enterprise*. No, not aboard, but atop it—and had been dislodged. That, he remembered—along with the last sight he'd seen before losing consciousness: a blast, well aft, which sent the saucer section careening out of sight. He hadn't been able to tell whether the blast had come from a Rengru weapon—or, worse, from the stardrive section, which Pike must have cast off for a reason. What mattered was that the ship was gone—

—and so was everything else from the colossal melee. It was as if the conflict had never taken place. No Rengru, no Boundless debris was visible anywhere, to the extent that anything could be made out.

He looked around, unsure of what to do. His gaze fell upon a white circle. An icy moon of the gas giant; perhaps it had been a full-fledged dwarf planet when the body was still a star. Now there was nothing special about it—except for the red point of light that had lingered before his eyes earlier. It appeared only when he looked at the orb; when he looked away, it vanished.

The jetpack on the Boundless suit could take him to it, he realized—eventually. It would take him a week to reach there, saving enough propellant to touch down safely. The armor could keep him alive during that time, and much longer.

It made as much sense as anything else. He was likelier to be found on the surface of a world, any world, than if he were floating like jetsam. Why *not* that world?

He called up the dialog allowing him to control the suit's engine. Only then did he realize that, imperceptible to him, his jetpack had been operating all along, driving him toward that particular ice planet.

He had set the course in his sleep.

CAPITULATION

May 2257

INCOMING TRANSMISSION (ENCRYPTED)

TO: CAPTAIN C. PIKE • *U.S.S. ENTERPRISE* • NCC-1701

FROM: REAR ADMIRAL TERRAL,
STARFLEET COMMAND

STATE OF WAR CONTINUES. *SARATOGA*, STARBASE 22 LOST. *DISCOVERY* IS STILL MIA.

WE DID NOT HEAR FROM YOU WHEN YOUR TWELVE-MONTH MISSION ENDED. REPORT WHEN CONDITIONS PERMIT, BUT DO NOT RETURN.

WE ARE EXTENDING YOUR MISSION,
END DATE TO BE DETERMINED.

END TRANSMISSION

39

U.S.S. Enterprise
Saucer Section
Little Hope

I'm dead.

No, I'm not. I just don't want to move.

Christopher Pike awoke to those thoughts—and to pain. He coughed. The air was stale, reminding him of another experience in utter darkness that he'd tried long and hard to forget. His thoughts grasped for something, anything else to light upon.

Freena. No, that was back then too.

Vina? Seeing her face in his mind's eye was nice, but also wrong.

He needed memories, not dreams—and his last recollection was of flying. No, not flying, but hurtling upward, toward the transparent aluminum port that sat in the bridge's overhead dome. Sailing up and out, like an angel—or someone with a jetpack.

Only he was not an angel, and had no jetpack. It made no sense. But he knew it made no sense, and that helped to clear his mind. As reason returned, he realized he had not broken through the dome at all. Rather, he was sprawled across it, suspended over inky blackness beyond.

Enterprise was upside down.

But it can't be upside down, he thought. *Can it?*

He lifted his head from the port and drew his fingers through his hair. It was matted with dried blood from where he'd struck it. And the not-very-heavy mass atop his legs wasn't crushed rock—but the stirring form of another person, similarly incapacitated. Sitting up, Pike squinted until he recognized who it was.

"Amin, are you all right? Wake up!"

His navigator rolled off Pike's ankles and moaned. "What hit me?"

"I think you hit me—and we hit the overhead. Only it's no longer overhead." Pike ran his hand across the port. It hadn't given way beneath their weight, but it didn't seem like a place to stay either. Indeed, the ship seemed to be undulating—gently, almost imperceptibly. "Any light around here?"

"Here, Captain." To his left he saw Nhan, her face illuminated by a handheld device. She crawled toward them.

"Over there," he said as she reached the edge of the dome.

She complied—and the rays illuminated a third body. "It's Raden!" The helmsman had struck the outer frame of the dome and was still out. Pike saw blood from Raden's left forehead lobe. "He must have hit hard."

"Careful getting to him," Pike said as Amin moved toward the Ktarian. "Either the artificial gravity's really confused, or we've landed—and I'm not at all sure we're on something solid."

Working together, they moved Raden off the edge of the dome. "He's light," Pike said. "So are we." They were clearly in a weak gravity well of some kind. Nhan lifted Raden onto the metallic composite surface and checked his condition.

"He's breathing," she said. "I think he's coming around."

Raden's eyes opened a fraction. Woozy, he spied Pike and mumbled, "Did . . . I leave . . . a mark?"

"Your head will be fine," Pike said. "We'll get you help."

"I mean . . . did *I* leave one . . . on the bulkhead?" Raden closed his eyes again.

I think he'll be all right, Pike thought. "How long have you been awake?" he asked Nhan.

"Never passed out. Believe me, I wish I had." She coughed.

"Oxygen, gravity, lights—they ought to be on battery." Nothing seemed to be working. "Where the hell are we?"

"No idea. I stopped paying attention when I threw up the second time." She shone the light off to the side. "Watch your step."

It was starting to come back to him. "I remember the inertial dampers going out," he said. "We got tossed like a salad."

"I'm begging you, Captain. Don't mention food."

"Let's get a head count."

With a light source of his own, Pike found the rest of the bridge crew—Dietrich, Nicola, and Galadjian—slumped but rousing against the bulkheads at various points of the bridge's circumference.

He checked on the older man. "You all right, Doctor?"

"Captain," Galadjian said, rubbing his head, "I should like to retire."

"I'm afraid the turbolifts are out."

"I did not mean to my room."

Pike shone his light above to what had once been the floor. Chairs descended like stalactites. "They stayed put. We didn't."

He decided to take advantage of his lighter weight. Reversing in his mind where things were located, he found his way to the environmental station. The light gripped in his teeth, he leapt for the top of the chair, hanging over his head. Grabbing it, he heaved himself up and reached for the station's console. An awkward minute in the dark later, he was lying atop the undersides of the control panels, his head and shoulders dangling underneath as he tried to work their controls.

"Everything's dead," he said. "Environmental systems' battery is offline at the source. Same for gravity."

"More victims of the shield feedback," Galadjian said.

Pike heard Amin speak. "How is that possible? Some of the battery systems aren't connected to anything."

"Yes," Galadjian said, sounding tired, "but the entire ship was part of the circuit. Results would be unpredictable."

Dietrich had crawled near the edge of the skylight. "Captain, I think we're floating."

"It doesn't feel like it," Amin said. "I mean it sort of does—like we're in gelatin."

"I said *no food*," Nhan growled. "And I definitely feel it. We're moving. Just barely."

Nicola had been trying his communicator. "I'm not getting anyone on the rest of the ship."

Down to just seven? Pike refused to accept the situation. He dropped to the deck—or, rather, to the overhead—as if he were hopping off his bed.

"Okay. One, we need to get life-support going again. Doctor, Dietrich, that's you. Two, we need to find everyone else—and get medical help for Raden and whoever needs it. Nicola, you're on it. Amin, let's go have a look where we are."

"What about me?" Nhan asked, no enthusiasm in her voice.

"Stay with Raden. And try not to move much."

She fell to her knees. "You're a saint, sir."

—

"I think we're going to be climbing a lot of ladders."

"The wrong way," Pike said as Amin ascended into the darkness ahead of him. At least the gravity made it a much easier ascent, though he could hardly feel a spring in his step given the circumstances.

He hoped that wherever she was, Una had survived. Better yet, that she was nearby, with a repaired stardrive section and ready to beam them all up. That seemed impossible, given the condition of the engineering hull and considering the masses of Rengru he'd seen assaulting it.

They passed another deck. "I keep having to think of everything in reverse," Amin said.

"Just count levels," Pike said. "It's easier."

Climbing ahead of them on the turbolift ladder, Galadjian and Dietrich disappeared into the primary hull circuit room, in normal circumstances the next-to-lowest deck of the section. Pike's destination was an earlier stop: the viewing lounge whose ports were designed to look down and out.

This time, the viewports were skylights—and something was lightly pelting against them. Pike glanced at the navigator. "Sounds like rain."

Amin handed Pike the tricorder she'd found. "It's working," she said. "You ought to at least be able to do spectral analysis through the viewport."

"Right." Pike dragged over a table and scaled it. He pressed his hands to the sloped port and stared out.

Oh, that's not good. He activated the tricorder and pointed it outside. *No, not good at all.*

"What is it?" Amin asked.

"You remember at the Academy," Pike said, "when they took you on that field trip to Saturn?"

"Yeah?"

"And the moon, Titan. Really cold, with the hydrocarbon oceans?"

"Yeah?"

"That's nicer than this." He handed the tricorder to her. "Look at our rain."

Amin focused on the results—and did a double take. "It's raining cyanide."

"I think the ocean we're on is methane or ethane. No land at all." He climbed down—and sighed. "This doesn't get any easier."

Amin nodded. She looked again at the tricorder. "Hey, I've got a working chronometer on this."

"That's something. How long have we been here?"

Amin looked—and laughed.

"What gives?" Pike asked. "Nothing could be funny about this."

"No, it's just—while we were knocked out, our one-year mission ended."

Pike shook his head. "Still not funny, Lieutenant."

40

U.S.S. Enterprise
Stardrive Section
Little Hope Boundary Region

"Captain on the bridge!"

"Inaccurate on both counts," Una said as she stepped gingerly into the crowded control room.

Ensign Yamata looked at her apologetically from one of the two stations. "I thought I had that right. I don't really work the bridge. You are acting captain."

From the other chair, Colt rolled her eyes. "She's saying that Christopher Pike is still our captain, Sam. And that this isn't much of a bridge."

"I'm sorry." Yamata stood and offered his seat to Una. "I'll get back to work on the transporters, Commander."

"Thank you, Sam." Una sat—and tried to focus on breathing. It had been twenty-four hours since she last slept. That was just as well, considering there were many times more people on board than there were living quarters. She had spent most of that time trying to stabilize the warp drive.

Her efforts had succeeded—helped, ironically, by the saucer separation. Main engineering had been on battery power since the crisis began; halving the ship had allowed the team to allocate more power to the antimatter injectors. The reaction had stabilized.

As soon as propulsion had been partially restored, she had directed the stardrive section out of the rift and into a thick nebular cloud bank for safety. She hadn't been able to learn what had happened to the saucer section; the last she had seen, a blast from one of the larger ships that had attacked the stardrive section had sent it tumbling. Attempts to hail Pike from within the cloud had been met with silence. Una suspected that he might be in hiding too.

Colt stared at a screen that showed little. "I wish we could see outside."

"Are you sure about that?"

"You're right. I didn't care for the look of those things at all. The second bunch. What were they called?"

"Rengru." Una had looked up the word in the primer from *Courier 5*. Once the Boundless's shipboarding attempts had failed, the beings had lost interest in the stardrive section—and departed to chase their true enemies.

"What a mess we've wandered into." Colt shook her head. "I don't know what's going on here."

Una had been working on it herself. "The Boundless attacked us. The Rengru attacked us—but they seemed to dislike the Boundless more."

"The Hellmouth food chain in action," Boyce said as he entered. Then he paused to gawk at the size of the command center. "Groucho Marx would ask room service to send up a larger room."

"I don't know who that is." Una gazed back, drawing ever more on her reserves of patience.

"It's all right. I'm working out of a sickbay that isn't much more than a first-aid station."

"You have a report, Doctor?"

Boyce consulted his manifest. "Seventeen injured, mostly in main engineering from the drop out of warp. A few knocked about in the attacks. All on rest and improving, except for a couple of burn patients, stable. I'm watching a couple of concussions."

"You don't have staff here, correct?"

"No, but I'll make do. Some hands have pitched in. Here's the roster." He passed her the manifest.

Una took a look. "Seventy-four?"

"Yeah. And I need so many of the billets for patients that you'll be stacking your off-duty people four deep."

"There are cots in the shuttles. They're not going anywhere."

Boyce frowned. "Not repaired yet?"

"We're working on the warp drive first—but either way, we don't exactly have a place to go."

The doctor grew animated. "We're going after Chris, right? There's a hundred people over there!"

"Ninety-nine," Una corrected.

"And the last we saw, it was spinning out of control," Colt said. "Right through where the Rengru and Boundless were fighting." She bit her lip. "It didn't look good."

Una nodded. She'd barely had a second to think about next steps. "Doctor, our mission in the Pergamum is officially over today—"

"But you're going to stay—to find the captain. We've got to!"

Having known Boyce of old, she tolerated the interruption. "I was going to say that we may not be able to go home—or anywhere—even if we're at a hundred percent. The Rengru look like they had the upper hand out in the Hellmouth, as you call it. If the saucer section is in there, there's not much we can do."

"This part of the ship has weapons."

"Which are best operated from a bridge we do not have."

She gestured around. "Starfleet's shipwrights aren't going to design a full 'battle bridge' unless they think we'd be likely to use it. Obviously, we haven't had to try this maneuver often."

Colt nodded. "Maybe they'll change their thinking after this."

"Or after the Klingon War," Boyce said, calming down. "I wonder if that's even still going on."

"You know what communications are like around here." Una pointed to her console. "That's another reason I'm not going to try to hail the captain again. The odds are very high that we wouldn't get through to anybody but the Rengru."

"The *what*?"

"We've been making all kinds of new friends," Colt said.

Boyce sighed. "Well, I guess that's what Starfleet wants from us, after all." He leaned against a support column, clearly spent.

Una smiled gently at him. "If Chris is here, Philip, we'll find him. For now, please take care of your patients—and send back any ensign you can find that's not on repair detail. We're going to need help creating new rotations and tracking consumables—for however long this lasts." She paused. "And get some rest, Doctor."

He grinned weakly. "I may have to climb into a storage locker to find space."

After he departed, Colt looked to Una. "I'm ship's yeoman—I guess I should help with that too."

"I need you with me. But you'll want to study this," Una said, passing her Boyce's manifest.

Colt scanned the names. "I just noticed something. During the emergency it was all hands on deck—even the transporter crews came down to help. So we have *every single engineer* aboard."

"No." Una shook her head. "All but one."

Colt studied the list again—and her eyes widened. "That means wherever the saucer section is, their only engineer is—"

"Yes," Una said, a tired but patient smile on her face. "We don't speak ill of other officers, Yeoman."

"Of course, Commander." Colt set down the manifest and returned to her duties. But Una caught her mouthing three words: *Heaven help them.*

41

U.S.S. Enterprise
Saucer Section
Little Hope

"Botany Bay?" Raden asked. "Sounds like it ought to be a storage unit off the terrarium."

"I think he's feeling better," Pike said, grinning down at the Ktarian. "What's the reference, Nurse?"

Surrounded by a dozen injured crewmembers spread out on mats on the ceiling-turned-floor of sickbay, a dark-haired woman looked up from the data slate she was holding. "Since our usual entertainments are nonfunctional, I've been reading to the patients," Gabriella Carlotti said. "For some reason, we keep coming back to shipwreck stories."

"I get it," Pike said, surveying the portable lamps on the deck. "Sure feels like we're camping."

"We're onto the *Flying Dutchman*," she said. "I was mentioning that one of the early descriptions of it was in *A Voyage to Botany Bay* from 1795. It was a ghost ship."

"Condemned to sail with its lost souls forever, never reaching port," Pike said with a dramatic flourish. He gestured to her slate. "Let me know if you get to one about a ship on a flammable sea under a poison sky."

Ten days after the forced landing, Raden seemed a little better, though his road back remained long. Among the many injuries sustained from the episode, his had been among the worst, and like others, he had not been able to draw upon the full medical resources of the starship. Galadjian had quickly gotten life-support working again, but not much else, meaning that much of the sickbay's diagnostic and curative equipment had no power. Carlotti and Boyce's other assistant, Yan, had been limited to handheld self-powered implements and hyposprays.

They had many of those, though the trick was reaching them, locked away in their cabinets, suspended above. With all the tremendous technology at their disposal, the most popular implement on every deck had been a stepladder. As easy as jumping was, Pike had found too strong a leap often resulted in a knock on the head.

The past week and a half had also been difficult for those in sickbay, forced to sit on the sidelines as Pike and the able-bodied fought to restore the basics. Raden appealed to Pike. "I never thought much about sea travel where I grew up, but these stories have me wanting to get back on the job. I'd love to pilot something on that ocean."

"You'd be disappointed," Pike said. "We're barely moving. The wave action is measured in centimeters."

"I never would have thought *Enterprise* could float," Carlotti said.

"You'd be surprised. There are many places where she would. Here, it's no problem—liquid methane is many times denser than water. But we'll have to restore more power before we can even consider leaving." Pike looked around at the other patients, listening intently. "So if you need something to do, think of ways of getting off this teardrop. It should be a fun little puzzle."

"Aye, aye," Raden said.

Pike rose and made his way past the patients into the hallway, pausing to step over the upper jamb of the propped-open doorway. Every automatic door aboard had needed to be pried and jammed open.

He saw Carlotti step out after him. "Thank you, Captain. You don't need to come by every day—I know you're busy, and it's an effort to get anywhere."

"Believe me, it's something I'm happy to do." *You have no idea*. "You don't have to read to everyone either."

"Well, the doctoring is done, and there's not much for them to do. The working data slates are tied up with the repair crew."

"Just tell me when you get to *Swiss Family Robinson*. I always liked that one." He turned to go, but paused to take a last look back at sickbay. "Anything else I need to know about?"

"Not since my last report. One hundred people still functioning, at various levels."

Pike stopped in his tracks. "You mean ninety-nine."

"No, I mean a hundred. There's the pregnancy."

The what? He turned to face her. "Did I know about this?"

"It would have appeared in Doctor Boyce's report to you at the appropriate time. Don't you read them?"

Pike shook his head. "He normally just tells me what I need to know."

"And brings the martinis. You know he wouldn't talk outside the report. Patient privacy. Besides," she said, brown eyes beaming, "I wasn't ready to tell anyone yet."

Pike did his second double take of the minute. "*You?* Wow. I had no—" He put up his hands and smiled. "I'll stow the curiosity. Congratulations."

"Appreciated."

"When?"

"Five months from now."

He took that in. "Okay."

"Yan knows," she said, referring to the other medical aide. "I'm fully checked out. No complications during the crash. But there could be other considerations."

"I'll say." Pike looked back at the sickbay with trepidation. "We're not exactly set up here for a baby, even under normal circumstances."

"I wasn't supposed to *be* here. The mission was supposed to end last week." She crossed her arms. "If Starfleet had kept us around here longer I'd have asked for a shuttle home."

He nodded. "We'd *all* like a shuttle home." He took a breath. "What are the other considerations?"

"I currently weigh a seventh of what I do on Earth. That might feel delightful for me in a few months, but it won't really be. I'll be losing muscle mass when I need it most. It's more complicated for the fetus. Our systems are evolved for Earth gravity. Here, there could be changes to circulatory, bone, and muscle-tissue development."

"Children were born in space before artificial gravity."

"Usually in conditions optimized for it." She gestured around. "These, as you say, are not."

"Understood," he said. For Pike, it was one more thing for him to deal with on top of many others, but for Carlotti—who already had a busy job—it obviously had more important implications. He wanted to sound as supportive as possible. "Tell me what I can do, beyond getting us out of here."

She had an answer ready. "Gravity boots. Find me a working pair."

"They're magnetic. Not really gravity."

"No, but for now, fighting to walk will keep me in better shape. If we stay here much longer, I'll need to try something else. Maybe we can build something involving an environment suit. I don't know how all that works."

"Someone will." He didn't add that he wished he had his engineers.

"But the best thing would be to restore gravity to even part of a deck."

"Which means we've got to get off the ceilings, first." Pike nodded. "Check, check, and check. I'm on it."

"Thank you, Captain."

"Stay well. Both of you."

He departed up the hallway, moving in and out of darkness as he went. The crew had broken out portable lights, stationing them at intervals. All of the smaller self-powered devices could run indefinitely, or at least longer than Pike hoped would be necessary.

And how long was that? Carlotti wasn't alone. *Everyone* who talked to him always wanted to know the same thing. Pike had thought it best in those cases to give vague assurances in confident tones, and then to move quickly along, acting like he was on the way to do the one thing that would solve all their problems. They'd let him get away with that—at least so far. Carlotti, however, needed specific help, on a deadline. It was motivation he could use.

While in space, Pike had always held isolation and claustrophobia at bay with simple facts. He had controlled his direction, his destination—and he had always been in contact with those back home. Those things did not apply anymore. He knew nothing of Una and his engineers, nor of his kidnapped scientists. Had he really seen a Vulcan salute during the battle? It seemed so hazy now. And he knew even less about Starfleet. All he knew of the Klingon War was that it had broken out a year ago to the day. Nothing more.

He had to keep moving, keep thinking about other things. Helping Carlotti; helping everyone. It was the only way forward in a place where there was nowhere to go.

Lithely scaling a ladder for the umpteenth time that day, Pike heard banging off to one side. He stepped into a corridor onto another deck. No one was to be seen. *Slow down, Chris. This isn't a ghost ship yet.*

More clanging, closer by, reassured him of his sanity. He

relocated one of the portable lights. The rapping was coming from a panel high in one of the bulkheads. Taking advantage of his lesser weight, Pike easily leapt upward, grabbed the panel frame, and turned a latch.

The panel door fell open, and Galadjian's sweat-soaked head appeared. "*Eureka*," he panted.

"What is it?"

"I have just . . . figured out . . . how to get out of a Jefferies tube."

"A week and a half. That's progress." Pike reached up to help the older man as he shimmied out. Having someone climb down his shoulders was barely a test here.

He allowed Galadjian time to catch his breath. "Do . . . other chief engineers do this sort of thing?"

"Some live for it." Pike gestured to the opening. "What did you find, Doctor?"

"It is as we thought," Galadjian said. "We were not able to raise our companions on the communicators in the beginning because of interference coming off the auxiliary power source for the emergency thrusters. They shut down when we landed, of course, but the *tsakat* event seems to have impacted the tokamak, which continued to generate magnetic—" He stopped and took a breath, clearly too winded to continue. "We should now be able to communicate within ship," he finally said.

Pike eagerly brought out his communicator, which he'd carried for days purely out of hope. "Pike to listening post."

Seconds later, a puzzled Nicola responded. *"Listening post. Glad to hear from—well, anyone!"*

"Small victories." He'd earlier moved Nicola and some equipment up to the ventral observation room near what was now *Enterprise*'s apex, in the hopes of hearing anything. "Is that portable receiver we put up there running? The off-the-grid one?"

Nicola was ahead of him. *"Yes, sir. Looks like it's just downloaded a message from Starfleet."*

Galadjian did not appear surprised. "The tokamak's interference would've blocked the extremely low-frequency subspace channel we occasionally get. Perhaps where we are in the Hellmouth is favorable for receipt from faraway sources."

"How lucky can we get? Nicola, read it."

"It's eyes only for you, sir."

"I don't give a damn. Give me the gist."

"It appears to be a few days old." He paused. *"Starfleet has extended our tour in the Pergamum, Captain."*

Pike closed the communicator and looked at Galadjian. "They're diabolical."

42

Varadah III

"Don't you love it?" Baladon asked, firing his disruptor rifle at the corpses again and again.

"I do," Kormagan said. "Yes, I do."

The humid air was thick with the smell she loved: incinerated Rengru. It was one of the few things she would stow her headgear for; others in her force had the same idea. She envied the troopers with more developed olfactory senses. Activating hers required disintegrating hundreds of Rengru carcasses—which is what they resembled, even alive.

The latest battle at Varadah III had supplied that much fuel, and more. The Varadah Gap was a narrow corridor, nearly a tunnel between expanses of nebular cloud so hostile and thick that neither the Boundless nor the Rengru could pass through. It had been named for the sole star system that lay astride it—a collection of a dozen worlds, most significant in size and laden with resources. Given the important places it led to, it was almost impossible that there would not be permanent war surrounding it. Kormagan had seen her first service in the campaign known as Fourth Varadah; they were on the eleventh now, and seven years in, it was far from over.

The Rengru would probably hold Varadah III again next week—but she had it now. The monsters had known they were outmatched, and had fought like there was no tomorrow. Rengru didn't retreat: why would they, when they multiplied so easily? She had seen it happen even in battle. Rengru got longer as they got older, adding limbs to their anterior sections; when danger struck, they could will themselves to split into two shorter—and somehow more energetic—beings. The bastion at Varadah III was entirely staffed by Rengru youngsters, suggesting they'd already been pushed to the edge. Kormagan and the Thirty-Niners had given them a final shove.

It was another make-good for the other waves, which blamed her gambit at Little Hope weeks earlier for their losing Varadah III in the first place. The engagement had ended with worse results for those who had joined her. Hemmick's carrier, crippled by *Enterprise*, had been destroyed by the Rengru as he tried to escape; his Forty-Fours had been forced to dissolve, his surviving warriors and ships melting into other groups. Quadeo's numbers had been halved. She had argued before the other wavemasters that Kormagan should lose her charter.

But that was before today's victory. "I guess we won't be merged with the Fifty-Twos now," Baladon said, continuing to fire.

"It was never going to happen." Not while Kormagan lived, anyway. The Boundless had no central authority binding her to their decisions; legitimacy sprang from the leader, and victories. As long as she had enough people and matériel to bounce back, she could keep her outfit alive.

Tragically, not everyone in her wave still was. Hemmick had not been the only casualty during the retreat. Kormagan had kept her forces in the game against *Enterprise* and the Rengru longer than anyone—even after the offensive had turned to a defense, and then a recovery operation. Her beloved friend Sperrin had stayed in until the end, directing the other troop modules to rescue would-be boarders while the situation deteriorated. It had been a fatal choice, as *Aloga-One* had been the final casualty.

The Boundless did not venerate the names of the fallen.

Only the living, and what they did, mattered. But Sperrin had been an example to everyone who had survived that day.

Another was Baladon. Ejected from *Enterprise*'s wayward saucer, his flailing form had been the very last pickup by any of the surviving troop modules—and he had reached it almost entirely by chance. She did not believe in good luck charms, but the would-be Lurian warlord was turning into one.

If she didn't count one small matter, of course.

"This almost makes up for losing *Enterprise*," Baladon said as he kicked a corpse.

"Not even close."

"Nothing you can do about it now. That splitting-in-two business—I've never even heard of Starfleet vessels doing that. I'm guessing the saucer spun into a rock. Or maybe a sun. That would have been entertaining to watch."

Guessing was all they could do. Little Hope was solidly Rengru territory now, a dreadful result considering how close she had come to a coup. Kormagan had only realized exactly how close when she reviewed the recordings of Baladon's actions on the saucer section. Spock's betrayal had disappointed her; she'd judged him more honest than that, but she also understood loyalty. In the end, his actions had not been pivotal; Baladon boarding a doomed *Enterprise* would have simply lost her a quality warrior.

The change in her appraisal of the Lurian amused her. The Boundless had unseated a few petty despots that had passed through; they had seldom amounted to much as soldiers. Baladon may have favored brute force more than was sensible, but he was smart, and solidly with the program.

"I admire the extent to which you've adopted our ways," she said as they walked between the pyres. "You've come a long way from—what was it? *Deathstrike*?"

"*Deathstruck*," Baladon said. "You might as well call it what it was."

"You don't miss being in charge of your own kind?"

"I see other Lurians now and again," he said. "It is enough. I detest foolishness. I despise incompetence." He spat at the fire. "The Boundless are more my kind than my species ever was."

To Kormagan, Baladon was the system working as it was supposed to. Rounding a path, the two beheld an opposing example. His head bare and face frozen in an agonized wince, an armored Connolly dragged a dead Rengru by its tail across the graveled ground. Robotically, he threw the mass onto the fire.

His eyes watering, he saw Kormagan. "*Please* let me button up. I can't stand the stench."

"This is the best smell in the universe," Baladon said, sneering. "Say, does anyone know if Rengru are good eating?"

"You'd die," Kormagan said. She looked at Connolly. "Back to work, Orange-Five."

"Why say it?" he responded as he turned to leave. "You're making me do it anyway."

Connolly had not been permitted freedom of motion since his attempted desertion atop *Enterprise*. The Boundless had no need for prisons when their battlesuits could serve as such, getting some valuable labor even as they punished. He had been made to fight at Varadah III, and somehow survived; the cleanup work was solely his.

Kormagan watched him work. "Where did we go wrong with him?"

"You have to understand what Starfleet is," Baladon said. "Back where I come from, the Federation—that's their bunch—is a collection of arrogant know-it-alls. It's a protection scheme: if you join, they'll frighten off your enemies with ships like *Enterprise*."

"They have more?"

"What, more *Enterprise*s? So I've heard. And they have plenty of other ships, though they may not be quite as good."

He chuckled. "Though I don't know how good *Enterprise* really was, considering!"

"Don't fool yourself. It was worth having." It was a bad habit of her fellow wavemasters to denigrate the value of territories they had lost, as if that minimized their failures. It was also an insult to those who had died. "An alliance with such people doesn't sound like a bad arrangement."

"You haven't heard the price," Baladon said. "Would you like to enslave your neighboring planet? You can't. Perhaps annihilate some ugly things passing through? You can't, not if they disapprove. The Boundless wouldn't be able to operate at all as part of the Federation. They would rather judge you than ally with you."

"They'll think again, if the Rengru escape the nebula."

"Maybe you should send Connolly back as your ambassador for common sense." He looked at the human, who had returned with another corpse. "How about that idea?"

Connolly looked at him wearily. "What?"

"Never mind," Kormagan said, motioning for Connolly's battlesuit to stop moving. "Are you ready to go back on the line?"

"I was already on the line today!"

"And you nearly died. You know our systems operate more effectively when the wearer takes command."

The human looked frazzled. "I don't want to be here either way!"

Kormagan shook her head. "I made a bargain with Spock in which I agreed to remove his people from combat. I don't consider myself bound by that now—and I won't honor it in your regard."

In truth, she had kept those former science officers she had control of in place behind the lines; their skills were too valuable to lose. But Connolly didn't need to know that.

Baladon walked up and slapped the human's face genially.

"You might as well give in, my friend. *Enterprise* is destroyed."

Kormagan saw Connolly's eyes narrow at that, but she did not know what that expressed. She came quickly to her point. "You don't want to fight another battle here? Fine. This wave needs reinforcing again if it's to continue. Our probes have reported a convoy of prospecting ships not far from here. I intend to take it. I've just appointed Baladon here as opmaster of *Krall-Three*. He has the experience. Will you join him?"

Connolly listened—and barely moved his head from left to right. "I don't want to help you capture anyone else."

"Then you'll remain here—even after I leave." She pointed to the blazing countryside. "I'll trade you to the Forty-Sixes for some small piece of equipment—or perhaps I'll simply give you to the Fifty-Twos, whom I think I will owe until my dying day. They will keep you here at Varadah III, and other planets, where you can fight all the time. You can be active or passive during it; it's up to them."

Baladon grinned. "Ah, there's no fun in being a puppet, Connolly. Fight for yourself—by fighting for us."

"What do you intend to do?" Kormagan said. She received an empty stare. "Suit yourself." Peremptorily, she turned. "Back to work."

Connolly's servos went into motion again, their noise nearly obscuring two words from him: "*I'll go.*"

Kormagan spun. "What's that?"

"I'll help you," he said, sinking into his armor's shell. "Not much else I can do."

"An intelligent life form!" Baladon slapped Connolly's chest plate. "Stealing ships isn't a bad life. And have no fear. We'll still get to fight now and again."

Connolly groaned. "But what's the point?"

"Why, that *is* the point!" Baladon gushed.

It was not, but Kormagan did not choose to tell them otherwise.

43

U.S.S. Enterprise
Saucer Section
Little Hope

Robinson Crusoe had made two lists.

Pike had never read the novel named for the character, and neither had most of his crew. As days dragged into weeks, however, the 1719 text—part of the complement of multiplanet cultural data preloaded into data slates aboard *Enterprise*—had seen a twenty-third-century revival. Pike had been too busy to catch even five words of Carlotti's first reading to the sickbay, but he had listened to the part of the encore where the literary castaway, having dealt with the immediate emergencies, had finally found time to sit down and really think about his situation.

Crusoe had prepared two lists about his predicament: one marked "evil," the other, "good." The order was both intentional and important, because the marooned mariner had used the second list to rebut every downbeat item in the first. To the "evil" point that he was without any defense against man or beast, Crusoe noted in the "good" that no enemies were around to be seen—and so on, all in an argument prodding him away from gloom and toward industry.

Pike thought about that as he returned to the room that had initially been dubbed the "listening post." That name still applied, given that it offered the best chance at an offworld signal reception—but the late popularity of naval stories had many calling it the "crow's nest," due to its location and ports looking out on the world of their exile. Whatever the name, Pike had found it was the only place where he felt comfortable dwelling on his fate. Anywhere else, he'd be brooding; being near the receiver gave him the feeling he was doing something. And it had ports, even if they didn't look out on much. He had come here before sleep every night, mentally adding to his own ever-growing lists of evils and goods:

We have systems that have suffered catastrophic damage.

But the saucer section is intact, and all crewmembers are alive.

We are on a world we cannot draw upon for any sustenance whatsoever.

But we have fresh air aboard, and stores for a crew twice our size.

We are upside down. Were we weightless, the ship's orientation wouldn't be an issue at all.

But were we under normal gravity, working would be a nightmare. This world has just enough to make it a mixed bag—as much help as nuisance.

We are without our engineering team, guided only by a man who could not pass a basic Starfleet examination.

But he is one of the most gifted minds of the age, and he is trying to learn.

We are far beyond known space, under skies that might be held by either the Boundless or the Rengru.

But we have seen no indication that anyone knows we are here, so perhaps they have moved on.

I have lost Number One.

He stopped there. He knew the correct answer—that he didn't *know* the stardrive section was destroyed, just as earlier in the year he didn't know that his science team might be alive. It was just that, as the weeks went on, the odds that it survived continued to decline.

Una had been his rock. His serene oracle and Mother Confessor, more aware of his faults than he was—and who often cared more about his future than he did. He needed her now. And not just her. He had the greater number aboard the saucer section, but no one he was close with. He had no Boyce, the father figure and drinking buddy. Even he and Yeoman Colt had shared deep conversations once in a while, though the gap in age and station sometimes left a gulf.

And Spock—well, the connection there had always been different, limited to whatever the science officer wanted it to be. But their conversations had always been rewarding.

Nhan was brash, operating at a higher level of intensity than he did; he couldn't feel relaxed around her. The same partially went for Raden, although he attributed that more to the Ktarian's nervous energy. The other new additions—Amin, Nicola—he didn't know much about at all. And of course, there was Galadjian, who had transformed from a famous celebrity to a vocational renovation project. Around all of them, Pike feared showing any doubts whatsoever. He had to be *the captain* for them every minute—even when he had no idea what to do.

Vina. Now there was someone a person could talk to. But that wasn't going to happen either. He was in the real world, in a real place.

A real, awful place.

More vile rain trickled across the port above. By popular acclimation, the crew had named their world of exile Defoe, after *Crusoe*'s author; that had been arrived at only after it was demonstrated the island in the book had no name. Nhan had suggested "The Foe" was a better pronunciation—and it certainly would have been apt. Stepping outside into the thin atmosphere without an environment suit would be fatal; apart from the chemistry, the temperature could freeze flesh in seconds. And while the methane sea below wasn't about to ignite with no oxygen present, neither was there anything of use about it.

Above, through the crow's-nest port, hung a dull gas giant; before it fizzled, it had been Defoe's sun. The now-moon Defoe hadn't yet tidally locked to the now-planet, further suggesting the two worlds' relationship was relatively recent. The pair appeared to orbit a common point with a brown dwarf. Amin had confirmed that it was the same system they'd fled toward in the battle, before the spinning started. Little else in the sky was of interest.

Pike shook his head. They were making so little progress. Power to the interior lights and food slots—that had been the last month's total accomplishment. Galadjian and an impromptu engineering group were still struggling with the thrusters, although it wasn't clear what good that would do. As weak as Defoe's gravity was, it was enough to keep them there. It wasn't clear thrusters would even break the considerable surface tension of Defoe's dense ocean.

All that left was the transceiver Nicola had brought up. Pike couldn't call Starfleet in the way it messaged him; that method was strictly one way, employing powerful arrays. The nebula had allowed for limited local subspace transmissions—but anyone still in the Hellmouth would likely be hostile. He'd tried a weekly transmission to Una on an encrypted Starfleet channel to no avail. Pike doubted his signal left the system.

"I'm sorry," he said to no one. He looked back down the nearby ladder well leading to the rest of the starship. "I don't think we're going to be able to do this anymore." He was going to have to take a chance—one he wasn't going to consult anyone about.

He adjusted the transceiver. The Boundless used a variety of subspace and electromagnetic-spectrum wavelengths for their probes, likely chosen for their performance in spite of the region's conditions. Nothing had been detected on any of these channels since the crash landing; he gambled that meant that the Boundless had left. If Number One lived, maybe she'd be monitoring them, waiting for her chance to return. Perhaps she was already in the Hellmouth, searching, just needing a faint signal to draw her near. He called up the Boundless channel he figured would be least likely used—a basic radio band—and thought of what to say.

His hand hovered over the controls. His attempt would put at risk one of the certain items on his "good" list: a lack of harassment by the Boundless and Rengru. The transceiver was weak, but what if the Boundless picked up the signal? And what of the Rengru? If they warred with the Boundless, wouldn't they monitor their frequencies too? Did they even do that?

The hell with it. Nobody can hear this thing anyway.

"*Enterprise* to *Enterprise*," Pike said, almost whispering like a criminal. "Come in, Commander Una."

For a minute, static.

"This is Pike, Number One. Do you read?"

Another minute. Nothing.

This is crazy. What had he just risked? He decided to cut off the unit and pray nobody had heard.

His fingers had barely reached the panel when he heard the words. *"I read you, Captain. This is Lieutenant Spock."*

44

Skon's World

To a child raised on Vulcan, snow was theoretical. And a bit aspirational.

It was a broiling night when the young Spock had first asked about a small white planet in the sky. The orb's high albedo, his adopted sister had told him, was explained by water trapped in the frozen state. Some existed as ice, a material familiar to him from his student visits to laboratories—but some as crystals that descended from the air itself, each frozen unit structured in its own unique configuration. After falling, large amounts tended to collect on the surface, sometimes presenting as powder, other times clumping into coherent masses easily shapable by the hand. For one growing up on a planet that had sandfire storms, the whole concept sounded like something out of a fantasy.

When Spock finally visited Vulcan's neighbor, he had already lost a good deal of the wonder that snow had instilled in him at that younger age. He had visited many frozen locales since—including, of course, the polar region of Susquatane. At every such turn, other pressing duties left little time to appreciate the aesthetics. Frozen water was frozen water, whatever its structure.

That had changed. Many weeks into his exile on a tiny ice world, Spock had yet to lose interest in snow. It had a way of altering terrain overnight—not the underlying topography, but the routes he had to take to explore the world. There weren't many other surprises; his armor systems had already mapped much of the surface during his long descent from space, finding little of interest beyond an ever-shifting landscape. Nothing existed above the ground except a thin, breathable layer of air that he could survive in for maybe a few hours before succumbing to hypoxia and death.

That left the snow, in all its various forms. His bodily needs tended to by his battlesuit, his mind was free to contemplate these simplest of surroundings—while occasionally thinking about the hallucination that had caused him to select this world over others. Surely, on a world of white, something so red would stand out—if it existed at all.

There had been one more activity open to him: checking his receiver for messages. It had always been a futile exercise. He had no intention of calling out to the Boundless for help, and certainly not the Rengru—but from the start, it appeared that neither of them had remained in the immediate region. He doubted his reception stretched much beyond the gas giant his world was orbiting.

So hearing Christopher Pike's voice had been both unexpected and welcome—more than enough to call him away from his late interest in snow hydrology.

"I still can't believe it," Pike said. *"Neither can anybody down here."* He laughed. *"Well, I guess we're 'up there' from your vantage point."*

"Not necessarily, Captain." Spock, always walking, looked up to the sky, always clear. "As we both orbit the same body, you are nearer its gravitational center than I am. So in that sense, I am the one above."

"It's definitely you, *all right!"*

That had apparently been in doubt early in their conversations. Pike had later spoken of worries that there might be some sort of Boundless trap at work. That Spock was a hostage, or that his voice was being simulated in order to learn the saucer section's location. But their mutual encounter on the hull of *Enterprise* during the battle, now clarified, was evidence enough for Pike that Spock was free.

"I'm sorry for shooting at you. You got flung off like a raindrop from a flying disc."

"No further apologies, Captain. You made no mistake."

Pike had already apologized for Susquatane, and much more. In an earlier conversation, Spock had explained some of his experiences with the Boundless, and what he knew of the disposition of the other science officers. He had less information about the Rengru, but shared what he knew. Every additional fact had prompted more expressions of regret from the captain. Spock thought recriminations were pointless—and worse, a waste of time that could be spent on other things. His ability to communicate with Pike depended on the facing and proximity of their two moons; there was a limited window available to them.

"You're sure you can't get back to orbit again?"

"Correct. I exhausted my fuel traveling to this world and decelerating to its surface."

"At least you've got a surface over there."

"There were nearer options available." He paused. "I cannot say why I chose this place." Rather, he did not want to say. "I have some months' reserves here before my battlesuit's resources give out. Boundless armor is designed in the expectation of prolonged military operations, but there are limits."

"And I thought we were deprived here. You're not even on solid food. I can't imagine. I'm sorry."

Spock forestalled another stream of apologies with a regret of his own. "I attempted to warn you not to enter this area when the wavemaster—my superior—asked me to come up with a name for the region that would be enticing. I suppose I failed in that."

"No, it worked. It was ingenious. We just didn't do what you wanted. So that's on us again!" Pike laughed. *"And I caught that the year next to the name was also a Talos reference."*

"That was coincidental, but it did give me the idea for the name."

"We decided to call the place the Hellmouth instead."

"Little Hope is the true Boundless term."

"Boy, that fits. I can see them wanting to change that. We'll go with that from now on, just to spite them."

"A common terminology is always superior."

"We call our little moon Defoe." Pike started to spell it.

"I am familiar with the name and the author's work. I see the association."

"What should we call your place? Crusoe? Friday?"

"I had already named it, Captain—coincidentally, in honor of an author: Skon, my forefather."

"That's what you call a grandfather, right?"

"Father of Sarek."

"Skon it is."

"I have chosen the construction 'Skon's World' to differentiate it from the much different planet in the Beta Quadrant. There are already two Delta Vegas, as you know."

"That's you, always thinking ahead."

Spock had been thinking quite a lot since their first contact. Pike had given him plenty of information about the saucer section's dilemma to contemplate during his walks, and he'd found one solution already.

"I have a way to address Nurse Carlotti's needs. Connolly's stowed research gear included a portable gravity-field generator for use aboard ship." Spock named the exact saucer-section storage chamber it was in. "While it was intended only to test the reactions of small samples to gravity, it is of sufficient power to activate a single panel of gravity deck plating. Replacement plating, likewise, should be in storage."

"We'll rip some off the ceiling, if we have to." Pike seemed delighted with the idea. *"We had no idea Connolly had that aboard. Some of the manifests are just on the main computer, and that still isn't up."*

Spock had been disappointed but not surprised to learn of *Enterprise*'s predicament. He understood what had happened. "I concur with Doctor Galadjian's theories. The ship's emergence from warp, shields running, into a torpedo detonation produced an inversion back to the projecting source. His *tsakat* approach may have amplified the effect, but I expect catastrophic results to *Enterprise*'s electrical and magnetic systems would have occurred regardless."

"No idea whether it'll help him to hear that, but it's good to know."

"The resultant damage to your circuitry can only be repaired by hand. With a full engineering crew and proper parts, your stay would still be many weeks. Without . . ." He did not finish the statement.

"The ship's a Frankenstein's monster, Spock. Galadjian and the others are pulling modules and cabling from the nonessential systems that work and plugging them into essential ones that don't. Doctor Good News is finding out a lot about elbow grease."

Spock figured that was some kind of Earthly idiom.

After a pause, Pike asked, *"About Galadjian. Did you know about his work performance issues last year?"*

Spock had not thought of the ship's engineer in months. "Please clarify."

"I don't think he'd ever held a hand tool before that didn't have a cube root function."

"I was . . . aware of some deficiencies. We served in different departments, so it was not my place to comment."

"You and Una covered for him. It would have helped to know."

"It was not an attempt to deceive. I did not wish to see

the ship's performance suffer." Spock went silent for a few moments before adding, "And I was reluctant to dishonor one whose mind was so accomplished."

"Should he have been here in the first place?" Pike asked. When Spock hesitated, the captain added, *"This conversation is private. I'd like your opinion—I've missed having it."*

"The dichotomization of science into pure and applied strains happens in every culture—and while conflict between them is unnecessary, it often occurs. Starfleet made *Enterprise* to be the greatest field laboratory of all. Certainly we must find a way to make a place for a mind as great as his."

"You're saying we may simply need to add more remedial training to the induction process."

"With the Boundless, I encountered many situations that my battlesuit was perfectly capable of responding to—if only I had fully understood how to work it. There may be a need in war to act without preparation. The ideal for science should be otherwise."

"Hopefully we can get back to being a scientific organization again," Pike said. *"Well, Galadjian's getting a workout now—but I don't think this was what he had in mind."*

Spock looked to the sky. "Defoe is about to set."

"Until next time then. I want to talk more about the Boundless."

"I will have the time," Spock said. "I have isolated and cataloged more than eight hundred different types of snow. Perhaps someone can make use of this data."

"You can publish it yourself. We're going to get this ship fixed, Spock—and then we're coming to get you. I swear."

Spock had heard Pike say that almost as much as he had heard him apologize. "I will await your next hail. Spock out."

45

U.S.S. Enterprise
Stardrive Section
Cloud Complex Zedra

"Shields up!"

Mann looked over at the first officer. "Say again?"

"Reflex," Una said, eyes focused on the small screens before her and the wave of Rengru fighters approaching. "Prepare to engage."

In the weeks since *Enterprise*'s separation, the engineers of the stardrive section had made progress on nearly every system but one—the shields, where all the problems had begun. That fact had required Una to look for "cool zones," where the nebular radiation was less intense. She'd found several patches in a massive cloud complex the Boundless probes called Zedra. The Rengru had caught on to her moves. The appearance of a single scout in their scopes invariably led to the arrival, hours later, of a wave of fighters, occasionally supported by one of the larger Rengru mother ships.

That didn't constitute a crisis, so long as the stardrive section could get underway quickly—but enough systems were still under repair that Una occasionally had to fight it out. While she would have preferred not to engage at all, the shield problem meant that her crew had an easier time on offense than defense. The phaser banks mounted above the hangar deck and flanking the underside ran on power from rechargeable batteries, and had suffered the least damage. Photon torpedoes were a limited resource, but had been useful at keeping the mother ships far away.

And Una had other tricks up her sleeve—but she guarded them jealously. The Rengru seemed to learn from every encounter.

"It's like encounter six," Mann said. Nhan's second, her skills as a tactician had been constantly needed. "We have twelve—no, eighteen fighters inbound. No mother ship."

"Mixed blessings. Save the torpedoes. Fire phasers at will." She toggled her comm system. "Colt team, go."

"On our way, Commander."

Flashes from the stardrive section's weapons lanced ahead on Una's screen, annihilating one Rengru fighter after another. But the remainder continued, undaunted.

"They're inside effective phaser range," Mann said, sitting back and shrugging. This was routine now; there was nothing more she could do. "Seems like this is a gap in the defenses, once shields are out—or if you don't have any to begin with."

"More for the after-action report to Starfleet. They're always designing something." Seeing the Rengru closing with the ship, she touched the comm key again. "We're going to have guests for lunch, Jallow. How's it going?"

The Tellarite robotics expert rushed in behind her. "I'm here, I'm here!" he said, breathless. "DOT-Sixes are ready to deploy."

"Excellent." She rose from her chair. "Put them out as needed. We don't have a lot to spare."

Looking up, she waited to hear the first thumps of Rengru landing on the hull. All things considered, Una felt it was better that she was the one that was here. Pike had always hated the little control room with its confinement and limited view outside the ship, likening it to what he called "submarine warfare." It didn't bother Una as much. It forced her to imagine the locations of her opponents, a chess match for her orderly mind to play out.

"There they go," Mann said, hearing the *thunk-thunk* of arriving Rengru. The next steps were always the same. Like cats clawing cardboard, their pincers would tear at the hull, trying to cause damage once they had purchase. They weren't eating the ship, though that had been the easy reference to draw upon. "The giant space termites are back at it," Mann added.

"Three are after nonessential areas," Jallow said. "One on the nacelles. Six near the dorsal phaser banks." His screen switched to a sensor view looking aft from the underside of the deflector dish mount. A small cluster of Rengru fighters clung to the hull with some limbs, tearing at it with others.

"I could fire and try to hit some—or shake them off," Mann said.

"No, they've positioned just nearby," Una said. "They're wising up, looking for ways to disable the banks." This might be preparatory to another attack, she thought. "DOT-Sixes to the phaser banks. Just a few."

"Aye."

The DOT-6 drones had been placed aboard *Enterprise* for "light housecleaning": damage from impacts made by nebular material that made it past the shields needed to be repaired without exposing anyone to radiation. The drones had survived the *Tsakat* Incident, but their external release ports had been another casualty of the catastrophic systems failure.

Since repaired, the ports secreted several small drones onto the hull. The little crawlers approached the areas just damaged by the larger Rengru and went to work, repairing the ship's flesh. The Rengru stopped what they were doing. Two fired their onboard disruptors at the newcomers; the others charged, tearing *Enterprise*'s robotic elves to metallic shreds.

"Our bugs against their bugs never works," Mann said.

"When they design the DOT-Sevens, maybe they should give them a phaser or two."

Jallow's enormous nose crinkled. "You really want *more* things crawling around and shooting?"

"We're just delaying them," Una said. With Jallow at her control station, she resorted to her communicator. "How are we doing, *Copernicus*?"

"Take a look," Colt responded. Una watched the feed from the ship's external sensors. A shadow crossed low over the hull—and then a shuttlecraft swept across, its angled nose chopping the Rengru from the surface like so many weeds.

Una nodded with satisfaction. "Galadjian has his machete, we have ours." The Rengru, amputated from the hull, tumbled wildly in space, trying to regain their bearings. "When she's clear, Lieutenant, fire away."

Mann did so—one short burst that annihilated everything. "Looks like we got them in time."

"Patching it up," Jallow said, dispatching more DOT-6s to the location.

*"*Enterprise *looks headless,"* Colt reported, bringing *Copernicus* around. *"It's kind of scary."*

"Hopefully it'll frighten off the Rengru," Una replied.

"I don't know," Mann said. "Those uglies out there might prefer it this way. They certainly can't leave it alone."

More precision flying from Colt and *Copernicus* shaved off three more Rengru. These her team took care of, using the phaser in the weapons pod that Una's engineers had improvised to give the shuttle a limited offensive capability.

Una nodded with satisfaction. She'd seen enough of the hull-top warfare with the Boundless that she didn't want to put any personnel outside toting phasers. The fact that the shuttles, too, had suffered maladies from the collapse of the *tsakat* had underscored that the pulse had impacted everything. But she had a ship full of engineers to bring to bear, and all but one of the shuttles now functioned. Twice before, Una had used them to repel the Rengru—and so far, none of the creatures had survived to report back that the ship's shuttles existed.

If they reported back at all, Una thought. *How did the things communicate?* Did *they*?

She needed to take a chance, try something different. She'd known that for a long time, but the need was becoming more urgent. Every attack had driven them farther and farther away from the region where *Enterprise* had split up. The Rengru never responded to hails; she'd stopped trying. She understood nothing of her enemy.

An idea struck her. She raised the communicator. "Yeoman, have you sighted the lone Rengru on the starboard nacelle?"

"Yeah. It's kind of pawing, trying to get purchase. We're discussing what to do. We don't want to do the ice-scraper trick there."

"I have *Copernicus*'s sensor view," Mann said.

Una leaned over and studied it. "Can you target just the toughest part of the Rengru, the hump on its back? Extremely low power, so as not to impact the nacelle."

"Give us a second."

It took ten. A blast from *Copernicus* struck the final Rengru squarely as Una had directed. The creature let go of *Enterprise*—and seemed to come apart. The structure housing the creature's rocket and disruptor emplacement snapped off, tumbling away. The writhing Rengru that remained seemed naked, a turtle out of its shell.

"Nice and surgical. Doctor Boyce would be proud."

"Coming around to finish the job."

"Negative," Una said. She pointed to Jallow. "A life-sign status check, please."

The engineer complied. "Same as usual—maybe dropping a little. We already knew they could survive the void."

Mann looked fraught. "Are we really going to leave it out there?"

"No," Una replied. "I'm going to take a page out of the Boundless's book."

"What page would that be? It looked to me like they lost that dustup back at the Hellmouth."

"Not that page. A different one." She spoke into her communicator. "Una to Lieutenant Pitcairn."

"Pitcairn." He'd been keeping station in the cargo transporter room, Una knew.

"I want to initiate a site-to-site transport."

She thought she heard him chortle. *"Excuse me, Commander. Did you say a site-to-site transport?"*

"I did." The technique, relatively new to the Starfleet menu, was extremely resource intensive, requiring a transporter to bring in a pattern and hold it in stasis while it prepared to send it somewhere else. "Is there a problem?"

"Not in theory, but we haven't used the transporter at all yet. Has something happened to Copernicus*?"*

"No. I want this transport to go to the brig." She thought for a moment. "And let's have security officers waiting when it gets there."

46

U.S.S. Enterprise
Saucer Section
Defoe

"This is a lot sooner than I expected to feel this weight," Carlotti said, a hand to her abdomen as she sat.

"These are the inconveniences involved in becoming part of a physics equation," Galadjian said.

Pike saw both of them smile—an expression seldom seen before word of Spock's survival spread. His science officer's suggestion had worked out perfectly. A square of gravity plating two meters across had been placed on the surface of the nurses' station; it was wide enough to hold a cot or a chair and desk, whichever she needed to use. "You ought to be able to get at least half the day in Earth gravity," Pike said.

"And I felt cooped up before," Carlotti said. "Maybe I'd better ease into it."

Galadjian passed her a remote control. "This may be used to adjust the intensity of the gravity field for comfort."

She tried it. "Oh, that helps. I'll ease my way up to normal gradually. Thank you, Doctor."

"My pleasure."

"And thank you, Captain."

Pike nodded and stepped out, followed by Galadjian. It was the end of a long workday for both of them, but Pike felt revived. They weren't far down the corridor when the engineer said the very thing the captain had on his mind. "In all this, it is satisfying to help one person."

"Yeah, no doubt." He looked at the older man. "I was a little afraid the fact the idea came from Spock would have—I don't know, put you back a little." Even the instructions Galadjian had used had been of Spock's design.

But Galadjian seemed unruffled. "The ideas cannot all flow from me, Captain. That was my mistake. Collaboration in the institute always meant that I directed, while the assistants tested. The discoveries were mine, but not always the difficult work."

"I'm sure you'd already paid those dues in your field."

"Yes, certainly." He looked to the tool kit in his hands. "But I have grown complacent. Between putting variables on a screen, and observing the result, many steps exist—stages I have often missed. To be present at every moment from concept to completion is refreshing."

Pike spied an upside-down door. "You want to stop here a moment?"

Galadjian squinted at the upside-down name beside the chocked-open door. "Doctor Boyce's office?"

"Yeah, I do some of my best thinking here." Pike stepped inside and reached up to a cabinet. Opening it, he gently removed a large medical kit.

"You are ailing?"

"Not as much as I would be if these broke," Pike said, opening the bag on the floor. He drew out a bottle and glasses. "Looks like Phil was in a cognac mood before he left."

"Then we will drink in his name."

Seated against the walls in a corner, they poured and toasted Boyce, and the missing. For the refill, the toast was to success. "First of a series," Pike said.

As they drank, they fell silent for several moments. Then Galadjian looked past his glass at Pike. "Do you know why I asked to join Starfleet, Captain?"

"I was thinking it had been on—well, a lark."

Galadjian's infectious smile returned. "This would be the worst whim of all time, would it not? To end in such a place?"

Pike laughed.

"I am an old man, Christopher. But when I was young, I grew up in Armenia. Under all the governments it ever had, the national symbol was a mountain. *Ararat.*"

Pike knew of it. "Where Noah parked his boat."

"Ah, you know the story. I sometimes feel we are in an ark now."

"And you're the only engineer who made it up the gangplank."

Galadjian looked down, self-effacing. "Two would have been of more help." He shook his head. "No, the importance of this is all the time Ararat was on Armenia's coat of arms, the mountain was in another country. It's a dynastic memory, from a time when the map of the world was different. It was aspirational," he added. "A dream."

"They wanted it back. Or to go back."

"Consider it. For hundreds of years, encoded in their symbols was an ancient desire to be elsewhere." Galadjian looked at the far wall. "I think that is what happened to me. All those thousands of equations, all those math problems were my own personal seal—and yet they symbolized real activity happening in another place. Nobody *needs* a secondary field projection for a warp coil, except somebody going somewhere. I think, perhaps, I really *did* want to be in the experiment after all."

"To Doctor O," Pike said, gesturing with his glass.

"I just should not have been in charge," Galadjian added. "I see that."

"Don't be so sure. There are many different kinds of vessels in Starfleet. On some research ships, you'd fit the bill perfectly."

Galadjian raised his glass. "Ah, but I wanted the best. *Enterprise* is the crown jewel."

"Halved and sitting upside-down in a poison sandwich." Pike downed his drink and mused for a few moments. "You know, your story made me think about what Spock told me about the Boundless."

"The force that captured him."

"Yeah. Thing is, they're not boundless. They're tied to something, longing for it. Spock didn't know what it was—but why would they still be here?"

"They, too, have an Ararat," Galadjian said. "Find it. The answer is there."

Pike didn't have any idea when or if he would have the chance to find out. Feeling the drink, he considered heading back to his quarters. Instead, a communicator beep told him what his next project would be. *"Nhan to Captain Pike."*

"Yeah, Nhan."

"We haven't been able to find you."

Pike studied his glass. "I am in an important meeting with the chief engineer. We are discussing the history of the Caucasus as it relates to interstellar menaces."

"Huh." A pause. *"Well, we're looking for him too. I was just talking with Spock. Lieutenant Raden has figured out a way to right the ship."*

Pike set the cup down. "You did say you wanted ideas from the crew, Avedis."

"By all means, let's hear them. I am tired of looking up at the toilets."

—

Pike sat in the crow's nest an hour later, fully sobered by what he'd heard. "You really think it will work?"

"I lack the computational resources in this battlesuit to

mount any more than a thought experiment," Spock replied from Skon's World. *"But the principle is sound."*

"That's what Raden said you'd say."

"We know the impulse drive remains down. We know thrusters are insufficient for the saucer to leave Defoe. We question whether firing the dorsal thrusters, currently under the liquid surface, can alone break the surface tension."

"Right. It hasn't been worth shaking everyone up again." Pike squinted at his notes from the meeting. "You're saying we fire *only* the dorsal thrusters on the front half of the saucer—"

"While firing only *the ventral thrusters on the rear half of the saucer, forcing the disc down into the ocean."*

"You want to flip it like a bar of soap." Pike still blanched at the thought of firing the jets currently facing the sky to force any part of the saucer farther under the surface. "You're sure we'll come back up again?"

"The density of methane relative to Enterprise *is a known variable,"* Spock said. *"The danger would be to those inside, who would, even under less gravity, be moved violently."*

"We already have scaffolds all over the place to work with the terminals that are operational. I guess we can invent some ways to keep people from being thrown about." He shook his head. "We just got Nurse Carlotti's office set up. We'll want to stow the setup we've made for her and bring it out again after—presuming—we succeed."

"My understanding is that the thrusters are not fully operational."

"I've delayed getting people out on EVA to inspect the units on top until we had a need. This is it. Good idea, Spock."

"Praise belongs to the sickbay patient whose idea Commander Nhan conveyed to me. I merely consulted. Mister Raden is strongly motivated."

"He'd love to salvage even one part of the ship. But I'm also certain he's anxious to get away from here. Everyone is.

The fact the war still seems to be going on back home only makes it worse," Pike said. "I know you'd thought it better that we remain to do science—but this isn't what you had in mind."

"Clearly not," Spock said. *"Opinions must evolve with the facts. What is the logic in staying away if there is nothing to come back to?"*

Pike looked at the chronometer. The conversation window was about to close again—this time for longer, as Defoe and Skon's World did their dance. "How are you faring?"

"I walked a glacial cirque today. The movement of nitrogen and water ices on this world suggests significant internal heat, either generated by radioactive decay or interactions with bodies such as yours."

"Enjoy yourself, I guess." Pike snapped his fingers. "Oh, yeah—a couple of things. We checked out that term you said the Boundless were using."

"K'davu."

"Right. It's not a Klingon word—and it doesn't turn up in any other language. But I guess it could be a personal name. You're sure of the spelling?"

"I am. It includes each of the first five characters of the Boundless alphabet, anagrammed. That is highly improbable, and suggests either that it predates the language, or that it is a later and purposeful neologism."

"The giant space army likes wordplay?"

"I cannot say, but thinking about it inspired my similar tactic with the probe."

"Then it was worth it," Pike said. "I almost forgot. Speaking of words, I'm sending something up on the data feed before we're out. *Robinson Crusoe.*"

"Appropriate. I do have the time."

"You know, I had never read it," Pike said. "Now, *there* was a guy who couldn't take a hint. He's nearly wrecked just getting from one part of England to another right at the start, and is shipwrecked again and enslaved long before he ever becomes a castaway."

"If our lives are any indication, Captain, travel has become no safer."

47

U.S.S. Enterprise
Stardrive Section
Cloud Complex Zedra

"What the—?"

Reading from a data slate, Una did not look up. "Is there a problem, Doctor?"

"When you said you had a patient for me to see," Boyce said, "this isn't what I thought you had in mind." The white-haired doctor stepped around the four guards armed with phasers to see the alien stalking around inside the stardrive section's brig. "It's positively grotesque!"

"It's a Rengru," Colt said, nonchalantly studying a tricorder.

"The things attacking us?" Reluctant to get too close to the force field, Boyce peered at the creature. Two and a half meters long, the ivory-white alien tromped about on dozens of multiple-jointed appendages. Before each wall, it stopped and curled its frame, slinking halfway up the bulkhead and probing with the tiny pincers at the end of its limbs. "It looks different from the things outside," Boyce said. "Slimmer."

Una nodded. "The whole flight apparatus appears to be artificial, riding piggyback," she said. "We beamed those portions into an engineering lab."

"And beamed this fellow here, I suppose." Boyce edged closer. The Rengru did not respond to his movements. Instead, it curled back down onto the deck and went exploring underneath the cell's sleep platform. "How did I not know about this?"

"I decided it was best to keep its presence aboard need to know," Una said, noting where the Rengru had gone. "The crew have enough worries."

Boyce's lower lip went sideways. "Yeah, this wouldn't win you many fans."

"I'm not trying to win a popularity contest."

In fact, matters of morale had entered Una's thinking. Too much time had passed since the ship separation, with too many deprived of their regular quarters and personal effects. It had worn on everyone. "I suppose we should feel fortunate that a brig was placed in this section," she said. "I'm not sure where we would have put the Rengru otherwise."

"Well, it's not rooming with me."

"Funny thing," Colt said, gesturing to the handful of items sitting about in the cell. "We were billeting people in the brig until about five minutes before it arrived."

"I think I'd move out too," Boyce said.

"We had to work in a hurry, or we'd have cleared the room entirely," she said, noting the clothing articles the Rengru was curiously clawing. "I don't think Ensign Zepton is going to want his laundry back."

Boyce watched the Rengru warily. "Is that all it's been doing?"

Una glanced at the creature. "If you're looking for it to snarl and crash into the force field, don't. It hasn't reacted to us at all. It was dying when we brought it aboard—and while it's improved since, I don't think it's at a hundred percent."

"How do you know what one hundred percent even looks like for—for one of *these*?"

"That's why you're here," Una said, approaching the doctor. She passed him the slate with her observations. "I want to know anything about it you can tell me."

Boyce gawked. "I'm not an exobiologist."

"We have seventy-four people aboard, Doctor. Name me anyone who's closer to being one, and I'll have them brought here."

Boyce scratched his head and grumbled. "I knew I got stranded on the wrong section."

"That's just because you left your cognac over there," Colt piped in.

It had suited them, Una noted, to speak and act as though the saucer section still existed. At least Boyce understood the circumstances well enough that he was no longer hounding her to search for Pike. She still intended to do that, of course—if the Rengru would ever let her.

Sorting through the images on the slate, Boyce asked, "How were these scans taken? The force field would block all but visible light."

"Sam Yamata recorded the transport pattern and dumped it into a file," Colt said. "Easier than an X-ray."

"Ingenious," Boyce said. After a few minutes of study, he looked up. "Well, I can tell you this: it doesn't eat people."

Colt looked to Una. "That's refreshing."

"I mean I can't find any trace of a digestive system at all." He stepped to Una's side and pointed at the image displayed on the slate. "Look at these complexes here and here. That looks like a thylakoid membrane—but what it's attached to is completely different."

"Photosynthesis?"

"Or something like it."

Una pursed her lips. "What if they harvest energies from the nebula itself?"

Boyce raised an eyebrow. "How would that work?"

"I'm not sure exactly. But there's obviously background radiation here of a kind that they flourish on." She stepped closer to the force field. "When we were parked in a cool zone earlier, it seemed downright sleepy. Now that we're moving through a cloud complex, it's livened up some."

Boyce frowned. Una knew he wasn't one for following lines of conjecture overly far. "Let's say you're right," the doctor said. "That whatever it needs is out there, and neither the hull nor a force field can stop it. We can use a process of elimination on the sensor data to find out what it does like."

"That would tell us how to keep it alive, certainly."

"But to what purpose? There are no sensory organs that I can see on this thing at all—except maybe touch, with all of those extrusions on each appendage. I assume you're looking to communicate with the thing."

Colt looked over at the Rengru. "We've tried talking to it—but I'm not sure it hears, much less understands."

Una couldn't accept that beings that had achieved spaceflight had no way of communicating. *Might as well have another go*, she thought, approaching the cell.

"My name is Una," she said. "Can you hear me? Do you see that I am trying to communicate?"

The Rengru wandered about, dragging Ensign Zepton's pants.

"You attacked us," Una continued. "Can you tell us why?"

Nothing.

"This is insanity," Boyce said. "You're not getting any change in behavior at all."

"There's already been at least *one*, Doctor." Una turned away from the cell. "When we grabbed it, it was actively trying to destroy the ship. Now, it's inside—and doing nothing."

"Maybe it doesn't know where it is," Colt said. "If it's never been transported anywhere before."

"Maybe."

Staring blankly at the far wall, Una tried to bring her mind to a restful state. Illyrians didn't sigh and didn't get frustrated. They focused and solved problems. She was not born one of them, but she had tried to emulate them. There were countless tiny details to consider in any crisis; each one had to be evaluated, prioritized, and filed away so as not to interfere with the others, clouding the thinker's path. After over a year in the Pergamum, her mind was becoming more like the nebula: strewn with debris, the debris of too many considerations. It was getting more and more difficult not to feel overwhelmed.

That was when Boyce interrupted her thoughts with a surprising bit of nonsense. A detail she would never have noticed—and, as it happened, one that would make all the difference.

48

U.S.S. Enterprise
Stardrive Section
Cloud Complex Zedra

"Commander," Boyce said, "the baby has a banana."

"What?" Startled, Una turned to see the Rengru back in the middle of the cell, contemplating the yellow fruit in its grasp. "Oh, I didn't know that was in there."

"Ensign Zepton likes his bananas," Colt said. "Probably had it in stasis all year, and brought it out to celebrate getting the warp drive working." She shook her head. "He won't like this."

Una stared at the creature. "Is it me, or is there something off about that?"

"Well, that's not how you eat a banana," Boyce said. "Those pincers are just poking holes in it. He's going to make a mess."

"No," Una said, squinting. "Computer, reduce room lighting eighty percent."

When the room dimmed, the others saw what she had seen. "Are—are the spots on the banana *glowing*?" Colt asked.

Boyce chuckled. "I guess they are. We were just speaking of photosynthesis, weren't we? Banana spots come from the degradation of chlorophyll. They're harmless—but they also fluoresce in ultraviolet light."

"Yeah," Colt said, "but where is ultraviolet light coming from?"

Una stared. Then insight struck. "The Rengru isn't just touching with its appendages. It's *seeing*." She took back the slate from Boyce and found the proper image from the earlier transporter scan. "The 'palms' of its 'hands'—each pod breaking down into smaller limbs—they're bioluminescent. We can't see the light it's emitting because we're human."

Colt held up her tricorder. "And this device can't see it because of the force field."

"But things fluoresce in the visible spectrum," Boyce said, "which means we can see the spots." He looked to Una. "Does this mean the Rengru can't see us?"

"Very possibly." Una restored the room lighting. "Our audio's piped into the cell beyond the force field so we can converse with prisoners. The fact that it's never responded could mean that it can't hear—but it also just might not know who's talking. And since it can't see us out here, we wouldn't be able to run any of the first-contact visual language protocols we've got." She looked to the guards. "Can we take the UV blocker out of the force field?"

"I don't know," one replied. "I don't think so."

"We've got a ship full of engineers," Boyce said. "Surely somebody can come up with something."

"Probably not without deactivating the force field," Colt replied. "I guess we could beam it someplace else and then back."

This is too much, Una thought. *We've been running for months. We have to take a chance sometime.*

In a firm voice, she said, "I'd like everyone to step back to the doorway."

Boyce gawked. "*What?*"

Colt stared at her, stupefied. "You're not suggesting letting it *out*?"

Even the guard who had spoken earlier shook his head. "Commander, that's not a good idea."

Una put up her hand. "I know what I'm doing. If I'm right, the Rengru has no context within which it can place us."

"The feeling's mutual," Boyce said.

"*Enterprise* was its target—and those Boundless warriors. I don't look like either one. There's a chance if it gets a good look at me, I'll be no more interesting than Ensign Zepton's pants."

"He dragged those across the deck!"

Una fastened a phaser to her belt. "Philip, we're never going to be able to search for the captain and the others—much less get home—unless we get past the Rengru. Not this one, but the hordes out there. They haven't given us any peace. Somebody has to take a chance. It's on me."

Boyce prepared to object—and then the wind went out of him. "Fine. But get Pitcairn on standby, ready to beam that thing back into space."

"Done," she said, picking up another device. "I'll let it have a look at me—and then run it through the universal translator's sequences. All the batteries—audio, visual, sensory. Maybe there's something it responds to."

Rank having won out, Colt and the guards retreated, with Boyce right behind them. Una stood several meters back from the Rengru. She brought her mind to rest and deactivated the force screen.

The Rengru immediately noticed—and noticed her. For several moments, it remained in position, facelessly facing her.

"My name is Una," she said, holding the translator in one hand, with her left near to her phaser. "I am a commander of the *U.S.S. Enterprise* of the United Federation of Planets."

Several of the Rengru's limbs lifted from the deck and pointed in her direction, their pincers splayed.

From the doorway behind the guards, Colt reported what her tricorder was seeing. "I can't believe this, but it just started emitting low-power ultraviolet laser beams at you. From its *hands.*"

"Echolocation. Lidar—radar with lasers. It's harmless." Una brought her free hand away from her phaser and raised it to the air. "I am not your enemy. Do you understand me?"

If the Rengru had coiled its body in an attempt to spring, she did not see it. She only saw it launch itself across the space between them, and the phaser blasts from the doorway ripping through the air. The universal translator clattered away as she lost her footing, knocked backward by a being that was heavier and more energetic than she had imagined.

"Tell them to beam it out!" she heard Boyce shout.

"Don't shoot!" Colt yelled. "You'll hit her!"

The Rengru writhed with her on the deck, trying to envelop her with its dozens of limbs. The whole thing was a hand, she realized, with hands at every fingertip. It existed to grasp and to hold—even as the guards and others tried to pry it off her.

"What the hell is keeping Pitcairn?"

"I can't get a lock!" a voice said—

—then she felt it. A sharp lance at the back of her neck, near the base of her skull. She felt her hair grow wet with blood.

"*No!*" Colt screamed.

The world swam—and then her whole body sagged against the frame of the Rengru. It had become a second spine, its limbs wrapped around her midsection and growing tighter by the second.

"She's losing consciousness," she could hear Boyce say.

Colt, again. "We've got to get this thing off her!"

"It's a dead weight!"

Una didn't recognize the speaker. She didn't recognize anything anymore. She felt intoxicated, dizzy, drained—a dozen emotions at once, all connected to fatigue in one way or another. She only wanted to sleep—and she knew she would have her way, perhaps forever.

But not before her eyes opened long enough for her to speak a single word to her companions:

"Wait."

49

Combat Module Carrier 539-Aloga
Varadah System

I guess I'm in trouble again.

Connolly felt as if he'd been called into the commandant's office at the Academy. Kormagan sat high on a platform surrounded by the nearer parts of the Pergamum nebula, or at least that was how the background appeared in Connolly's interface. He had heard from Baladon of the existence of such a staging area aboard the lead carrier, but he had never been inside. He had no idea what he'd done wrong, but life had lost its ability to surprise him.

"Enter, Bluesub." Kormagan turned her chair. "Would you like to hear a little of what you've done?"

Not really, Connolly thought. But he stared upward and saw a familiar sight.

"*The Dandy*, a ship of escapees from a penal facility called Thionoga," Kormagan said. The images shifted to display moments from the Boundless boarding party's assault. "Desperate characters. They'd booby-trapped an entire wing to explode when our people entered—but you not only disabled the mechanism, you convinced them further resistance was pointless."

I was scared out of my wits, he did not say.

The picture changed again. "Then there was the ground exfiltration of those short blue things that had set up a colony inside the nebular boundary. They went underground and would have suffocated when their scurry hole collapsed—but you were able to get the troop module's sensors to figure out where they were in time to reach them all."

"It's the actual thing I was trained for," he said, choking on all the irony that entailed.

The image changed again. "Then another group of prisoners—you people outside the nebula are big on prisons. They were being transferred by someone called the Enolians. Their guards decided your ship had been hired to set the convicts free—and released poison gas into the detention area." An image flashed past of an armored Connolly carrying convicts, one over each armored shoulder. "You located and destroyed the gas jets, hauled out half the unconscious on your own, and administered aid aboard the troop module before the exfils even got to Processing."

"These things are problems?"

Kormagan laughed, and the stars and clouds returned. "Since you started doing exfiltrations, *Krall-Three* Blue Squad has seen a zero casualty rate for exfils. And the other squads' rates have gone down to zero, too, due to your example."

"We're all competitive. I just suggested something else to compete over." He began to think this was what he was being called on the carpet for. "Baladon says unless we break a skull now and again he'll get a bad name, but I just can't do that."

"Well, he's not getting a bad name. In fact, he's getting a commission. I'm naming him captain of *Carrier Urdoh*."

"*Captain?*"

"Recruit to captain in less than a year. I wouldn't have believed it either. It turns out that all Baladon needed to be an 'exemplary pirate,' as he put it, was a crew that knew what it was doing."

Connolly nodded. The Boundless as an organization might be many things, mostly bad—but Connolly had to admit that it was an unparalleled engine for recognizing and rewarding merit. Even better than Starfleet, where he had nearly died of boredom in Academy classes he hadn't really needed, and on officer details that didn't put his talents fully to use. He knew the reason, of course: the frenetic churn rate of personnel. War was the great organizational accelerator, and constant war was the defining feature of Boundless life.

He wondered if the conflict with the Klingons had changed anything at home.

"There wouldn't have been an opening on *Urdoh*," Kormagan said, "but Gallous is getting past his prime, and they're trying to launch the Six-Ohs."

That puzzled Connolly. "I'd heard that new waves never had anything to trade. What would you get for a captain?"

"Mmm. That's your doing too. You remember the talk we had on your return to Varadah III?"

I remember I was terrified to be back there. "Refresh my memory."

"That we could commoditize prospective recruits, making them into assets for trading."

"Draft picks. What are you getting for Captain Gallous?"

"The second, third, and fourth ability-test scorers from their first five exfiltrations. Fifteen soldiers for an old campaigner!"

Connolly remembered what he had been babbling nervously about that day. "Remind me to speak to you about free agency some time."

"You've turned yourself around, Bluesub—or Connolly, if you prefer." She'd never called him by his name before. "I don't think it's just because you hate the smell of burning Rengru."

It wasn't. He had not fully accepted that *Enterprise* had been destroyed, of course; unlike the Boundless, he knew what saucer separation was. His fellow Starfleet officers apparently hadn't let the cat out of the bag about that capability either, given how Kormagan and Baladon were acting. But he had seen the Rengru tearing at both halves of the starship, and the creatures still controlled Little Hope. If either part of *Enterprise* yet existed, the chances for anyone aboard either section were poor.

It baffled Connolly that so many starships wandered into the Pergamum, given the reputation of the place—but the phenomenon was familiar. People still wandered into the Delphic Expanse even though they knew better. He had concluded the Boundless were the lesser of the evils awaiting such travelers—and that humane treatment could go a long way toward keeping the army's victims from harm, at least in the beginning. As the only human on *Krall-Three*, he'd appointed himself director of the concept.

It was, of course, a dodge, an attempt to live with his conscience amid an intolerable situation. "Gently enslaving" was no different from enslaving; those he captured were still sent off to face possible death. But they had a better chance than if the Rengru had found them.

His efforts had made him a subaltern two months earlier—and now, he learned, something else.

"Baladon is going to *Urdoh*," Kormagan said, "and so are you. I'm appointing you opmaster of troop module *Urdoh-Two*, strictly in charge of recruiting. No more stops back here to fight the Rengies—barring the unexpected, of course."

Connolly was glad she couldn't see his face within his headgear. "You're giving me a *ship*?"

"I'm not worried about your past. Opmasters can't run off with the troop modules—they're just barely warp capable, and as you know, the modules have their own flight crews. But you'll run a platoon of twenty-five—and get me some of those 'future draft picks' I need. I'm bartering for the resources to get the new *Aloga-One* into service faster."

Connolly stared at the projections of stars, bewildered. He'd been in the Boundless the better part of a year, and in that time had made more progress through the ranks than he had in his whole Starfleet career. It was just in a service he'd never intended to join—and doing something that offended him. "Can I say no?"

"Of course," she said. "You've faced the Rengru—you've earned that right. But I would be disappointed if—"

"I have two conditions."

Kormagan laughed. "What is it with you Starfleet people and bargains? Spock didn't keep to his. Why should I accept yours?"

"Hear me out," Connolly said. "One, my ship won't attack any Federation vessels. Period."

"I thought you were going to say 'Starfleet' vessels. Is there a difference?"

"It's hard to explain. Kind of military versus civilian."

It was clear Kormagan didn't understand that difference either, which was no wonder. But she considered the offer. "You wouldn't have been sent after any Starfleet vessels. I trust you, but not that much." She leaned over in her chair. "You do realize I would simply send other units against such ships?"

"Yes, I expect that." *They'll just do it anyway,* Connolly thought.

"Agreed, then. Your other?"

"I want to know exactly what the hell this whole war has been about. I think Baladon knows more than he did, but he's not saying anything."

"Ah! As opmaster, you're entitled to that." Kormagan waved her hand—and Connolly's jetpack activated, lifting him up to her platform. She rose and walked to the railing. "Listen well, brother-in-arms, for it is a story handed down by the generations. *Why we fight . . .*"

50

Combat Module Carrier 539-Aloga
Varadah System

"'Your duty honors all of us,'" Connolly read from the message Kormagan had introduced onto his interface. "Who was Eudah again?"

"One of my greatmothers—female ancestors." Kormagan gestured. "She lived long ago, in a place I have never been. But we all remember."

The words disappeared from before Connolly's face—and, in their place, he saw the nebula rotate and move, expanding around him as if he were traveling. All along the way, Rengru symbols infested the clouds. At last, an opaque bank swelled to consume Connolly's platform, revealing what lay beyond: a single white star and a multicolored world.

Kormagan spoke with reverence. "You wish to know the meaning. There it is: *K'davu.*"

So that's it. The planet looked huge, with several colossal supercontinents divided by narrow oceans. "I've heard the name. I thought it belonged to a person, a god."

"Some see it as such. In a sense, they're right. We are its creations."

"It's vast."

"Not large enough. Six sentient species arose on K'davu. The Rengru rose first, on the Northern Mass. They had already developed advanced technology by the time the other peoples of the world achieved intelligence."

Connolly noticed something in his peripheral vision. Turning, he saw five figures approach him from the darkness, walking on nothing. One resembled Kormagan without her headgear; another, the armorer Jayko. Two of the others represented species he had seen while with the Boundless. But the fifth, a nearly transparent bipedal being with a glowing heart, was unfamiliar. "Who is that one?"

"She is of the Taaya, whose domain was the oceans."

"I've seen the others with the Boundless, but none like that."

"They are with us. Dreston is one. The Taaya cannot remove their headgear. You must have noticed he communicates over his armor's public-address system in person."

Connolly nodded—and wondered. As trapped as he had felt in his armor during the year, at least he could come out of his shell for a breath once in a while. Dreston and those like him were entombed.

"The other species ruled the southern lands," Kormagan said, directing attention back to the globe. "And not very well. We five developed technology for one purpose: to fight with one another. We did so for millennia, while the Rengru watched and did nothing." She paused. "It turned out they were waiting."

"For what?"

"For their chance, I suppose. One day they left their domain and attacked. Not just my kind, who lived nearest in the tropical zones. But under the seas too—and as far away as the polar icecap. And in all cases, they acted as they do now. I will not show you images of that."

Connolly didn't need to see any. "The same thing? Enveloping—and the stab to the back of the neck?"

"Only our people were not armored. Not yet."

Connolly's eyes narrowed. "I always wondered—after they envelop their victims, what happens after that?"

"There is no after that."

"Do they devour them? Take their knowledge somehow? Use them for—"

He stopped as he saw Kormagan step away, offended. "Don't be obscene. We don't care what they do. They end our people's lives. That's enough."

Connolly understood. He'd had to fire on a number of Rengru-compromised warriors himself during his service. He could only imagine the carnage the creatures could wreak on so large a world of civilians.

"The conflict united the Five. We collaborated, shared what we knew—using a new language, created to honor our shared love for K'davu. We stole technology from the Rengru, to modify our own."

So that's where that habit started, Connolly thought.

"But there was only so much we could take—or invent for ourselves. The situation reached a stalemate. Our past intramural squabbles had never threatened to destroy the beauty of K'davu before; against the Rengru, they did. And so began the Great Project."

"The one Eudah talks about in her message."

"Correct. The Rengru had both spacefaring and warp technology, but had never used it for some reason," Kormagan said. "If you ask me, they were waiting until they had finished us off. But our people acted first. We stole that tech—and set off in search of more."

Connolly watched as five starships launched from various locations on K'davu. They did not resemble the current Boundless carriers, but he could see some similar influences. "Wave One," he said.

"Wave One," she said, voice full of pride. "Eudah's

daughter—and so many more of K'davu's children—set out looking for an edge, something that would vanquish the Rengru without destroying the homeworld. But, of course, the menace followed." Rengru vessels, large and small, lifted off from the northern continent in pursuit.

Connolly's view followed them—and as K'davu grew smaller, he now saw something that hadn't been there earlier: masses of Rengru orbital shipyards with armed space fortresses.

"The Nest began as a Rengru attempt to bar Wave One from returning. The blockade has grown and grown. But so have we, replenishing our numbers through childbirth and recruiting, building ships and dividing into new waves."

"You became the Boundless."

"And we bound our enemies. Over the years, we've contained the Rengru to the inner regions of the nebula, surrounding K'davu. We may never retake our world, but we will see that the Rengru are never unleashed upon the universe."

Connolly took a deep breath as he gazed again on the sea of markers indicating the current positions of the Boundless waves and the Rengru emplacements. Would this be what became of the Federation, if the Klingon War continued and metastasized? Surely there was another way. But he could not help but feel that if there was a correct side, the Boundless were it.

She looked to him. "You understand now."

"I do."

"Would your Starfleet be willing to help our crusade?"

He flinched. "They're not big on crusades. It's not really a good word in our culture. Bad history."

"We live with our bad history every day." She took her seat and pointed to the deck below. "An opmaster should be able to find his own way down. Report to Baladon and join *Urdoh*."

Connolly looked at the star map one more time before

jetting gingerly to a soft touchdown. Before he left, he asked another question. "What happens if you win?"

"What?"

"If you exterminate the Rengru, take K'davu back. Will you release us all then?"

Atop her platform, Kormagan sat motionless. At last, she responded, "Ask us *then*."

51

U.S.S. Enterprise
Saucer Section
Defoe

"I'd like to say it feels good to be back in the captain's chair," Pike said. "Or, rather, somewhat adjacent to it. But this is pretty strange."

It was a scene no Starfleet training exercise had ever prepared him for. The three officers in the command well dangled, suspended, meters in the air near their upside-down seats and controls. Workers had fastened bungee harnesses to the deck over their heads, and at multiple points to the frame of the dome below. Bobbing, even in low gravity, over a big transparent opening to the sea was unnerving, at best.

"Carabiners holding," Amin said at the helm.

Suspended near the other seat, Nhan asked, "Why am I doing this again?"

"Carlotti's orders," Pike said. "She doesn't want Raden on any thrill rides, so Jamila's covering for him. And I'm not lighting engines without someone at navigation."

"And, oh, yes. I volunteered," Nhan said. "That'll teach me."

Only one other person was on the bridge—or rather, on the bulkhead. Galadjian was netted sideways to the wall, just beneath his engineering station. Looking up, he could monitor it. "I'm not sure what the awards committee would think if they could see me now," he said.

His was the low-tech solution they'd chosen for many of the ninety-nine aboard; officers were slung, snugly wrapped, in sleeping bags or other fabric envelopes affixed to the bulkheads. All the efforts were to prevent another round of injuries from up becoming down suddenly. Pike didn't want the weak gravity to lull them into a false sense of security; sudden acceleration and a rough stop were expected.

"All decks sound off," Pike said. He listened for and received the desired responses—and then made one direct call. "Carlotti, are you ready?"

"As I'll ever be." Further along in her pregnancy, she was strapped into the most elaborate mechanism they'd fashioned, a gyro chair affixed to a column in sickbay.

"Let's roll, Jamila."

"Aye, Captain." Amin touched a control—and for the first time in months, engines on the saucer section activated for more than a second-long test.

"Thruster engine warm-up complete," Galadjian said, looking up at his interface. "Readings nominal."

"Configure boosters," Pike said. According to Spock and Raden's plan, they needed to activate specific ones, oriented upward and downward, in order to flip the ship. "Ten percent power, Lieutenant."

"Ten percent power, aye."

The saucer rumbled around them.

"Still stuck," Amin said.

"Twenty," Pike said.

"Twenty, aye."

Pike made the mistake of looking down; below, the frigid methane heaved and churned. It was what he was afraid of: breaking the surface tension would require more oomph than might be healthy for his passengers, considering that he intended to instantly crash-land again.

"Ventral thrusters thirty percent, dorsals twenty. Alternate every second. Let's shake this thing free."

Amin did as ordered—and the saucer section groaned and rocked. "I think it's working," she shouted over the din.

Pike's body pitched sideways along with *Enterprise* as a wretched creaking sound assaulted his eardrums. "Fifty percent to both—and hang on!"

The saucer continued to tip—momentarily bobbing on its side, a movement that jerked Pike away from his chair and its controls. Methane streamed down the exterior of the skylight, which allowed in light for the first time in months. Amin, barely clinging to her control station, shouted something inaudible and punched a key.

A sudden lurch—and *Enterprise* slammed back into the sea, right side up. Bouncing in his personal suspension system, Pike called out, "Cut thrusters!"

The engines juddered and died. Quiet came more quickly than Pike had imagined possible. He hadn't been conscious for the saucer section's stone-skipping landing on Defoe months earlier; it had been violent, from what Nhan had said. This time, the woman looked a little green—but otherwise okay.

"That was amazing, and we did it," Nhan said, pulling at her harness. "And as soon as I get out of this thing, I would like to be excused."

Cheers wafted up from down the open turbolift shaft. "All decks report," Pike said. As the responses came in, he couldn't help but smile. A small thing, in the larger scheme: flipping over a bug that had been on its back, flailing. But now, they again had the chance to go somewhere.

Or not. "I wouldn't count on the thrusters for much more," Amin said. "Not until we get back to spacedock."

"But they fired, didn't they?"

"Not exactly their standard operating environment."

"It may not be necessary," Galadjian said, struggling with the wrapping he was suspended in. "Now that we have righted the saucer, we can finish the repairs on the fusion reactor that powers the impulse drive."

"What good does the impulse drive do?" Amin asked. "It's not multidirectional—it just points aft. We need to go up, not forward—and the thrusters alone may not be able to hack it."

"Enough," Pike said, detaching himself. "We'll move on that next. For now, let's take the win." Then he placed his feet on the deck—and sat in his chair.

It felt marvelous.

Skon's World

"You wouldn't believe the difference," Pike said over Spock's comm system. The captain was ebullient over the righting of the saucer section, and excited to be broadcasting from his bridge, now the uppermost portion of the vessel. *"I don't know what it is,"* Pike said, *"but I'll take weightlessness in a heartbeat over living in a ship where down is up."*

Spock might have made some comment about the phenomenon, but he was marveling at a discovery of his own. Skon's World's tallest mountains, a kilometer high, loomed ahead of him across a glacier flow field rich in nitrogen ices. It had been his destination for months, but finding a route had been difficult given the changeable and sometimes treacherous landscape. Nothing posed a danger to his battlesuit, but he had been forced to rethink his path many times.

Summer was coming for Skon's World, and the moon's close approach to the gas giant had brought subtle but detectable changes. The glaciers were shifting—and his sensors detected ever more quakes. Earlier, he had thought it ironic that he was using Boundless technology to take the same kind of seismic readings that he had been taking before his capture. He didn't have as many thoughts about the Boundless anymore, although Pike often found subjects that were tangential.

"Hey, did you finish Crusoe*?"* Pike asked.

"Among other texts," Spock said, clambering over an ice barrier. "I found irony in that the title character was leading an expedition to capture slaves when he was shipwrecked."

"Yeah, I saw that. Served him right."

"It is also curious that his rescue of the native he calls Friday was not benevolent, but premeditated, as part of a plan to make another his slave. He sees no shame in the enslavement, because it is a means to an end."

"And that's how the Boundless looked at you and our crew."

"Precisely." Spock paused on a ledge. "Only, there is a curious thing. Crusoe is deeply conflicted over shedding blood to capture his slave—but he feels he has been forced to it by circumstance. The Boundless wavemaster I dealt with, Kormagan, likewise seemed to harbor some regret. Perhaps it was weariness that I detected; they are many years distant from whatever started their war. But there may be some faint acknowledgment what they are doing is wrong."

"You're stranded on a deserted ice world, and you're trying to reform whole civilizations." Pike laughed. *"Whatever keeps you busy, Spock."*

"I suspect you intend to jest, rather than patronize—but you may encounter the Boundless again after you escape, Captain. You may draw upon my analysis."

"Of course. Noted."

Pike left the topic of literature and began talking about possibilities for *Enterprise* to escape, now that the saucer section was righted. Galadjian and the others faced a new, different set of problems, which Pike described in detail, along with some of their working theories. Spock listened politely, but was far more interested in the mountain farthest to the east.

It might be an ice volcano, he suspected; being present on the surface for its eruption would be a rare moment of scientific significance snatched from a year—indeed, a career—that had gone off track.

And there was something else about that place, something he hadn't mentioned, and wouldn't.

"The window's closing. Keep us apprised on your battlesuit's status," Pike said, sounding confident. *"We'll get to you before time runs out. I know it now."*

Spock thanked the captain and signed off. In fact, his consumables in a couple of categories had already run out, given the battlesuit system's inability to find any useful resources in the air or on the surface of Skon's World. He expected the other levels to drop to zero before long. But as long as his existence served to motivate Pike and crew, he would say nothing.

Enterprise reaching space again was not the means to an end. It *was* the end. As for Spock's end, that would come soon enough. He had just one last question to answer first.

52

U.S.S. Enterprise
Stardrive Section
Cloud Complex Zedra

"I never expected to hear myself say these words," Philip Boyce said. "As acting captain, I hereby call this senior staff meeting to order."

He looked around the little table in the engineers' briefing room. In another time or place, Boyce might have expected a chuckle or two at that, or at least a smile. *Nothing.* Not after all that the stardrive section had gone through—and not after what had happened to its commander.

Weeks after the Rengru's assault, Una was still in the brig—only on the other side of the reactivated force field with the prisoner. She had lain comatose since that horrible day; the Rengru, having impaled the back of her neck with something, had locked its limbs around her like a second set of ribs. It, too, seemed dead, or at least dormant—yet Una somehow remained alive, sustained, at least in part, by her connection with the creature. He was at a loss to explain the mechanism. All he knew for sure was that there was no separating the two without killing the first officer. He didn't have the equipment or facilities, much less the knowledge.

So she had stayed there, perversely cocooned with her attacker ever since—with the force field in place in case the Rengru rose to maraud the ship. Guards remained posted, and Boyce had gone inside the cell to check on her six times a day.

It had been twelve times a day, but there now seemed less and less reason to go. And he had other worries.

"As chief medical officer, I'm ranked as a commander, but not in the regular chain of command," Boyce said. "But that entire chain is now either off this ship, or incapacitated. The yeoman reminds me that I had line officer's training many moons ago, though not the full command course—and with Jallow and the rest of our fine engineers having their hands full keeping the ship running, I get to catch the falling scalpel."

"I wouldn't object if I could," an exhausted Jallow said. "Between the Rengru, the nebula, and the running, we're held together with duct tape."

"Always a place for tape in my line of work," Boyce said.

He let out a deep breath and looked around the table. They'd not had formal meetings because there hadn't been time, and there were so few to attend. Mann, Pitcairn, and Jallow, all covering for multiple departments—with Colt running between, handling everything else. Boyce usually saw them enough daily to cover everything. This time, however, he had graver topics to discuss—beginning with Colt's report on her latest shuttle action.

It wasn't a good one. "*Herschel* took some bad hits this last go-around," Colt said. "They've adapted to our shuttles-as-defenders tactic."

"Do the Rengru know we have one of their kind aboard?" Mann asked. "Would they respond?"

"We don't even know how to tell them."

Boyce nodded. "There's been no change whatsoever in the condition of the commander *or* the Rengru prisoner. Whatever she hoped to learn about communicating stopped right there, weeks ago."

"Are you still reading brainwave activity?" Colt asked.

"It spikes and goes away. It usually vanishes when we move her for the daily intravenous feeding—almost as if the movement disturbs her concentration, if that makes any sense." He shook his head. "It doesn't to me. If I had the full sickbay—"

He stopped. It wounded him that he hadn't been able to do anything for Una. He and Number One hadn't always seen eye to eye—Boyce the devil on Pike's shoulder, her the angel—but he missed her voice and her steady presence.

"Speaking of feeding, what are our stocks down to, Lieutenant Mann?"

"Running low," she replied. "We never expected to have to feed and water so many for so long, even with the machinery able to assist. We've been rationing for months—and looking for ways to go into generation-ship mode, recycling everything." She eyed Boyce. "I don't think that's really an option."

"And that's the main reason I called you all here today. I've spoken with many aboard, and sounded a lot of people out. It doesn't look like our situation is tenable to remain in the nebula. We've never seen those Boundless ships again, so our science crew is gone—and as much as it pains me to say it, I don't think we're going to be able to help Captain Pike, if he's out there." Boyce's chest tensed up after saying the last phrase. Before that moment, he hadn't allowed that Pike's survival wasn't guaranteed.

"We're leaving," Colt said, morose.

"If the damn Rengru will let us," Pitcairn said.

Mann punched her fist. "We've never taken it to them—gone for one of the mother ships. They've never been made to hurt."

"That's because they've usually got things crawling all over the hull for us to deal with," Jallow said. "We're flat out of DOT-Sixes."

"And that's why we're talking," Boyce said.

"Unless we're talking counterattack," Mann said, "we're just wasting more time. Forget the DOT-Sixes. We should just go at them!"

Colt shook her head. "Commander Una didn't want us to go after the mother ships, Trina—not when we didn't know why they wanted us in the first place."

"Does it matter now?" Mann asked. "Look what trying to talk to them got her!"

Colt shouted at Mann in response—and Boyce slapped the table. "Hey, hey. Let's stop this, before I sedate everyone here." *Myself included*, he thought.

The speakers calmed down. Pitcairn looked to Boyce. "Is any help from Starfleet possible? We're overdue."

Boyce shook his head. "We last heard from Starfleet months ago. It's only a partial, but it says the Klingon War is still on and that our mission has been extended." He frowned. "You know what I think of that. As far as I'm concerned, I'm going to do what Chris Pike did nearly a year ago this time—I'm going to assume those orders are outdated and void."

Colt appealed to him. "But the Rengru—"

"—are going to attack us whatever we do. I think we have to pick the shortest direction with the least nebular garbage in the way, and run like hell. If the Rengru want to fight it out—then, Lieutenant Mann, you'll get your way. One last foofaraw."

The table went silent.

"Of course, 'foofaraw' is one of those terms we learn in medical school," he said. But there was no lightening the mood, not now.

"I'll—uh, get the crew ready," Pitcairn said, rising. "I think you'll want to distribute new self-destruct codes."

Boyce coughed. He hadn't thought of that. "Yes, once I figure out where they are."

Colt didn't look up. "I can help with that."

"I suppose they'll go to Mann and yourself, Mister Jallow. And, er, me."

Colt shook her head. "We're really going to do this, aren't we? It's going to end like this?"

No one answered. Boyce started to stand. "I guess let's—"

Colt's communicator chirped.

Snapped out of her funk, she opened it. "Yeoman Colt."

There was no response.

"Yeoman Colt. Who is this?"

That question was met with a strange sound, almost a gurgling. Mann leaned over. "Where's the call from?"

Colt looked at the display—and almost dropped the communicator. "It's Number One's device!"

Boyce grew enraged. "That's a sick joke! Some damn guard down there—"

"Hello," drawled a voice that sounded vaguely like Una's, only flinty and slowed down.

Colt's eyes widened. "Commander, is that you?"

"No," came the response. *"I mean—I don't know what that means."*

53

U.S.S. Enterprise
Saucer Section
Defoe

Not every night for Pike ended with a talk with Spock. Sometimes, given the relative positions of Skon's World and Defoe, days would pass with no possibility for contact. At other times, the window to talk was during what passed for Pike's sleep cycle. He had made those calls anyway, yielding them to other crewmembers only after weeks had passed.

Rare were the days that both began and ended with a chance to converse with Spock. Alone on a bridge that still saw activity only infrequently, Pike would sit at the comm station, going over the scheduled repair plans in the morning—and then evaluating their success with Spock when the day was done.

But whether he discussed shipboard matters or classic literature, Pike's intent was always the same: to draw the science officer out, to keep him engaged. To give him a reason to go on, to remain connected while exiled in a frozen wasteland.

Increasingly, Pike wasn't having much luck.

"Galadjian's really getting into the game," Pike said, well into describing the morning's plans. "We've had a lot of chief engineers, all with one thing in common: they knew how to tear a starship apart and put it back together again. This guy barely knew anything—and he's old enough to be my father, to boot. Yet he's made a choice. He can be dunsel, or he can act like a cadet. He's hustling around everywhere. I already saw him this morning with the team working on the transporters."

"The situation . . . is motivating."

"And the low gravity doesn't hurt. Remind me to retire to a small planet. With better restaurants."

Spock did not respond.

Under normal circumstances, nonresponse by Spock to levity was, itself, a response—a statement of who he was, and where he came from. This wasn't that.

Pike tried another tack: asking Spock to recall his interactions with other *Enterprise* crewmembers while with the Boundless. That usually forced Spock to speak in greater detail, given that it might be useful knowledge if the saucer section ever took to space again. But Spock had already described every encounter he had remembered, and had nothing further to say about the Boundless and their tactics.

Still, Pike pressed.

"Captain, I am incapable of helping in this matter."

Captain was a normal word for Spock. *Incapable* was not. The officer Pike knew would always find *something* to contribute, reflecting, even obsessing, over tiny details. The Spock he knew compared and contrasted the morals of interstellar army generals with eighteenth-century fictional characters. He wasn't *incapable.*

Pike heard activity down the turbolift shaft and checked the chron. "We're starting to run real duty shifts up here again. I guess I should get going," he said. "What do you have planned today?"

"Walking."

"Any place of interest? That volcano you told me about?"

"It is distant."

"Far from a volcano is a good place to be—even an ice one. Stay safe."

Pike waited to hear a response. None came. He signed off.

—

"I wish you could hear him, Gabrielle," Pike said, pacing around sickbay. "Maybe you make the call one night."

"Until you get the turbolifts and transporters working or can pipe it down here, I'm not going anywhere," Carlotti said. Seated at her desk atop the section of gravity plating, she patted her growing middle. "Ladders are a delight I will know again—*after*."

"Look, I'm no counselor. All I know of Vulcan psychology comes from serving with him. I can't even see him—he's just a voice. But I really think something's wrong. He's drifting on me." Pike looked over at the medical bays, finally empty of patients. "I wish he'd give us a real report on his health. But he hasn't been willing to send his diagnostics to us in weeks."

Carlotti didn't seem surprised. "Folks in my line have faced patient rebellions as long as there's been spaceflight. During the Apollo 13 disaster, the ship's commander removed his sensors. The reasons he gave we still contend with today: discomfort, power consumption worries, and jealousy over personal privacy."

"If Spock's been in one of those suits most of the year, I doubt anything will make him more comfortable—and power hasn't seemed to be a problem for him." Pike thought for a moment. "But privacy? Yeah. I could see Spock not wanting us judging his condition by analyzing his vitals."

"That was the big one for Jim Lovell, according to his book."

"I missed that week. I wore out early on the shipwreck stories."

"Understandable."

Pike looked back at her. "He's been on that iceball longer than he was with the Boundless, and in that armor for all of it combined," he said. "I don't care how well designed he says that outfit is. He's just surviving, not living."

She shook her head. "There are plenty of people whose functioning and mobility depends on technology—"

"And they live productive lives. I know. It's just—"

"He's disengaging. And that is not Spock."

"Right."

"He's suffering isolation, deprivation, and probably post-traumatic stress from the Boundless," she said, reaching inside a compartment of her desk. "I think we'd all be hunkered down and hiding after that." Carlotti passed him a slate. "There are a number of batteries that gauge mental health—even for Vulcans. Take a look, maybe ask some questions."

He studied the information. "This will help. I'll also try to get the call linked down here one of these days."

"Just fix the damn turbolifts," she said.

"On the list," he said, making for the door. "Thanks."

"Oh," she called out, "and if all else fails, ask about family. That usually gets most people talking."

—

Pike yawned as he finished relating to Spock the events of the day. "So we're at dinner—nice to eat *on* the table, rather than under it—and the raging debate is whether saucer sections were ever intended to launch again. Raden, who's finally out of sickbay, is certain they never were, because the impulse engine only points out the side, and it seems to have taken everything out of the boosters just flipping the ship. And, of course, there's no warp drive."

Pike waited to be scolded for saying something Spock

already knew. When nothing came, he continued. "Suddenly, Galadjian slaps the table and cries 'Eureka,' like he does, and begins talking about surfing and methane and volatization."

"Volatilization," Spock corrected.

"Yeah, that was it." He tried to draw him out. "What is that again?"

Spock did not answer.

"Anyway, Galadjian rushes off to work on formulas, drafting not just Raden, but Nhan."

"The commander."

"Of security. That's right. No idea what they'll come up with."

Pike looked sadly at the data slate Carlotti had provided. He had asked questions from the batteries earlier; Spock had kept to one-word answers for most of the conversation. The captain had felt guilty while quizzing him, and wondered if Spock had sussed out his intentions.

He decided to go for whatever reaction he could get.

"We've been scanning for any more messages from Starfleet, but we've had nothing for months. I sure hope they've found *Discovery*—and Michael Burnham." He paused. "Do I remember that correctly, that you two grew up together?"

"Adopted by Sarek," Spock said. *"He said . . . he expected us to be . . . friends."*

"Right," Pike said, having definitely remembered. "You two did good work at Sirsa III."

"As . . . ordered."

Pike nodded. "That was it? No catching up?"

For moments, only static.

"Captain . . . I have a request."

I bet it's no more nosy questions. But it was a start. "What can I do for you?"

"In my quarters . . . there are tomes of Vulcan philosophy."

Pike nodded. He could see Spock wanting them. "Are there copies in the ship's computer?"

"No. The elders feel . . . sacred meaning cannot . . . survive digitization."

"Understood. Maybe I could read them to you."

"You would not understand them. So I ask . . . please image the pages."

"Sure. And your elders?"

"Are currently . . . not here. Spock out."

The abrupt cutoff startled Pike—and the nature of the request worried him. He shut the slate off and toggled the internal comm system. "Pike to Galadjian."

The man sounded as if he'd been awakened. *"Yes, Captain?"*

"I just ended a call with Spock, Doctor."

"How is he?"

"Out of time. If you have a plan, Doctor, get it ready. Because whatever it is, we're doing it."

54

Logistical Support Station 539
Near Varadah

"Human, wait!" Baladon clanked up the hallway, trying to catch up with Connolly. "I've never seen such an intemperate young fool—that wasn't of my own blood, at least. Are you sure you're not a Lurian?"

Connolly stopped and swiveled, an armored finger in front of Baladon's nose. "Stow it, 'Captain'!"

Baladon blinked. "I have killed people for less," he said aloud to himself. "Why can't I kill him?"

"Because I know what I'm doing." Connolly turned. "But I also know what I'm *not* doing." He looked from doorway to doorway. "Where the hell is Kormagan?" He reactivated his headgear just long enough to see the leader icon appear on the interface map.

LSS-539 was the largest single vessel affiliated with Kormagan's wave: a floating foundry and shipyard, with significant sections devoted to research and development. He had already seen dozens of tech workers toiling in one sector; almost certainly, some of the other members of *Enterprise*'s science crew were there. He would have given anything to talk to them, to see how they were doing—

—but he had a more important mission. Connolly rounded a corner and entered a vast chamber. "*Kormagan!*"

Standing before the future *Aloga-One* troop module, the

wavemaster did not look back. Connolly had no doubt that she was aware of his presence; Kormagan stayed buttoned up much of the time, and he would have displayed in her interface. But she continued to confer with those around her until Connolly, Baladon in tow, barged into the gathering.

"We had a deal," Connolly said, confronting her.

"I am busy, Opmaster. And even if you can't keep your head in the game," she said, using a common expression for remaining in headgear, "you ought to be able to recognize another wavemaster."

The armored figure nodded. "Quadeo, of the Fifty-Twos."

"Connolly, *Enterprise.*"

"So you're the one," Quadeo said, sounding impressed. "Kormagan's traded half your catch next year for the impulse engines for this ship."

"Yeah, well, don't count on it." Connolly only glanced at the thrusters going into place. "I said I'd do what you asked, Kormagan. But I'm not going to let you spread this nonsense of yours any further!"

"Dreston, talk with the wavemaster. I need a minute." Kormagan took Connolly aside. "Now, what are you talking about?"

He pointed to Baladon. "He said our next mission was in the Wenavee Notch. I checked the star map. That's not in the Pergamum!"

"In the what?"

"It's what outsiders call the nebula," Baladon said, stepping closer. "And the reason it's not in the nebula is because it's in a notch. I should think that would be self-explanatory."

The gap was on the far side of the nebula from where *Enterprise* had entered; odds were that if he had gone, Connolly wouldn't have been able to get a distress signal back to Starfleet from there. That wasn't the issue. "You told me your kidnappings have always been in the nebula. This is not in the nebula."

"I never said that," Kormagan replied. "We're at war. I'll cross the galaxy if I have to."

Baladon shrugged. "It was my idea. That region's always been good pickings for the Lurian privateers before—always prospectors wandering around. It's available and it's close. I chose it while the carrier was in for service—and the human went berserk." He clapped a hand on Connolly's shoulder. "I really think it would be for the best if you let me kill him."

Connolly gawked at him. "I'm your only friend!"

"So it would be a sacrifice for the good of the service."

"Enough!" Kormagan pointed to Quadeo, over with her other staffers. "I have *that one* trying to swipe my veterans and sniping—not behind my back, but in front of me—to the other wavemasters. I have a roving bloodbath going from one planet to another in this infernal star system. I lost so much prestige with the *Enterprise* blunder that I'm surprised I'm not carrying dead Rengru. And I have you two debating about where it's right to recruit from!"

"I'm not debating," Baladon said. "Really, I don't even have to kill him. Knocking people around is quite effective. I do wish you'd let me try it."

Kormagan threw up her hands. "I don't have time for this." She turned back toward the others.

"We had a deal," Connolly said, tromping after her.

Baladon followed. "I told you, you're just going to antagonize her if you—"

An alarm sounded in the chamber. Every warrior whose headgear was deployed froze; something was coming in over their interfaces. Connolly and Baladon quickly buttoned up.

"The Rengru," Kormagan said, thunderstruck. "They're all leaving!"

Quadeo echoed her surprise. "My ground forces on Varadah VIII say the Rengies just took off in the middle of a fight. *A fight they were about to win!*"

"To operations," Dreston said over his armor's public-address system, a necessity since he could not breathe without his headgear deployed. He pointed to an aperture across the factory floor. The wavemasters led the way. No one minded that Connolly followed; nobody was paying attention to anything beyond the baffling news.

The place was like Kormagan's sanctum, only with dozens of Boundless working the spherical staging room, studying the great enemy's latest moves. And these made no sense whatsoever.

"A complete evacuation," Dreston said. *"And not back through the Varadah Gap."* In a bewildering move, the Rengru mother ships and fighters weren't falling back to the nebular corridors leading to K'davu and the Nest. They were diving headlong into a massive cloud complex.

"That's a dagger to nowhere," Quadeo said. "It's madness. We'll be able to consolidate here and pick them off as soon as they return."

"*If* they return," Kormagan said. She hadn't said much, Connolly noted. Instead, the wavemaster stared at the movements represented above, trying to make sense of it all.

"Who cares if they return?" Quadeo pumped her armored fist. "Such a blunder!"

"The other wavemasters are calling in," Dreston said. *"They say it's a chance to make sure the Rengru never take the Varadah Gap again!"*

"It's even more than that," Quadeo said. "The dilithium here alone is enough to supply our waves for a century—free for the picking!" She moved to leave, pausing to slap Kormagan's shoulder. "Don't be the old fool who gets left out!"

Quadeo departed, and several warriors followed. Dreston stared at Kormagan. *"She's right, Wavemaster. We can't miss this. Orders?"*

"This is wrong," Kormagan said. She pointed. "What's that small force over there?"

"Over where?" Dreston asked, a little irritated. *"Oh. That's the remnants of the Rengru force that hit us at Little Hope."*

"That was months ago. What are they after?" Looking up, Baladon squinted. "It doesn't seem like we have anything over there."

"We don't. The probes say they've been blundering about ever since, K'davu knows why." Dreston appealed to Kormagan. *"Come on. Let's pick a planet, before they're all gone."*

"No," the wavemaster said. "Look at the Rengru force, the one that just left Varadah. They're cutting through to Little Hope."

"There's nothing there *either!"*

"The Rengru disagree." Kormagan walked under the artificial nebular clouds. "That other probe data is delayed. I'm betting those other ships that have been looking for something have found it—and it's at Little Hope."

Dreston stood motionless. *"I should have gone with Quadeo."*

"What a display of loyalty," Kormagan said. "Fine. Take the rest of the wave and occupy a planet."

"That's more like it! Which one?"

"I don't care." Kormagan turned to Baladon. "Your ship is at the closest carrier dock, right?"

"Huh?" Baladon said, startled. "Er—yes. I find walking overrated, armor assisted or not."

"Fine." Kormagan pointed to Connolly. "You got your way. You're not going to the Notch." She saw Dreston off and hurried toward the exit.

Baladon and Connolly turned to follow. "Would you be so kind as to explain to me what's going on?" Baladon asked.

"Kind?" Connolly blurted. "You were just talking about killing me."

"The mildest of japes. Humans have no sense of humor."

But within his headgear, Connolly was smiling. The Rengru knew something—and Kormagan thought she knew what it was. He did too.

Enterprise was still out there. And if it was, there might just be a chance to save it.

55

U.S.S. Enterprise
Saucer Section
Defoe

"I do not violate any code of Starfleet conduct by saying that this idea stinks," Pike said from the command chair. "And regardless of what may happen in our future careers, know that we have provided the service with jokes for centuries."

With the thrusters ailing from their earlier escapade, another solution had been required. Defoe's gravity was weak enough that the saucer didn't have to launch vertically, like a rocket, but the impulse engines did need to be angled downward for a launch to be effective.

Thus, the plan. Strictly speaking, they did not intend, as Nhan had bluntly put it, "to ride a flaming fart to orbit." Defoe's methane sea would not, could not, burn without something to react with. But it could be vaporized, made to expand by an energy source no one aboard the saucer section had considered before Galadjian: the ship's phaser banks.

Pike looked over to the engineer. "It's your boat, Doctor."

"The sea is fine today, Captain," the engineer said. "Let us discover if this boat can fly. Mister Raden, impulse drive at one percent."

A mild jolt from behind.

"We're moving—barely," Raden said. On the main viewer, the placid chilly sea responded with the lightest of wave reactions.

"Commander Nhan, as helm boosts the impulse power, fire the ventral phaser banks in a dispersal spray downward and forward, increasing in intensity according to the guidance I have provided."

"Happy to," Nhan said, glancing at her instructions. "I've wanted to shoot at something for months. This crappy moon is an excellent choice."

Pike had seen Galadjian's notes to Nhan and Raden; he had characteristically boiled down a mass of imposing equations to something simple for wider consumption. "Mister Raden," Galadjian said, "you may increase power according to the program."

Another boost from the impulse drive—and Nhan fired the phasers. For several seconds, Pike noticed nothing.

"Five percent," Raden called out. "Surface is getting choppy."

"The phasers are shaping a channel of aerosolized methane beneath and ahead of us," Galadjian said. "Can you confirm, Ensign Dietrich?"

"It's there," she called from the science station. "And expanding, just as predicted."

"Excellent. Continue with the procedure."

As the saucer section pushed harder across the surface, Pike saw the static line of Defoe's horizon cloud up and disappear. Then he felt himself tip back as the vessel's bow gently angled upward.

"It's working, Doctor," Raden said. "We're starting to break surface tension. Pitch elevation, three degrees."

"We're surfing the gas. How'd you ever think of this?" Pike asked.

"We use phaser-powered analytical nebulizers in modern

plasma spectroscopy," Galadjian said. "Here, we create our own nebula to return to another!"

"Constant fire continuing," Nhan said.

"Impulse ten percent, pitch six degrees."

The saucer section shook as it surged across the dense, endless ocean. Pike had been aboard a speedboat once where the bow had risen into the air; he'd felt then as if the craft was about to launch into space. With a ramp of expanding methane to angle the impulse engine downward, the saucer section had a chance of doing exactly that.

Whatever happens, please don't let us flip over again!

"Impulse fifteen percent, pitch . . ." Raden looked back. "Captain, we've reached our escape angle!"

Pike looked to Galadjian, who winked and pointed his finger in the air. It was time. "Raden, go!"

Raden increased power—and Pike grabbed his armrests. The saucer section wobbled, but righted as it went gradually skyward. "Hold on, people," he said—and not just because of the thrust: he could feel the Defoe's meager gravity lessening.

And then . . . space. And cheers.

"Fusion reactor is performing correctly," Galadjian said. "Gravity plating coming online. It will be at full power in thirty seconds." That was another fix that had taken months, completed just in time. "I hope you have all been doing your calisthenics."

"You did it," Pike said, speaking to the entire crew. Then he looked to Galadjian. "*You* did it."

The doctor nodded—and leaned back in his chair, contemplating not the space outside, but his terminal.

"Thrusters seem to be cooperating a little better now that we're out of the soup," Raden said. "I think the manifolds fouled a little during the flip."

"I like being able to turn around." Pike looked at the main viewer. "Anybody see us leave?"

Nhan shook her head. "Doesn't look like it. It's not much of a vacation spot."

Pike already had somewhere to go. "Set course for Skon's World, full impulse. Let's get Spock!"

Skon's World

The cryovolcano erupted again, spewing its mix of ammonia, water, and methane in a colossal plume. For nearly half a year, it had been Spock's destination—and as his resources ran low, he had feared he would not reach it. It was the last spectacle he was ever going to see, the last moment when nature would break from its quiet majesty to speak loudly and firmly, declaring the presence of the physical laws of the universe in a symphony of science.

It had also been where, during his time in space, he had last seen the red light of his waking dream. It had been only a spark by then, heading toward the mountainous region and then disappearing. By the time Spock had landed, the planet's rotation had carried the volcano to the opposite side of the globe, necessitating his walk.

He had not decided how close he would want to get to the mount; his armor decided for him, its armatures finally giving out less than a kilometer from the active cryomagma field. He had been losing heat for weeks, and his oxygen reprocessor was fouled to the point where the air in the battlesuit was little better than the thin, frigid haze that clung to the surface of Skon's World.

Spock had always known what he would do next—and even debilitated by his ordeal, he did it.

With the governor not functioning, Spock found it easy to extract himself from the battlesuit. Like petals opening on a flower, the armor blossomed outward, hinged modules peeling away from him one at a time. A lobe of armor plate here, a stowed weapon there. He clambered out and fell on the snow, wheezing. His muscles carried their own weight for the first time in months; were it not for the weak gravity of Skon's World, he might never have moved again.

But there was something else to do.

During his first conversation with Kormagan on the mobile processing center, Spock had learned that the clothing he was wearing on Susquatane was stowed amid his gear. Disregarding the vile condition of his Boundless-provided tracksuit, he quickly put it on.

Not for warmth; regardless of his attire, he would shortly freeze on Skon's World, if he didn't asphyxiate first. He had another reason. He was gratified to see his tricorder, but not surprised. Kormagan had said that, since it was not a weapon, it had been left with his personal effects. It was all he needed.

The battlesuit stood nearby, as if at attention. Spock stood too—rockily, uneasily, fighting for breath as he turned to face the volcano.

He would not meet death as a Boundless soldier, cast away. It would be as a Starfleet science officer, doing his job to the end.

He turned the tricorder on and started taking readings.

56

U.S.S. Enterprise
Saucer Section
Approaching Skon's World

"Closing on Spock's estimated position," Raden said.

Pike was up and pacing. A hundred technical systems and subsystems aboard the saucer section had been impacted by the disaster at Little Hope. Three things had gotten most of their attention: survival, escaping the surface of Defoe, and defending against any Boundless or Rengru who might be lurking above.

But one system beyond that was sure to be needed—and had posed its own problems. The transporter rooms in the saucer section were powered by the fusion reactor and could function without access to the rest of the ship, but their capabilities weren't robust. That was by design: since a separated saucer's needs related to evacuation, most of the emergency transporters focused on sending signals, not beaming people aboard. The units that could transport both ways had been hampered by a shortage of functional datacores and working sensors.

"Lieutenant Dietrich is helping to work the panels," the relocated Galadjian called up. *"Sensors are having a hard time finding life signs."*

"They could never pierce the battlesuits before," Pike said. Spock had told him that was one of his armor's features. "The suit itself ought to be easy to find. It's big enough."

"Understood. Stand by."

White and clouded, Skon's World grew in the main viewer. Pike had trouble containing his glee. "I've been waiting months to make this call. Nicola, hail Spock."

"Channel open."

Pike smiled. "Spock, I hope you can stand some good news. We'll be overhead shortly."

Nicola listened to his earpiece—and frowned. "No response, Captain."

"What is it, Vic? Don't tell me our equipment's gone wrong again."

Nicola shook his head. "We're getting the receive signal from the battlesuit five by five. He's just not answering."

Pike looked to Nhan, who shrugged. "Even Spock sleeps sometimes."

"Then he'll wake up here from a bad dream."

Pike took a deep breath. Escaping from Defoe had been a victory; regaining Spock would be a second. He'd put off thinking about after that.

Would Spock be the first step toward rescuing the rest of his crew—or the only one he would save? It would depend on how fast it took the crippled saucer to make it home. Just over half his crew was still out there somewhere. He'd come back in a spacetug to pick up their trail if he had to.

More of Skon's World emerged from night. "Doctor, do we have that damn lock yet?"

"No, Captain. You know what shape our sensors were in."

"The whole planet's an ice sheet. Can't we eyeball it to start the fix?"

"You can see what we can. Some kind of eruptive event is going on. Hundreds of square kilometers are clouded by vapor and crystals."

Pike peered at the globe ahead. "Well, what do you know? Spock's volcano is going off." He chuckled. "Well, that's better than sending up a flare. Doctor, that's where he is."

"Not too close, I hope," Raden said.

A few moments later, Galadjian reported back. *"We've found it. Stand by."*

Pike looked expectantly at the icy moon—

—and saw a wave of Rengru fighters emerge from behind it, racing his way.

Four members of the bridge crew swore at once. Pike called for a red alert and ran back to his chair. "We've picked up right where we left off," he said. "What is it with these guys?" He touched the control on his armrest. "Doctor, get him out of there, now!"

Nhan looked back at him. "More contacts!"

Pike had already seen them. Rengru mother ships: two following the fighters—and more, climbing over the southern and western horizons, disgorging fighters of their own.

And *Enterprise*'s saucer section had no shields.

"Evasive maneuvers?" Raden asked, rattled.

"Not until we have Spock." The moral quandary—save one or save all—hit him only after he'd answered. "Weapons!"

"Phasers we have," Nhan said. "But I can't speak for targeting."

"Do your best. Fire at will."

Ergs of the saucer section's precious energy lanced out at the careening Rengru, striking a fighter here and there. It wasn't nearly enough.

"We're surrounded," Nhan said, enemy ships large onscreen. She turned back from her station to face him. "Sound boarding alarm?"

Several thumps on the hull indicated that was the right decision. Pike called out again. "Doctor, I need an answer! Is the transport complete?"

"We have the battlesuit," Galadjian said. He sounded baffled. *"Just the armor."*

"You beamed it and not him?"

"He was not inside. He seems to have climbed out of it. We're still looking."

No, Pike thought. He sank back in his chair. Skon's World was barely visible on the main viewer, so numerous were the Rengru outside. Nhan was already up, holding her phaser. He waved for her to wait. "Nicola, give me the hull view."

Where they had once seen Boundless boarders—one of whom Pike now knew to have been Spock—the bridge crew now saw Rengru at the airlock. Pike reached for his phaser. "Another last stand," he said.

Something made Nhan turn. "That's weird," she said. "The airlock just opened. That portal was secured."

"They've got a slew of limbs. Maybe one's a lockpick."

"No," Nhan said, checking her monitor. "They used an access code to get in. A Starfleet access code."

Pike gawked at her—and then heard a skittering noise from behind. He turned to see the first boarder, crawling up out of the turbolift shaft from the deck below, where the airlock was located.

The Rengru looked different from the ones that Pike had seen attacking *Enterprise* in the battle, months earlier. It seemed smaller, missing the shell with the thruster and phaser. But while it had no weapon, it did bring a demand. *"You will come with us, Christopher Pike."*

That the Rengru knew his name was not the most surprising thing, nor the fact that it spoke in crisp, clear Standard.

It was whose voice it was. He stared at the creature. "*Una?*"

57

Skon's World

Spock meditated.

It was the first time he had done so outside his battlesuit since the beginning of the year. Every breath nearly choked him. His eyes watered; just as quickly, the tears froze. He blinked repeatedly and brushed away the frost from his face, only partially protected by a fabric mask.

Stubby pillars stood all about, making the snow fields surrounding the volcano seem a temple to its might. Logic told him they were ventifacts, pitted structures abraded by high-velocity ice crystals; similar ones shaped by sand were found on Vulcan and Earth. But he had no desire to catalog them, and he took no solace from their beauty.

He thought about the words of the Vulcan philosophers and wondered what death would feel like. His *katra* would remain here, with his mortal form, vanished into nothingness. Perhaps it was not worth saving. Perishing so young, he had accomplished little of what he had intended to.

Everything, all his promise, had come to nothing. Whatever had pushed him to join Starfleet, to come to this nebula, had driven him to his death. Whatever had possessed him to flee the Boundless had been a mistake. Whatever had led him to Skon's World had been a phantasm, the product of hypoxia. Nothing more.

His eyes beginning to crust over, he thought of a warmer place: his home, and of his mother, and father. And—

It glowed. Crimson, and magnificent, hovering above.

No. Not here. Not now!

He did not want to see it—and yet, he had sought it, crossing a whole world on foot. It had been Spock's way, ever since that terrible night so long ago when the hovering phantasm had appeared. He would shut it from his mind—until his inquisitive brain demanded that he think on it again, and research.

What was it?

Why had no one ever seen it?

And why had it appeared to him *and, evidently, no one else?*

It was one of those times when his curiosity had gotten the better of him that he had found a similarly shaped fantastic being in the cultural texts of Earth, putting a name to the thing that both frightened and fascinated him.

The Red Angel.

Three words, describing something that could not, should not, exist. The being that had pointed the way toward young Michael Burnham, whose life was in danger—only never to appear again, except in his nightmares.

It had shown him something important then.

If so, logic said it must have some purpose now. A purpose he could not ignore.

He forced his eyes open and raised his tricorder to the air. Around him, time slowed, the colossal volcanic eruption fading into nothingness. It was no apparition; his tricorder was reacting to *something*. True, it was reacting by spewing nonsensical data—but that was a reaction. He lowered the tricorder—

—and in the same moment, the Red Angel descended toward him. It took his hand. Spock felt warmth as his fingers touched the rounded surface of the being's head. A helmet? He did not know.

But he knew what to say.

"Your mind to my mind."

The Red Angel spoke. *"Your thoughts to my thoughts."*

Then it was no longer an angel that Spock saw—just red. Fantastic, powerful signals, blazing rubies in deep space. One after another in the Milky Way.

Seven!

A supernova. Spock in the supernova, or was it the Angel? And then—

—nothing.

No, not nothing. But it *felt* like nothing. A deathly cold—more bitter than anything he had just experienced. And he saw before him landscapes. Hellscapes, one after another.

Earth, desolate and destroyed.

A world he knew but had not visited: Qo'noS, of the Klingons.

Vulcan, its glories snuffed out.

Andoria, returned to nothing.

World after world. Every native dead. Murdered—by what?

He could not think on it—for he was not Spock. Or not the same Spock. He was a child again, cowering in his bed. There it was again, the Red Angel, hovering above. Planting—forcing—into his mind a cacophony of information. Letters, numbers, images, equations. Like the dead worlds, one after another, until his mind, or something else, exploded—

—and Spock fell to his knees in the snow.

Alone.

He was dying—and so, too, would the universe.

After the year he had endured, that, alone, made sense.

OBLIGATION

October 2257

INCOMING TRANSMISSION

TO: CAPTAIN C. PIKE • *U.S.S. ENTERPRISE* • NCC-1701

FROM: VICE ADMIRAL K. CORNWELL, STARFLEET COMMAND

EARTH IN DANGER. DEFENSES BREACHED. STARBASE ONE POPULATION ANNIHILATED. KLINGON INVASION IMMINENT.

NO CHANGE IN *ENTERPRISE* ORDERS.
DO NOT RETURN. REPEAT: DO NOT RETURN.

IF THIS GOES BADLY, CHRIS, MAKE SURE PEOPLE KNOW WE WERE HERE.

END TRANSMISSION

58

U.S.S. Enterprise
Saucer Section
Orbiting Skon's World

Since entering the Pergamum Nebula at the beginning of his original mission, Christopher Pike had received a total of five messages from Starfleet over the extremely low-frequency subspace band. He had never gotten one while he was on the bridge—until now. Naturally, given the way things had been going, it was horrid news.

And it couldn't have been of less use to him, given that the bridge was under occupation when he heard it.

". . . do not return." He looked up from Nicola's screen. "Somehow, I don't think we'll have any problem with that one."

The Rengru on the bridge had multiplied, wandering about, poking and prodding inanimate objects with their appendages. Two had run Raden and Amin completely out of the helm area. They weren't being violent. Just . . . creepy. Getting into everyone's personal space. Tapping at computer interfaces not entirely randomly, but without much effect.

And answering questions in incredibly frustrating ways, but with the most pleasant voices.

"That's the helm," Raden said. "Don't mess with that!"

"Follow the directives," the Rengru said, two of its limbs raised and again sounding just like Una.

"You're already aboard," Nhan said. "Why do more of you keep landing on the ship?"

"Follow the directives."

"What directives?"

"Follow the directives."

Nicola's brow furrowed. "Do you mean we are to follow your directives—or that following directives is what you're doing now?"

"Follow the directives."

Standing amid the milling Rengru, Pike gawked at the scene. It was like someone had let loose a herd of alien sheep onto his bridge. He had intended to direct his questions to the first one that had entered, but they'd gotten mixed up.

"Listen, why do you all sound like Una?" he asked.

"You will come with us, Christopher Pike."

"We've covered that. Accompany you *where*?"

"Follow the directives."

"Great." He looked to Nhan. "How many of these things are on the hull?"

She edged past the Rengru studying her terminal and tapped some keys. It did not respond when the interface changed. "Five hundred or so. Give or take a million."

"And they're not ripping into the ship."

"Just grabbing hold."

Pike shrugged. "I'm not even going to ask how many are inside."

"Hell, I'm just glad they know how to close an airlock door." Nhan still held her phaser; ordered to do nothing with it, she found her seat and collapsed in it. She propped her feet on her workstation, jostling the Rengru. "Spock said these guys were incredibly dangerous, right?"

Pike nodded. "He said they never talked to him. He didn't think they *could* talk—or hear."

"I'm not sure about that." Dietrich had her tricorder out.

"The sounds are coming from some of their limbs—the ones they put in the air when they talk. The tiny little pods are vibrating at audible frequencies. I think some of their hands may be functioning as ears too."

"Good work." Pike was glad he hadn't sent all his exobiologists to Susquatane. He looked to Nicola. "Try Galadjian again." The captain had given a general order that the Rengru were not to be resisted once their numbers became apparent. Since that time he had heard from other decks that they were dealing with visitors too. But nothing from Galadjian and Dietrich over the intercom.

Pike remembered his communicator. He reached for it and flipped it open, only to startle half a dozen Rengru who coiled in his direction, appendages chittering. *"Follow the directives, Christopher Pike."*

"That's a new formulation, at least." He showed the communicator around, as Dietrich had done with her tricorder. "Not a weapon."

He had no way of telling if they were satisfied with that answer or not—only that they had made no move to tear into him. So he toggled the unit and spoke. "Doctor, where are you?"

"Greetings, Captain." Galadjian sounded like a man who'd entered the wrong theater door and wound up on stage during an opera. *"I apologize for the lapse in communication, but things are decidedly strange here."*

Tell me about it. "Spock, Doctor. Did you get Spock?"

"Oh, yes! He materialized just seconds before our other guests arrived."

Pike's eyes bugged. "Were you going to tell us about it?"

"We were busy. He is quite ill."

"Did you beam him into sickbay?" It was on the same deck as the main transporter room, but no short walk with a patient.

"We are in sickbay now. But we did not transport him. The Rengru carried him."

Pike looked at the others, baffled. "They *carried* him?"

"Once they understood we were trying to move him, yes. In fact, they carried Lieutenant Dietrich and myself as well. These beings are very nimble and quite strong." He paused. *"I did say things were strange."*

"How is Spock? What's his condition? Have they done anything to him?"

"Follow the directives," said another voice across Galadjian's mic.

"That was not me, Captain," Galadjian said. *"It is not Commander Una, either, though you may be forgiven if you—"*

"That's enough," Pike said, closing his communicator. "I'm going down there!"

He moved toward the turbolift shaft—only to find his way blocked by two Rengru, their vocalizing limbs lifted and pointed his way. *"You will come with us, Christopher Pike,"* they said in unison.

Pike gestured toward the turbolift. "If you guys know anything at all about Una, you know she'd want to help me. And Spock." He took another step toward them. "Now are you just going to talk like her, or act like her?"

The Rengru faced one another for a moment—and then, abruptly, snaked toward the captain. "Hey, wait!" Spun sideways by the Rengru, Pike saw Nhan bolt upright, phaser in hand—and several other creatures rising in response. A second later, the two Rengru stretched upward, catching Pike under his arms with several of their limbs and lifting him from the deck like living crutches.

Nhan gawked. "Captain, should I—"

"It's all right. Looks like I'm going for a ride too." The pair skittered toward the turbolift shaft, toting Pike in midair. "Mind the store, everyone. Giddyup."

—

"He was in hypothermic shock when these—uh—*things* brought him in," Carlotti said. "We've been working to stabilize him."

Pike looked past Carlotti to the diagnostic table where Yan, her aide, ministered to Spock's supine form with a medical device. The scraggly-bearded Vulcan's garb had been stripped and dumped in a corner. To the left, a Rengru plodded about, looking at the walls.

Spock moaned.

"He's conscious?"

"He's been in and out," Carlotti said. She nodded, allowing Pike to come near.

"I'm here, Spock. It's Captain Pike. You're home."

Spock seemed to be whispering. Pike didn't want to interfere with the nurses' work, but he wanted to hear.

"Earth. Qo'noS. Vulcan. Andoria."

"What do you mean, Spock?"

Spock said more planet names. But Pike picked up some of the same ones again: *"Earth. Qo'noS. Vulcan. Andoria."*

"Spock, we're still in the Pergamum Nebula. Over Skon's World. We just picked you up."

Spock's eyes opened. "What time is it?"

"I—" Pike had no idea. He looked back. "Why does he want to know that?"

Galadjian stood in the doorway to the intensive care unit. "His battlesuit may have failed. Perhaps that is why he got out of it."

That made sense.

"We got you in time," Pike said, reaching for Spock's hand. It was frigid.

"I cannot meditate," Spock mumbled. "Not here."

He looked to Carlotti. "What in the world?"

"Delirium," she said. Her brow furrowed. "It's an unusual case. His heart rate was sky high when he came in—almost as if something had terrified him. It might have even kept him alive."

Pike looked over at the Rengru, which seemed to be patiently waiting. "Spock, I want to stay with you—but we've got boarders. I have obligations."

"I have obligations," Spock repeated.

"Okay, yeah. But right now, you need to—"

"Time. What is it? Am I in it?"

Pike let go of Spock's hand—and the Vulcan's eyes closed. He stepped back to allow Yan to move to that side of the table and continue her work. "Keep me posted, Nurse."

He moved toward the exit—and the nearby Rengru moved in his direction. *"Follow the directives,"* it said.

"This again."

"Follow the directives, Christopher Pike."

Pike moved out into the corridor—as did Galadjian, who had a Rengru tail of his own. The hallway bustled with Rengru, who wandered about various passing crew without harassing them.

But not without unnerving them. Galadjian asked, "Captain, what is happening? Are we under occupation?"

"They don't seem to be menacing—at least not intentionally. Though I'd think twice before telling them you intend to go somewhere."

A mild bump resonated through the deck. "Unless I miss my guess," Galadjian said, "I think we are *all* going somewhere."

"I'd better get to the bridge." Pike looked to the Rengru tailing him. "Come on, Creepy. Find your partner. Let's get this over with."

After an uncomfortable ride on living stilts up the turbolift shaft, Pike was back on the bridge and rubbing beneath his arms. "If you guys are going to keep this up, we need to look into saddles."

Raden looked back. "How is Spock?"

"He's—" Pike stopped. "You know, I'm not really sure. But he's here—and he's alive." He looked forward at the main viewscreen. "And we're moving. How are we moving?"

"It's not me, Captain." The Rengru were still at the helm station. "I don't think the thrusters fired either. You know the state they were in. We're making smooth turns."

Pike frowned. "Give me a look on the hull again. Topside, aft."

Hundreds of Rengru—still in their space-traveling configuration—were arranged around the circumference of the rear half of the saucer section. Their onboard booster rockets were firing.

"They weren't grabbing the ship to take a bite. They were getting ready to push," Pike said. "But we can't go far like this."

As if to answer, the Rengru at the helm lashed the interface with one of its limbs. A jolt shook the bridge. Ahead, all saw the saucer section overfly Skon's World, heading past it.

"I can't believe I'm saying this, but they've just figured out the impulse drive," Raden said. "The Rengru outside are just setting direction."

Pike watched as Rengru mother ships grew in the viewscreen—and parted, admitting the saucer section into their midst. "We're heading into a convoy."

Several Rengru spoke in unison. *"You will come with us, Christopher Pike."*

"Yeah," he said, resigned. "I think we got that."

59

Combat Module Carrier 539-Urdoh
Little Hope Boundary Region

Kormagan thought she knew the Rengru. It was impossible to battle an enemy for decades and not understand something about how they operated. She could never know how they thought, of course—the monsters' use of technology was the only evidence they had minds like other beings at all. But she knew how they acted and responded, and what had happened at the Varadah Gap had not tracked with that at all.

Abandon an important corridor to K'davu and its vital resource worlds, for what? To revisit an old battlezone?

It made even less sense when *Carrier Urdoh* reached the edge of the Little Hope rift—coincidentally, not far from where Kormagan's wave had lain in wait for *Enterprise* months earlier. The wavemaster had ordered Captain Baladon not to simply barge in, but to dispatch stealth probes into the region. They'd found much of the Varadah force there—and something else.

"That's *Enterprise*, all right," Baladon said from his seat on the bridge. "Or the front half, anyway. And we count twenty-seven Rengru mother ships surrounding it." He turned his head to face Kormagan and smiled toothily. "A veritable menu of delights. Which one should I go after first?"

"Don't be ridiculous." The carrier was hopelessly outmatched.

At the Lurian's side, Connolly—who, like Baladon, rarely kept his headgear deployed outside of battle, no matter how often Kormagan chided them—simply stared at *Enterprise* in wonderment. He'd said nothing. As opmaster for *Urdoh-Two*, it was his right to be present on the bridge—and Kormagan was now glad he was. "I thought you said *Enterprise* was crippled, damaged beyond repair after it broke in two. What's it doing there?"

Connolly didn't avert his eyes from it. "I thought the same thing you did. When the recon probes didn't find it after we evacuated the first time, I assumed it had been destroyed—or fled." His brow furrowed. "Maybe they ran and just got found."

"They couldn't have gone far in that configuration," Baladon said. "Not without warp nacelles."

That made even less sense to Kormagan. "If they'd tried to flee the rift on impulse, our probes in the clouds would have seen them. Could they have landed on some pebble here?"

Connolly seemed reticent to say much more about *Enterprise*'s capabilities. Baladon rolled his eyes. "Just answer, human. You've got nothing to gain now."

"Fine," Connolly said, shaking his head. "That part is not really designed to take off again. I mean, I *guess* it could, but I can't imagine how. I'm a scientist, not an engineer."

"It's obviously moving with the convoy." Kormagan looked more closely at the surveillance imagery. "It looks like the Rengru fighters are pushing it—but I can't imagine they'd be enough to more than turn it."

"Sensors detect impulse drive activity." Baladon looked to Connolly. "Somebody's got to be aboard that thing running it."

Kormagan saw Connolly's eyes widen at that. "Did the probes detect life signs on *Enterprise*?" he asked. Detecting them was a major part of the Boundless's recruiting operations.

"Didn't get in close enough," Baladon said. "They've kind of got her wrapped up."

That was an understatement. Kormagan looked more closely at the visual feed in her headgear's interface. "I don't understand. I've never seen the Rengru throw this much materiél into one operation before."

"You think that's the interesting part?" Baladon guffawed and slapped his armored knees. "You're both missing the obvious."

Kormagan glared at him. "*What?*"

"They're not trying to destroy it anymore. They're keeping it for themselves."

Kormagan had been so bewildered by the size of the force and the reemergence of *Enterprise*, she'd given little thought to that part. "What would Rengru want with a starship?"

Connolly looked confused. "Am I missing something here? I seem to remember them starting a fight over it. I'm pretty sure I was there."

She ignored the sarcasm. "They were trying to deny us the ship. That's what they always do. But they only take raw materials for themselves. Piracy isn't their tactic at all."

"Yeah, I guess we're the tech scavengers, not them," Baladon said. "Unless it's something they can't resist using."

Kormagan couldn't imagine what it might be. The whole idea defied any precedent. Rengru built things for themselves, only and always.

Connolly seemed lost in thought, she noticed. "Do you know what it is?"

"Who, me?" He appeared to come out of his haze. "I don't know what you're talking about."

"Just like Spock," she said to Baladon. "He would never give away anything about his ship's technology. Something about a First Directive."

"Prime," Connolly volunteered. "You're not technically

the kind of civilization that we'd use it for, but meddling in your war qualifies as something we wouldn't do."

Baladon chortled. "I thought you'd left all that business behind. Seems to me you've all been working for us for the better part of a year."

"Under duress."

"O blithering fool, you don't know what duress feels like."

Kormagan put up her hands. "Enough! If only all our recruits fought the Rengru the way you two fight one another."

Connolly shrugged. "It kills the time."

"I'll say," Baladon said, rising from his chair. "Are we finished here? Jayko fooled with my armor lining again and it's been chafing me for weeks."

Connolly blinked. "You're going to leave *Enterprise* to the Rengru?"

"We can't fight them." Baladon looked to Kormagan. "We can't, can we? Because it would be a pleasure."

"No, of course not." Kormagan had but one carrier. She turned to depart. "Set a course back to the Varadah Gap. We can see whether or not Dreston just got us the dregs."

"Wait!" Connolly said. "I don't want to lose it again."

"It's lost," Baladon said. "They may have traded the whole Varadah Gap for it—but it's theirs." He tilted his head. "You've been thinking about *Enterprise* for months. Isn't it better this way, knowing it's gone? Now you can focus on being part of the Boundless."

"But the people might not be gone."

"If they're on a ship full of Rengru," Kormagan said, continuing to walk, "they certainly are."

"But they could have beamed off before—"

Kormagan stopped and looked back. "Could have what?"

Connolly froze. "I . . . said that they could have gotten off the ship."

"How?" She advanced toward him. "You said they probably couldn't land and take off again. And there are no shuttle-bays on this portion of the ship. We've known that ever since analyzing the imagery from *Deathstruck*!"

"Still wrong," Baladon said.

Connolly fidgeted. "There are escape pods. That's what I meant."

"Then why didn't we see them from either half of the ship months ago?" Kormagan got right up against his armor. "You said they could have *beamed* off. Do you have some capability that you haven't told us about yet?"

Connolly went white—and Baladon slapped his forehead. "Oh, this is rich. Simply tremendous!"

"*Baladon . . .*"

"They don't *know*!" Baladon's armored arms went to his midsection as he bellowed with laughter. "*The Boundless don't know!*"

Kormagan grew cross. She barked, "What in K'davu's name are you talking about?"

Baladon wiped away tears. "I assumed you'd have found out long before you captured me. Did you ever wonder how *Enterprise*'s teams got down to Susquatane?"

"The same way everyone does," Kormagan said. "We knew about the shuttles."

"Yes, we landed in shuttles," Connolly said. "They dropped us off and flew back to—"

"Give it up, little human." Baladon shook his head. "No, I guess if the Boundless had never caught a Starfleet vessel before, they wouldn't know. I certainly couldn't afford one on my ship."

Kormagan's arms shot out, her hands grabbing the collars of both Connolly's and Baladon's armors. "*Talk!*"

"My pleasure," Baladon said, putting his hands up and smiling. "Let me tell you about *transporters . . .*"

60

U.S.S. Enterprise
Stardrive Section
Cloud Complex Zedra

"Here comes Rengruna," Boyce said to Amin.

"I heard that," Una said, entering the tiny control room. She smiled from beneath the Rengru's head, which covered hers almost like a hood. "You know, Doctor, just because I've melded with an alien being, we shouldn't sacrifice decorum."

"Duly noted." The name had started circulating mere days after Una reawakened—and while she understood it to be a lighthearted way of making the crew feel more comfortable about her transformation, she didn't think it should come from senior staff.

She didn't count herself in that category. She'd been compromised, and she didn't expect the crew to follow her orders. That they largely had deferred to her reflected a combination of factors. The behavior of the Rengru outside had completely changed—and hers hadn't. That, plus general exhaustion, had once again made her Number One on the stardrive section—if carrying a particularly ungainly asterisk.

Boyce rose from a command station where he had not had much to do lately. "Same picture outside as always: Rengru mother ships galore. Just sitting there—the way we like it."

"Thank you, Doctor."

"The 'bridge,' if this closet can be called that, is yours." As

Boyce tried to edge past her on the way out the door, the Rengru limbs extending from her conjoined partner reshaped to let him pass. He shook his head. "If we ever get home, remind me to retire. This ship is altogether too weird for me."

Life had not been any more normal for Una over the past several weeks. Their captive Rengru's attack, she had come to realize, had not been that at all. She knew from their shared intelligences that it was following a preternatural drive directing it to unite with bipedal beings. Boyce had initially treated the Rengru as a parasite, and her as the host—but that didn't seem right. Nor was *she* the parasite, though somehow during her coma the Rengru had reduced her need for sustenance. She was still searching for the proper metaphor.

What she did know was that, during her slumber, her neural pathways had adapted—or been made to adapt—to the Rengru's presence. It served as a second spine, now, rising from the small of her back and curling over her like a headdress. Several of its limbs clutched her in a bear hug, keeping it affixed as she moved—with the rest of its appendages free to manipulate objects. She found that she didn't have to concentrate much to make use of them.

The more important discovery had been that the Rengru had some kind of channel open to others of its kind. It was not, she suspected, telepathy; it seemed to be an evolved system, somehow making use of the many different kinds of energetic emissions crisscrossing the Pergamum. It was also why, she believed, the Rengru seemed to favor some regions over others.

They had certainly been great in number in the space near the stardrive section—and, indeed, had been amassing for what might have been a decisive strike when Una's joined companion reentered the conversation, literally. She'd found herself understanding what she was "hearing"—and not just eavesdropping, but participating.

Rengru social order seemed to be based, as near as she could tell, on a theory of governance Boyce had called "Any More Bright Ideas?" While there were cells of behavior organized around starship construction, fortress building, and other activities, much of that ran on automatic. Tactical insights rarely occurred, but when they did, many of their number took notice. So it was that when her Rengru familiar opened a conduit for communication, she found herself talking to parties that were not only stunned to hear from her, but fascinated by what she had to tell them.

And willing to tell her something Rengru scouts had known of for some weeks, but decided to ignore: strange radio communications between two moons of a failed star in the area where the saucer section had disappeared.

"The armada's back," Mann said, pointing to her monitor. She smiled. "They've brought company!"

Una already knew. She closed her eyes and mouthed the words as she thought them: *Follow the directives.*

Eyes opening, she typed a quick message and sent it, before turning to Mann. "Lieutenant, I'd like the room."

"Aye, Commander."

Then she waited. Waited for the cheers to break out aft of the control room as others saw the saucer section arrive. Waited for the alert that her particular guest had transported over. Waited for the next roars to die down, as everyone came out to see him as he made his way forward.

And waited for Christopher Pike to be able to speak after he saw what she had become.

"*Una?*"

"Welcome aboard, Captain. We have a lot to talk about."

61

Combat Module Carrier 539-Urdoh
Varadah Gap

Baladon's mouth had caused more than a stir. Kormagan had ordered him to turn *Carrier Urdoh* around, whereupon it had raced back to the Varadah system, and the many Boundless operations underway there. Busy plundering and consolidating positions, the other wavemasters had been most reluctant to respond to Kormagan's appeal to meet. But Kormagan had activated a rarely used emergency power, calling for a confab of all the wavemasters in the area. It put at risk her own prestige and position—but she clearly considered it to be worth it.

Connolly understood why. It had been the reason behind all the *Enterprise* abductees remaining silent all year: every technological capability the Boundless learned about made it all the more likely that they would redouble their pursuit of the starship. Since Connolly's months with Baladon's traveling press gang, he had come to think that transporter technology would be the worst thing in the universe for the Boundless to get their hands on. They would kidnap at will, then, whole populations from ships and settlements—and possibly beyond the confines of the Pergamum.

So he had tried his best on the flight back from Little Hope to make it seem like Baladon was telling a tall tale—until it became clear that was no longer tenable. Baladon had noted that a little general information about transporters had been in the database from his pirate ship. While Kormagan had sworn that her people analyzed everything, she'd concluded, after checking, that Baladon was telling the truth.

"They didn't look very carefully," she had said, upset with her team. "They weren't very impressed with you."

"I am wounded," he had replied.

Knowing there was no way to deny the existence of transporters—and that a supreme meeting was coming up, Connolly had realized there was another play. One that required him to stop his denials and start selling instead.

As a soldier, Connolly had seldom seen the carrier's briefing room; the Boundless method was to throw troops at trouble and instruct them on the way, if it told them anything at all. Designed for a platoon of twenty-five, the carrier's briefing room, by all accounts, had never seen so much brass. Insignias announced the leaders of waves from the venerable Thirty-Twos—which existed almost in name only, now—all the way up to the latest outfit, the Six-Ohs.

Connolly was on display—and Baladon—as Kormagan made her case. She had stowed her headgear, for a change, so as to more emphatically make her case—and so had several of the listeners whose anatomies allowed it. It made it all the easier for Connolly to tell that not one of her colleagues wanted to be there.

"After Little Hope, I'd think you'd be afraid of more boondoggles," declared Gavlor of the Fifty-Sevens. "You're telling me that these Starfleet people have on *Enterprise* the ability to move matter—"

"Including living beings," Kormagan said.

"—including living beings, from one place to another, by converting it to energy and beaming it through space. Why is this the first I've heard of it? We'd have gone with you on that operation months ago!"

"We all would have," said another.

"I was there, and I didn't even know," Quadeo said, pointing accusingly at Kormagan. "I think she was going to keep it for her own wave!"

Intimidated before, Connolly spoke up. "She didn't know about it because I didn't tell her. I didn't want you to capture *Enterprise.* If you'd succeeded, you'd have found out about the transporters anyway."

Old Barson from the Thirty-Twos was skeptical. "Can this really exist? In all the ships we've captured, we never heard of it before."

"We invented it back in the last century," Connolly replied. "It was only in our most advanced ships for a long time."

"It's really very unfair of them to hog it," Baladon said, standing off to the side. "The privateering profession would be far more civilized if you'd share." Kormagan gave him a bad look.

"This is nonsense," Quadeo said. "Kormagan, you've finally lost your mind. You have brought us here with no evidence, wanting us to listen to the fantasies of these people. You might as well surrender your charter, because when word gets out about this to the rest of your crew—"

"And how will that happen, I wonder?" Kormagan asked.

Connolly clapped his hands together. "Hey, wait. I just remembered something. *I can prove it.*"

Kormagan regarded him warily as the human called upon his armor to produce the compartment with his personal effects. His clothing from Susquatane was there, as were a couple of his scientific instruments. And something else. "This device takes visual recordings," he said. He looked to a forward screen. "Does that interface with the armor systems?"

A quick connection later, they were all looking at a field of snow. "My friend Ghalka took this on Susquatane the day before you all—er, dropped in."

Kormagan frowned. "What are you doing there with that stick?"

"I'm—uh—driving snowballs to center field. I was going to show my friends back home that I was still keeping in shape for the season."

"What season?"

"That's what *I've* been saying. I missed the whole thing this year. Just watch."

The image showed Connolly throwing snowballs into the air, striking them. Some went farther than others; some disintegrated. After a couple of swinging miscues, Quadeo asked, "Are we supposed to be impressed by this?"

"Hey, it's just a fungo bat. But Susquatane's snow worked pretty well." He pointed. "Now, here it is."

Connolly's past self smacked a fly ball high into the sky. The person taking the video turned the imager to follow its motion—and captured a living being, materializing out of nowhere: Spock. Noticing the snowball falling toward him, the Vulcan snatched it from the air. Wearing a wooden expression, he pointed toward the imager.

"I guess I'm out," Connolly said, embarrassed.

"What just happened there?" Quadeo said. "Is that a trick?"

"No trick. See?" The video continued to run, showing Ghalka handing the imager to Connolly. He pointed it at her just long enough for it to record her dematerializing. "She had to go back up to *Enterprise*. It was a shift change."

A sea change is what Connolly saw when he looked back at the others. Mouths hung open—and within seconds, the room was abuzz with heated conversations. Connolly shut off the recording and smirked. "So I guess you believe me now, huh?"

62

Combat Module Carrier 539-Urdoh
Varadah Gap

"This is a calamity!" Barson declared. "The worst of all disasters! What could the *Rengru* do with this?"

Baladon snorted. "What *couldn't* they do? If they knock down our energy shields, they can put Rengru aboard this very ship."

"Yeah," Connolly said. "That's right. We board other people's ships all the time using the transporters." He pointed to Baladon. "That's why the captain here didn't stand a chance against us. He had to do things your way, punching holes through hulls. We could have beamed right onto his bridge."

Baladon nodded. "It would have meant less property damage."

"The Rengru could board our vessels," Quadeo said, less vocal now. "But we have shields."

"The Rengru manage to breach your shields all the time," Connolly said. "And as soon as they're breached?" He made a *whoosh* sound and waved his hand. "They could beam you out into space or into a sun. Or into their ships—where they'd be waiting."

"This device works through starship hulls," Gavlor said. "Astounding."

"Of course. It's the whole idea. And transporters can

send other things too. Back last year, Baladon was firing his little photon torpedo at us. We could have beamed one into his lap!"

Baladon laughed. "You know that Starfleet is too weak willed for that." He faced the others. "But yes, they could become potent weapons—in the *right* hands."

"Or the wrong ones," Kormagan added.

Connolly saw an opportunity to press. "It's not limited to starships either."

"What do you mean?" Quadeo asked.

"The transporters can be installed anywhere. I had one down the hall from my room at the Academy." He gestured grandly. "Think of it. You put together another of your wonderful ground assaults, perfectly executed. And as soon as your forces are near enough—"

"Can I make the noise?" Baladon asked.

Connolly ignored him. "Suddenly you're out of your armor altogether. Maybe you're a kilometer in the air, or in the middle of a room full of knockout gas." He stared directly at Quadeo. "Or full of Rengru, if you prefer."

She put up her hands. "Stop. Our armor has energy shields too."

"Great! You'll be able to look around longer when they beam you into an active volcano."

Quadeo's voice quavered. "You have this power, and you *don't* use it as a weapon?"

"Of course not," Connolly said. "It's called a *transporter*."

"I take back everything I've ever thought about the Lurians. *You* are the dumbest people I've ever met."

"Yeah, well, we invented it, you didn't."

Kormagan faced Connolly. "How would they exploit this thing? Is it a device that can be removed? Replicated?"

"Not easily," he said. "It's a room. The Rengru could wreck it if they're not careful. So could you."

Gavlor shook his head. "I'm convinced. We can't let the Rengru have this thing. Where are they now?"

Kormagan looked to Dreston, who spoke up. *"Our probes in Little Hope say the convoy just entered Cloud Complex Zedra, at the far end."*

"They're going slowly. Why?"

"The saucer section only has impulse engines and thrusters," Connolly said. "Besides, this nebula of yours tears the hell out of our shields—and *Enterprise* didn't have any, back when you attacked it before. Maybe it still doesn't."

"That means she can be boarded," Kormagan said. "What are the odds the Rengru can exploit this thing?"

"I don't know," Connolly said. "It looks like they've gotten the impulse drive working, but this would be totally new to them—and a foreign ship's data system, to boot."

"The Rengru control the ship," Quadeo said. "Maybe some of your people bartered its secrets for their lives."

"The Rengru don't barter," Kormagan said.

"And my people wouldn't either," Connolly said. "Our practice is to scuttle ships before they're exploited by others."

"Clearly, they failed."

"Yeah, well, *I* won't." Connolly had wound up. It was time for the pitch. "I'll destroy the ship—but not until after I get you the keys to K'davu."

The room went quiet at the word.

"Excuse me?" Kormagan gawked at him. "I was going to recruit the others to hunt and destroy *Enterprise*, just as the Rengru had attempted to do. What are *you* proposing?"

He gazed coolly upon her. "You asked me once before if I'd give you the secrets of *Enterprise*."

"And you wouldn't do it because you weren't one of us. Not yet."

"I never will be. But I don't have to be one of you to think that the Rengru winning is a bad thing. I can do something about that. Like I told you again and again, I'm a scientist. I understand transporter technology pretty well—"

"You can build one for us!"

"Not *that* well. My work's in a different discipline. But if you find me a few of my fellow *Enterprise* crewmates, we might be able to get aboard, download the transporter schematics, grab some of the relevant equipment, and blow up the ship, right under the Rengru's nonexistent noses."

"Why would you do this?" Barson asked. "It hasn't sounded to me like you've much loyalty."

"Oh, I have plenty—just not to you. But it happens that our interests are aligned here."

Kormagan frowned. "Spock tried to work a similar deal, to save the people aboard the ship. They're almost certainly gone now. What would you want? Freedom for your crewmembers, I assume?"

"Yes—but it won't be like that. We'll help you figure out the transporters—and use them against the Rengru. On one condition." He crossed his arms. "Win this war—then come help us with ours. You want us to help you to defeat the Rengru? *Promise you'll help us defeat the Klingons!*"

63

U.S.S. Enterprise
Saucer Section
Cloud Complex Zedra

Since Spock's move to the intensive care unit—and without much else to do with Rengru piloting his ship—Pike had found himself keeping to the pattern he'd established when the two were separated by tens of thousands of kilometers. Only rather than sitting by a communicator, Pike sat by Spock's bedside, talking.

Spock had not always been awake—and when he was, it wasn't easy to tell. He had rarely said anything that made sense, continuing to mumble planet names and other things. It was incoherent. He'd sounded like one sweating out a fever—only Vulcans didn't have sweat glands, and Spock's vitals had stabilized long before. His body was back from Skon's World, but not his mind.

For a change, Pike had news he hoped would bring it back.

"*Enterprise* is reunited," he said. "Well, not really—we're not able to put the sections back together, not out here." It was far from an automatic process, Pike lamented; the designers had assumed any calamity great enough to require a saucer to separate would have resulted in a stardrive section that was either unusable or destroyed. "But we're in the same place, and we've been transporting people back and forth."

Fused with a Rengru, Una had somehow tapped into the life-forms' collective intelligence and prevailed upon the creatures nearby to deliver the saucer section to her. Time was of the essence, she'd said, because the Rengru had intended to destroy both halves of *Enterprise* to deny them to the Boundless—and if other Rengru forces who weren't in communication with her stumbled over the saucer section, they might stick with the original program. The Rengru seized the saucer instead, following her directives specifically—even to the point of offering assistance to any injured crewmembers aboard.

"That's why they helped Galadjian walk you in here a few days ago," Pike said. "I expect the ride was a little rough, but Carlotti says it might have saved your life."

Spock turned his head on the pillow, continuing to mutter as he looked at the bulkhead.

The directives had included walking Pike to the transporters as soon as the saucer section entered Cloud Complex Zedra—and then stepping outside the room while he beamed across to the engineering hull. They'd followed that practice since, as others had passed back and forth between the sections. Una's mind-sharing with "her" Rengru had not given it full access to her knowledge, and she'd decided to avoid introducing them to the idea of transporters while the subject could be avoided.

"All that she's been through, and she's still thinking about the Prime Directive," Pike said. He looked at the back of Spock's head. "I'm sure you'd do the same."

No reaction.

"She told me everything, Spock—everything she thinks she knows about the Rengru and their fight with the Boundless. Galadjian was right. K'davu is the Boundless's homeworld, the place they've been fighting to reclaim. But there's something they don't know about it—and they'll never know, because to communicate, the Rengru have got to make physical contact—

and hold it, for as long as it takes for the joining to occur. The Boundless are all armored. And like you told me, whenever anyone's armor is breached by a Rengru, the Boundless blow them away."

More to the point, Pike said, so much time had elapsed since the war had begun that even the Rengru themselves had forgotten about any need other than to fight it. Una had convinced them that they'd gotten an innocent bystander—and had offered her services to mediate. But first, she'd demanded delivery of the saucer section.

"I don't know if that was a feint to get us back, or not—but the Rengru seem to be cooperating so far. She thinks they really do believe something has gone wrong, something in the basic order of things."

"No. No." Spock's mutter grew more audible. "It has not happened yet."

Pike looked to him. "What hasn't?"

Spock returned to naming planets. Pike sighed.

"Una feels there's only one way to fix it," he said, plowing ahead. "It's something the Rengru would never think of themselves—and something they'd never do on their own. It requires us. And not just us." He clasped his hands and leaned forward, talking more closely into Spock's pointed ear. "It turns out we had aboard the one item she needs to make things work. You brought it to us, Spock. *The Boundless battlesuit.*"

Spock turned and fixed his eyes on the overhead. "Earth," he said. "Qo'noS."

"Spock, you have the key. Galadjian's actually got engineers to work with now—they've certainly seen a change in *him*! But while they think they can get the unit juiced up again, the systems don't respond to anyone." He paused. "It needs to hear from *you*."

"Vulcan. Vulcan. Vulcan."

Pike looked down and shook his head. "I'm sorry this happened to you, Spock. I feel like I failed you. But we really need—"

"*Vulcan,*" Spock said more emphatically. He turned his head toward Pike. "It is . . . the keyword."

He closed his eyes, let out a breath, and went to sleep.

64

Combat Module Carrier 539-Urdoh
Approaching Shennau Corridor

"I'm delighted to see you, Evan," Ghalka said. Wiping away tears of happiness, she looked to her other three *Enterprise* companions. "I never thought I'd see *any* of you again. But what the hell is going on?"

Connolly smiled, happy to see her—as well as Gupta, the ensign who had been kidnapped from the polar camp. He had only encountered the other officers, Godwin and Haddad, once since their abduction, so he was glad to see they were in one piece—and more excited to tell them his news. "Didn't the Boundless explain? They're going to put a team on *Enterprise*—and you're going with them." He pointed to the glowing red light on all their shoulder assemblies. "You're my squad," he said.

"*Enterprise*?" Ghalka blurted, before looking nervously around at the other squads gathering on the carrier's muster deck. "They told us it was destroyed!" she whispered.

He quickly explained about the discovery of the saucer section—and the fact that the Rengru controlled it. Seeing the others' faces fall, he quickly apologized for getting their hopes up. "We don't think there's anybody left on the ship—but we don't know what happened to them either. There's still hope."

"But boarding?" Godwin asked. "Why us? We haven't been in the fighting since near the start."

"The Boundless want us to board *Enterprise* and help them get everything they want to know about the transporters."

"Transporters?" Ghalka was baffled. "I'm a biologist."

"And I'm in security," Gupta said. "If I didn't know disruptors inside and out, I'd probably be fighting Rengru rather than building weapons."

Connolly expected this reaction. "We can still operate the computers, right? I told them I needed everyone we could find, because some of the doors and systems have coded locks—and it takes at least three crewmembers to scuttle the ship."

Haddad's eyes went wide. "But we want to go home."

"And that might happen if we help the Boundless. But it won't be aboard *Enterprise*. That's lost. We just have to deny it to the Rengru."

"I can't scuttle the ship," Ghalka said, looking self-conscious.

Connolly tried to look supportive. "Ensign, we have to, or else the—"

"That's not it." She leaned close to him and mouthed, "*They never told me how to do that.*"

"Me neither," Connolly confessed. "But how hard could it be? The impulse drive still works. We just point it at a sun—or get one of the Boundless to tote one of those tactical nukes aboard."

Connolly pointed over to the other squads gathering. Kormagan was there, as were several of the wavemasters who'd been at his briefing. It was Boundless practice that their greatest generals took the field along with their newest recruits; this grouping, however, was top-heavy.

"These are the all-stars," he said. "Total first-string. Just them and us. And if it works—and the transporter tech helps them beat the Rengru—they've promised to help us defeat the Klingons!"

All four of his crewmates reacted at once to that. "Less than a year ago he's swinging a stick at snowballs," Ghalka said. "Now you're running your own foreign policy?"

Godwin shook her head. "Lieutenant, you are *way* out on a limb here."

"We've been exiled to a nebula, kidnapped, and made to walk around in these things all year. Court-martial is not really on my sensor screen at the moment." Connolly spoke with determination. "Look, if any of you have seen the Rengru fight, you know we can't let them defeat the Boundless. They could go after the Federation next—and if the Klingon War is still going on, that could be a deathblow."

The others nodded.

"The Varadah Gap's fallen. This thing could be ready to break in favor of the Boundless once and for all." He pumped his fist—and then studied the wooden faces of his armored crewmates. "Are you in?"

"We're going to take a meeting to decide your sanity," Godwin said. "But we've never had any choice about where we went, and this'll probably be no different."

"Good," Connolly said, taking it as a victory even though it wasn't a sentiment to feel good about. He patted the light on his shoulder. "Just remember, for this one, you're Red Squad, I'm subaltern."

"You would pick red," Ghalka said.

"Not funny," Gupta responded.

Connolly excused himself to give them time to talk. Similar gaggles were going on all around—only rather than conversing with one another, the wavemasters were on comm with their waves, coordinating the upcoming attack.

Kormagan spied him. "We've got everyone we wanted. Your little talk worked."

"Pieces in motion?"

"Pieces in *action*. Probes say after the Rengru convoy left the cloud complex it went just where we thought—farther up the Shennau Corridor." It was a narrow bottleneck leading right to the Nest, and because of that it was a place the Boundless never struck. Until today. "Three waves have already hit them to slow them down. Four more are coming in."

"That's . . . a lot. And fast," Connolly said. For a force without central command, the Boundless could move quickly when faced with an existential threat.

"There's more to come. I don't know if you really comprehend the scale of the operation that's being mounted. The Rengru convoy grows every kilometer it gets closer to the Nest. They really think *Enterprise* is worth having—and if any of the Boundless didn't think so at Little Hope, everyone does now. A lot of people are risking everything because of you."

Connolly's mouth went dry. "I don't know what to say to that."

"Just get us in and out," Kormagan said, her tone icing. "If you get aboard and change your mind again, we'll treat you as if a Rengru got you and blow you away."

"Noted."

He ambled awkwardly away. It had never dawned on most of the Boundless that a final defeat of the Rengru could even be an option. Looking around the deck at the animated discussions of the other wavemasters underscored for him how important success could be.

"You Federation people," said a figure inside the doorway to the bridge. Baladon stepped fully onto the deck. "A few months running about and you turn everything upside down."

"Something like that. Why aren't you flying this thing?"

"As soon as we run into the Rengru, I'm back to being a boarder. I asked Kormagan to let me come along. This *Enterprise* has become a bit of an obsession for me. Third time is blood or nothing, as they say."

Connolly studied him. Baladon didn't look his usual, smart-aleck self. "What's wrong?"

"I saw your little reunion over there. Others are not so fortunate."

"What do you mean?"

"I received word before we left Varadah," Baladon said. "Just before the Rengru pulled out, a troop module belonging to the Forty-Eights went down with no survivors. Two of my brothers were on it."

"Baladon, I'm sorry." Connolly thought for a moment. "Wait. Weren't you always talking about how you used to threaten them?"

"Yes, but the decision to kill them should have been mine."

"Some weird Lurian custom?"

"No. Just me." Baladon crossed his arms. "There is something else. The others of my species within the Boundless are declining in number every day. The loss of buffoons is no danger to the gene pool, but it occurs to me that *I* might wish to procreate someday. Being the last Lurian alive here might be an impediment to that."

"That just dawned on you, huh?" Connolly smirked.

"These antics have been fun, but if we successfully take the transporters and defeat the Rengru, I could be convinced to found that colony planet and retire."

"Well, we're not done yet. Klingons first, remember?"

"Details." A chime announced that the carrier toting the troop module was approaching the Rengru convoy. Kormagan left her group to hurry forward. Baladon nudged Connolly. "We won't be deploying until the other waves clear the path. Why not come look at some delightful carnage while we wait?"

"Just a second." Connolly looked over at his Starfleet companions. They nodded to him approvingly. *They're on board*, he thought. He turned back to Baladon. "Yeah, I guess I have a minute."

"Splendid." Baladon walked with Connolly toward the bridge. "So, these Klingons. They'll be just as much fun to fight, I hope?"

65

Combat Module Carrier 539-Urdoh
Shennau Corridor

Standing aboard *Carrier Urdoh*'s bridge, Kormagan had never seen anything so majestic—or so dreadful.

The Rengru had protected *Enterprise*'s remnant with everything they had in the region, seemingly willing to endure whatever attacks were necessary to get it back to the Nest. She had obliged them—and more. One after another, Boundless warships leapt from the cover of the cloud banks into the Shennau Corridor. They struck at the Rengru mother ships, dealt whatever damage they could, and darted quickly back into the pillars of dust. Most of the Rengru vessels held position, but occasionally some peeled away in pursuit, thinning out the numbers protecting *Enterprise*'s saucer section.

That had been the plan Kormagan had concocted back at the Varadah Gap summit—a strategy terrible in its costliness. She had never fancied herself anything other than a competent warrior, trying to make good on the promises made so long ago to their K'davu progenitors. "Wavemaster" was as far as there was to go, and now she understood the reason. What right had she to risk so many of the Boundless's ships and personnel—on a hunch? On the basis of some nefarious threat posed by an alien technology?

Setting eyes on *Enterprise* reminded her of the answer. The Rengru's interest was all the convincing she needed. It *had* to be valuable. And now, thanks to her sacrifices, the echelons of Rengru covering the saucer as it traveled were thinning. *No, not just thinning.* She toggled her interface to magnify what she was seeing.

"There's our in," she said, pointing to Dreston, who sat in the captain's chair vacated by Baladon. "Every time one of our carriers strikes off the convoy's starboard quarter aft, the mother ships on the port side of *Enterprise* shift to cover ground vacated by its pursuer."

"So we hit away from the shift," Connolly said.

"I never know what you're talking about." She gestured for Dreston's benefit. "Coordinate with the Fifty-Eights across the corridor. We'll come in parallel and deploy the troop modules when the gap opens." She looked to Baladon. "Satisfactory, Captain?"

He laughed. "You think like a true Lurian pirate."

"Thank you—I suppose." She looked more closely at *Enterprise*, and the Rengru half-ringing the saucer. "Those forces on the hull are serving as attitude-control rockets. I don't think they will be able to disengage quickly to oppose us."

"Agreed." Baladon nudged Connolly. "It's time, my young friend. Button up." Both deployed their headgear.

"I like the look of both of you better that way," Kormagan said. It was time to head for the troop modules. She felt the gravity of the moment. "In K'davu's name," she said, "let this be the day when—"

A chime sounded, heralding a text message appearing in her interface:

ATTENTION, BOUNDLESS. ATTENTION, KORMAGAN.

Five-Three-Nine-Aloga-One-Gold-Five. She didn't immediately recognize the call sign. An icon indicated the party was using an identifier that had since been reassigned to a later recruit. "Who is this?" she said aloud into her mic.

I AM SPOCK.

What? She looked again at the sign—and remembered. She piped the message to the others on the bridge. "What do you make of this?"

"Spock?" Baladon asked.

"Spock!" Connolly shouted.

AND YOU ARE CONNOLLY AND BALADON. IT IS AGREEABLE TO HEAR YOU, LIEUTENANT.

"And no word for your old subaltern?" Baladon asked. "I am disappointed in—"

"Shut up," Kormagan said. She checked the identifier tags on Spock's transmission. The signals were definitely coming from his battlesuit. "Spock, where are you? Why can't we hear you?"

I PREFER NOT TO SPEAK. I AM HIDING ON *ENTERPRISE.*

"He made it!" Connolly said, gleeful.

"Impossible," Kormagan said. "You were hurled off the saucer, like Baladon."

YET HE IS STILL WITH YOU. I FOUND MY WAY BACK AND BOARDED. BUT I WAS TOO LATE.

"The Rengru had control?"

CORRECT.

She frowned. She had no way of confirming where he was. With his governor deactivated, her interface would not be able to track him, even if *Enterprise*'s hull allowed it.

"Spock," Connolly implored. "The crew. Tell me about the crew."

LIEUTENANT, I REGRET TO REPORT THE RENGRU SPARED NO ONE. THE ACTS THEY COMMITTED WERE UNSPEAKABLE.

Kormagan looked past the glowing words in her interface to *Enterprise*'s saucer section, still partially surrounded by Rengru. "What do you want, Spock?"

I HAVE WAITED FOR THE BOUNDLESS TO APPROACH IN THE HOPES OF COMMUNICATING. MY POWER RESERVES ARE ALMOST GONE, AND I FEAR THAT RECHARGING AGAIN WILL DRAW THEIR ATTENTION TO ME.

She understood.

"Spock," Connolly said, "we're just about to—"

"Quiet," Baladon snapped. "Say nothing. It could be a trick!"

"The Rengru don't do tricks," Connolly said. "You both told me that."

Kormagan looked to the others. "Spock has already deceived me once."

I DID NOT DECEIVE. I BOARDED THE SHIP, AS I PROMISED—AND WILL DELIVER IT TO YOU NOW.

"How?"

I AM CONCEALED IN THE SECURITY CHECKPOINT NEAR THE DORSAL AIRLOCK. WHEN I SEE YOUR APPROACH, I WILL UNLOCK IT AND ADMIT YOU.

"If you're that close to the exit, why don't you just leave?"

ILLOGICAL. I HAVE NOWHERE TO GO, AND WOULD SOON BE FOUND.

"That certainly sounds like Spock," Connolly said.

MY WORK IS INCOMPLETE. *ENTERPRISE* IS BETTER OFF DESTROYED OR IN THE HANDS OF THE BOUNDLESS. IF THE RENGRU EXPLOIT IT, THE GALAXY IS IMPERILED.

Kormagan definitely believed that. "What's the defense like there?"

MINIMAL. JUST SUFFICIENT TO OPERATE THE BRIDGE, BUT TOO MANY FOR ME TO DEFEAT ALONE.

"Stand ready, Gold-Five. We're coming for you."

STANDING BY.

She closed the channel, allowing her to speak without her correspondent hearing. The news was incredible, the timing unexpected. "Can we believe any of this?"

Connolly was emphatic. "Spock doesn't lie. And the Rengru don't trick."

Baladon concurred. "I would say we just received a gift. But if you don't trust him, there are other airlocks to enter. As long as the accursed thing doesn't start spinning again."

Kormagan wasn't worried about that. Her eyes were again on the battle outside, and the trails of tumbling shrapnel that used to be ships belonging to her people. One way or another, they had to act. "We'll chance it. Dreston, await my command and move in. Move!"

U.S.S. Enterprise
Saucer Section

Three Boundless squads from *Urdoh-Two* landed on the saucer's hull. Kormagan expected it was by far the most heavyweight assault ever assembled. She led four wavemasters, and Quadeo, who would accept no subsidiary role, led four more—while Connolly was again attached to the hull, this time leading his former *Enterprise* teammates.

"No reaction from the Rengies on the hull," Quadeo transmitted. *"They're not even responding."*

That made Kormagan correct, but she didn't mention it to her rival. They were past internecine disputes now. "Converge on target," she said, pointing up the slope toward the saucer's center. Connolly was already most of the way there, with Baladon at his side.

"I should be the first aboard," the Lurian said, shoving. *"It's my right."*

"What if it's a trap?" Connolly asked.

"Quite right. You should be the first aboard."

Kormagan tuned them out by opening another channel. "Spock, we are here."

AS AM I. ENTER QUICKLY. YOU WILL ALL BE REQUIRED.

Within a second of reading the message, Kormagan saw the airlock open. An armored figure was visible in silhouette for several moments—long enough for her interface to identify him.

"Step it up," she called out to the others. The Rengru on

the hull certainly had noted their presence; it was likely those inside had as well.

She arrived at the airlock after Connolly and Baladon had already entered. Inside, past a darkened lounge, was an open portal leading to a shaft of some kind; her companions were already inside, flying upward on their jetpacks. Above them, Kormagan saw their benefactor step off the top ladder rung into a brightly lit aperture.

Moments later, Kormagan set foot, weapons drawn, on *Enterprise*'s bridge. The round room was brightly lit, with a railed-off circular area recessed into the floor at the center. A control room—

—but no Rengru. Just Baladon, walking cautiously about on alert, and Connolly, standing next to what she presumed was the captain's chair. And seated in it, the warrior that had opened the airlock.

"Where are the Rengru?" she asked as her companions filed in behind her.

Quadeo entered. "Not seeing anything on the other levels."

"Well?" Kormagan moved into the command well in front of the chair. "You said there were invaders here, Spock. Connolly said you never lie!"

"That's true. But you see, the thing is—I'm not Spock." With a whir, the seated figure stowed his headgear, revealing a stern-faced older human with dark hair. "Captain Christopher Pike, *U.S.S. Enterprise*. And the only invaders here . . . are *you*!"

66

U.S.S. Enterprise
Saucer Section
Shennau Corridor

This battlesuit makes my butt too big for this chair, Pike thought. *I hope I don't have to get up in a hurry.*

Of course, he had no intention of being anywhere other than where he was—even with several members of the Boundless looming menacingly around him. Their immediate attention was on one another, anyway.

"If you *Enterprise* recruits are thinking about betraying us, think again," one of the Boundless said. Pike's interface had previously identified the speaker as someone named Kormagan. "His battlesuit's governor may not work," she said, "but yours do." She made a gesture—and five of the warriors froze in place. Head protectors retracted into their battlesuits, revealing Connolly and four other crewmembers. "I do not doubt your loyalty, but I must sort this out."

"I doubt their loyalty," said another Boundless member. "This is some kind of trap!"

"Patience, Quadeo." Kormagan walked in front of Pike. "What, did you think to lure us here and decapitate our command? The Boundless are eternal, Captain. One rises to replace another. Succession is what we're best at!"

"You've got me wrong. That's not what I had in mind at

all." Pike interlaced his fingers. "I wanted to meet the people who thought they could steal my crew."

"Just grab him," Quadeo said. "We'll put him in a suit for real and throw him at his Rengru friends!"

"Maybe later," Kormagan said. "Don't forget why we're here." She looked to Connolly. "Are you going to help us, or must we do this the hard way?"

Pike drew a blank. "What's she talking about, Lieutenant?"

Immobilized, Connolly quickly explained that the Boundless had come in search of transporter technology—and that they intended to scuttle the ship afterward. "I didn't think you were still alive, Captain."

"We all are—barely. We thought the same about you. I'm glad to see you all." He nodded to Connolly. "Nice beard, by the way."

Kormagan looked to the space battle raging outside. "I can't believe the Rengru left you here alone—or will spare us much more time. Give us what we need, Captain Pike. The transporters!"

"Well, I can tell you they work. That's how we got everyone off the ship so I could have this little conversation in private." He smiled, adding, "But they haven't gone far."

"That's enough," Quadeo snarled, pushing past Kormagan and pointing a weapon in Pike's unprotected face. "Stop with the games!"

"No games," Pike said, gaze not on the barrel, but the main viewscreen beyond. "In fact, here comes the rest of our crew now."

The Boundless turned toward the screen and saw the other half of *Enterprise* racing toward them. Rather than attack it, the Rengru mother ships opened a lane for it to pass through—an event that clearly alarmed Pike's guests. For a moment, it looked as if the engineering hull was going to collide with the saucer section—until at the last second, it swooped overhead.

"Where'd it go?" Quadeo asked, pulling the weapon away.

"Just passed behind us. You'll see it return in a second. Keep watching."

The stardrive section soared back into view just ahead of the saucer, traveling more slowly and in the same direction. A blue light flashed beneath the hull—

—and the whole saucer section shook. "Is that a weapon?" Kormagan asked.

"Everything we do that moves things, the Boundless thinks is a weapon," Connolly said. He'd been agog, marveling at the whole sequence. "They don't know what a tractor beam is, Captain."

"That's a shame," Pike said, "because it's pretty useful. You see, we're on impulse only, and our maneuverability is shot. But while our engine section may not be able to push us, it can definitely pull us."

The acceleration, mild at first, was fully noticeable. To the alarm of the Boundless, the engineering hull surged forward, the saucer in tow.

"We've got to get out of this thing," one of the other Boundless said. *"Now!"*

"No," Pike said, "I don't think so. You've had months to get to know my people, but we've just met. I don't want you to leave just yet."

"We are leaving," an infuriated Quadeo said. "I don't care about any stupid transporter."

"I think you'll stay."

Quadeo's disruptor was in his face again. "And how will you stop us?"

"Oh, *I* won't. But someone else will." Pike spoke into the air. "Mister Spock, are you with us?"

Everyone on the bridge heard the response over the intercom: *"I am, Captain."*

"It turns out I'm not the only one aboard," Pike said to the others. "I have a gaggle of engineers down in sickbay, huddled with an old acquaintance of yours. Lieutenant, if you're feeling up to it, I'd like you to have the honors."

"Thank you," Spock said over the intercom. *"Boundless units: Freeze."*

Pike continued looking at the barrel of the disruptor—and realized that its owner had no way to operate it. He stood carefully, dislodging himself from his seat and edging around Quadeo. *All* the Boundless on the bridge were statues now.

"Way to go, Captain Pike!" Ghalka said.

"Credit where it's due," Pike said, pacing about his new museum of metallic art and ignoring the howls of complaint from the Boundless. "Back when he was stranded, Spock told me all about you. He said that even your leaders—your wavemasters—had these governors on their battlesuits." He rapped at the sphere over Kormagan's shoulder.

"That got me thinking," he continued. "You stole our scientists, but not our engineers. I didn't have access to them myself for months. But once we were reunited, I brought them a little gift: Spock's battlesuit." He regarded his armored arm. "Your manufacturing is really something. Even though Spock took a laser torch to his governor, our people were still able to figure out how it worked. And what channel it operated on—and how to issue a signal of their own to your units on the bridge."

Connolly looked at him. "Can *we* move, sir?"

"Spock, can the team down there figure out who's who?"

There was a pause. *"This is Galadjian. We are working on that now."*

Pike wasn't surprised to hear the engineer's voice. Spock

wasn't even back at ten percent—but in his lucid moments he'd insisted on helping. The captain hoped this was part of the way back for him.

"When our carrier sees we've been out of contact, they'll fight your signal," Kormagan said. "Whatever reprogramming you've done, they'll reverse!"

"We're not some tour group that wandered in," Pike said. "I have some of the best computer operators in the cosmos. You characters just steal stuff."

He turned to face the viewscreen, where the nebular clouds were flying by as the convoy picked up ever more speed. "You also seem to like to steal people. Well, now I'm stealing all of *you*!"

67

U.S.S. Enterprise
Saucer Section
Approaching the Nest

Leaders of the Boundless loved to posture, claiming that they had never known fear. Kormagan thought that was nonsense. Across her decades of service, fear had saved her more than once, driving her away from situations where there was no hope for survival for her troops, much less victory.

Nothing she had ever felt compared to what she was going through now. From her stationary position, she had watched the screen as the Rengru convoy—now a pair of flying chevrons, forward and aft—protected both halves of *Enterprise* as they soared ever faster. Boundless carriers had kept up for an hour, only to fall behind as the formation reached depths of the Shennau Corridor no Boundless member alive had seen.

The saucer's bridge, already crowded, had grown busier still, as more of the *Enterprise* crew entered via the shaft to something Pike called a "turbolift." Pike and his vile engineers had sadistically manipulated the battlesuits of the Boundless, forcing the wavemasters plus Baladon to all stand to either side of the command well, heads facing the screen—and the doom that certainly awaited them all.

But she could still see Pike—and that gave her a chance. "Captain, can you order my headgear to be stowed? I wish you to see my face."

Pike called someone on his communicator and made the request—and seconds later, was staring into her eyes. "You have something to say?"

"Captain, I have underestimated you and your people. This I regret. But you are making a grave mistake." She looked to the screen. "Clearly you have made some kind of—*alliance* with the Rengru." The words curdled in her mouth. "It is misguided. You're taking us to the Nest, where the Rengru will tear us apart!"

"Is that so?"

"You don't know, Captain. We don't even tell our own people, because it's too horrible. The Rengru inject feeding tubes into the backs of their victims' necks—and devour their brains. Then they implant their young in the empty skulls!"

"Wouldn't it make more sense if they implanted the young first and let *them* devour the brains?" Pike looked around to his crew. "I mean, I've heard some scary monster stories in my day, and what really sells them is logic." He pointed to the air. "Now, Vulcans—you'd think they'd be *great* at writing horror."

"Stop being foolish," she implored him. "You are in immediate danger!"

"Eh," he said, turning to look at a data device a human held before him. "Sorry if I seem a bit distracted. We didn't want you to see a ship full of people and Rengru when you got here, so I had to move most everyone to the stardrive section." He shook his head. "This whole thing has played hell with the duty rosters."

Kormagan's eyes goggled. "Did you say the Rengru were aboard?"

"Yes. They left. I asked them to."

"You did *what*?"

Pike shook his head. "You've been fighting forever—and yet both of you know jack squat about the other. It's time that changed." He spoke to the air. "Commander, whenever you're ready."

Forward, beneath the large screen, the air itself began to glow. It was like the effect she'd seen on Connolly's video, but the being that materialized was not. It was a human female, partially enshrouded by the limbs of a Rengru clinging to her back.

Words of disgust streamed from Kormagan's stilled companions. "What is *that*?" Quadeo said.

Pike approached her. "I'd like to have you meet my Number One, Commander Una." A human dressed as Boundless greeted a human wrapped within a Rengru. "I'm sure you're glad to be back on the bridge."

"It has been a while," the black-haired woman said. She faced the Boundless—and several of the Rengru appendages writhed, recoiling. "There is nothing to fear."

"Do you say that to us, or to *that*?" Kormagan asked.

"To you both." Una glanced at the limbs, which settled at her side. "This meeting is long in coming." She looked to Pike. "Captain, the Rengru have given me an updated navigation report."

"I'd tell you to take your station, but neither of us are really designed for the furniture right now. Lieutenant Amin, take the commander's information."

The Rengru-human hybrid walked right past Kormagan. It was a horrible, mesmerizing spectacle—but what was on the screen was worse. The nebular corridor had ended, with the Rengru mother ships peeling away to reveal a vast floating complex of space factories and shipyards.

"The Nest," she whispered. It was the black fortress, the innermost seat of Rengru defenses. No Boundless force had threatened it since the waves were in the double digits. Her worst fears were realized. "Pike, I implore you. There is still time to stop!"

"Why would we want to stop?" Pike asked, his back to the screen. Then he looked back. "Oh, that? That's not where we're going."

Kormagan and her colleagues watched, forcibly transfixed, as *Enterprise*'s stardrive section towed it closer to—and *through*—the elements of the floating Rengru megalopolis. Soaring beyond, into another bank of nebular clouds, completely black.

And then: stars. Young and bright, within a pocket in the heart of the vast nebula complex. The *Starship Enterprise* veered toward the nearest, traveling as fast on impulse as the tow would allow.

"Increase magnification," Pike ordered.

"Magnification, aye."

A single globe orbiting the star appeared first as a tiny dot—growing, eventually, into something all the wavemasters immediately recognized, even though none of them had ever laid eyes on it directly.

"*K'davu*," Kormagan whispered.

She said no more. But her thoughts were alive with the words of one long dead—and the words she had always longed to say: *We are coming home, Greatmother Eudah.*

68

U.S.S. Enterprise
Saucer Section
Approaching K'davu

Still armored, Pike clanked off the pad in the main transporter room. "Thanks for bringing me down here," he said to Pitcairn. "We have *got* to get those turbolifts fixed. Connolly tells me I can just jetpack up and down the shaft, but I'm afraid of becoming a human torpedo."

"We don't mind the work," Yamata said, standing next to his boss. "We're just glad to be back on station."

"And doing what we can without full power," Pitcairn added. "We'll have rewritten the book this mission on how to operate with half a ship."

"Save room for a few chapters," Pike said. "We're taking the whole tour group down to K'davu, so you'll be beaming them down here first before sending them on their way."

"Yeah, I guess all our shuttles are in the wrong section," Yamata said. "And I'm not sure our guests would even fit through the doors."

Pitcairn smiled. "Sure you don't want to try another saucer landing?"

"I see the ordeal hasn't hurt your sense of humor," Pike said. The *Enterprise* had barely gotten aloft. The saucer would never make it out of a real gravity well.

He'd been even more curt with the Boundless, who were

still imprisoned on the bridge; Federation first-contact specialists probably would not approve of his handling of them. He didn't care. "First contact" in this case had meant the Boundless kidnapping nearly a sixth of his crew for the better portion of a year, and the second contact hadn't been any better.

Yamata pressed a control—and Una and a still-armored Connolly materialized. They stepped down to meet Pike. "Our guests are . . . resigned," she said. "They don't like me very much, but K'davu has them spellbound."

"They're not too happy with me, either," Connolly said. "I think Baladon's about to rupture something."

"The Lurian, right?" The frozen Baladon had also asked for his headgear to be stowed. "Tell him it's payback for his torpedo way back when."

Connolly looked pensive. "I've told Number One what I know about K'davu, Captain. The others and I would like to go along."

"Still asking for the away missions. That didn't work out so well the last time." Pike shook his head. "Boyce and Carlotti want to check all of you out, to see if you're suffering any of the same effects that Spock did."

"I get it—but we'd like to see how this plays out. It's kind of personal."

That, Pike understood. But he had a condition. "If we're going to visit another world, I want my scientists to do some science. Bring your equipment."

"Yes, sir!" Connolly said, cracking a smile. "Now I just need a change of clothes. You wouldn't believe how much I've been looking forward to that."

"You'll have to wait a little longer," Una said. "You'll need an environment suit on K'davu. It will make sense when you get there."

Connolly's face fell. "Then I guess I keep this damn thing on."

"Sorry," Pike said. "But come to think of it, I'll need to get out of this thing for a few minutes. I'll be right back."

Exiting the suit was easy, thanks to his engineers' instructions. He walked quickly down the hall to sickbay, where Boyce, newly restored to his domain, gestured to his lone patient in the ward. "He won't sleep—and he won't let me medicate him. Maybe you can talk sense into him."

Pike found Spock sitting up in bed, rubbing his hands together. He started with the good news. "It worked perfectly, Spock. I wish you'd been up there to see it—the Boundless leaders are powerless."

Spock looked at Pike. His beard had been trimmed, the captain saw.

"Do you understand me?" Pike asked. "It's done. And you gave the command."

"I . . . just said a word."

That was true: the engineers had done all the rest. It didn't matter. "You earned a share of this. And I'm willing to take you down to K'davu with us, if you want. In an environment suit, of course." Pike had changed out of the battlesuit intentionally so as not to confront Spock with his prison for the past year.

Spock's eyes focused on something Pike could not see. He began mouthing words again—only this time, soundlessly. After a few seconds, he looked at Pike and spoke. "Captain . . . I *cannot*."

"Okay. I don't want to push you. How are you feeling, Spock?"

"I have . . . bad dreams."

"I didn't know Vulcans had them. I guess everybody does."

"My mother said that." He shook his head. "I cannot tell . . . when I am awake."

"From what the doctor says, you nearly always are." Pike looked to Boyce out in the examination room. The doctor shrugged. "You weren't even in charge of your own body most of the year—and stuck on that snowball for a lot of it. Anyone's sleep patterns would be wrecked."

Spock started to say something—and stopped, gripping his hands together more tightly. "I will control this—and return to duty. But not yet."

"All anyone could ask."

"You have obligations," Spock said. "Meditate—I mean, *mediate*. Find the peace between them."

"If it's there to be found. Una thinks so." Pike rose. "Stay strong, my friend."

Boyce followed Pike out into the hall. "It's like he never came back from where he went, Chris."

"What did you expect, Phil?"

"I expect *Spock*." Boyce pointed a thumb back at sickbay. "I read Gabrielle's notes about him from when he was on Skon's World—and took a look at the medical reports Galadjian's people were able to coax out of the battlesuit. He was under physical and emotional duress, yes, and we could tell. But he was coping—right until he got out of that armor. What we beamed off that ice sheet was someone else."

Pike growled in aggravation. "Are you talking alien possession on top of everything else we've had to deal with? Because I have about reached my limits on this mission."

"I don't mean that. It's Spock's body, Spock's mind. But his predicament and ours was one level of problems. He's worried about a lot more than that." Boyce stared at him. "Come on. You started having your own moments, two years ago. You know what it's like to be here—*and not here*."

Pike blinked, and the face returned, unbidden: *Vina*.

He patted the doctor on the shoulder. "One existential crisis at a time, Doc. I've got a war to end."

69

K'davu

Kormagan's colleagues had once thought Starfleet's transporter to be a fantasy. It was real. She had just watched several of her companions vanish from the bridge of *Enterprise* when she felt a tingle of energy herself. For an instant, she caught a glimpse of a different room—empty, antiseptic—until things shifted around her again.

K'davu, meanwhile, had been real to the Boundless, even though no living soul had ever visited. It was only when the transporter glow faded that she realized what the real fantasy was: the version of the world they thought they knew.

"Where are the glens?" Barson asked. "Where are the waterfalls?"

Where, indeed? Still unable to move, Kormagan looked in every direction she could—and tried to remember the images she'd been familiar with since childhood. She knew the cities of the Southern Masses looked different for each of the five original Boundless species. The tree-homes of the Jaulawa. The coral castles of the undersea Taaya. The manicured gardens of her own people, the sun-loving Phannak.

Standing on one of the middle terraces of an escarpment, she looked down into what had apparently once been a wide river valley. Now it was a canyon-laced desert, populated by immense towering shapes of bone. Enormous ribbed shells half a kilometer high and several kilometers long lay partially buried in the sand, resembling the bloated bodies of giant slugs. The structures stretched across the former floodplain, climbing hills and partially disappearing in gullies.

And scurrying betwixt and between: Rengru. Seeing them, she realized the edifices resembled gargantuan versions of their bodies—only with the limbs interlocking. *Are these their temples, their hives*?

"This is not K'davu," declared Quadeo. "These are the abattoirs of the enemy. Pike is their agent!"

Kormagan had not seen the Starfleet captain on the terrace—until now. He materialized in front of her, still wearing Spock's battlesuit. The miscreation he called Una arrived separately and approached to greet him. She looked different: more of the Rengru's limbs wrapped around her, shielding her human frame from the sun.

"*Enterprise*, we're all down," Pike said. Kormagan heard those words—but not the response, as his headgear was deployed. "Pitcairn says he's going to take the transporters on both halves of the ships offline for a few minutes," he said aloud. "All the radiation out here's giving the phase transition coils a stomachache." He looked to his companion. "But we should be able to entertain ourselves. It's your show, Number One."

"Thank you, Captain." Una nodded to him—and at the same time, the part of the Rengru crowning her head appeared to bow as well.

Pike pointed at it. "Should I call him One-and-a-Half?"

"It actually doesn't have a gender—or a name. In a sense, all the Rengru in the area are with me, in gestalt. I must say the voices have gotten a lot louder here."

"No surprise."

Kormagan couldn't understand Pike at all. "If you value your officer's life, you should kill them both. She has become a monstrosity!"

"Pipe down." Joined by Connolly and the other rescued Starfleet crew, Pike turned to address the assembled Boundless on the terrace. "Our engineers have sent commands to your battlesuits," he said, "disabling your jetpacks and all weaponry. We're not going to walk you around like puppets, but we will if we have to. And believe me, I won't feel at all guilty."

He gestured—and Kormagan found herself able to move her limbs for the first time in hours. Finally able to turn, she saw that the bluff rose behind her, with dark openings here and there on the higher levels—but there was no getting up there without her jetpack.

"I know what you're thinking," Pike said. "Forget it."

Flexing her tensed muscles, she turned to face him. "Why do you remain hostile to us? You have the upper hand. Pettiness soils your victory."

"That's rich, coming from you."

"We're an honorable people, operating in a dire circumstance."

"Circumstances that you extend to plenty of others who just happen by." Pike's tone was full of disdain. "We've got people in our part of the galaxy who'll run you over to succeed in their crazy quests. We've had about enough of them too."

"It was *you* who came to this nebula," Kormagan said.

"That doesn't mean we're volunteering for your cockamamie—"

"Christopher," Una said, interrupting his response. "This is not productive."

Pike went silent for a few moments before asking something of his colleagues. "Godwin, how's the weather?"

"Improving quickly," Godwin said, holding some kind of instrument in her gloved hand. "That radiation shower is ending fast. We should be able to unbutton soon."

"What's that mean?" Pike asked.

"Stow headgear," Connolly replied.

"Ah. It's my first walking arsenal." As Connolly and the other scientists set up their equipment, Pike strolled the wide ledge. "Una tells me this is K'davu," he said to the Boundless. "Look familiar to any of you?"

"It does not," Kormagan said. "We know the surface of K'davu from images in our database. This place looks nothing like any of them."

"You saw it on approach. You all thought it was K'davu then."

"That was an assumption. We know our world sits in a safe harbor within the nebula—"

"Like you saw."

"—enshrouded by clouds, preventing transmissions. Our probes have never penetrated them. The Nest we passed is actually one of many Rengru space structures covering the approaches to the harbor. We use the singular because no Boundless has ever lived to see more than one and tell the story."

She gestured across the blighted landscape. "I thought, judging by the landforms we saw from orbit, this might be the fertile valley of Drissh. It's clearly not that." Kormagan shook her head. "I don't understand why the Rengru would protect this world if it were not K'davu."

"It *is* K'davu!" Barson yelled.

Kormagan looked back at the old wavemaster. "What?"

"Don't you all get it?" He walked before the others and gestured to the enormous structures, lesions on the land. "This must be K'davu. That is what you have brought us here to see, isn't it, Pike? The Rengru have deformed this world, remaking it in their own beastly images."

"No," Quadeo said. "I refuse. This is a twin planet, one of the other worlds in the harbor. He wants to fool us into thinking our cause is lost!"

"I told you I was tired of quests," Pike said. "If I can actually resolve one, I'll do it." He gestured to Una. "Or rather, she'll do it. Are you ready?"

"I am," Una said. "We are."

She walked down the rise to the next level. Reaching a plateau, she stood alone, arms and Rengru limbs raised. Seconds later, many of the Rengru that had been wandering about below bolted up the ridge toward her.

"Move, fool!" Kormagan said, reaching for a weapon that was not there. "You'll be killed!"

But Una was *not* killed. The herd slowed as it approached her. Joining her on the terrace, the Rengru circled about the human, occasionally touching tendrils with the creature connected to her.

Una looked out on her growing herd—and faced the Boundless. "They say it is time. And they say there is someone to see you."

As if in response to her words, the ground quaked. Across the lands visible from the terrace, one giant shell after another ruptured down the middle, yawning open. Some of the structures released bursts of gas, which curled up into the air as clouds.

Other shells, it could now be seen, were composed of giant interlocking ribs. They curled backward until they were entirely vertical; then the ribs descended into the ground, revealing new landscapes previously hidden within the shells. Geysers erupted—and resolved into fountains, their gushing water flowing into the former river basin through orderly canals.

It took mere minutes for a new world to take shape. Yellow here, orange there, green everywhere: the arbors of the Jaulawa, the pinnacles of the Vis-kals.

And, yes, the gardens of Kormagan's kind.

"They're cocoons," Pike said. "For whole civilizations.

We've spotted thousands of these things, spread all across the planet. They're in the oceans too."

"The solar maximum cycle here is measured in days," Una said, "and changing all the time. The desolation you saw before is what this world *would* look like—without intervention." She turned to watch as the Rengru retreated from her side, dashing off into the newly revealed lands.

Kormagan looked back at her companions. They had seen it too—and were as thoroughly agog as she was.

Shaking, Gavlor pointed. *"There."*

Half-orbs within many of the settings yawned open, revealing first individuals, then multitudes. People, spreading outward to inhabit the new landscape. Kormagan increased her interface's magnification, trying to see what they looked like. Her eyes settled on a single figure stepping onto a hexagonal surface. It floated into the air, carrying the rider aloft—and was soon joined by others, rising from other places. One even rose, dripping, from the new stream.

Una climbed back up to Kormagan's level and stood in wait for the platforms. The five shapes levitated to a stop on the patch behind her. The bipedal riders who dismounted looked like her, only different: more fully enshrouded by the Rengru arms, to the point where their faces were almost completely covered. Kormagan was mystified—

—and baffled further when one of them spoke in the language of her people. "It is safe, now. Show yourselves, those that may."

Pike looked to Godwin, who consulted her instrument and gave a hand signal. In response, the captain stowed his headgear. After testing the air, he nodded to his companions and to the Boundless. "Go ahead."

Kormagan was too fascinated to object. After her headgear withdrew into her armor, she took a deep breath. It nearly intoxicated her: the air of a world she had never known.

No. A homeworld. "This *is* K'davu," she said.

"It is," said the arrival that had addressed them. "I was told true. I have waited so long—and you have come at last." Rengru limbs peeled back, revealing the face of another of Kormagan's kind. "My name is Eudah."

70

K'davu

Una had planned for this moment for weeks. It had been the goal ever since her joining with the Rengru, since coming to understand what they were, and what they wanted. There was only one way, she had concluded, that the Boundless would ever accept what she had learned.

They had to be shown.

"The Rengru cannot communicate normally with others not of their kind," she said. "It requires a physical union. They told me of what existed back here on K'davu, and how it had changed. When Lieutenant Connolly told me of your message from Eudah, Wavemaster Kormagan, I thought it was only right that the Rengru ask her to attend."

Kormagan gawked at Eudah—and the other four riders, all Rengru-joined, each representing one of the five founding races of the Boundless. It could not be *that* Eudah, not possibly. But she had to find out. She spoke tentatively, voice quavering. "*Thank you for what you are doing, daughter. The Rengru are destroying our lives.*"

"*Your duty honors all of us,*" replied Eudah. She smiled. "I wrote those words. Long ago, to Virell, my beloved daughter, as she went off to space."

Kormagan fell to her knees. "*Greatmother?*"

Eudah stepped forward and touched Kormagan's forehead. "I see your face, and I see my child, from long ago."

Kormagan looked up, eyes tearing. "How is it possible? You—"

"Should be dead by now. It could be said of this entire planet." Eudah turned to look out at the alluvial plain. "After the First Wave left K'davu, the Rengru grew ever more frantic, rushing our continents. They knew something we did not: that our star above was about to enter a period of greater, more frequent radioactive emissions, intense even for this nebula. K'davu would have been completely cleansed of life—had it not been for the Rengru."

"This has happened before," said one of her companions, whose golden features were vaguely avian. "Many times, long before our recorded history. Our historians learn more about those times every day. The Rengru are driven now, as they were then, to find us when they know the time is coming—and to protect us."

"Nonsense," Quadeo snarled. One of the Vis-kal species, the wavemaster had vaguely lupine features, Una thought—and a temper. "Why would the Rengru do *anything* for us? What do they get out of it?"

"Your survival," Una replied. "That is all they want. To help their neighbors in need."

"It's coadaptation," Ghalka said, mesmerized. "Two species adapting, cooperatively, to deal with a change in the environment." She looked to Eudah. "I've never seen it happen in so short a time frame. How long has the solar cycle been hostile to life?"

"Hundreds of years. I was here then. Our southern peoples came together as one to battle the Rengru, not knowing what they intended. When they did bond with individuals," she said, clearly horrified, "we killed them before they could communicate. It takes months—sometimes much longer—for the bond to take hold. Few have minds organized well enough to adapt quickly."

Pike chuckled. "They'd never met anyone who grew up with the Illyrians."

Una moved past the praise. "It was an accident that they tried to bond with me at all. I have two legs. They just didn't know the difference."

Eudah went on. "After the space travelers departed, our defenses fell at last. They charged—and bonded with us. Enshrouding us, protecting us. Not in time to save all from the sun, but many. They have spent the last decades helping us rebuild our world so we can live on it."

One of Eudah's other escorts gestured to the Boundless battlesuits. "The Rengru are our own armor against death. When the rays are bad, they protect us doubly, with the structures you saw before."

"And the joining offers other benefits," Eudah said, "such as long life. But I must say I feared I would never see the day when our children returned." She reached for Kormagan with one of her Rengru limbs.

Kormagan swatted it away. "*No.*"

She got to her feet. "I am not Virell. We are not the First Wave! Five hundred and more have come since, all trying to get back to you. All opposed by the Rengru!"

"Whom you were organized to fight," Una said, thinking it was her responsibility to speak for them. "The Rengru don't recognize much nuance on their own. There are only bipedal beings to be saved—and bipedal beings trying to stop them. Their initial fear had been that you would disrupt their work to save those left on K'davu. Once you had killed enough of them, they began building defenses—and extending their boundaries ever farther beyond K'davu. They constantly tried to bond with one of you, to communicate—"

"But you kept killing anyone that they 'compromised,'" Connolly said.

Kormagan looked sharply at him. "You were with us."

"Only to keep you from hurting people. And then to help my own."

"Same difference." Kormagan turned her wrath back on the natives. "The Rengru have technology. Why did you not have them send us a message?"

"Messages, here?" Pike asked. "You know how well they travel in this nebula."

"And the Rengru would never understand the mission," Una added. "They communicate like everyone else does in the Pergamum—locally. The will, the drive to transmit something like that would never have made it far. They had to find an agent."

Kormagan wasn't accepting it. She railed at Eudah. "Why didn't one of you make the trip yourself? You could have found your daughter—before she gave her life in your name."

Eudah gasped. "Did she? I had hoped—"

"She was one of the *first* to fall. She inspired all of us!"

"I—" Eudah's words caught in her throat. "I would have left if I could. But the Rengru joining causes biological changes—changes that mount over a long term, binding us to this place. We could never survive parting from this world."

"The Federation has medical experts," Pike volunteered. "We could help with that."

"Someone would have to ask. We are happy here." Eudah nodded to her companions. "Our communion with the Rengru has enriched all our lives. No one has ever asked to be freed."

"Of course not!" Quadeo grew enraged. "Who would, with eternal life on the line?" She faced Eudah. "So you left us out there to die, trying to save you from *them*!" She pointed to the Rengru crowning Eudah. "This has all been a mistake. It's all been for nothing!"

"Not for nothing," Eudah said, visibly unnerved by the conflict. "Yes, the war is a mistake—but it can end now. And you can all come home, and live with your people again!"

"Join you?" Quadeo spat. "Not if it means becoming *like* you. I would never accept existence in such a disgusting form!"

"You could not live here otherwise," one of Eudah's companions said. "Not unless you remained in your armor during the storms. Could you live like that?"

Connolly laughed. "They've done it for decades."

"Silence," Kormagan said, clearly fraught. "We will decide this ourselves!"

In unison, Pike and Una nodded to Connolly. This was a time to stand back. A family matter.

The oldest of the Boundless stepped forward. "I think I would try," Barson said.

"*What?*" Quadeo blurted.

"I am old, child. The Thirty-Twos are the oldest of the surviving waves—yet they were the last stop for me. I entered service a hundred years before." He looked to one of Eudah's colleagues—a member of the Vis-kal species, like him. "I do not expect eternal life. But I would live among my people for the last days of it."

"*We* are your people," Quadeo shouted.

"Quiet. Let me think." Kormagan looked long at Eudah—and then at her allies. She could read their faces; several were hypnotized by the cityscape. "I don't think Barson will be alone in thinking that," she said, "and I can see others of our people following along, once they know."

"And you?" Eudah asked.

Kormagan shook her head. "I won't stay here. I can't be Boundless and accept a prison, no matter how wonderful it appears. But I will put the choice to the rest. If they come here, and you make your case, I will not interfere."

Eudah nodded. "That is all we could ever ask."

"A monster, a traitor, and an old fool," Quadeo said. She got in Kormagan's face. "Your command is ended. I'm going to find a way to go back and return with all the waves. And purge this misbegotten planet!"

"The Rengru will stop you," Pike said. "With or without our help."

"Then you will die too!"

Kormagan reached out and grabbed Quadeo's metal collar, yanking her near. She growled as she shook her fellow wavemaster. "You will do as I say, little recruit. Or I will end your insults once and for all!"

Quadeo locked eyes with Kormagan—and appearing to see reality, nodded. Kormagan released her, and she staggered away—

—only to speak into her battlesuit's collar. "Cargo pod twelve, deploy!" The armor's caddy ejected a coconut-sized sphere, which escaped Quadeo's hands and bounced on the rocky ground. She dove for it. Before anyone caught her, she reached it and twisted its halves.

"Freeze!" Pike commanded, activating a control as he did. Immobilized, Quadeo pitched forward, bruising her face in the dirt. "What have you got there?"

Una reached for the black item, fallen from Quadeo's grasp. Kormagan hurried to her side—and confirmed what she had already surmised. "It's a bomb!"

71

K'davu

"A bomb!" Pike didn't wait before making the call. "*Enterprise!* I have something to beam into space!"

"Stand by," he heard through his suit.

"I can't stand by!"

"It was what we were bringing for *Enterprise*," Kormagan said, "had we needed to scuttle it ourselves."

Bleeding and bruised, Quadeo laughed. "I'll settle for all of you. I've given my life to fighting Rengru. I'll do it now if it means making sure this plague doesn't spread!"

"No good, Captain," Pitcairn said. *"We're still offline—and when we restore power, we'll only be able to receive, not send."*

That settled that: Pike couldn't beam a bomb *to* his ship. He looked to the others. "Is it armed?"

Kormagan nodded. "The second she activated it." She glanced at Pike. "You wouldn't have caught it when you disarmed us. The Slammer-Nine's reactants are held in stasis, and wouldn't have scanned as dangerous until mixed."

"That's refreshing. How long?"

"Five minutes. Maybe."

"How big?"

"We cleaned the sites at Susquatane with these."

Damn it, I was afraid you were going to say that. "Pitcairn, I want you beaming people up as soon as you can," Pike shouted.

"Aye, Captain!"

He looked to Eudah. "You'd better warn your population."

"Doing it now," she replied, looking fearful. The Rengru down in the valley were moving frantically. "It takes much longer to shield the cities than to uncover them."

Then five minutes won't do. Pike looked up and around. No ships, no anything—and the natives' flying platforms weren't fast at all. "What have we got?"

Connolly called out. "Look here." He knelt beside the geocorder he'd brought to study the planet. "Those tunnels atop the escarpment—they're mines."

Eudah nodded. "From the days when we plundered K'davu for resources."

Connolly pointed to the display. "There are shafts going down. Pretty deep."

"Yeah, but they're staggered," Pike said, regarding the readings. "We can't just pitch it in. If the bomb lands on a ledge, the whole ridge blows out onto the valley!"

"No, sir. Look—tunnels that hook." He traced the outlines with his finger. "They used J-tunnels to contain the old underground nuclear tests on Earth."

Contain. That was all Pike needed to hear. He reached for the bomb.

His move startled Una. "Captain, wait! Maybe the natives could help."

Eudah gestured to her flying platform. "Solar-powered. They would fail before they got far." She looked to the valley nervously. Many citizens were still out and about.

Connolly started to stand. "Sir, I've used the jetpack before—"

"And you ran half dry getting to *Enterprise*. Galadjian topped me off." He buttoned up his armor and pointed to Connolly. "Give me maps if you can."

The "Aye, sir!" was nearly lost in the rumble of Pike's

engine—and he himself nearly bought it against the escarpment wall before he righted his course. The Boundless battlesuits, Spock had told him, were designed for the novice—and at flying, he definitely was. But Connolly knew how the machines worked, and seconds after a chime announced the arrival of underground maps, the lieutenant was online telling him how to feed the legs of his journey into the autopilot.

Pike arced high—and soared into an open pit, evidently an air shaft. Darkness enveloped him as he careened near one wall, and then another—only to flip head-over-heels and decelerate.

"First base," Connolly said as Pike hovered over a surface that would have been invisible if not for his battlesuit's interface. *"Go left!"*

A slight jog to the left and Pike was descending again. The Boundless were skilled at communicating locally through some of the worst mediums around; Pike was thankful for that fact as his position was reported back to Connolly.

"Second. Left again!"

Another jog, another plunge. "Connolly, use what fuel you've got and beam out. Put the Boundless on Eudah's platforms, if they'll go—"

The shaft ended before he could finish. *"You're on the level,"* Connolly said. *"Two lefts and you're home!"*

"I said go! That's an order!"

Pike's impulse was to run through the horizontal section, but the ceiling was too low for the immense battlesuit—and his time too short. The jetpack wasn't designed for lateral travel on a world with gravity, he soon saw—slamming against walls and ceilings as he went.

The far end arrived before his systems sensed it. He struck hard, protecting the orb with his arms as he fell. Dazed, his system alarms screaming from the impact and low fuel, he paused to catch his breath, and question his sanity—

—but only for a second. Yes, he was in a mine again, but he wasn't going to stay this time either. *Hell, no.* He clambered to his feet and rounded the turn, ducking all the way.

Finally, his battlesuit's laser sights detected the end up ahead. He bowled the beastly marble and turned to make his way out.

Pike was strangely thankful the bomb had come with no timer attached; he didn't need the motivation, especially not when the jet-fuel warning was impetus aplenty. He took the route back to the vertical shafts on foot, allowing—at the cost of his complaining back—the battlesuit to curl him into a crouched run.

By the end of the first of the two vertical shafts back to the surface, he was nearly dry. "I don't think I can do this," he called out. No one answered. He felt only acceleration, saw only darkness, heard only—

Chris, I'm with you.

Pike blinked. Vina's voice.

He saw a pinprick of light, still so far ahead. A tiny star at the center of a nebula of hardship. The jetpack sputtered, and he continued to rise—even as he saw an alarm appear. A sensor had reported back by subspace a fact heading for him in milliseconds: a detonation.

"*Shields activate!*"

Pike went up—and part of the mountain did, too, seeming to heave and churn. A jolt struck his personal shields, knocking him sideways—then upside down, and every way possible. The force quickly exceeded the shields' capacity. He felt weightless for an instant, prone and powerless, riding the back of the shockwave.

And then, just as he began to fall, he felt something else. Something clamped about his midsection. Above, through the miasma of light and churning dust, he saw divers heading for him. No, not divers—it only looked like he was drowning.

They were people in battlesuits, as he was, riding what little fuel they had in a quickly forming chain of arms and legs to gently guide him clear of the blast.

His crew.

Completely spent from the experience, Pike barely felt it when the group landed, fuel exhausted, on one of the lower terraces farther out from the escarpment. He rolled on his side to see the ridge venting columns of smoke from several high apertures, but otherwise most of its shape remained.

Una reached him first.

He tried to focus on her. “I told . . . you all . . . to get out.”

“I’m afraid we all work for someone who has very stern rules about this sort of thing.” She smiled gently. “*Leave no one behind.*”

72

Combat Module Carrier 539-Urdoh
The Nest

Kormagan gazed out upon the Rengru spaceyards with awe. Weeks earlier, the scene before her eyes would have been military intelligence of the highest value. Countless probes and scouting missions had been sacrificed over the generations, none getting more than a glimpse.

All had changed. Her target, for so long, had become—*what*? Not her friend, but perhaps just a simple fact of nature. The Rengru were the sea that had kept her from K'davu, the storm that had claimed so many of her ships. But they were the water without which all life on her homeworld would have perished. She could not like them—but neither could she resent them for acting in her people's interest. The fact that they had been unable to communicate their intentions owed entirely to the prowess with which those like Kormagan had executed their duties. She could hardly blame them for that.

Since meeting Greatmother Eudah, she had seen the woman a couple more times. Already a mythic figure for many members of the Boundless, Eudah had made it her mission to welcome all who chose to visit K'davu, whether they did so to find out about their origins, or to look into joining with the Rengru of their free will. The prospect still frightened many, and repulsed more; Quadeo, humbled, had crawled off, filling her carrier with those who wanted nothing more to do with the idea of K'davu. The others, meanwhile, at least had an example of the result. Barson had risen from his coma after what she had been told was an unusually short assimilation period.

"The creatures," Eudah had said, "have learned from their connection with Commander Una. The change will not be so harsh in the future." Indeed, Barson was immediately active, and had seemed no different to Kormagan afterward. He was, of course. Kormagan had no more chance of relating to him than she had with Eudah. Members of the native species who had once united as the Boundless had become, together with the Rengru, something else: the K'davites.

Kormagan had spent the intervening time spreading the word and ferrying back visitors—and taking care of another project, one that had just come to fruition. She spied Captain Pike entering the bridge—he in yellow and black, accompanied by Connolly in blue and black. *How odd their uniforms look,* she thought. It was amazing the Federation held any territory at all the way its warriors were outfitted.

"Connolly tells me you've got some news for me," Pike said.

"I have kept my word," Kormagan replied, stowing her headgear. Armored life had remained second nature. "Captain Baladon has collected on this vessel the last of the remaining recruits—" Seeing Pike's reaction, she stopped. "The last of those we took from Susquatane," she finished.

Pike gave a guarded response. "How many casualties?"

"None."

Pike's eyes widened. "Excuse me?"

"None. The other wavemasters moved your scientists to rearward positions quickly after we realized their merit," Kormagan said. "Of them, only Spock and Connolly saw combat for extended periods."

The captain smirked at Connolly. "How'd you get so lucky?"

"I guess they just thought I was a man of action," Connolly said.

Pike's eyes narrowed. "There were security officers on Susquatane too."

"All alive, all here," Kormagan said. "They ran the gauntlet, Captain. They had been well trained before we ever met them."

"I guess that's a compliment." Pike looked out at the shipyards of the Nest, where space-fitted Rengru worked with Pike's crewmembers to reconnect the two halves of the ship. He remarked on it. "That's not supposed to be doable outside of spacedock. I guess we're learning things on this trip after all."

The connection would not make *Enterprise* whole, Kormagan knew. She'd come to understand the ravages it had suffered—some at her own hands—while in the nebula. It was a miracle it still flew at all. She'd been right all along: Starfleet's technology was superior, its engineers greatly talented.

Maybe we should have recruited them instead, she mused. But that was a thought that belonged to another time. New circumstances were at hand, requiring her to make an offer.

"I made a bargain with Opmaster— I mean, with Lieutenant Connolly here, before. He got me aboard *Enterprise*, as promised, and while it didn't work out as I expected, we reached K'davu and the war's end." She looked behind her and saw that the pallet she'd requested had been delivered. "Have a look."

The humans stepped toward it. "New armor," Connolly said, running his fingers over the gear. "It's nice."

"I can't depart the nebula until my people have made their choices to either settle here, or leave," Kormagan said. "So my forces will not be able to join your war against the Klingons immediately. But you may take that unit and the forging instructions and place your own battlesuits in mass production. We will join you when we can."

Pike stared at the gear, puzzled, and then looked at Connolly. "You made this deal?"

The younger human nodded. "I thought we could use the help."

Pike faced Kormagan. "Thanks, but no, thanks."

"What?" Connolly said, startled.

Kormagan asked the same thing. "We're still a powerful force."

"Yeah," Pike said, crossing his arms. "I've got no doubt there. What I do doubt is how you got that way. I'd never be sure which of your warriors was there because they got pressed into it—or whether that armor was made by someone who got ripped from his family."

"You do know that we've been arranging the departures of others we've captured, correct? Even Baladon's Lurians."

"And that's well done. It's also overdue. You cost nearly a year out of my crewmembers' lives, and the rest almost died trying to get them back." He shook his head. "Maybe one day we'll meet again—Connolly tells me you're thinking of going exploring, now that you can. But for now, we're good."

Kormagan only partially understood. "I thought you were in great need."

"Not that great. It's like I told my admiral—it matters *how* we fight, and with what."

"Very well. The choice is yours."

Pike's communicator chirped. "Pike."

"Captain," Nicola said, *"Doctor Galadjian reports we are ready to get underway."*

"Not until I hear from the other doctor about Una."

"You are now," said another human voice. *"Boyce here. Once she was done coordinating the work with the Rengru, Una simply asked it to disengage from her—and it did."*

The news startled Kormagan and Pike both. "Is she all right?" Pike asked.

"She warned me she'd be in a coma again for a while, and she is. But she's able to live on her own—she wasn't connected as long as those people on K'davu."

"That's good news. Pike out." He looked at Kormagan. "Will your people be more likely to embrace the Rengru if they think it's reversible?"

"It depends," Kormagan said, looking outside, "where people decide their home is."

"And where's yours?" Connolly asked.

"I'm not sure. But I think I may be wearing it." She deployed her headgear and departed the bridge.

73

Warship *Deathstrike*
Acheron Formation

"This is a cruel, cruel joke," Baladon said, kicking at garbage. "I can't believe you brought us back to *Deathstruck*!"

Connolly smiled at him. "I thought it was *Deathstrike*."

"Have a look around. You tell me!" Baladon stalked about, avoiding debris. "Most of the bridge stations are torn out, we've got half a dozen airlocks where they shouldn't be, and we don't have a single torpedo!"

"Maybe that's for the best," Connolly said. "Hey, you still have a chair."

Baladon collapsed in it. "This is not even remotely fair. The Rengru helped you people get back underway. You agreed to lead us out of the nebula—and brought us to this. You never told me Pike was a sadist!"

"You don't have to take it. We just thought those troop modules you were in were pretty cramped—and we were headed this way anyway."

"I feel all my old nightmares returning. I am cursed."

Once it had become apparent that the Boundless were no longer in the piracy business, Baladon had gathered up as many of the Lurians as he could find. Their casualty rate had been significantly higher than that for the *Enterprise* abductees, but then, his people had seen more combat, and also had the handicap of imbecility. One of his cousins posted with another wave had taken out a troop module while juggling grenades.

"I don't suppose you want to take *any* of my people back with you?" Baladon asked.

"We're kind of full up—and I'm not sure what they'd do. Here, they've got a project." Baladon's crewmembers were belowdecks, receiving the replacement equipment *Enterprise*'s engineers had beamed over.

"Some project. It will take us months."

"Yeah, well, we'd like a head start."

Baladon laughed. "You are a true pirate, Connolly. You sell yourself short with these people. You should come with us."

"No, it's not me."

Baladon knew Connolly had been regretting his actions ever more in the days since rejoining his crew, especially as he had learned the fates of others he had served with—and had helped to abduct.

Connolly spoke again. "You remember Malce, the Antaran from my first squad?"

"You mean the little sniveling one?"

"You can call him that. I wouldn't. He ran headlong into a Rengru fortress on Varadah II."

"I don't remember the Rengru having a fortress on Varadah II."

"They don't. He ran in with a sack full of Slammer-Nines on his back."

"Huh," Baladon said. "I wouldn't have thought he had it in him."

"Well, it shouldn't have happened." Connolly looked down. "The longer I've been free, been back on *Enterprise*—and knowing now the whole war was a mistake—the more I feel I should have fought harder against the Boundless. Shouldn't have cooperated, shouldn't have tried to make deals with Kormagan. And I definitely shouldn't have traded people around like they were outfielders."

"What is it with you Federation people, always courting misery?" Baladon asked. "You couldn't have resisted. *I* wouldn't have let you resist. Your acts would have gotten you nowhere, and would have been seen by no one."

"I would have known."

"Bah!" Baladon stood and clapped his hand on the human's shoulder. "There will come a time, friend Connolly, when you learn that we are all just microbes in the muck, living to eat and breed. All else is in your imagination."

"Well, I can imagine doing something different then. If there's a next time." He looked out the viewport at *Enterprise*. "I'll tell you, though, I've asked Captain Pike for a more active role. No sitting around on the bridge when big things happen."

Baladon laughed. "Are you sure you're really a scientist?"

"Babe Ruth pitched and batted. So can I." Connolly snapped his fingers. "Speaking of career changes, I nearly forgot. I brought you something." He pulled a data slate out of his satchel.

"Parting gifts? Lovely. And I didn't even clean the place up."

"That week I spent in sickbay trying to teach my body to live without the armor, I found out people had been reading an ancient Earth book about shipwrecks."

"And you wish me one. It improves."

"No, this was the author's follow-up," he said, handing it to Baladon. "*The Life, Adventures, and Pyracies of the Famous Captain Singleton*."

"A pirate?"

"Who had enough of the life, and went straight and settled down. That's still the plan, isn't it?"

Baladon scratched his chin. "Spock had said something about a planet that might be good for my people—Garadius something. We might go take a look."

"I remember that place. Maybe it's still uninhabited. What if you get there and find that somebody else wants it?"

Baladon grinned. "*That* is not an impediment."

74

U.S.S. Enterprise
Outside the Pergamum Nebula

"The war is over. Enterprise *is recalled from Pergamum Nebula. Destination to follow."*

It had been short, as all their transmissions from Starfleet had been. And sweet—that was a change.

The news of the cessation of hostilities had arrived just as *Enterprise* was limping out of the nebula, using a Boundless-suggested route that took them through the Acheron Formation with far less drama along the way. The timing made for a psychologist's buffet of mixed feelings.

Relief, of course, for the war's end—and for the end to their isolation.

They had spent months longer than the appointed year in the body, and their stay had been difficult in the extreme. And yet, as bad as all the experiences of *Enterprise*'s crew had been, as more accounts came in about the traumas back home, a mixture of anger, grief, and regret filled the corridors.

Hell had been visited on the Federation, and they had been away. Kept away, Pike felt—where they'd wound up in the wrong war. Many aboard questioned where they'd been, and what they'd done. Pike had thought to remind others that the Boundless had been trapped in a mistake for centuries—but he'd decided that was better left unsaid. His crew was smart. People could figure that out on their own.

It wasn't long after *Enterprise* began making its way home that the transfers began. Shuttles dispatched from the ship on a nearly daily basis, sending some away in exchange for their overdue relief officers; others, like Raden, to be with family or friends impacted by the Klingon War. The young Ktarian had shown true dedication despite his injuries, but Pike had missed his longtime helmsman. His command hadn't been the same without a Tyler on the bridge.

And others were entertaining opportunities to help rebuild the fleet. No one had as many offers as Galadjian, who had resumed holding spirited conversations with a team that idolized him now more than ever. The tale of a prize-winning theoretician crawling around Jefferies tubes and teaching himself starship repair with a data slate had spread far beyond *Enterprise.* Pike expected to hear any day that he was heading for his own Starfleet Corps of Engineering command, continuing *Enterprise*'s game of chief engineer roulette.

Possibly the best reason for leaving was Carlotti's, as she had begun her leave with her new child. He didn't know whether she, or any of them, would be back. Whatever happened, for the next few months a much different crew would run *Enterprise*, presuming Starfleet didn't take one look at its damage and decommission the thing. But he still had Nhan, Connolly, Colt, and many others—

—plus the two he cared most for, and had been most concerned about of late. He stood at the door of the first one, and got ready to wait. Spock had taken ever longer, lately, to respond to the request to enter.

The door opened to admit Pike to a darkened room. He looked about. Spock kept tidy personal quarters normally, but this seemed different. Unlived in. The bed appeared unused.

Spock sat on the floor, staring at nothing. His candles remained on the shelves, unlit. Pike asked anyway. "Meditating?"

"I . . . cannot meditate."

Pike edged his way into Spock's view. The science officer didn't look up. "We've missed you on the bridge lately."

Seemingly lost, Spock spoke to the air. "What time is it?"

"Not that time."

Pike knew that Spock had barely slept in weeks—continuing to cite the debilitating nightmares. Boyce could do nothing for him. Spock had tried to return to his station during the journey from K'davu, but he had grown so ineffective that often he just sat on the bridge, hand covering his mouth as he looked at his terminal. Pike thought it might be to cover the mouthing of words, which, while better than mumbling, had never subsided.

He saw a data slate on Spock's table. It was still active. "Still working on Defoe, I see."

"Yes."

From past attempts at conversations, he knew that Spock had been trying—intentionally or not—to retrace his life from his exile on Skon's World, including reading things he had read during that time. But this, Pike saw, was a later Defoe work. "*A Journal of the Plague Year.* Didn't we just live through that?"

"No. It is . . . about . . ."

"I know. The black death." Pike reached down and shut the slate off. "Spock, you should be reading cheerier stuff. Doing cheerier stuff."

"I have been . . . drawing."

Pike looked over at the desk before deciding not to look at his art. It was too private, and Spock's condition was not something amenable to a pep talk—from a captain, or a friend. But there was one thing he and Spock shared. Sitting in one of the Vulcan chairs nearby, he clasped his hands together and spoke into the darkness.

"Spock, I want to tell you something. I've had moments like these too. I nearly got crushed as a kid—" He paused.

"No, it's not that. It's more recent than that. It's Talos IV, Spock. I was there, and I think I still am. Buried, under all that rock."

He looked over at his friend. Spock was mouthing words, not fully listening.

Pike looked away at the ceiling. "I see that place, Spock. I see Vina all the time. You were there, Spock. Do you see them?" He looked to him. "You knew to use Talos IV as a code I would recognize. Do you remember that?"

Spock clasped his own hands in front of his face, the same way Pike had. "I remember . . ."

"I don't dare bring it up because I know they'll lock me away, pull me off the ship. And I have obligations. These people need me, Spock." He leaned over, toward him. "You need me."

"You . . . need me," Spock parroted.

"Yes, Spock. We need you."

"Captain . . . I request you . . . take me to . . ."

"Take you where, Spock?"

". . . a facility. Where I can be helped."

Pike simply breathed. It was the only thing he'd asked for in weeks.

"Sure thing, Spock. I'll take you."

Eyes wild, Spock grabbed the captain's hands, surprising him. "I will take you, Christopher Pike. To be helped."

"No, Spock. *I'll* take *you*. You'll get help—and I'll see you again. I swear."

—

Pike felt he had already been made a liar—this time, by obligations to a larger number. Starfleet had not approved the captain's absence, and he could not leave his post until he got the rest of his crew all the way home. Boyce had accompanied

Spock aboard shuttle *Copernicus*, delivering him to a mental health facility on Starbase 5.

The doctor was available because Carlotti's relief had arrived, but also because he had no patients left to tend. Una, with no more reminder of her Rengru joining than a light scar on the back of her neck, joined Pike on the observation deck.

"Good evening, Number One."

"And to you. I wanted to let you know that the final turbolift has been repaired."

"That is the best news I've had in a year and a half." He stretched against the viewport. "Why'd we put it off so long?"

"Too much else to fix," she said. "There still is. We attempted to bring the holographic systems up again today—that was a mistake."

"I saw what happened to the lights—I was afraid it was Defoe all over again. I think the ship's in about the same shape as her crew."

She nodded. "Well, there's something they won't mind. I got word: Starfleet's awarded Extended Tour Ribbons for everyone aboard."

"That's the least they should get. Anybody who helped get that saucer section aloft is an honorary engineer in my book." He looked to her. "How's our acting chief science officer settling in?"

"Connolly is . . . *always right*. And anxious for action."

"Before the Boundless, he was a little headstrong. I thought the last year would have humbled him some, and maybe it did, a little. But he seems to have taken his survival as a sign to push even harder. I just hope he doesn't flame out." He thought for a moment. "It's probably not a big deal. It's not a permanent step-up."

She nodded. "How long do you think Spock will be gone?"

"However long it takes."

"He does have months and months of leave accumulated."

"I hope they can reach him. Nothing I've told him since K'davu has gotten much reaction. Not when I told him about the war—or when I said *Discovery* had been found."

"Oh, I think he's hearing," Una said, rubbing the back of her neck. "But maybe he's like I was with the Rengru. He's hearing too much."

He looked at her. "How?"

"The Illyrians' and the Vulcans' minds aren't that different. Hit them with anything that *can* make sense, and they'll find a way to sort it out."

"But if it doesn't make sense . . ."

She took his hand. "They're going to help him, Chris. And we'll all get home, and you can ride a horse."

Pike took a deep breath. "Believe me, I'm going to take a few months and just—"

"Captain, this is Nicola."

"That's probably Boyce calling in," he said to Una. "Have we received a signal, Lieutenant?"

"Not one, sir. *Seven.*"

Seven? "We'll be there. Pike out."

Una and Pike looked at one another. "Seven? What could that mean?" she asked.

"I know exactly what it means," Pike said, already heading for the turbolift. *"No rest for the weary."*

Epilogue

Spock meditated.

No, he could not.

Earth. Qo'noS. Vulcan. Andoria.

Earth. Qo'noS. Vulcan. Andoria.

Time went forward.

He saw backward.

No, that wasn't correct.

He saw forward.

Time went backward.

No, that wasn't logical.

He could not meditate. Not here.

Christopher Pike would take him home, to be helped.

What home? No Earth. No Qo'noS. No Andoria.

No Vulcan. No Vulcan. No Vulcan. No—

No, not yet. It had not happened yet.

When was "yet"? What time was it?

What was time? Was he in it?

He could not meditate.

He had obligations.

He could not meditate.

Earth. Qo'noS. Vulcan. Andoria.

Christopher Pike had obligations.

Christopher Pike would take him to be helped.

Then he would take Christopher Pike to be helped.

It was not logical—but it felt correct.

The story of Spock's vision and Captain Christopher Pike's response continues in Season Two of *Star Trek: Discovery*.

ACKNOWLEDGMENTS

The first season of *Discovery* left a major blank to be filled: the period of the Klingon-Federation war when *Starship Enterprise* was not on the scene. I was delighted that Margaret Clark asked me to fill it, and appreciate all her work in editing the book. Thanks also go to Ed Schlesinger, Scott Pearson, and the whole Simon & Schuster team.

There is no book without Kirsten Beyer, fellow *Trek* novelist and staff writer on *Star Trek: Discovery.* She somehow carved time during the second season's shooting schedule for extensive conversations with me about what the *Enterprise* characters might be doing during their first-season exile. My appreciation also goes to John Van Citters and the staff at CBS for keeping me in the loop on the series as it was being written and shot.

My first brush with *Discovery* came at the very beginning, when David Mack asked my thoughts on his plans for the first novel in the line, *Desperate Hours.* That book, which includes Pike and Spock in prominent roles, was helpful in writing this one, as were many others that touched on Pike's *Enterprise.*

Thanks go to Brent Frankenhoff for proofreading—and much appreciation, as ever, to proofreader and Number One on my bridge, Meredith Miller. Thanks also to Allyn Gibson for a timely assist.

Ken Barnes, one of my oldest friends and the person who

really got me into *Star Trek* eons ago, helped immeasurably by participating in my thought experiment about the predicament *Enterprise*'s saucer section finds itself in. Another contemporary, Army vet and *Trek* fan Michael Singleton (who shares a name and rank with the title of Daniel Defoe's follow-up to *Crusoe*), helped greatly as a sounding board on the Boundless and their ways. When the stuff of your car-ride debates in high school finds a way into your professional work, you're under a lucky star!

ABOUT THE AUTHOR

John Jackson Miller is the *New York Times* bestselling author of the acclaimed *Star Trek: Prey* trilogy (*Hell's Heart*, *The Jackal's Trick*, *The Hall of Heroes*) and the novels *Star Trek: The Next Generation: Takedown*; *Star Wars: A New Dawn*; *Star Wars: Kenobi*; *Star Wars: Knight Errant*; *Star Wars: Lost Tribe of the Sith—The Collected Stories*; and fifteen *Star Wars* graphic novels, as well as the original work *Overdraft: The Orion Offensive*. He has also written the eNovella *Star Trek: Titan: Absent Enemies*. A comics industry historian and analyst, he has written for franchises including *Halo*, *Conan*, *Iron Man*, *Indiana Jones*, *Battlestar Galactica*, *Mass Effect*, and *The Simpsons*. He lives in Wisconsin with his wife, two children, and far too many comic books.